BEFORE AND AFTER MICHAEL

JEMIAH JEFFERSON

ROCK PAPER TIGER

SEATTLE, WA

Published with the assistance of Rock Paper Tiger, Seattle, Washington.

Photography by Amanda Rebholz

Design by Jimmy Presler and Steve Libbey

Special thanks to Cecilia Cannon, Heather Reddy, Jeremy Boutwell, Myrlin Hermes, Nená Rawdah, Jenny Blenk, Garret Cook, Konner Knudsen, and Lara Haehle. Your help and encouragement mean everything.

ISBN 978-0-9830611-1-3

Second printing August 2018

10 9 8 7 6 5 4 3 2 1

Printed in the United States of America

he is no hero
he is a god in my eyes
the man who is allowed to sit beside you -
he who listens intimately to the sweet murmur of your voice

—Sappho, trans. Mary Barnard

1. A BOY CAN DREAM.

May, 2007, Lower East Side, Manhattan, New York City.

"So what do you think—power bottom?"

"Michael Kaminsky?" Drew responded with surprise, although he and Jesse had been staring at the same person for the last few minutes. "I don't even know if he's gay."

"Oh, no, he's gay all right." Jesse dusted off his hands, nodded decisively, and stretched back in his seat. "Maybe he doesn't know it. I mean, hell, I don't *really* know about him for sure. I just met him today, same as you." He sighed longingly. "He's hot though," he added. "And I think he's got a li'l crush on you."

"A *crush?*" Drew laughed dismissively. "Whatever, Jess."

A dozen yards away, in the disarray of the nascent stage, the rangy figure of the lighting technician paced back and forth. Every few steps, he would stare up into the rafters, shining thin red laser beams at the ceiling, and writing down measurements and notations in a notebook dwarfed by his massive palms. Michael Kaminsky was undoubtedly tall, dark, and handsome, but also sported a wild tangle of untamed eyebrows, clunky eyeglass frames, and a blue broadcloth shirt tucked in despite the warmth of the day. It was plain he assumed he'd be ignored. He effectively was, but for the focus from the theater's third row aisle seats. The construction crew carried wooden beams and metal tubing on the stage. Shouting to each other, they moved past him without a glance. Michael deftly avoided them, ignoring them right back, focused on his calculations. Despite his height, his posture was ramrod-straight; despite gangly limbs, he moved with economical grace, keeping himself out of the way with half-steps and precise pivots on the balls of his feet, as exacting as a ballet dancer.

Jesse pulled at the sweaty neck of his T-shirt, shrugged, and rolled his eyes at Drew's airy tone. "Don't play dumb. Everybody gets a crush on you."

Drew answered, "Huh. Well." The director of the play, the set-building crew, even the guy who had come to deliver water that morning – they'd all let their eyes linger on Drew, looking him up and down, startled or dazzled or knowingly amused. "I do look good today," he admitted. He stroked a thumb down his tie, smile flashing a hint of brilliant white teeth.

"Heh!" Jesse snickered. "That's funny, Mister Farrow. If only they could get a look at your feet, they'd run screaming."

"Last night you might have been screaming, but you weren't running," Drew murmured distantly, eyes focused unwaveringly on the stage, on the tall glider in the glasses and tucked-in shirt.

"Truth." Jesse sighed again. "God, he's foxy. I wonder what *his* feet look like."

"Big," Drew guessed.

In unison, he and Jesse chuckled and snorted in a pleasantly juvenile, comfortable way. "I wonder what he's doing later," Jesse said idly.

"Who knows," Drew teased, "but tonight, I think *you* should be home. Takeout and a movie; first night of construction. It's a ritual."

Jesse grimaced, eyes flicking to Drew and away again. "I thought I gave up rituals when I stopped being a Catholic."

"You never stop being a Catholic." Drew sighed. "Anyway, do whatever you want; I'm not your jailer. You don't have to if you want to do something else; I've got to go to sleep early, so *I* can't go out."

"Okay, okay. I'll be there. You big baby."

"Good. I'll make it worthwhile." Drew lay his hand against the back of Jesse's neck, not quite a friendly pat and not quite a caress, but somewhere in between. Jesse's eyes drifted closed for a moment as he enjoyed the touch, the connection. "Now, I gotta run. I've got a client meeting before the producer's lunch. And you better get back to work, too."

"True," Jesse said, smiling again. He quickly stood up, bent over Drew, and pressed a quick, light kiss against his mouth. "See you tonight, *cugino*." This last, he whispered; it was important to keep their other connection, as cousins, discreet in the workplace. He sauntered into the aisle and back toward the stage.

Once Jesse left, Drew returned his attention to Michael Kaminsky. The tall man had turned away. Maybe he'd seen the kiss; maybe he hadn't. Maybe he'd been disgusted by it. Drew really didn't know the guy, and it wasn't worth his time to wonder if Jesse had inadvertently offended him.

It was time for Drew to get back to his life, his *real* work, not this enjoyable sideline in theater. His days (and often his nights) were occupied in wrangling investment strategies and estate tax loopholes. He much preferred these brief indulgences in the creative world. He wasn't a performer, just a producer. This was as close to the magical world of make-believe as he got; his role was to secure financing, to know the right people, to grease the right palms. Even if he was interested in backstage mechanics (and backstage drama), he didn't have time to get involved. He just needed to sign the checks, and try to keep the production on budget. A lot of the time, it was fun, exec-producing plays; he thrived on the stress, the hurdles, the complications, and yes, the drama. If he ever felt himself growing disenchanted, he could remind himself that he was only spending the money his father had left him, not the money he'd made on his own. He gleefully imagined how much his father, the esteemed businessman Alistair Farrow, the staid and driven "Portuguese powerhouse" of international import-export, would be horrified at the idea that his money was being thrown away on *contrasensso . . . that nonsense*.

Alas, he'd never know; he'd been dead for years.

With amusement, Drew watched Kaminsky stare at Jesse as the shorter man ambled by, his bowlegged stride taking him a little closer than was polite. Kaminsky's expression was furtive, but also startled, intensely alert, almost scared. When Jesse reached the back of the room, he bent over his own toolbox, lifting his lusciously round behind directly into Kaminsky's sight line.

Jesse stood up again, grinning, eyes innocently wide and shining, holding up his power drill. Kaminsky dropped his stare immediately, shuffling clumsily out of the way. He got creamed by two guys carrying a six-foot plank, and stammered nervous apologies.

Jesse caught Drew's eye, nodded, and winked. *He's gay*, he mouthed.

Drew got up, chuckling, and put his suit jacket back on, thinking, *Well, I bet he is now.* Jess could turn the Pope gay.

Drew walked down the aisle, screwing his Bluetooth earpiece into his right ear. Anticipating the bright transition of sunlight out on the street, he paused just outside the door to slip on his sunglasses, an involuntary smile tugging at the corner of his mouth. He hoped the lighting designer would be all right, having to work with a firecracker like Jesse. Jesse wasn't just a flirt; he was an outlandishly talented savant of sexual chemistry. Still, he managed in many ways to remain a sweet, curious kid. It was a deadly combination that Drew himself hadn't been able to resist. He was just lucky enough to have gotten there first.

In the men's room, Michael Kaminsky locked himself in a stall and stood there, facing the wall, taking deep breaths to calm himself. He held out his hands and stared at them. His fingers were trembling.

He turned and sat on the toilet seat, closing his eyes, trying to center himself, to practice *pranayama*. His mind cleared, only to be flooded again with the memory of the painfully beautiful set crew member, that bright-eyed jewel of a boy who seemed perfectly aware of what Michael was thinking. That wicked, knowing smile had been too much for Michael to take, and he had turned on his heel and made a beeline to where he could be alone and get ahold of himself. Was that a look meant for him? Was that incredible creature flirting with him? He could only accept that it must be the case. And then the way that Jesse had kissed Drew, so casual, so knowing, a gesture born of lengthy intimacy, had upset Michael even more.

Unbelievable. So Jesse was "that way" too. (Good Lord, so very.) And not just that — he was obviously *with* Andrew Farrow, the executive producer, who, if anything, was even more confidently gorgeous, if more obviously and blatantly so, the neon to Jesse's warm candle. It wasn't fair that two such incredible men would already be off the market. Not that he was looking.

But . . . *pooraka*, inhale*; rechaka,* exhale*.* Of course he was looking. It was okay to look—no, it was *great*. He chastised himself for using the wrong language even in his own thoughts. It wasn't *"that way."* It was queer. Like him. He owned that; he was that, and more. Every day he actively reminded himself that it was real and right and perfect and beautiful. And yeah, he was looking, and that was real and right and perfect and beautiful, too.

It was supposed to get easier every day, and just become a part of him, but his psyche rejected that comforting terminology. He knew good and well that every time his eyes fell in love with a guy, his heart would end up falling out onto the floor. He did not know what to call it; it just didn't seem like something anyone could have in common with someone else. *Queer*, at least, defined something.

But Jesse Landon and Andrew Farrow looked more like each other than they looked like him. They belonged together.

He pressed his trembling palms together, closed his eyes, and held himself that way until the trembling stopped. "You're all right, Michael," he said to himself. "Just think it through."

He needed somebody. Wanted; okay, wanted. He didn't need anything. It wouldn't make or break him to have a boyfriend. Or a lover. Or even a random fuck. *Oh, God, a fuck.* Michael's head spun again, and he gulped in a deep breath and held it. It was all right for him to acknowledge that need. He was a man, a healthy young man, and he craved sex with other men. There was nothing wrong with him. There never had been. But sometimes he felt incomplete.

It was just a *feeling,* not a fact. He was a complete, blessed, sacred being. One who got horny sometimes.

Make that all the time. And that, too, was okay.

Michael exhaled and stood up, squaring his shoulders. Working with that particular set builder was going to be an issue. Michael was just going to have to deal with it; his role in the production was too important for him to bail, or even avoid the set during the construction phase. He needed to be there; the director had specifically requested his expertise, and Michael oversaw his own wiring as a matter of course. Indeed, Michael was getting paid a good chunk of change to light this show, more than he'd ever been paid for a lighting job before, and his designs would be at least as important as the script or the actors. *Viridian* was *his* show, too; he'd been corresponding with the writer for over a year, bouncing design ideas off one another as the play was written. He couldn't allow himself to get distracted at the sight of a nice-looking ass, or eyes the color of gold-dusted chocolate, or the kind of thick, dark, effortless hair that invited the touch.

Or thinking of what it looked like when Drew Farrow touched it. Grabbed it. Pulled it tightly.

He took one more deep breath, held it for a count of five, and exhaled, "Just be cool." Checking his watch, he realized it was time to leave for the first production lunch at the Spotted Pig, a hyper-trendy place where Michael had never been. If he could spend a few hours with strangers, talking about technical concerns, it stood a good chance of keeping his mind off those walking definitions of "out of his league."

Upon emerging from the men's room, he climbed down into the house instead of remaining backstage. Hiding in the shadows, he observed the builders, a plainly capable crew of varied men and a few women walking back and forth, shouting, drilling, hammering, and standing while staring at the ground with arms akimbo. It was like the official set crew pose; perhaps it enhanced spatial cognitive processing. From a battered old boom box tucked backstage, Lynyrd Skynyrd could be heard in the gaps of noise between rounds of electric shrilling. Michael could sit and watch this process for hours. He loved being in theaters, in shadows, backstage, or in the spaces between rows of seats, but only when a show was being put together or in performance, from backstage or a control booth, high above the crowd. It just seemed so absurd that a magical illusion could be created out of such dust and noise, and always Skynyrd for some reason.

The set foreman stood in the space between the first row of seats and the stage, hauling cables out of the hidden space there. Michael approached and casually asked him, "Excuse me, I'm wondering — that guy? Jesse?"

Michael pointed out the young man, who, immersed now in work, bobbed his head in time with the music, though there was no way he could possibly hear it. Michael almost sighed out loud at the sight: the slight wiry frame, corded forearms, and a prominent, rounded behind, obvious even through baggy jeans.

"Yep, what about him?"

"Just curious," Michael replied. "Is he part of the standard crew?"

"Yep, he's here for the full build and dress."

The next sixteen days, then. Michael thanked the foreman, fetched his attaché case from the locker in the box office, and left as quickly as he could. He felt different than he had that morning; his thoughts sideways, like he was stoned on something that merely nudged him into a parallel state of being. It was all that deep breathing, he decided.

All of the major producers of *Viridian* were already there when Michael arrived at the restaurant. The director, Larry LaPonte, a bigwig in his own underground, barely profitable way. The set designer and buyer. Sound and costume designers. The writer, Lavinia Hermann, who introduced him as "Michael Kaminsky, lighting savant." As he squirmed under their intense scrutiny, she went on to brag that Michael was the one who was going to turn this little play from a vaguely interesting, stylistic, off-off-Broadway exercise into something worthwhile. The cast and the set were secondary concerns; they'd just be bodies, occupied space, while all around them a painting in lights would create an immersive environment that had no regard for the division between stage and audience. She and the director both wanted rainy-night urban streets, and parklands in summer, and the stark silver-white of an operating room (or at least, the way operating rooms looked on TV). Easy. Michael was more than certain that he could do that, but he needed instruments of his own design, and construction that had great flexibility and ran cool.

"And this, of course, is Andrew Farrow, the main angel investor." LaPonte smiled wolfishly. "We labor for *this* man."

Everyone applauded, and Michael tried not to stare. He had been warned that he was risking falling in love once an hour when he moved to New York, but it hadn't even been an hour since the last time.

Farrow was about forty years old, medium height (not average; nothing about him was average), clad in an impeccably tailored suit and good shoes, his stance confident and relaxed. The jacket of his gray three-button suit had the lower buttons undone over a white shirt—no, very pale green—and a solid dark blue tie, a dull-silver tie bar biting neatly into it. All of it looked expensive, but too tasteful to be forbidding. Obviously, Farrow had a lot of money, and had always had a lot of it; he didn't consider it interesting enough to celebrate or reject.

His face and body showed the same care and fortune. Farrow's tanned face was so smooth and well-kept it was shiny, like he'd been buffed with a chamois. It still bore the tough, masculine grain that came with shaving for twenty years, maybe even twenty-five. His smile was almost too dazzling to look at, with those Hollywood-white teeth, those cheekbones, thoughtful creases at the corners of warm green-hazel eyes. And his voice, a rich, smooth baritone with just the faintest trace of a lisp, and deeply amused by the whole business.

"Please. You make me sound like I'm much nicer than I am. I happen to know for a fact that this show *will* turn a profit. How can it not, with such talent on board? Shall we order? I'm starving."

Most of the producers didn't actually eat anything, but Andrew Farrow neatly gobbled up his lunch while listening avidly to the director and costume designer's conversation. Michael ordered a risotto, which arrived in a huge bowl, too hot to eat. Eventually, the producers rose from their chairs and mingled about, greeting others in the restaurant that they knew, rearranging themselves at their own table. Michael looked up from his risotto, finally cool enough to eat, and saw Andrew Farrow standing right in front of him, extending his hand. "I thought I'd introduce myself properly."

His grip wasn't quite as hard as Michael had expected, and Michael knew he was holding on too hard and too tight in response, and quickly took his extremity back. "Andrew Farrow. Good to see you again. What's it been—two hours?" He punctuated with a grin and a roll of his eyes, as if to say, *This is ridiculous.*

Michael felt enormous and clumsy, even still seated. He instinctively ducked his head and laughed a little too much as he stammered out, "More like a hundred minutes."

"Indeed," Farrow replied, and he sounded amused. "Do you prefer to go by Mike, or Michael?"

"Michael, please."

"You can call me Drew. Just never Andy."

"Okay," Michael said, a bit dazzled, looking past Drew's left shoulder so that he wouldn't keep staring right into his eyes. He reminded himself that he mustn't slouch, or let his mouth hang open, or pick at his cuticles.

"Your portfolio is very impressive," Drew said. He had an incredibly sexy voice, too. Undoubtedly he also smelled and tasted delicious, had an IQ of 200, saved innocent children and puppies from burning buildings, won dance contests, and created soufflés that made Martha Stewart puce with envy. And he was buttering *Michael* up. "You won quite a few awards in school, I see."

"Uh, thanks, thank you . . ."

"But this is the real world," Farrow continued, frowning a challenge. "This is New York theater. You think you're up to this?"

On this, Michael had complete confidence. "Absolutely," Michael replied firmly, frowning back.

"Good." The smile returned. "I look forward to seeing your work." Somehow even these neutral, innocent words, enfolded in Drew Farrow's whiskey-velvet voice, sounded like a sexual challenge.

"I, uh," Michael said, "look forward to impressing you." Farrow nodded and continued away toward the bar, where he greeted the staff by name. Michael's risotto had gotten cold, but it was still one of the most delicious things he'd ever eaten.

At the conclusion of the lunch, Michael shook hands all around, and exchanged contact information with those who didn't already have it. Drew Farrow somehow arranged it so that he came up last. He held out two business cards between fore and middle fingers, his smile confident and predatory. Michael examined the cards—one all business, color and glossy—and the other plainer, brown ink on white laid, listing a phone number, email address, and chat-service user I.D., all different from the ones on the business card. Andrew L. Farrow, financial services consultant, versus plain Drew Farrow; Michael wondered which one was in control.

"Call me any time," Drew said, "for . . . whatever."

"Thank you," Michael said again, handing over one of his own simple, cheap business cards, still bearing his college email address. "Um . . . here. Very nice to meet you. I look forward to seeing you again."

"The feeling is mutual," Drew replied.

"Feel free to call *me* any time," Michael added.

"I *will* feel free," Drew replied, laughing softly.

Michael sighed when his gaze was finally released by the financier, but even so, he did not fully relax until he was on an uptown train, safely out of sight.

He thought it through some more, and came to the rapid decision that, for his own sanity and self-respect, he had to ask out either Drew or Jesse, just for coffee or a walk; nothing that screamed "hookup," but could easily become one. It was one of those challenges he was supposed to demand of himself. But which one first? And perhaps, just to be bold, he should ask them both out; they wouldn't both accept, probably neither would, but at least he'd have done it instead of slinking away with guilt like a scald on his heart. Time to challenge; time to change. Just because they seemed to be together didn't mean that they were exclusive, right? He must no longer assume.

Michael stopped by his former shared office at IUSL, on the Morningside Heights campus of the City University of New York, and picked up the last of his textbooks. No one was there at the time, but already someone had moved into his space, with papers and sticky-notes strewn all over the desk that had once been Michael's. Nostalgically, he stroked the edge of the desk where he had sat almost every day for the last six months. His post-grad research in laser optics was complete, certainly complete enough that he knew he wasn't interested in it anymore for the moment. He had crossed his T's and dotted his I's well enough so that he could take the next year off and figure out exactly what he wanted to do. Was it theater lighting, or was it optical laser physics, or was it something else entirely?

Laden with books, he headed home, stripped down to his undershirt and briefs, ate a raw zucchini sandwich, and slid the books haphazardly onto the bookshelf. His first year out of school had officially begun. Financially buoyed by steady payments from a pair of patents he'd developed, he could simply enjoy life, enjoy New York, explore his inner self and recharge his own batteries, and still help out his parents with their medical bills. He had been in school non-stop for more than twenty years, but these days, when he tried to come up with a Ph D. topic, his head fogged in, rapidly coalescing into fleeting images of men dancing, naked, wobbling cocks and flexing ass cheeks. And smiles.

He wanted to join them so, so badly.

It was still early in the evening, the sun a grenadine stain behind the trees on the horizon. He could go out tonight. He knew it'd probably be good for him to go out, dance, have a drink or two, listen to some new tracks, and maybe get picked up. It was appropriate to celebrate the start of the new job. But he didn't feel like drinking, or dancing, or the negotiations involved in finding a sex partner—if not because of their issues, then because of his own. He wasn't fluent in the wordless language of glances and gestures that all the other gay men seemed to have had memorized from birth; he didn't know how to tell just by looking at a man whether he was compatible or willing. It was easier to stand back and watch, and then go home and think about what he might have done, what he'd seen, and the methods of particularly skillful seducers. He liked to observe. He paid attention. He brought it home and went over it in his mind, forming his own opinions.

Tonight, though, he didn't want to interact with strangers, even if sex might be his reward. He could always reward himself, and be his own DJ to boot.

He put on a new mix CD he'd gotten in the mail from a girl he knew who worked at Warp, and spread out his yoga mat on the floor in front of the bathroom. The mix disappointed him; instead of pure electronica, it was all a bunch of acoustic guitars and soft, intimate male vocals. Grizzly Bear, Gravenhurst, Lambchop, and the like. Michael didn't object to it, but it wasn't what he was expecting. He guessed this was what getting old felt like, that kind of reflexive rejection of that which is unexpectedly new. But Michael had already settled in the lotus position, concentrating on his breathing; he had to sit still and have the experience, and found that he quite liked it.

Just be patient. Relax. Take it. Yes, now it feels good.

At the thought, all the hair on his body quivered. He had never heard those words spoken to him before, not aloud. He had heard them in his fantasies a thousand times. He knew that was how it should be. He imagined the phrase being spoken by Drew Farrow. Drew's voice, all smoke and honey and leather.

Michael planted his palms on the yoga mat, extended his legs, and lifted his hips into the air, his body forming a perfectly triangular downward dog. His breath slithered through his teeth, and he imagined bowing down to Drew's cock. Oh, and maybe Jesse bowing to it, too, his perky little ass pointed up and out, Jesse's thickly muscled forearms straining to prop him up, head down, blood rushing into his skull, filling out those cherry-red lips, making him dizzy and suggestible.

Lifting one hand off the mat, balancing himself on the other, Michael smoothed his hand down the front of his body. His supporting left hand quivered, but he maintained the pose as he poked his fingers under the waistband of his underwear. Almost directly underneath the head of his penis, hot and swollen, rose up to meet his fingertips. Shifting so he carried his weight more evenly between toes and palm, he took hold of the head of his dick, squeezing it lightly between thumb and forefinger. He was shaking too much. This couldn't last. But he didn't let go until he felt a slick of wetness under his thumb, pressed out from the head of his dick. He loved that, and felt joyous wonder at the natural lube that came from him, manufactured through basic animal lust.

He put the hand back down, dropped his hips, and smoothly rose into upward dog, staring fiercely at the ceiling, then lowered himself even further, making his back scream from the strain, until he brushed the yoga mat with his dick. Lowered more, relaxing, lying on his stomach, the cool ribbed texture of the mat brushing his cheek. Without turning over, he felt for himself again, pulling his cock out of his briefs, stroking it, caressing it, pulling on it. Shifting his weight onto his shoulders, he lifted his hips again, just enough so that he had room for his arms to move.

Then he felt ridiculous. He rolled over and sat up, got onto hands and knees, pulling off his shorts. With a smooth movement, he rolled the underwear into a tight ball between his palms, and tossed it into the open laundry hamper at the side of his bed. Keeping his head low and his eyes closed, he crawled the short distance from the door of the bathroom to his bed. Instead of climbing up onto it, he rested his head against the futon mattress, arched his back, and pushed his forehead into the bed, over and over again, squeezing his dick hard.

He lightened his grip, measuring out the amount of pressure he'd felt from Drew's handshake earlier. He slid his hand down the thickening shaft of flesh, quivering as he felt himself respond.

"Yeah," he whispered, "oh, yes, please . . ."

He could do it all with his eyes closed, bent over, face squished into the bed. He stripped off his undershirt and spread it on the edge of the bed, underneath and in front of him. From the third drawer underneath his bed frame, he retrieved a bottle of cheap drugstore lube, tippled a little over his fingers, and took a deep breath. This would be good; he'd been waiting for it all day, holding back and holding back. He could have come straight home and done this, or he could have even taken a few minutes in the restroom at his office, or . . . hell, just pulled one out in the toilets at the theater. But he hadn't. He wanted things to be as perfect as they could; he wanted to be on his knees, bent over, with his face shoved into the bed. Finally allowing himself, he let his cool, slippery fingers slide down the sides of his cock.

It took nothing at all, barely a stroke up and down, for him to break. The orgasm barely hit him; it was just a match struck, and quickly sputtered out. Still, he ejaculated, thick and plentiful, against the white ribbed fabric of his undershirt. He sat back for a minute, catching the mess before it dripped, and again balled up the dirty shirt and tossed it into the hamper. He was far from done. He could do more; he *would* do more.

In the bathroom, beside the tub, Michael knelt on the bath mat, ass in the air and his weight on his shoulders, lubing up his favorite butt toy, a slim, curvy prostate stimulator. He slid it inside, calm until it contacted his most tender spot; after that, the hand smoothing up and down his cock trembled. The bath mat was smelly and needed washing; his bathroom floor wasn't the cleanest, either. It just made him hotter, to imagine being forced down here onto the floor, and for him not to mind because he was so turned on; he'd never say no. Not to him. Not to . . . well, pretty much anyone, really . . .

But Drew. God, that mouth.

Yes, and maybe Jesse, too. Would Jesse throw Michael down on the floor and *insist*?

Probably if Drew told him to, he would . . .

Michael gasped so hard he choked and coughed, hissing, "Oh, fuck," his hand and his belly suddenly sticky with come. He let it stay, crawling back to bed with the toy still sticking out of his ass, lying down on his back, his whole body shaking hard. He'd have to be careful—he'd almost bitten his tongue this time—but he needed another one. Again.

It was one of those nights from which he'd wake up raw in the morning.

2. KIND OF BLUE.

Andrew Farrow got home by six-thirty, sun only now slanting towards the west. He was starving. He'd left work at five-fifteen and headed to the gym with a couple of his colleagues to talk over tomorrow's business while engaging in some brief, high-intensity weight training, then left them behind to run on the treadmill for thirty minutes. He'd had a run in Central Park in the first blush of morning while it was still cool outside, and eight miles would hardly even make him break a sweat. His next marathon wasn't until late July, but he relished the exertion and the focus on his breathing and stride.

It was time for him to buy new shoes; his current pair had begun to chafe around kilometer 7000 on the treadmill. He had managed to avoid a blister, but it wouldn't be a good idea to wear those shoes again tomorrow. As usual, he'd give the busted pair to Jesse; they were still wearable, and they shared the same size.

While he climbed the flight of stairs that led from the foyer, he listened to the message left earlier that evening at his personal phone number. His ex-wife Denisse had called, asking if he'd sent in the final paperwork to approve the sale of the house they'd once shared, reminding him that it was due tomorrow. She added a hello for Jesse, and said she hoped Drew was having a nice day. She never said goodbye before she hung up. She had only said goodbye to Drew once, at the end of the day that he told her they shouldn't be married anymore.

He decided not to reply to the voicemail, only to get the

paperwork couriered over tomorrow. Then he and Denisse would truly be done, ten years after the beginning of the end of them. She'd moved on gracefully. The sins and mistakes of the past were behind them. They even pretended to still be friends.

In his kitchen, Drew set down his gym bag and slowly drank a bottle of coconut water, allowing himself a few minutes to relax and get lost in his thoughts. Denisse called these states "the quietudes." Jesse called them "Blue Steel" if he was being catty, "the aquamarines" when sympathetic. Drew could remain motionless for hours, sitting in a chair, standing in the middle of a room, lying in bed, or polishing off a fifth of scotch without noticing. He kept himself busy as much as possible these days so that he would have fewer opportunities to do that. And Jesse helped, too; his mere presence kept Drew rooted in the present moment.

Jesse wasn't home yet, and so, Drew took the opportunity to brood.

Endings that weren't endings; beginnings he'd seen before.

When Drew was in junior high, he played sports of course, but also stayed after school helping the teachers and the librarians, math tutoring, even being a detention monitor. He enjoyed the extra credit, certainly, but mostly he liked to have an excuse to stay behind after almost all the other students were gone. Once he'd determined that the coast was clear for a few minutes, he'd sneak into the girls' bathroom, lock himself in a stall, and masturbate furiously, touching himself all over, fantasizing about all the girls he'd like to fuck, what they'd look like or sound like, what he'd look or sound like. When he reached the age of opportunity, he found that he had difficulty keeping an erection unless he continued touching himself, caressing his own body, from thighs to the back of his neck, biting and sucking on his own hand. He'd dismissed his own gaze, the one that lingered on the bodies of the more well-built of his fellow athletes, as mere aspiration. He spent less and less time with other boys, happily surrounding himself with an eager fan club of adoring girls. In college, at Yale, Denisse was perfect, the answer to all his prayers, a smart, funny jock with gorgeous, bouncy dark hair and a perfect level of non-competitive ambition. And they had real sex, too — real, phenomenal, lusty sex, as long as he was touching himself as much as he was touching her. In college, too, he found places he would go and be touched by different hands, feel other sensations, grow addicted to the feel of a stubbled chin scraping his belly, the rank scent rising from their two bodies, the low growling voices. Denisse followed Drew to NYU; they matriculated, married. He moved into finance, she into city planning, and that summer he accepted his first invitation to an all-male vacation house in Fire Island Pines.

Years of this. She genuinely never did know; she never did suspect, apparently, even when he came home at three in the morning, bleary-eyed from blow and with his asshole raw. She got pregnant, then miscarried while, across town, Drew was being sucked and fingered by some nameless man in a filthy gas station men's room. He came and signed her out of the hospital, brought her roses and pain medications, and told her everything. She shouted at him, and cried a little, but was surprisingly calm as she kicked him out of the house.

Drew didn't understand the level of forgiveness necessary for her to find it in herself to remain friends with him. It was ten years ago, and time healed, but still. He hoped to God that he and Jesse would never have to attain the level of cool, thoughtful acquaintanceship that he had with Denisse—the slowly diminishing invitations, the politeness, having to decide to watch a lover drift away on the arm of someone else, or to look away.

If nothing else, he and Jesse were solid, had been since the very start. There were few untruths between them, as far as he knew. He was getting older, but so was Jesse; getting older with him. So what if Jesse looked at other men, all of them younger than Drew—all of them Jesse's own age? Jesse had chosen *him*. It worked. It was working. And Drew looked at other men, too, and touched them, and that was all right; touching was all right, violated nothing. Just touching; no further. No kissing, no fucking, but touching was okay. Monogamous, but realistic.

Drew shook his head and put the empty bottle into the sink. He knew that if he had to, he could face it. If Jesse someday chose someone else, Drew could survive. He could endure anything, really. This was the lesson he had hoped to learn when he first started running. Now he could run a hundred miles, if he wanted to; he could run all day and all night, and still be alive at the end. He just had no desire to do that anymore; a marathon was plenty. At the end of a marathon he could go drink beer, eat pizza and ice cream cake with Jesse, curl up to sleep with him, wake up the next day with Jesse already applying ice packs to his legs.

Each footstep on the squeaky floor between kitchen and sitting room echoed through the bones of the townhouse. Flipping light switches as he went, Drew restarted Miles Davis's *Kind of Blue* on the stereo, disk still in the machine from last night. With the cool, familiar sounds of vibraphone and brush-drum humming from speakers in the corners of several rooms, he went to his bedroom's walk-in closet to change. He paused, nude before the floor-to-ceiling mirror on one of the closet walls, examining his body closely, checking to see if any part of him needed work. He looked good all over—thick, smooth muscles on his arms, shoulders, chest, thighs, strong hips and groin, abs firm and defined, body hair kept in check—until his critical gaze reached his ankles. From there down, he was a mess of scars and hardened calluses; the flesh and bones of his feet were gnarled from wear and impact, toenails blunt nubs in bruised beds. Still, that was a point of pride, too. He liked his ragged and tattered feet best of all.

While he still sat on the dressing room bench, sliding his striated feet into sandals, he heard the front door open and the muffled jangling chaos of Jesse's keychain as he let himself in. Momentarily Jesse ambled into the bedroom, an overstuffed messenger bag weighing down one shoulder. Drew stood up to greet him with a quick hug, just a grasp of Drew's hand on Jesse's arm. "Hey," Jesse said wearily. "Cool if I take a shower first?"

The layered reek of sweat dried on sweat rose off Jesse. The younger man's hair was filthy, stained with flecks of paint, sawdust, and dull dirt; the same evidence was streaked on his cheeks, like he'd been too preoccupied to even rinse his face before leaving the theater. "Please do," Drew said, stepping back and grimacing. "Do us both a favor."

Jesse rolled his eyes at Drew as he walked to the bathroom. "You stink sometimes, too," Jesse grumbled.

"You like it." Drew followed, not too closely. "I'm ordering in Japanese," he said. "You want noodles or sushi?"

Jesse stripped off his T-shirt, turned on the shower tap, and unfastened the buckle on his belt, shimmying his baggy jeans over his thighs. Drew enjoyed having the opportunity to openly stare at Jesse taking off his clothes. Even though Jesse could only occasionally be bothered to visit a gym, he managed to stay in good shape, strong but slim, his chest still mostly smooth but for some long, stray hairs surrounding his nipples and navel. All the scars and damage that were confined to Drew's feet were evenly dispersed over Jesse's body. He wore several fresh new bruises along his arms and ribs, and two of his fingers were bandaged. Still, he was gorgeous, his lean muscles shaped by building, skateboarding, biking, climbing any tree or rooftop he could reach; a vigorous young body, built for roughhousing and sex. His finely-featured face, with its shapely red lips, as pretty as a girl's, could still pass for that of a teenager. "Cold udon," he said, scratching his hair. "And a seaweed salad. What's that called again?"

"*Wakame*." Drew started to say something else, but Jesse had already gotten under the water and showed no signs that he'd heard. Drew shrugged and left the room. Jesse needed his space.

The order arrived before Jesse emerged from the shower. Drew was tipping the delivery man at the bottom of the stairs when Jesse peeked out from the French doors at the top, gleaming clean, wrapped in one of Drew's white terrycloth robes, sloppily tied, nothing on underneath. The delivery man, young, Asian, with indie-rocker shaggy hair and a pierced eyebrow, looked up at Jesse and nodded acknowledgment. Jesse just chuckled and disappeared.

"What was that all about?" Drew asked, bringing the bags to the kitchen and setting them on the counter. "Do you know that guy you just flashed?"

"Don't you recognize him?" Jesse had found the *sake*, and busied himself pouring some into champagne flutes. "We used to run deliveries together last year, back when I worked for Fresh Direct. His name's Ichi, like the killer. Pretty cool guy."

"Huh," Drew replied. He pursed his lips, letting annoyed jealousy dissolve unspoken. "Set the table, would you?"

Jesse whined a little. "Honey . . . I don't feel like eating at the table. Can't we eat in front of the TV? On the couch. I'm too tired to want to sit up straight. Please?"

Drew let out a long-suffering groan. "Just don't make a mess." He grabbed a serving tray from the top shelf of his rack of cabinets and put the takeout boxes onto it, unconsciously squaring the corners and perfectly aligning the chopsticks in parallel.

"Promise I won't," Jesse said amiably, poking chopsticks into the box containing Drew's food, and drawing back with a grimace when he saw that it was chicken. "So, what's the movie?"

Drew let his shoulders relax. "*Les Enfants Terribles.*" He recited the title with a practiced accent, and Jesse smirked. "Written by Cocteau. Not directed by him, though."

Jesse rolled his eyes and sighed. "Ehh. Cocteau again. How many of them are there? We've seen them all by now, haven't we?"

"I thought you enjoyed them," Drew replied quietly. "You were all hot for *Orphée.*"

"No, I like them. I do. It's just that you like them more." Jesse softened all of this with a smile, a suggestion of husky laugh. He carried the drinks over to the viewing room and set them onto a low table beside the long, rectilinear sofa. Drew followed with the tray. "I was kind of hoping you'd taken a chance and got a *Nightmare on Elm Street* movie or somethin'."

Drew laughed. "Okay, Jess. Fair enough. You get to pick the next one we watch."

Jesse arched his eyebrow warningly. "I'm gonna remember you said that. I'm gonna make you watch *The Doom Generation* again." Grinning, he waited for Drew to groan in dismay at the memory. "Let's get started now, though; I'm really tired. I probably won't last too long tonight." Jesse plopped down and slurped his full glass of *sake* in one gulp.

"Not drinking on an empty stomach, you won't."

"Well, gimme my food then . . ."

"I'm gonna slap you," Drew said mildly, moving toward the television and DVD player. Chuckling, Jesse pulled the top off the container of noodles and began shoveling them into his mouth with a deft hand on the chopsticks. Drew grinned, hiding it behind his hand. "For God's sake, you're not supposed to serve *sake* in glasses like that. Unless it's in cocktail form."

"But a flute keeps the *sake* far from your fingers, so it doesn't get warm," Jesse pointed out. "There's a method to my madness, Miss Post. Or is that Ma'm'selle Chose tonight? See, I remember my high school French, too."

"Fuck you."

Jesse finished his entire meal within minutes, then sat back and relaxed, sipping his drink, studying the film. "Why are they wearing shorts in the snow?" he asked.

"They're supposed to be schoolboys."

Jesse snickered. "They're thirty-five."

"Hollywood magic. Shush."

"Why can't I talk? It's subtitled." Jesse's attention was already wandering, three minutes into the picture. Drew ate slowly, despite how hungry he was, taking time to savor each bite. Jesse perked up momentarily. "Oooh. *He's* really cute."

"That's Édouard Dermithe. Cocteau's lover."

"I just bet he was."

"It didn't work out between them. Anyway. Could you maybe watch the film?"

"Okay, film, right, yes," Jesse grunted comfortably, and leaned into Drew a little bit. Drew was glad that the food in his mouth muffled his sigh of pleasure. Shortly, Jesse altered his position, resting his legs across Drew's lap. Drew gently rubbed and kneaded the soles of Jesse's feet, clean and strong and innocent of scars. "I've got a pair of shoes for you," Drew remembered.

"A new set of old-and-busted? No, thanks. I took the other ones you gave me to the Salvation Army. I'll buy my own kicks. When I need 'em."

Drew washed down the last bite of *yakitori* with a mouthful of cold, cloudy wine. "Whatever. What's up with the hand injuries? Did you lose your work gloves?"

Jesse's attention had wandered back to the film, where the crazy blond brother and sister lay in the same bed. "Huh? Oh, I got distracted. I didn't lose 'em. It's just a couple of little cuts. This movie is *weird*, man."

"It's Cocteau. Of course it's weird." Drew promised himself that he'd watch the movie again some other time, when Jesse wasn't around. He was distracted, too.

"Got a hard-on for *Cock*-teau, don't you?"

"Shut. Up. Jesse."

"You're gonna slap me," Jesse added, and laughed faintly.

"Yes, I will," Drew agreed. When Jesse sat up again, he let his lips play across Drew's mouth. Drew kissed back, but without force.

Still, the feeling was wonderful. Drew never grew tired of the way it felt when they kissed. So many years now, eight officially, ten if you counted from when they first kissed, when they probably shouldn't have been kissing. From when Jesse was way too young and Drew had pushed him away in alarm, scared of that intense, damaged child, scared of how instantly he himself had responded to Jesse's seemingly innocent flirtations. They hadn't been innocent at all, and Jesse had known that Drew liked it. Liked *him*, despite the impossibility of it.

It was still so good—the soft warmth of his mouth and the moist surprise of the tip of Jesse's tongue, always interested in exploring, even the territory that he already knew. Jesse's mouth was always and never the same. The same mouth that Drew had first tasted when Jess was only sixteen . . . and . . .

Jesse's desperate whisper, *Please.*

And Drew had muttered, *Stop it; you're my cousin.*

And Jesse whispered back, *I don't care.*

You're just a kid.

Ha . . . You *don't care.*

And here they still were, and now Jesse was twenty-seven, and Drew turned forty in August.

Drew pulled back from the kiss with a sigh. Jesse's innate scent had begun to reassert itself from behind the polite mask of shower gel and shampoo, mingling with the nautical odors of the seaweed and sweet soy sauce he'd just eaten, and the silken texture of his tongue had dredged up a decade's worth of memories of desire.

But now for some reason Jesse was absorbed in the film again, so Drew watched him instead. Jesse's overgrown locks of vaguely wavy dark hair had become shaggy at the edges, still damp from the shower. His face presented a few freckles in tiny clusters across olive-tanned cheeks and the Roman nose with the double-crooked bridge. His lips flushed deep rose from kissing, outlined with a faint mist of dark stubble. The images on the television screen swam over Jesse's golden-brown irises, and his nostrils flared in unconscious response to what he was seeing.

In the movie, the characters had gone to sea without Drew remembering how they'd gotten there. He was fluent in conversational French, but not so much that he could follow the dialogue without watching. He slipped his arm around Jesse's shoulders, holding him near, accepting Jesse's head nestling under his chin, and turned his attention back to the tableau playing across the plasma screen.

The siblings seemed to be in bed again, the brother prone and unconscious, or faking it. The sister lustily ate crayfish, and plucked the meat from a shell, murmuring assurances. Then she fed her brother the crayfish, the camera focusing tightly on his mouth, her fingers poking the slippery tail of the crustacean again and again, insistently, between his glistening, ridged lips.

"Jesus," Drew whispered, chuckling, a hot thrill running across his skin. Moments like these were why he treasured Cocteau in the first place.

"That's it," Jesse murmured. He sighed, and rubbed his cheek across the base of Drew's neck. He grabbed one of Drew's thick, heavily furred forearms, and said, "This is ridiculous. I can't deal with this anymore. You know what the ritual is actually about, and it's not watching this cracked-out movie."

Drew grabbed Jesse by the shoulders, and forced him down onto his back on the couch. He kissed him several times, sharply and aggressively. Under Drew's lips, he felt Jesse's curve into a satisfied grin. Nonetheless, Jesse tried to cross his arms over his chest and offer resistance, but it was too awkward, and he just tangled himself in the sleeves of the immense bathrobe.

"Okay," Jesse said.

Drew pulled at the tie holding the robe closed, and once it was loose, he slid his hands underneath, up over Jesse's ribs, providing just enough pressure that it wouldn't tickle him. Jesse gazed up, smiling, calm and pleased. He'd gotten some attention. Drew took each of Jesse's nipples between thumbs and forefingers and twisted them, just roughly enough. Or so he thought. Rather than bucking against him or howling in protest, Jesse just kept that gentle smile. "Aw, now you're mad," he whispered.

"No," Drew replied, shaking his head, dipping his mouth back in for another kiss, his hands sliding possessively over Jesse's lithe, smooth torso, thumbs delving one after the other into the shallow reservoir of his navel.

Jesse sighed, and pushed his hands up underneath the hem of Drew's shirt, his slim fingers cold. It didn't feel good at first; it felt like Drew was being nibbled by tiny damp newts. To distract himself, he tugged the shirt up and off over his head, then loosened the drawstring on his linen pants. When he caught a glimpse of Jesse's face, he saw an expression more distracted than he'd expected, almost bored. "Can we just go to bed?" Jesse asked.

"Yeah, yeah," Drew replied. He sat up, found the remote. Jesse got up.

By the time Drew made it to the bedroom, Jesse lay on turned-down sheets, nude, staring into space and stroking a distracted hand up and down his stomach. Drew slid out of his clothes, draping them over a chair. Joining Jesse on the bed, he took Jesse's hand and guided it down to his half-hard dick, as if showing him what to do. Jesse closed his eyes, but didn't take direction; he let his fingers splay out over his own genitals without taking hold. Drew lay beside him, and kissed the side of his face. Jesse responded by stroking Drew's skin with the same light, petting touch that he'd used on himself.

Drew took Jesse's shoulders more forcefully, denting the muscle with his fingertips, and kissed Jesse's lips, opening his mouth with his tongue. If Jesse wasn't going to grab himself, Drew would do it. He took Jesse's dick in his hand and squeezed firmly. When Jesse barely responded to that touch, Drew changed tactics and instead gently kissed the various bruises and scrapes on Jesse's body. Shoulder, elbow, knee. Drew held up Jesse's arm and kissed the tips of his bandaged fingers.

Jesse liked that. He arched and moaned softly, touching himself again. "Seriously. Are you mad at me?" he asked.

"I already said I wasn't. Should I be?" Drew took Jesse's dick in his fingers and kissed the vulnerable, supple tip, lightly applying a touch of wet tongue. Jesse was a grower. Drew wanted to see it. It might take a while, at this rate, which surprised him; hadn't it been Jesse who suggested bed? "You want me to be? I can be angry, if you want."

That brought another sigh from Jesse, resigned, disappointed. "No . . ."

"What do you *want*? Or do you want me to use my psychic powers to figure out what you want . . .?"

"No. It's like . . . I'm . . . just touch me. It feels good. I need that."

Drew relaxed onto his side, half-propped up on one elbow, fingers stroking up and down Jesse's torso, from collarbone to treasure-trail, turning back at the thick black crop of pubic hair. "I want you to tell me what's on your mind," Drew said quietly, but firmly. "Whatever it is." He didn't have to add that anything that would distract Jesse from easy sex was a big deal. "You feel okay?"

Jesse nodded, and as Drew's fingers circled the small patch of rough scab on his shoulder, bit the edge of his lip as if fighting off a sudden pang. It wasn't pain; shouldn't be. "Yeah, I'm . . ." He suddenly opened his eyes and gazed at Drew, then glanced away with an embarrassed smile. "I'm just having dirty thoughts. About someone else."

"That's what I thought," Drew said. "That's okay, you know. I don't mind." Jesse laughed freely, as though a weight had been lifted from him. Drew kissed the hollow of Jesse's throat, and finally let his stroking touch move down to the base of Jesse's penis. "Do you want to tell me about it?" Drew added.

Jesse shifted his hips, spreading his thighs a bit; Drew stepped up the pace of his fingers circling Jesse's cock, tightening, but moving slow. "Like, talk dirty to you?" He laughed again, languidly, arching his hips, fucking Drew's hand. Drew's mouth began to water. "Get you hot and kinked out, get your cuckolding jollies in for the week?"

The younger man's voice dissolved in shaky laughter, seized hard by his own self-directed desire at the same time that Drew held his hips down and lifted Jesse's cock to his mouth. "Oh, Jesus. You know that's right . . . You wonder, too. You want to see me with somebody else. What's it like? *Me taking someone else's dick.*" Under Drew's restraining hand, Jesse's lower abs tensed, and he opened his legs wider still. Drew angled one arm under Jesse's left knee, lifting it up, exposing him. "Think about it. God, what would it be like? Would you like that? Watching me ride some other cock and making you watch, right? Are you into that?" Jesse quivered all over, his lifted leg shaking. "Those big hands. Man . . . I wondered all day how he must taste. Imagine him on his back with those long legs in the air."

Drew said, "Hmmm," lips vibrating on Jesse's cock.

Jesse's breath hissed between his teeth. "I thought about him fucking you, too. Him spearing you on his cock. Oh, Drew . . . God. That's nice. Would you like that? Take some other man's cock for me?

Oh . . . would you do that? Would you do that for me?"

He fell abruptly silent, and Drew raised his head to look up at him; his hand on Jesse's cock was slippery all of a sudden, warm fluid overflowing his fingers. Only after the fact did Jesse let loose his melancholy-sounding orgasmic moan.

"Real good," Drew said. "I want some, too."

Jesse smiled, eyes glazed, cheeks flushed bright red, the tip of his tongue slicking the corner of his mouth. "I want *you* to do to me what you want *him* to do to me," he whispered. "I want to feel what you want to do to *him*. I want to jack off to that tomorrow." His body was still shaking, as though he were still coming, somewhere, on some plane of existence.

The older man sat up, and reached for one of the white cotton hand towels that he kept in a neat stack in a wire basket next to the bed. Once he'd wiped his hand clean and dry, and dropped the towel into the small covered hamper that he kept underneath, he scooted to the edge, and lightly tapped the floor with his foot. "Over here," he commanded softly. "On your knees. Suck this."

"Pretend I'm someone else," Jesse suggested, grinning as he climbed down.

Drew didn't reply, only firmly grasped the back of Jesse's hair, and pushed him forward between his legs. Jesse emitted a series of pleased puppyish growls and whines, and took half of Drew's length into his mouth at once. Drew held the back of Jesse's head still, and arched his hips back and forth. He hardly dared to look down at Jesse's face; the sudden vicious strength of desire fulfilled was almost too much. But that was Jesse down there, bangs fringing down over his face, obscuring his eyes but framing the wet, reddened lips stretched around Drew's cock, the rounded end pushing out his cheek. Jesse inhaled deeply through his nose, and let out a long groan of protest. Not a real one, but one to let Drew know that he was reaching his limits. Drew thrust a fraction harder, while he could; and imagined a set of clunky black glasses slipping down over a big, sensual nose laboring to breathe, darker eyes, fuller lips . . .

"Oh, fuck. Oh, my God," Drew hissed, clamping his eyes shut; the orgasm looked like a sudden slash of forked lightning against the darkness. The lightning traveled up his spine, spreading slowly as heat through his limbs, over his face. Jesse whine-moaned again, but Drew held him still, stroking his throat, not releasing him until he'd swallowed.

As soon as he was free, Jesse relaxed backwards, sighing, his tongue dangling from his mouth. "Goodness gracious, Mr. Farrow," he murmured. "You know we're not supposed to do that."

Drew collapsed back onto the bed, aftershocks shivering through him. "It's a rare treat," he sighed. "Savor it."

"Gross," Jesse chuckled.

"Get up here. Good Lord, I need a hug."

Jesse climbed up, and dragged the bedding over him, over Drew's opposite side. Drew pulled the sheets up to his shoulders, and took Jesse into his arms, holding him close. Jesse squeezed back, kissing Drew, transmitting the taste of his semen back to him. He held his damp forehead against Drew's, his tongue tracing gentle circles inside Drew's mouth. He used to swallow all the time, and kiss him like this afterward. Perhaps he had only done it this time because he fantasized about doing it with someone else. It was splendid, nonetheless, the sticky spiral kiss, and yes, Drew had been thinking it, too.

Almost at once, they both shuddered, and broke down laughing. They gazed into each other's eyes, separated by only a few inches, simmering in the intimacy.

"So, do I know this person?" Drew asked softly, brushing Jesse's hair out of his eyes.

After a moment's hesitation, Jesse shook his head. "No," he said.

"Do you want to fuck him?" Drew asked, gently gripping Jesse's hand.

"I don't fuck anybody but you," Jesse replied. He squeezed back.

"But do you want to?"

"Of course I do," said Jesse. He smiled. "But we don't do that, you and me." He frowned in realization. "Wow, we haven't gone out in a long time. When was the last time you had a back-room hand job?"

"What about you?" Drew responded. "Did you get a hand job

from Ichi the Killer?"

Jesse laughed. "No, I wish," he said. "He's straight." He squeezed Drew's hand again. "I would have told you if I did. I have never fucked around on you, or gone behind your back." His eyes lowered, and he nodded thoughtfully. "And that's good. I trust you. That's why I can eat your come." He chuckled faintly, and stared at Drew. "But . . . you know . . . what if?"

"What if."

They both went quiet then, and ran their hands over each other soothingly, relaxing into twin puddles on the huge bed, flanked by two walls of huge windows, the blue evening light diffused through sheer rice paper screens. It was just nine o'clock, but the sun had barely set. Summer was nearly here. Drew was tired, though; at this time of the year, even when he wasn't in training, he'd get up an hour before sunrise so he could be out running when it came up. It had been a full day, and he had come really hard. Harder than he had in months.

With a quiet clearing of his throat, Jesse stirred, and sat up, smoothing his hair back. "Where you going?" Drew asked, sleepy and irritated.

"I'm going to the other room," Jesse replied. "Going to sleep." He kissed Drew. "I'm sorry. Even though I pretend you don't, you wake me up when you get up." He slid over to the side of the bed, and stood up, arching his back and stretching his shoulders. "I'm on the set tomorrow from nine to nine-thirty. Twelve-hour day. You know." His satisfied cock dangled, still lengthy, between his thighs, and Drew resisted the urge to smack it like a cat attacking a swinging cord. "You should come down after work, if you want."

"Yeah . . ." Drew drawled, sliding his hands back under the covers. "Dinner afterwards?"

"We'll see. Maybe just a few drinks."

"And a back-room hand job?"

Jesse smirked and rolled his eyes, then bent over and kissed Drew's forehead. "'Night. Sleep well. Run good in the morning."

"I will," Drew said, and watched his boyfriend gather up his clothes and walk out, naked and barefoot. The townhouse had five bedrooms, two converted into Drew's home gym and home office, one guest room, and one room that was more or less Jesse's own disaster area. In the five years they'd lived together, in this house, Jesse had slowly gravitated towards having his own room, even though he originally claimed he didn't need one.

Despite how relaxed he'd been five minutes ago, Drew found himself seized with that kind of end-of-the-day restlessness that often took hold of him when Jesse wasn't there. Jesse always, almost always, slept in Drew's bed with him; almost always, they fell asleep together. But sometimes Jesse needed his own space, his own area of cluttered privacy, his own bed, and his own bills to pay. They both agreed on this. But they were never far away from each other; never someplace that needed shoes to be put on for them to be together.

Drew got up, went to the bathroom, and brushed and flossed his teeth. He was sad to be rinsing Jesse's flavor from his mouth, but it had to be done, especially at his age. He took care of himself. He returned to bed, holding a pillow.

3. THE JOKER AND THE THIEF.

The next morning Michael arrived at the theater at 8:45, a full forty-five minutes before call, hoping he could verify the rigging diagram without a bunch of construction crew underfoot.

It was going to be a long day.

He hadn't gotten to the end of the first column of his equipment checklist before the door at the back of the house opened. Jesse came into view, a rectangular moment of sun behind him, wiping his face with the back of his hand. His slightly bowlegged walk was more of a casual, limping swagger, weighted down on one side by a large duffle bag. He was wearing the same paint-stained, blue-black jeans he'd worn the day before, a threadbare but body-hugging cycling jersey, and heavy, clomping steel-toed industrial boots. He hadn't shaved, the dark mist of stubble thicker than it had been yesterday, making Jesse look like a dissolute 18th century prince turned pirate. Michael sighed and marveled.

"You're here early," Jesse grinned. He sat on the edge of the stage and set down the duffle bag, pulling out an enormous Thermos bottle. "You want some coffee?" he asked. "I always bring coffee to the stage. That's my superstition."

Michael watched as Jesse set up the Thermos and a half-dozen mugs, all of them different and bearing the weathered patina that came from a thrift store shelf. "Sure," Michael said, cracking tension out of his shoulders. He didn't have to be so uptight; Jesse didn't bite.

"Got a guy who roasts it for me, back in the old neighborhood.

He got a shop over there, 18th Street, good pignolos, zeppoli, shit like that, you know?" Sudden thickening boroughs accent out of nowhere. Michael breathed it in like a scent. For just an instant, Jesse looked up and their eyes met. "Pick a coffee mug. Tells me your personality."

Once Michael had chosen a mug (one with a *Gone With the Wind* graphic badly printed on it), Jesse poured for him. "Good choice. I just got that one last week. It's new; never been used here before." He nodded again, thoughtfully. "You like things clean."

And, Michael thought, *I'm a screaming queer.* "Thanks. So what are *you* doing here so early? Construction call isn't for a while."

"Like I said, bringing coffee," Jesse explained. "I was up, anyway. I had kind of a hard time sleeping." He looked back toward the stage.

"Excited to start working?" Michael guessed.

"Something like that." A smile curved the edge of Jesse's mouth. "You want to give me some pointers about the rigging? Because I've seen the set model, but I'm still not sure exactly what you're going to be doing."

"Oh – yes – right. That. Well, I'll show you." Michael bolted the rest of his coffee down as he went out onto the stage. "My plan is a combination of traditional incandescent lighting overhead, and adding LED follow spots and pans lower to the stage floor, lighted floor panels, and six vertical columns there, there, and there. Also, there'll be additional rigging required for the house, because there'll be hidden spots in six places at the back of the room, and sixteen floods overhead. The thought is that during the waterfall scene, the overhead grid will be in sync with the columns on stage, so that it'll look as though there's water rushing overhead and down onto the stage, so that the audience is actually underneath the waterfall."

Jesse just chuckled, and shook his head, like he'd told a joke that Michael didn't get. It didn't matter; Jesse was standing right there, being *him*. Sweaty hair had dried into locks and half-curls, finger-combed into the kind of messy shapes that styling products were meant to emulate. He didn't need to be well groomed; he was naturally attractive, his features delicate and beautiful, and yet undeniably masculine. "I'm sorry; I'm boring you," Michael said.

"No, not at all," Jesse said. "I'm mostly just kind of amazed. Have you been doing this long?"

"I've done stage lighting couple of times," Michael replied, walking away and picking up his rigging diagram and checklist from where he'd set them on the floor. "Mostly I've been in academics. I went to Carnegie Mellon for undergrad, then transferred to City College to work on my Ph.D., but . . ." Michael shrugged. "I got bored with my dissertation. I want to do more practical, applied tech. I want to use the stuff I built."

"You *built* all this stuff? What, by hand?" Jesse's eyes went wide.

Michael felt a warm quiver of pride go up his back, even as he despaired that he'd ever get back to work. "Mostly these days I design systems. I helped develop practical applications for ultraviolet LEDs. For anti-counterfeit measures. Got a couple of patents." He shrugged. "It's a little money."

"Wow," said Jesse. He seemed impressed, even humbled. "How old are you?"

"Twenty-seven," Michael admitted.

"Wow, me too," Jesse said brightly, and sighed. "I... haven't even graduated from college. I'm, like, five credits short. I just don't feel like it, you know? I hate writing papers. I'm not dumb, but I just like to work. Y'know. Have a job, get paid."

"Yeah," Michael said softly. "I get it." He pushed his glasses up onto the bridge of his nose.

"Anyone ever tell you that you look like Clark Kent when you do that?"

"Not usually," Michael replied, his cheeks suddenly hot. "That would imply that I'm Superman underneath."

Jesse grinned. "Aren't you?"

"Mr. Landon, if you please," came a shout from stage left.

Jesse glanced over his shoulder at the set foreman frowning at him, arms crossed over his chest. "Better get to it," Jesse said sheepishly, and turned away. Michael let out a heavy breath he hadn't known he was holding.

He spent the morning obsessing over Jesse. That amazing face, entirely built on imperfections. That compact, wiry body, obviously much stronger than it looked. Michael couldn't stop watching him, even if only from the corner of his eye, from up above on a ladder, peering around a corner. Every element intrigued him: the smile, the laugh, the frown of concentration, lips pursed tight as though sucking on something. So he was a dropout. So he was staunchly working-class; in a different world, under different circumstances, Michael would have been, too. Jesse was obviously bright, engaging, and well adjusted. He'd probably have to be, to be dating an alpha-male titan of industry like Andrew Farrow. Michael sighed, reminded himself of his place, and forced himself to concentrate on his work.

The rest of the day was a blur of work for Michael. Problems kept cropping up. He hated knowing that he'd proposed a lighting design that was more ambitious than practical, and in an attempt to control his anger and frustration with himself, he kept his head down and his focus tightly on what was directly in front of him. Rather than taking a break at dinner with the others, Michael worked through, grinding his teeth and ignoring the growling in his stomach.

Nine o'clock came, and the construction crew cleared up the loose elements on the stage, stowing them safely away to continue tomorrow. Michael looked up to see Andrew Farrow, gray suit artfully rumpled and hair utterly perfect, standing at the front entrance to the stage, eyes shining as Jesse walked over to meet him. They smiled at each other and kissed on the lips.

Michael's chest burned with jealousy. He didn't want to see that. Oh, but at the same time, they were really beautiful together. Standing side by side, under the bright house lights, they resembled each other in a way. Drew was an inch or two taller, his big movie-star head crowned with thick mink-brown hair, neatly combed and pomaded into submission, contrasting with Jesse's tousled mop of nearly black. But they had similar features, similar ears, and the same arm-to-torso-to-leg ratio. They were cut, one sharp-edged and one asymmetrical, from the same cloth. Had they seen each other across a crowded room, and felt an innate attraction to another who looked so much like him?

"Let's go. I could use a drink," Drew said, and put his arm around Jesse, guiding him out. Michael watched them stride together until they disappeared, sighing for the solitary night ahead of him.

The next day, Michael did not arrive early; there was no point. He knew the score.

Today was serious business. Conversation was minimal, replaced by the shrill of power drills and a barrage of hammers. The theater grew very hot even before noon, hoarding the heat from outside. Michael chewed mint gum and continued his dusty, picky wiring task, occasionally rewarding himself with a quick glimpse at Jesse's undiminished beauty. It didn't make him feel any less hot, but it kept a smile on Michael's face and a quiet joy in his heart.

Around eleven-thirty, Jesse set down his power drill, and announced, "I'm too hot; I'm taking five. Anyone needs me, I'll be in the dressing room." No one even looked up, and Jesse went backstage, wiping his face with his shirttail.

After trying for a few minutes, Michael had to admit that he couldn't focus on the wiring diagram. He was too hot, too. Nobody would notice if he took a break. He was in the crew but not *of* it, not really part of that shaggy gang of builders.

Treading lightly and carefully, he followed in Jesse's wake.

In the dressing room, bolts of cloth leaned against the wall. Some unfinished costume pieces had been marked out on pattern-paper and were held tightly in place with gleaming pins. The costumers were nowhere to be seen; probably out smoking, huddled in the sparse shade under the awning of the print shop next door.

Jesse was on the bench where the actors could tighten bootlaces or take five between scenes. He had taken off his paint-stained, sweat-soaked T-shirt, and lay with his arms stretched over his head, wantonly exposing his dark-haired armpits, stretching the skin over his chest, which glistened with a fine sheen of sweat. Biting his lip at the sight, Michael had a sudden impulse to take one of the sewing pins and slowly insert it into Jesse's skin, just below the collarbone, to keep it in its beautiful place. Jesse's form was neat and elegant in a way that his disheveled clothes disguised; such linear veins running down his arms, such perfect quarter-sized dusty-pink nipples. His torso seemed hairless but for the sprinkling of sparse black hair that thickened over his belly, a trail of coarser hair leading teasingly underneath the white elastic waistband of his underwear, an inch or two of which was visible above the top of his filthy jeans.

Glancing at Michael, Jesse smiled, shy but friendly, almost innocent, eyes soft like a storybook woodland creature's. He could have gotten away with a smoldering, lascivious look, lying there exposed and vulnerable. *Kiss me right here; ravish me.* But he only looked calm and relaxed, his shoulders shifting, arms up. Michael turned away and swallowed. "Sorry; I didn't mean to disturb you," he murmured.

"You didn't," Jesse said. He took a deep breath and released it as a luxurious sigh as he closed his eyes. "I just needed to lie down. It's fucking hot out there."

"Maybe you should bring one of the fans in here," Michael suggested, focusing his eyes in a corner of the room. A tent of cobwebs in the corner wore a heavy, blonde mantle of sawdust. Just looking at it made him want to sneeze. He fought off the urge; he didn't want to get microscopic flecks of spittle and germs on Jesse's immaculate bare chest. Oh, but he did, he realized; he did. Suddenly the thought of sneezing all over Jesse was painfully erotic. Would he flinch, or accept it with this same lazy calm?

The answering chuckle from Jesse just intensified his longing for release. Michael was glad that he was facing away so Jesse couldn't see the size of his erection. It ached; he could feel it pressing tight against his inseam. "No way," Jesse replied. "With all that dust on the ground? I'd just be asking for an allergy attack."

"Asking for it," Michael echoed, chuckling too. How obvious was he? "Can I get you anything? Maybe some ice water?"

"No, it's cool. I've got some." Jesse angled his head back, indicating a clear bottle of Volvic, its surface dotted with fat droplets of condensation rolling down and puddling on the floor next to the bench. "There's some more in the fridge if you want it."

"Yes, I know," said Michael. He got a bottle of water, opened it, and cleared half of it before the cold refreshment kicked him in the back of the head. It felt good; he had been far thirstier than he thought. He took a deep breath, steadying himself, and walked back toward the door. "Thank you for reminding me." He had to get out of here before he compromised himself and offended Jesse. And Andrew Farrow would probably be offended if he knew how Michael was staring at Jesse, wanting him so much his mouth watered. Wanting him so much he wanted to attach his skin to the bench with pins, a thousand of them; to tack Jesse down to the peeling leatherette and take his measure.

"Any time," Jesse replied. And laughed again.

Michael walked back toward the doorway.

"Hey, Mike," Jesse called after him. Still laughing. Jesse obviously knew. He thought it was funny.

Eyes closed with impatience. "Please. It's Michael."

"Michael! Oh, sorry. *Michael*." Slowly, sensually. Like he was testing the syllables in his mouth. He knew. "Do you want to go get a drink tonight? We're going around the corner to the Lit Lounge after we knock off."

"Oh . . ." Michael paused at the doorway, tempted to look over his shoulder to get a last glimpse of that splendor of skin. "Yeah. I'd love to. Thanks."

"You're so polite," Jesse said in a whisper, a stage aside that the audience was clearly meant to hear. "I love that."

That afternoon Jesse was too busy to steal more than an occasional glimpse of Michael, let alone talk to him; the frustrated urge became longing, and then hunger. Jesse ached to tell him how great he looked, wearing a faded black Nine Inch Nails T-shirt instead of his long-sleeved button-down shirts from the days prior. Michael had nice arms, very long, beautifully defined without being hugely muscular, furred with dark hair that extended onto his wrists and the backs of his hands. The hair looked soft and touchable. But the man himself was intently occupied, running wires, taping them down, testing power levels. Michael didn't even go with the rest of the crew to grab a quick dinner. He hadn't gone to dinner last night, either. It drove Jesse crazy; didn't the guy need to eat? He spent the evening fantasizing about what kinds of food Michael liked, and how great it would be to cook for him—a nice big bowl of angel hair pasta with truffle oil and asiago, to fatten those skinny bones; or maybe a sweet, ice-cold gazpacho and a pile of frozen grapes and blueberries, fed to him one by one.

The day went on and on, a dusty, grunting haze of lifting and holding, hammering and drilling. The set crew worked as fast as they could without hurrying; rushing to build something that people stood on, or underneath, was an invitation to danger. Maintaining the balance between haste and care required tremendous concentration.

Finally, the strident, hoarse buzzer of the big union clock mounted at the back of the stage made ten heads snap up as one. Ten minutes to clear up and mark where they had left off. Jesse made haste to gather and replace all of his tools and bits, and when he had signed the time sheet, he looked up to see Michael standing right beside him, smiling uneasily and clutching his silver briefcase to his chest as though it contained government secrets. Jesse grinned at his eagerness. "You ready?"

"Ready to roll," Michael replied.

Jesse laughed, wondering if Michael had any idea how sweet and naïve he appeared, and angled his thumb towards the backstage door.

The company poured out onto the street. Jesse loved these moments when the crew all got together after the day's work was done and went in a noisy mob to take over some bar. Moments like these, much more so than opening night or the performances, made Jesse love set construction more than any other kind. The built-up soreness in his palms and back vanished. He worked with his hands for a living; he paid for leisure with his sweat and his diligence. And Michael gazed with wonder at it all, as though he had never been in such a group.

The company quickly traversed the two blocks to the graffiti-covered door of the Lit Lounge, and packed themselves in to the dark, noisy, boozy space of the downstairs bar. It was too early for bands to play, but the DJ had the new Wolfmother single cranked to a glass-rattling volume. Jesse immediately danced to it, banging his head and making choppy swimming motions with his arms. He knew he looked like a goof, but he just had to dance. Michael watched him with a grin. "I fuckin' love these guys!" Jesse shouted, his words mostly smothered by thudding bass. "Are you into Wolfmother?"

"I don't know who this is," Michael said, exaggeratedly moving his mouth so that Jesse could read his lips.

"It's–" They were in danger of being left behind by the rest of the group, heading back through the bar towards the upstairs room, where a conversation was possible, if still unlikely. A couple of large booths were promptly occupied. Michael ended up perched on the end of a booth, still holding his briefcase to his chest, still grinning, looking around him as though he couldn't believe his luck. Or, Jesse realized, nervous as hell. "It's Wolfmother," Jesse answered, leaning in close to Michael's ear. Michael nodded, uncomprehendingly, his grin melting down to an anxious half-smile.

"I'm sorry; I don't usually listen to music like this," he shouted apologetically.

Jesse pouted. "That's okay," he replied. "What are you into?"

"What?"

"What kinda music do you like?"

Michael shook his head uncomprehendingly.

Jesse sighed and gave up. There was no room for him to sit. "Hey, I'm going to get a couple of pitchers for everybody," Jesse yell-offered, standing up again. "Do you like light or dark?"

"What? Oh, uh, anything! Thank you!" Michael's eyes darted everywhere, trying to take in the entire darkened room and every detail in it. His grip on the briefcase was turning white at the edges.

"Any time," Jesse said, turning away, heading toward the bar, letting out his breath in a sigh. This was one of those times where he wished he were Drew; Drew would know what to do in this situation. Drew always knew what to do, always got what he wanted. Almost always. It was tempting to call him and ask for advice, but Jesse shook off the idea. He'd figure this one out himself, and if he fucked it up, oh well. Michael was just a guy, if a little cuter, more interesting, and a lot brainier than most. And more accomplished, too. And polite. . .

Seizing his hair with dismay, Jesse groaned at himself as he approached the bar. He just didn't really know how to do this. He had forgotten how to talk to a guy he liked, if he'd ever really known. When he was a teenager, if he wanted to fuck someone, he just asked them, "Wanna fuck?" and the answer was either yes or no. And with Drew–well. Whole different situation. (Allies, first, then friends. Then everything wonderful in the world. And then lust, later. But that wouldn't work here. What was he even *doing*?)

He returned bearing two foaming pitchers, one light and one dark, and poured with a practiced hand for anyone interested. He gave Michael the pale pilsner, judging it a safer bet. Jesse sank onto the edge of the booth next to Michael. "Cheers," he said.

"Cheers," Michael replied. They clinked the rims of their pint glasses together, and took a swallow in unison. Michael visibly grimaced.

"Not a fan of PBR?" Jesse asked with a smile.

Michael stared critically at the glass. "Not really," he admitted. "Not really a beer drinker in general."

"Why didn't you tell me to get you something else?"

"What? Oh. No. I like beer. Just fine. I like... Guinness..." Michael shrugged, back to nervous.

"Hey, yeah, me too." Jesse rolled his eyes. "Everybody likes Guinness; it's like liking puppies."

Michael made a face that was almost like a smile, a sound that was almost like laughing, wasn't either. "Sorry I'm so ordinary."

"No, no, you're not. That's not what I meant. You're really . . . not ordinary . . ." Jesse desperately cast around for something interesting, but not too intimate, to discuss. The room banged loudly with the sounds of the Yeah Yeah Yeahs; not quite as metal as Wolfmother, but still making it impossible to speak with normal tones. He reached forward and lay his hand against Michael's chest, right at the base of the throat. When Michael's eyes widened in slight alarm, Jesse explained, "This way you won't have to yell so loud for me to hear you. I want to talk to you! So, like, how'd you start doing theater?"

"Oh. Yes." Michael smiled, and it seemed sincere for once. Under Jesse's palm, the plain black fabric of Michael's T-shirt was cool, slightly moist with sweat. "I started in high school, and I picked it back up again when I went to CMU. I've always liked it. It's something different from my usual life. It's more creative."

Jesse smiled. Under the edge of his palm he felt the deep, slow, steady steps of Michael's heartbeat. He could see that now, Michael was watching him intently. Jesse studied back, noting Michael's coarse features, big nose and thick, plush lips, and those wild, heavy, tangled eyebrows. Without thinking, Jesse put out his fingertips to touch the skin of his forehead, testing his theory that the fur never did interrupt itself, only hesitated and grew tentative in the middle. Michael drew back, shoulders quivering with self-conscious laughter. "Hey! Don't poke me in the mono brow . . ."

Jesse added his laughter. "I'm sorry. It's cute."

"Stop it." Michael, eyes lowered, still smiling, picked up Jesse's hand and placed it back on his chest.

The music poured into the silence. *Wait. They don't love you like I love you.* Jesse closed his eyes and sighed along with it. He had thought that he was sick of this song, but something had changed. *My kind's your kind.* His throat tightened, and he nodded his head forward so that his hair hid his face for a moment. When he flipped his hair back, Michael was watching him with club lights sparkling in his eyes.

When Jesse finally spoke, his voice was so quiet that Michael could only have heard it through the contact of palm on heart. "Where did you come from?"

"Pennsylvania. Place called Altoona."

Jesse nodded. "What's it like?"

"It's a small town," Michael said. "Boring. Depressed. Hasn't had much money or much life since the Sixties. Nothing much goes on there." His smile turned briefly to a smirk, and then disappeared altogether. He pulled steadily at his beer, draining half of it.

"Your folks still there?"

"Yeah. Mother and father. That's it; I'm an only child."

Jesse nodded and looked at the table. "Yeah, me too," he said. He took his hand back, refilled both of their pints, and put his hand back on Michael's chest. It felt comfortable there.

"Are your parents still over in Brooklyn?" Michael asked.

"Nah . . .They're both dead," replied Jesse off-handedly. He still couldn't make eye contact with anyone he told, but at least it didn't trouble him to say it.

Still, Michael's eyes widened in dismay. "Oh my God! I'm so sorry. What happened? If you—I'm sorry, it's none of my—"

"Car accident." He lifted his eyes to Michael's, smiling calmly. "Black ice. Huge crash on the BQE; killed nine people, ncluding both of them. Gotall the parental loss over with at once."

Michael blinked, eyebrows drawn all the way together. "Jesus."

"It's okay. It was a long time ago," Jesse said, amusing himself by repeating to himself *mono brow, mono brow.* "It doesn't bother me anymore."

That didn't seem to comfort Michael at all; the brow remained undivided. He had gone visibly pale. "Oh. Still. God, that's... terrible."

"It's just something that happened in the past. Time goes by. You keep going." He drank a bit more, then laughed, trying to ease the aching tightness in his face. "You know what? It's dumb to try to talk up here. Let's go out to the patio; the music isn't so loud down there." He jumped out of his seat, glad to be moving, and Michael got up, too, following so close behind it was as if he were afraid of getting lost.

The back patio was sparsely populated, caught in the dip between two waves of drinkers, and Jesse easily claimed one of the rickety wrought-iron tables, edged by metal folding chairs illuminated with graffiti. Michael glanced back into the club. "I'll go get us some drinks, to reciprocate," he offered. "What do you want?"

Jesse grinned at the fancy word. "Right on. Gimme two double vodka and Cokes."

"Two double . . ."

"I want two of those. Doubles. They're pint-sized."

Michael raised his eyebrows. "Maybe just one at a time?"

"It's okay; it's New York. Seriously, bring me two. Saves time." He shooed Michael away with flicks of his fingers.

From here, Jesse could see into the art gallery in the back of the club. This month featured black and white photographs of a Middle Eastern nightclub, with lots of shirtless brown boys dancing on tables. If the photos weren't so kinetic, they might be the kind of thing that Drew would like. He made a mental note to tell Drew about the exhibit; Jesse couldn't afford to buy any of the photos, but the thought of Drew buying one comforted him.

Michael returned with a double handful of pint glasses with straws. "I got two, too," he said, setting down his bounty on the table. "Coke and double vodkas, and let me say that sounds like a frightful combination; and for me, two sangrias. Extra fruit."

"Oh, a sweet sangria for a sweet señorita." Jesse rocked happily on his chair. Michael gracefully folded his height into the opposite chair, extending his legs under and alongside the table. The legs went on and on, ending in scuffed dark brown Doc Martens that looked like they were older than he was.

"I could use the vitamin C," said Michael.

"You know, you should really eat more," Jesse grinned, drawing his closed fingers near to his mouth. "Ya too skinny. *Mangia, mangia*! I'm Italian. Ya gotta eat." He dropped his gaze to the table. "Half Italian," he clarified. "But I figure it's like bein' Jewish; if your ma's Italian, you're Italian . . ."

Michael just stared at him. "I love how you can just drop it," he said. "Just be like, 'Oh, yeah, both of my parents were killed in a car accident, but whatever.' You know?"

"It's a coping skill," Jesse countered, shrugging. "Anyway, let's not get into it. It's a long story and it's grim, and that's not how I wanna feel tonight. I want to know about *you*. What made you come here? Besides the fact that this is the *only* place. The city: where dreams come true every day. I should know; I'm not really a native, either." He gulped his cocktail and waved one hand. "I'm from Brooklyn, y'know? And not the glamorous parts, either. It ain't the same. When I was growing up it seemed like thousands of miles away, like Hollywood, or Paris, or somethin'. But I always like the 'why are you in New York?' talk, and everybody here from somewhere else always loves to tell their story."

"Right," Michael replied. He sipped uncertainly at the sangria, his eyes on the table. "I always wanted to live in New York. I came here on a school trip when I was in fifth grade and we went to the Museum of Natural History, and I just fell in love. I'd never seen someplace so alive; it made *me* feel alive. I fought hard to get into to school here, but I had to get my bachelor's, and then get some grants before it became possible. It's not like we had any money for me to go to school; I'm a scholarship kid. And I just I wanted to get out of Pennsylvania altogether. First I just thought I wanted to get out of Altoona, but when I was in Pittsburgh, I realized that, really, it wasn't just a big city I was after. It was New York."

Jesse grinned and nodded encouragingly. "But you worked it out," he replied. "You made your dream come true. So, you in school right now?"

"No," Michael answered. "I'm taking a year off. At least a year. Maybe I won't even go back. I don't know; sometimes I wonder if I should."

"You'd go back to Altoona?" Jesse asked in surprise.

"Oh, fuck no," Michael replied quickly, and they shared a

laugh. "No. That's not gonna happen. I meant back to college full-time. I mean, I'm supporting my parents, but I will not live *with* them, or anywhere *near* them, ever again."

"*You're* supporting *them*? Really?"

Michael grimaced. "Basically. Huge medical bills, both of them; they're both sick, and have been for a couple of years. So I pay for the house. It's not that bad. Cheaper than assisted living. But no," he said, shaking his head, "I'm never going back there. They're still in the same house I grew up in. I just couldn't be there anymore. Maybe it's selfish."

"I don't think so," Jesse said quietly.

Michael continued, as if he hadn't heard. "I had to come here to find out who I really am. I'm not just a son; I'm not just a student. I'm trying to change myself without changing myself. Becoming more me and becoming less me at the same time. Do you know what I mean?" Shaking his head, Michael sighed. "It's all still kind of new to me, you know?" He swallowed, and muttered, "I'm, y'know . . . gay. Obviously."

"Cool," Jesse murmured, then snapped out of his daze. "Oh. Yeah. Me too. Also. Obviously."

Michael's shoulders slumped. "It's still really new for me to say that to somebody."

"Somebody you don't even know very well yet," Jesse prompted.

"To somebody who . . ." Michael said slowly. "Looks like you."

"What, like a dork?" Jesse laughed.

Michael opened his eyes, and leaned back. "Now you're just making fun of me."

"You're just so serious." Jesse smiled gently at him, and took Michael's wrist in his hand. "I'm just a regular dude. Just another kid in the city, tryin' to get by. There's nothing to be afraid of. You can tell me anything," he said. When Michael met his eyes, Jesse nodded patiently. "Really, I don't judge."

Both men solemnly drank for a while. Five or six more people had come out to the patio, lighting up Marlboros and loudly complaining about a stalled subway train. Michael cleared his throat, and asked lightly, "So how long have *you* been out?"

"Forever," Jesse replied with a shrug. "I mean, to myself. I hate to say that it was never that big of an issue for me, but it really wasn't. It was just true. I mean, everything about me was fucked up, anyway; that was just one more thing. But *that* made sense . . ."

"What do you mean? How could everything about you be fucked up?"

"Oh, you know what I mean. You were a kid too, once."

"Oh, *that.*" Michael rolled his eyes. "Yeah, okay. I was a four-eyed caveman with one eyebrow and giant feet, and I was a snitch, and I smelled like pickles."

Jesse chuckled sympathetically. "Totally. I was the class shrimp, and I smelled like *garlic*. And got my ass kicked, like, every single day for all of third *and* fourth grade. And my dad hated me—" Jesse grimaced, annoyed at himself for saying that. Alcohol always drowned his inhibitions. "Well, no, okay. He didn't hate me. Not much." He laughed. "No, he did."

The look of pale concern was back. "Jesse, I'm sure that's not true."

"No; he told me. To my face. Repeatedly. He told me to fight back at school, but I tried that and I *still* got my ass kicked. And then I'd go home and it was worse there. Me, and my ma . . . Then *she'd* hit me for making *him* mad . . ." He rolled his eyes. "Fuck it. I'm still here; they didn't win. One crazy Italian parent and one crazy, drunk Irish parent that thought he was Jake La-fuckin'-Motta. Fuckin' delusional. I didn't have a chance. Whatever. *Any*way." Jesse stared longingly at the smokers, the dancing lit tips of their cigarettes.

"I'm sorry he hurt you," Michael said softly.

"Oh, he straight-up beat the shit out of me. Among other things." Jesse rubbed the crooked bridge of his nose.

"For being queer?"

Jesse shrugged. "Among other things. I got plenty for a bully to pick on." He held up a warning hand. "No pity, okay? It doesn't help me. Just keep goin'. That's all you gotta do. Just live through it."

Their eyes met, and Michael reached across the table, hooking his pinky finger around Jesse's. "My father never hit me, but I almost wish that he would have," Michael said very quietly. "He just stopped talking to me. Or looking at me. My mother just . . . she cares, but the person she cares about isn't the person I am. She thinks I'm something else. As long as I got good grades, and kept getting grants and winning prizes, that's the extent of it. I stopped talking about myself; I only tell her what she wants to hear. She was upset when I moved, for some reason; I don't know why. They still don't . . . know," he added. "I don't want to tell them. It's like they don't deserve to know. They don't know me."

"It's fucked, isn't it?" Jesse murmured, and Michael nodded. A moment of silent, sad understanding settled around them. "The aquamarines," Jesse added.

"It's a hard world for little ones," Michael quoted quietly.

Taking a deep breath, Jesse shook himself, smiled, and took a drink. "From *Night of the Hunter*. I know somebody else who quotes from movies all the time." He seemed briefly more uncomfortable than he had been when discussing abuse, nervously licking his lips. "Yeahhh . . . anyway, yeah. New topic. Can I see you without your glasses on?"

Michael didn't protest, slipping off the frames and handing them to Jesse. Of course Jesse put them on, but rather than spouting the usual cliché about how blind Michael was, he looked over the tops of them, holding them at the corner and arching his eyebrow light a naughty secretary. "You know," Jesse said, handing back the glasses, "you really do have to do something about those eyebrows. I love 'em, but they're insane."

Michael arched one eyebrow. "Wow. Really, Jesse."

Jesse gave into uncontrollable laughter. "No . . . I'm not trying to fuck wit' cha. But you are a handsome, fly fox, and with a little threading, you could be sublime, I'm telling you."

Michael snorted. "A handsome, fly fox. Sounds like a fishing lure."

"Christ, you really are a hillbilly," Jesse teased, drinking, crunching ice noisily between his teeth. "Just kidding, just kidding. Nah, you're gorgeous. Seriously."

"That's my line." Michael narrowed his eyes. "Don't you *have* a boyfriend?" he asked.

Jesse shook his head, tamping down a flutter of alarm in his chest. "Um," he said. "Not, like, anything for you to worry about."

"I don't think you're being honest with me," Michael said. "How can I trust you?"

Dark eyes flitted to a corner of the room. "Okay. Like I said, it's not something you should worry about. I've got a thing, but . . . we're not married. Not exclusive."

"I guess that's good," Michael said, eyebrows raised, looking unconvinced.

"Yeah, it is," Jesse replied, "because I'm gonna kiss you now."

He leaned over and put his mouth against Michael's, hardly even pressing lips against lips in his haste. With surprising ease, Michael obligingly opened his mouth, his tongue moving effortlessly, hungrily, into Jesse's mouth. The cheap wine of the sangria was dry and bitter against the corn syrup sweetness on Jesse's palate; he sucked Michael's tongue until he tasted citrus. He let go and sat back, taking a deep breath. "Okay?" he asked challengingly.

Michael licked his lips, and said, "Again."

The chill plastic lenses Michael's glasses flattened Jesse's cheek. This time, Michael sucked his tongue, his lower lip, trailing the flesh briefly against his teeth. Immediately responsive, Jesse kissed back harder, but Michael broke off and leaned back in his metal chair with a pleased smile. He took his glasses off, and wiped them on a napkin wet with condensation. Jesse rocked back in his seat, spreading his legs, giving the aching lump in his jeans some breathing room. "Whoa," he whispered. "You are a good fuckin' kisser." His blood flared like gasoline at the touch of a lit match, and he wanted a cigarette with all of his being. "Who the hell *are* you again?"

"Just another kid in the city," Michael said. "You're the one who's a good kisser. Of course you would be," he added, and Jesse smiled and nodded, as if the praise was brand new to him. "And now it's time for me to go home. You, too."

"Your place?" Jesse asked. His tongue felt odd, lips slightly numb. Two beers, two double vodkas, empty stomach, hot day. He wanted to fuck.

"No," Michael said, "you're going to your home, and I'm

going to my home. I'll get a taxi."

"But I rode my bike."

"And I think I saw it locked up inside the theater. It'll keep until tomorrow. C'mon, let's go. Before you do something you regret."

"Please . . ."

"Heh. No. You've *never* had to wait, have you?"

"Uh . . . not really."

While they stood on the sidewalk together, Michael held Jesse up against his body, back to front, and Jesse clearly felt the long, hard ridge of Michael's erection against his back. Through clothes, Michael's cock felt like a knife handle, a sword grip, a tire iron. Long arms held Jesse, hugging him, securing him and keeping him from wavering on his feet, hands gripping Jesse's sides, sliding up to his armpits, down again. The scent of Jesse's sweat rose, tangled with Michael's own spicy-dirty-nutty odor. Jesse's head fit under Michael's chin, if he slouched. He turned and they kissed again, soft lips this time, tender and curious, hands in each other's back pockets. Michael's body was as cool as a cocktail. Jesse didn't even notice that Michael had flagged down a cab until it halted sharply before them.

Michael opened the door and bundled Jesse inside. "I'll see you tomorrow," he whispered. "Looking forward to your coffee."

"I'll make it special for you," Jesse mumbled.

Jesse didn't remember anything about the cab ride to 61st Street; he found himself climbing the long staircase up to the main living area of the townhouse, suddenly alert, desperate to piss, rushing toward the half-bath just off the staircase to one side of the kitchen. HIn mid-stream, he suddenly came back to himself, sober for a moment, then just as abruptly wasted all over again. He held one hand against the wall in front of him so that he didn't pitch forward into the toilet. With his Irish genes, he felt no nausea, and a quick splash of cold water on his face as he washed his hands was enough to bring him back to himself.

He meandered into the kitchen's dark, echoing space, trailing his hand along the countertop of polished honey-colored stone and the pristine enamel surface of the stove. Though his appetites had been stirred, he only briefly considered trying to find something to eat. He didn't need food; he needed contact. Cold surfaces; hot hands. He could eat in the morning.

Jesse walked unsteadily into Drew's bedroom. Drew was asleep in front of the TV, playing *A Place in the Sun*. On-screen, Elizabeth Taylor spotted Montgomery Clift across the room, and rushed to him, heedless of his social discomfort, his ill-fitting cheap tweed suit, seeing only his beauty and promise.

Drew lay very still on the bed, his body a diagonal ridge under a single pale, striped sheet, his regular slow breaths soundlessly rising and falling. His eyes were closed, mouth slightly open. Without speaking, Jesse smiled to himself, and untied his boots. When Jesse unzipped his jeans, Drew's eyes fluttered open at the tiny shirring of metal teeth. He stretched in bed, reaching for a glass of water on the bedside bureau. "Hmmm," he said, taking a swallow, and glancing at the clock as he set the water glass down beside it. "There you are."

"Here I am." Shaking his head, Jesse kicked off his jeans, underwear bunched inside them, and pulled his shirt off, tossing it on the floor beside pants and boots. He climbed onto the bed beside his lover, sitting up on his knees, his penis the sudden center of all attention in the room. "Touch this," he demanded.

"Magic word," Drew murmured, staring at Jesse's cock, completely hard, standing straight up, the tip reddened and moist.

"Now."

Drew smiled. "That's the one." He drowsily reached out, caressing the flesh from the top down, curving his hand around it. Jesse's breath hitched, and he abruptly began breathing hard. "You're actually home earlier than I thought you'd be," Drew said. "You smell like cigarettes. Were you smoking?"

"Nah . . . I was out at the Lit Lounge. You know, that rock club a few blocks... ah... down the street from the theater." Jesse couldn't keep himself from helping out, touching too, lacing his fingers through Drew's as they enclosed him, tightening his hand. Squeezing to relieve the pressure, or to increase it. "Out on the back patio."

"I see," Drew replied softly. He let Jesse take over stroking himself, and took Jesse's balls in his hand instead. Jesse swept one hand over the top of his head, arching his back, quietly wanton as he pulled on his dick. In the cool, conditioned air of the room, his nipples were tight and rigid, and Drew ran a hand up Jesse's belly and chest to brush one with his thumb. Jesse whined through gritted teeth, and stroked himself more firmly. Drew took Jesse's hand off his penis and replaced it with his own lighter, less insistent touch.

Jesse moved his hips forward, the skin on his dick straining against Drew's palm. "Harder. Please."

Drew's ceased all motion, but not pressure. In fact, he tightened his fingers. "Maybe I'd rather be asleep."

"You wouldn't be watching a Monty if that were the case."

"I thought you'd be out late." Though the edges of Drew's voice were soft, his cadence was clipped. "You didn't call me, so . . . ."

"Don't be mad. Here I am." Jesse bit his lip, took Drew's active hand, and brought it to his mouth, wetly licking Drew's palm and putting it back where it had been. "I'm just . . . really . . ." His mood plummeted so suddenly that he felt dizzy. He sat on the bed, folding a leg underneath him, afraid to lie down. Drew let him settle, but immediately resumed stroking Jesse's penis, still watching him with narrowed eyes.

"You stink, Jess."

"Sorry," Jesse muttered. "Please. I just need my lover right now. Do you love me? You're all I've got. I talked too much. I forgot how much it hurts. I'm so messed up. Do you still love me even if I'm this messed up?"

"Shh." With one hand, Drew caressed Jesse's hair. With the other, he stroked maddeningly slowly up and down Jesse's cock. Abruptly, he tightened the caressing hand in Jesse's hair, drew his stroking fist down, opening his fingers to Jesse's balls, and holding the straining cock steady, brought it to his mouth. He slid it past his lips, running his tongue around the already slippery glans, humming with his own private satisfaction. The fingers released Jesse's hair, smoothing down his torso, pressing a thumb into one nipple. They moaned in unison. Jesse's fingers combing through the hair on the back of Drew's head, adding a slight pressure downward, the soft wordless gasp that shuddered through Jesse's teeth: these were the syllables of tenderness spoken between them for years.

"Thank you . . ." Jesse mumbled.

"I do love you," Drew paused long enough to comment. "You know that." His voice was gravely and thick, throat slick with Jesse's pre-come. Without letting go, he took another drink from his water glass, and got back to sucking.

"We're all so fucked up," Jesse sighed. His balls tightened in Drew's hand. "I forget how much. I just got so lonely tonight . . ." Jesse shuddered in a deep breath.

Drew lifted his mouth off Jesse's cock, and circled the base of it, just above the ligature of the testicles, with his fingers. His expert touch simultaneously stilled Jesse's orgasm and kept the blood from escaping, forcing it to the purpling head. Jesse yelped in distress. "Oh yeah?" Drew said, same tone of voice, steady and silky and under complete, level control. "What'd you do?"

Jesse let out a long sigh, eyelashes fluttering. "I . . . I kissed . . ." He broke off before he said the name, laughing silently, amazed at his own inhibitions. He even kept his eyes closed so that he couldn't see Drew's reaction. "This one guy."

Drew's brow furrowed dangerously. "Who?"

"It's been so long since I kissed anyone like that . . . anyone but you . . . but he needed it. I had to."

"Oh, did you?" Drew asked. "Did *he* really need it, or did *you*?" He lowered his mouth over Jesse again, sucking in, and only then releasing the base of his cock.

Jesse's moan came from deep in his stomach, hands grasping and sliding uselessly across Drew's shoulders. "Uh—! I'm coming— that's it—"

Just before the spunk jetted out, Drew took his mouth away, and cupped his hand neatly over the crown, catching the fluid spurts against his palm. The sounds coming from Jesse's throat sounded like crying; his legs jerked in spasm. Drew whispered to Jesse, "So fucking horny. Yeah, that's it. Ahh. There you go. All better."

When Jesse could open his eyes and see clearly again, he saw that Drew's skin was covered in goose pimples, all of the abundant fine brown hair standing at attention. The older man's upper lip was drawn back from his teeth in a lustful grimace, eyes glazed in concentration. Jesse held Drew's head between his hands, trying to raise him up so that they touch put their lips together, but Drew angled back out of Jesse's grip, wiping his hand across Jesse's belly, wiping his own semen into the fine line of hair. He tightly grasped the hair at Jesse's crown again. "Now," Drew murmured, all quiet menace. "Make it worth my while to stay up late. Let me fuck you."

"Okay. Yeah. Absolutely." Jesse nodded quickly, his wet, sensitive dick twitching and tingling all over again. He wished that he could be the one to fuck Drew — he'd love to feel the hot clench of musculature inside Drew's hard ass — but he wasn't one to complain when an opportunity presented itself. Having Drew's cock inside him, filling him up, forcing him to come to terms with himself; yes, that would soothe his broken heart, make him push the memory of his parents back out of his mind where it belonged. Better to think of a sexy man, hot for him. (Michael. That kiss, scratch of unique whiskers against his face, the glasses, the boner. Altoona. The escape. Michael. Worth it.)

He shoved the bed sheets away from them, curled over, and mouthed Drew's cock without using his hands. He sucked hard. Drew's groan was all the reward he needed in the world. "Fuck! What is the matter with you?"

"Hmm, nothing," Jesse mumbled, kissing up and sucking down. "Just fuckin' missed you. Missed this dick. Wanted it in my mouth. Needed somethin' to make sense." He paused, reaching down under the bed, returning with lube and a condom. Drew's cock, spit-wet and thickly wrapped with veins, awaited his touch. "Now," Jesse said, quickly sheathing his prize and draping it with ribbons of lubricant, "do what *you* want." He stroked down the length of the erection with one hand, and wiped the excess lube across the base of his balls, his perineum, and slid two fingers inside himself. He was loose and relaxed. He wanted this.

Drew swung one leg over him, settling on top, between Jesse's thighs, shaking his hips back and forth to open Jesse's legs. Jesse raised his thighs along Drew's hips, up to his waist, higher.

"More. Knees up." Drew pulled his hair some more, slid a finger into his mouth. Jesse tasted his own come, and grimaced, his mood and his mind slipping away again. *Poor Michael, alone, knowing that I have this, knowing that it's wrong. I don't know how he knows, but he does.* Drew sharply pinched Jesse's nipple to gain his attention. "Here. With me. C'mon."

When Jesse was in the position that Drew wanted, only then did he grace Jesse's mouth with a kiss, softer than Jesse had anticipated. He arched against Drew's body, feeling every faint quiver in the muscles along his core, along his arms. He kissed Drew's forearm, overwhelmed again with love. "You're the best thing that ever happened to me."

"I know," Drew said. He pressed his slick cock head against Jesse's asshole. "And I love you more than anything in the world. But," he paused, snapping quick, hard kisses against Jesse's face and neck, "tell me what you want."

"Ah. Yes. *Yes*," Jesse sighed. He groaned as he felt himself penetrated, breath shuddering. Even if he was ready for it, eager for it, his body always reacted with surprise. Suddenly he wanted everything at once, arching toward Drew, panting desperately. Drew gently wiggled his hips back and forth to relax him, clutching one of Jesse's buttocks in his hand. "Just do it to me," Jesse begged. "I can take it. You *know* I can . . ."

The fuck was easy. He was so ready for it, hungry for it, the hot, hard pressure coring him, the simple delight of having his legs spread open. "More! Yes! Ah!" Drew fucked harder, though not faster, and for a while, until he got used to it, Jesse lost the ability to speak in more than abbreviated, choked moans. But Jesse was nothing if not adaptable. "God, I needed this . . . needed to come home and get fucked . . ."

Drew drove in harder still, deeper still, so deep that Jesse couldn't breathe, discomfort and lust closing off his throat. Drew relaxed, just for a moment, then filled him again, holding Jesse locked in place, the helpless recipient of sensation. They hung suspended for a long moment, both silent and still; then Drew shuddered and moaned, his voice rising, almost astonished. Jesse hung on, absorbing Drew's shaking, riding out his orgasm, knowing that eventually it would spin itself out and allow him to breathe again. He could always take this, and more. He rubbed one hand down Drew's spine, and as soon as he could, he murmured, "Yeah, that's right. Oh, you fuck so good. I got you. I'm right here."

Too soon, it was over. Drew squirmed away, tossing the rubber, and quickly returned to Jesse's side, enfolding him and smothering his face and shoulders with the kisses Jesse had been craving all day. Not Michael's kisses, his abundant lips; he wanted

Drew's curvy, sleek mouth, always so smooth and hot, the way he always sought a certain corner of Jesse's lips, or lightly touched the tip of Jesse's nose or the point of his jaw. Drew knew him, and Jesse knew him right back. They were everything to each other. It had just been a kiss; it didn't diminish *this* at all.

Poor Michael; he should have something like this. Michael shouldn't be alone. Maybe he picked up tricks all the time and had a perfectly satisfying life; maybe it was none of Jesse's business. Though Michael hadn't kissed him like it was none of his business.

Jesse and Drew relaxed in a sweaty cuddle, still touching each other's cocks, but without any particular intention. "So, what happened?" Drew asked softly.

"Told someone about Mom and Dad dying," Jesse replied. "I shouldn't have said it. I thought I could be cool about it . . . I thought I had a handle on it, y'know? I thought I was over it."

"You're not supposed to get over it," Drew remarked. "Just . . . manage it."

"Yeah, I know." Jesse frowned, and edged even closer. Drew nuzzled his forehead. "So I just ended up talking to and kissing this guy. I kinda liked him, though." Jesse met Drew's eyes, watching anxiously for his reaction. "We kinda connected."

"That's okay," Drew said. "I love you; I don't own you. You can do whatever you want. Just tell me." His smile was too slight to crinkle the corners of his eyes; he looked and sounded at least half asleep. "As long as it's okay for *me* to do whatever *I* want."

Jesse heaved a sigh of relief, and snuggled even closer, damp bodies touching from collarbone to pelvis. "You know what I want?" he murmured, a fingertip brushing the faint silver strands at Drew's temples.

"A younger boyfriend?" Drew joked, catching Jesse's hand and kissing the fingertip.

"No." Jesse smiled and rolled his eyes. "I want you to come out to the bar tomorrow night." He took his finger back, and used it to trace a line down to Drew's navel. "'Cause I miss you, too. And hey, get to know the crew a bit; they're people, too."

Drew laughed faintly. "Sure," he said. "Just not at that skanky club. It smells like piss and beer."

"Most nightclubs do."

Drew kissed him again. "Not my scene," he said, raising his eyebrows fractionally. "But I can't tomorrow night; too much shit going on tomorrow. Let's try for Saturday night. We can meet at L'ete. Anyone who wants to can join us. They have a good martini there. And I can stay up a little later when I've planned to." He glanced ruefully at the clock and sighed. Jesse picked up the crumpled bed sheet from where it had fallen on the ground, and added the light summer bedspread on top of them both. "It's midnight. I'm gonna regret this."

Jesse nodded and yawned. He wouldn't have moved for a million dollars. "How 'bout we both sleep in till nine. You're an executive; you don't have to be there at seven every day. You can go running in the afternoon. I want to wake up next to you. Make you breakfast. It's been ages since we did that. Remember? Like in the old days." He got a kiss, and gave one back.

4. THE SECRET ROOM.

The first shock of cold water against his inner thighs was nearly the best part of a swim. Michael never hesitated or tried to acclimate himself; he stepped right in, teeth held carefully together, and shuddered with pleasurable discomfort. Helpless groans backed up in his throat. He held them there until his head was underwater, then he released them in a gush of silver-green bubbles.

The water enveloping his body surprised his skin, but his muscles knew what to do, launching him like a dart towards the far side of the pool, pushing him several meters before he buoyed up and caught his breath again. His velocity cleansed and purified him, washing away the persistent sensation of sticky sweat that had clung to him since last night, and lifting his spirit to more exalted things. He had never needed a swim so badly in his life.

He couldn't even remember his ride home on the subway last night, only the sound that his shoulder made slamming against his front door; the jangle of keys on the linoleum floor; his own rough, raw panting. Just the abrasive brush of his underwear as he'd dragged it off made him come so hard the tears streamed from his eyes. He touched his penis with reverence. He'd held it against Jesse, right on his back, feeling the ridge of spine alongside it, the hard, lean muscles of Jesse's ass against the tops of his thighs. He made a mess on the floor, on his shed clothes, on his blankets. Before he could even think to get online and try to troll for a spontaneous hookup, he fell into one of those sleeps that comes on like a black velvet hood being thrown over his face, drawstrings pulled tight; he woke in sunlight, in a wet spot that extended from one edge of his bed to the other.

Though he hated to admit it, Michael knew he was falling for Jesse.

Michael had been in love before, hopelessly every time, in the sense that there was "no hope." With girls, more than once. (He'd even felt desire for them, had even had sex with two of them, but it never felt right, and left him feeling guilty, confused, and ashamed.) Mostly with boys, most of them straight. He never claimed to be one of those impossibly lucky people who had never fallen for someone who could never return the emotion. But Jesse . . . the way he'd opened up, his attention and kindness . . .

Swim it off. Maybe there was a chance. Those eyes, that look, that kiss. But Jesse was already impossible. Already hopeless. Because of Drew. There was simply no way Michael could hope to compete with that.

Michael shoved himself through the water, but the water itself wouldn't be shoved; it still held him afloat, still swirled so beautifully in response to the movements of his limbs, and it would not be bullied. It would not allow Michael to act the bully. After ten laps of fighting, he relaxed and concentrated on his stroke, on his breathing, his buoyancy, the past streaming behind him. Soon he was transported back into joy. He would see Jesse again, be in his presence. Jesse existed, and Michael had gotten to kiss him. Life was wonderful again.

After an hour's hard swim and a hot shower, Michael finally felt clean, relaxed, sane, alert, ready to head down to the theater again. Toweling off, he sat on one of the wooden benches in the locker room and pulled his phone from one of the zipped compartments in his aluminum attaché case. He only meant to check the time, but he saw that he had a text message from a number he didn't recognize.

Hey it's Drew. Let's get together tonight.

Michael went absolutely still for a moment. What did he want? Had he found out? Was he angry? He saved the number and immediately sent a reply, amazed that his fingers weren't shaking. **Sorry, I have plans after work. Another time?**

Lunch then. Meet me at the Russian place at the corner of E 2nd + 2nd at 12:30.

Michael stared at his phone in confusion. Could it be that urgent? **Should I bring the wiring budget? I have the docs with me.** He finished drying his hair, and quickly pulled on his street clothes.

While he was still zipping his jeans, his phone pinged again.

No not a work lunch. I'd just like to spend some time with you. If you're not into it, show up anyway, and we can talk shop, but I really would rather not.

"Jesus," Michael whispered. He felt weirdly cold all over, then very hot, and his heart jumped like a whipped racehorse. *This is how it's done,* he thought. *This is life. This could be your life.* Before he could overthink it, and convince himself not to, he thumbed out **OK see you then** and sent it.

No reply. Apparently, when Drew Farrow told someone to do something, he expected it to be done, and didn't bother with sociable thanks. Michael finally put his phone back in the briefcase, stared at the ceiling, and exhaled, "What . . . the . . . hell?"

It was nearly ten. Jesse had gone a while ago, bright-eyed and with a spring in his step, as was typical the morning after a good, solid fuck. He had made his stage coffee, poured a cup for Drew, kissed him, and left before Drew was fully awake, before he could ask for any more details about last night.

As far as Drew knew, Jesse hadn't kissed another man the whole time they'd been together. Or, if he had, he never admitted it. So either he suddenly decided to test the bonds of their agreement, or else he was a liar. And Jesse was a shitty liar. Maybe it was just a signal to Drew that as long as they were honest, a little low-contact messing around wouldn't jeopardize anything.

Drew sent Michael a text. *Two can play at this game, kid*, he thought. When Michael finally agreed to meet him for lunch, it brought a satisfied smile to his face. It wasn't a kiss he was after, but it was just as harmless. And this could turn into a very hot, very fun game, if they both kept themselves honest and under control.

It was long past time for them to try taking another lover, anyway. He couldn't imagine ever growing bored with Jesse, but restless? Absolutely.

Usually, Drew went to his day spa on Saturday mornings to receive his weekly haircut, barber shave, facial, body groom, foot massage, and manicure, but they would see him whenever he called, with an hour's notice. He needed to be impeccable when he met with important clients. He not only needed the physical perfection, but his own awareness of it, that additional boost of strong, blithe self-assurance that accompanied it, to not only put the clients at ease, but seduce them, get them to surrender their trust to the financial consulting firm where he worked. What he did was theater, too.

By noon, he was as close to the illusion of perfection as he was going to get. His lightweight, dove gray suit and white shirt had been expertly pressed, the subtle odor of cedar still clinging to the garments. Plain black oxford shoes had been polished to a matte sheen; silk socks taken directly from the tissue they'd been packaged in. Tips and thanks were given and received. Drew stood outside on the sidewalk for a few moments, ostensibly checking his cell phone, so that customers coming in to the spa could witness the kind of care they were about to receive. Drew got a general discount on all of his services there because he drove in so much traffic. Last year he had turned down an offer to model for their magazine ads. It was better for his business if people thought that he rolled out of bed looking like that. No one really wanted to know how much work went into his appearance; the painful, sweat-soaked hours in the gym and on the track, the sour taste of tooth-whitening gel, the dull stinging at the sides of his face where the barber's straight razor had expertly peeled off a microscopic layer of dead skin.

He got a taxi down to East Second, using the ride to scroll through the last ninety minutes of financial news on his Blackberry. Once the cab came to a stop, though, he closed off that part of his mind and opened another. He hoped he still remembered how to do this, but reassured himself that it was probably easier, for him at least, than riding a bike.

Michael waited on him already, perusing the menu through the café-bar's front window, and turned to him with an expression of startled wonder. "Hel-*lo*!" he said emphatically, his voice almost a gasp. "Wow! Forgive me; I'm really, really underdressed."

Drew laughed. "No, no, it's fine. I'm going from here to a client meeting this afternoon. This is just the usual level of primp I give when papers are going to be signed. You look perfectly fine."

Michael glanced down at his blue checked shirt and black jeans, and sighed. "Well, okay. What's good for lunch here?"

"Oh, we're not eating," Drew said. He smiled. "Come this way."

The café-bar he had chosen was an adequate place for food or drink, but Drew thought of it specifically for the red brick building to which it was attached. He punched in the code and the front door unlocked itself. Two doors down the hallway, on the left, was a small room, perhaps once a janitor's closet, but now empty of anything but linoleum floors, fingernail-scraped walls, and a bare, yellowish bulb dangling from the ceiling. The door of the closet locked from inside. Someone kept it reasonably clean, but Drew could only imagine what bodily fluids, and how much of them, spilled on that floor every week. Rumor was that somewhere else in the building, a powerful dominant lived, and cleaning the secret room was his (or her) masochists' task.

"Wow," Michael breathed.

"Found out about this from the director of the first play I did," Drew said, glancing up at the lightbulb. "I always wonder if one day, it'll just be gone. All the best secret places get discovered. Ruined. Or just removed altogether." Drew removed his jacket, hung it on the doorknob. His eyes sought out Michael's; the tall man looked dazzled and dumbstruck. "Hand jobs okay?"

"Oh, my God," Michael said quietly.

Drew rolled his eyes with an impatient sigh, and unbuttoned the fly of Michael's jeans. "Are you just very new to this?" he asked.

"Um . . . I'd say, yeah. For sure. For absolutely sure."

"Don't think about it. Just do it." Drew unzipped his own trousers, then handed Michael one of the handkerchiefs from his inside pocket. They were monogrammed *DF*, to distinguish them from his *AF* (for Andrew) handkerchiefs, which he never used for himself; they were the hankies he could produce if a woman began to cry in his presence, which was nowhere near as rare an occurrence as he'd like. The *DF* ones, he mentally labeled *dick fluid*. Drew Farrow's dainty fucking dick fluid. "Make sure you don't spill any. Not on my clothes, not on the floor. If you want to lick it up, be my guest; I'm clean." Michael's cock was a hot, rigid shape in Drew's hand. "Okay?"

Michael leaned over, trying to kiss Drew. Drew carefully avoided him, showing no alarm or distaste. "No kissing. I only kiss my boyfriend."

"Oh," Michael said, and his cock lost half its hardness immediately.

Drew arched his eyebrow, applied pressure, pulling Michael's cock all the way free of his shorts and the jeans, stroking it out long. "Even if he doesn't show me the same courtesy," Drew murmured, pleasurably petty. At Michael's expression of dismay, and the further softening of his erection, Drew laughed softly and nuzzled the tip of his nose against the underside of Michael's chin, blowing hot breath at his larynx. "I'll be quiet now," Drew promised. "Work those hands on my dick. Let's get off."

Michael's grasp, clumsy and eager, felt wonderfully stimulating; not Jesse's touch, not Drew's own; unpredictable, soft skin and rough fingertips, so new he barely knew what he was doing. "You smell so good," Michael mumbled.

"Mmm-hmm," Drew agreed without hearing what he agreed to. He licked his palms, reapplied them to Michael's crotch, tangled with hair and the agitated throbbing of his pulse, rolling the shaft of the penis firmly between his palms, making it grow longer and longer. This was a nice one, a good one, a cock Drew would really enjoy in his mouth. Too bad this was just a hand job, but divine; exquisite. *I love you, Jesse,* Drew thought. *Thank you for giving me the idea to do this.*

Michael pulled the lightbulb chain, darkness surrounding all at once, and in the absence of light Michael's mouth came down on the side of Drew's face, the side of his neck. He had to bend so far forward to do that, and keep his feet on the ground and his thighs spread, that he slipped a little, and ended up slammed against the back wall with Drew pressing his chest against him, his hands now jerking on Michael's cock, one after the other. Drew would have liked to see Michael's face, but the darkness was forgiving, comfortingly close.

"Let me know when you're about to come," Drew said.

"Ah—uh-huh, ah, um, okay." Michael gasped again. He suddenly produced so much seminal fluid that it solved the lubrication problem, or would for a moment, anyway.

"Harder. Do me harder. —*Yeah*. Ah, like that." Drew could smell the other man's lust now, bestial and yet rarified, rising from his groin. "Wish I could lick your balls," he added. "You like that?"

"I don't know," Michael sighed. "I—oh, now, now."

"Don't stop," Drew commanded, letting come flow over his fingers, just a bit, before blotting the moisture with his handkerchief. "Get me off. Nobody ever licked your balls before?"

"No," Michael said sadly.

"Maybe I could be the first," Drew said. Convulsing, quickly and sharply, he tapped his skull against Michael's sternum. He fell silent for it, but he felt that he was coming in buckets, like a pier-splintering wave crashing into shore. Without seeing it, he didn't know how much he'd actually come, but it felt amazing, anyway. And Michael's long fingers tightened in his hair for a moment, just a perfect moment of sharp sensation elsewhere.

But back to real life.

Drew reached up and turned the light bulb on again. "Okay," he said. "That was great. Again sometime?" He smoothed his hair back down again, but with its enthusiastic waves, he would have to comb it before he saw clients. He decided not to get angry at Michael for it; the sensation had been more than worth it.

"Sure," Michael breathed.

Drew smiled at him, zipped up, and handed Michael the handkerchief that Drew had used on him, as if gifting him with his own spunk. Michael blinked behind his smudged glasses, and said nothing as Drew picked up his jacket and left the room, left the building. He still hadn't emerged by the time Drew had hailed another taxi to take him further downtown.

Yawning, he checked his Blackberry again. He sent Jesse a text: **I could use a kiss right now.**

He arrived at the hotel where the deal was going down, located the restaurant on the thirty-ninth floor, and was shown into one of the private rooms in the back with a view of the stippled, sunlit city spread out like a blanket behind the windows. His clients had already arrived, with three other men in attendance. They had not yet been seated, and Drew introduced himself and shook hands all around. By touch, two of the unknown men were lawyers, and the other was an accountant. All to the good. The more people he had to advise, the more comfortable he was. Half the enjoyment he got from his profession was the ability to subtly work the priorities of one man against another to his own advantage.

This particular deal looked like it was going to be a cakewalk, based on the way that the client, and his accountant, gave Drew the unmistakable stare of interest and desire. A slight flaring of the nostrils, a quirk of the eyebrow, that unconsciously mercenary glittering in the eyes as they looked him up and down. He responded to their attention with a slow smile, parting his lips to show his perfect teeth. "It's a pleasure," he said. "Shall we get down to it? I highly recommend the mesclun salad."

They all ordered it.

"Do I look all right?" Michael worried.

Jesse was all too happy to give him a close, intense examination. Michael had put on the same plain light blue button-down shirt and nondescript black slacks that he had been wearing when Jesse first met him, crisply pressed and still bearing a faint odor of dry-cleaning chemicals. He had even brought nice shoes to change into at the theater when they finished work. Michael's hair, like Jesse's, was still wet from the hasty shower he had taken back at the theater, and combed straight back from his broad, smooth forehead, with a hint of a widow's peak at the center. Excitement blushed his clean-shaven cheeks.

Michael seemed genuinely anxious, so Jesse made a show of picking nonexistent specks of lint from Michael's shirt front, dusting off invisible dandruff, even looking into his ears and up his nose, like a grooming ape. Michael squirmed, but didn't laugh until Jesse undid the collar button, then the one below it, exposing a swath of hairy upper chest. Jesse gently slid his hand across the skin, and released a third button, just for good measure. It didn't expose too much; the sunset-stained evening remained very warm, and they were in Chelsea. He unfastened Michael's cuffs and scrunched the sleeves up over Michael's forearms. "There," Jesse replied, nodding with satisfaction. "That's better."

"Thanks," Michael sighed sincerely, and looked at the small rectangle of painted and laminated wood above the door of L'ête, the only signage the establishment had. "Well, I guess we should go in. We're already late."

"Don't worry about it," Jesse reassured him. "He won't mind. He's expecting a bunch of people, anyway." He boldly pushed against the door and went in ahead, blinking as his eyes adjusted to dim lighting. The tables themselves were illuminated with taper candles enclosed in slim glass cylinders, but standing just inside the doorway, no patron's features could be clearly made out. L'ete was discreet, elegant, and comfortable, with curved booths and long-pillowed couches along the walls of the hallway that fed into the main body of the bar. The barstools had oversized seat cushions, wide enough to support two sets of hips, as long as they were narrow. The air held a compelling scent of jasmine and ginger, lime and juniper, and a subtle but unmistakable hint of male sweat. Connie Francis crooned "Fly Me to the Moon" on the stereo. At the bar, a couple of young women, too angular and tall to be anything but models, leaned and chatted animatedly with the stoic, muscled, slick-haired bartender opening a bottle of Taittinger champagne. Behind the women, middle-aged men in Brooks Brothers shirts or designer T-shirts jostled calmly, waving twenty- and fifty-dollar bills, which the bartender ignored. When Jesse turned to glance back at Michael, the technician's eyes were huge and animated behind the lenses of his glasses, as if he were trying to take in everything at once. He kept his arms pressed tight against his sides, and walked almost on tiptoe. Jesse smiled. Michael was out of his element, but he was keeping himself together. "This is totally Drew's kind of place," Jesse explained wryly.

It only took Jesse a moment to spot Drew. He sat at a booth, drinking a glass of water and folding the vulnerable pink sheets of the *Financial Times* as if displaying his plumage. Jesse nearly laughed. There was no way Drew was actually reading the paper without his glasses, not someplace this dark. Drew wore a cream-colored shirt, so scrupulously plain that it had to be expensive, with no tie and the first two buttons undone, sleeves scrunched up as Jesse had done to Michael, but the sleeves only went partway up his muscular forearms. His face gleamed, as freshly shaven as Michael's, probably an hour ago in a corporate men's room; his curved lips pushed out in a pouty moue of concentration. For a little while, Jesse remained silent, unwilling to share the sight. *That's my man.* They had barely seen one another since Wednesday morning; Drew at the office until eleven some nights, and Jesse either collapsing unconscious by ten or out at the Lit with Michael and the rest, but mostly with Michael.

"Hey, I see him," Michael whispered in Jesse's ear, bending

down a little to do so. He placed one hand against Jesse's back, between his shoulder blades, producing a different, warmer thrill. Michael didn't move forward, either. "God, he is so hot," Michael murmured.

"I know."

"How do you stand it?"

"I just thank God every day," Jesse replied. "Not literally. Well . . . yeah, literally. God or whoever is taking his messages these days."

Michael rubbed Jesse's back a little. "I would, too. On my knees." He let out a faint laugh.

"Oh, I do . . ." Jesse chuckled too.

Michael's hand stroked up over Jesse's shoulder, then around it, drawing him in close. He spoke into Jesse's ear, the tickle of breath on hair and skin making Jesse's skin quiver. "That face. Those hands! Incredible. He looks like . . . just the *perfect* man. Like he's out of a catalogue."

"He just looks that way," Jesse said, rolling his eyes. "He's not . . . the perfect . . ." He shrugged, stalling for time as he sought for the right words to describe it. "He's plenty flawed. He's just really . . . groomed."

"Well, also, he's really naturally handsome," Michael maintained.

"I know, I know."

Michael drew back a little and sighed again. "I'm sorry. I'm nervous as hell."

"Don't be! It's fine; it's just Drew."

"But he's the angel," Michael insisted.

Jesse snickered. "Oh, he's no angel!"

"Oh, I *know*," said Michael.

Jesse kept smiling, but it suddenly felt odd. "Do you?" he murmured, not loudly enough to be heard over the music. Impulsively, wanting to get it over with, he grabbed Michael's free hand and pulled him towards the booth where Drew sat. "Let's get a drink."

"But—! Jesse—" Michael's voice rose to a sulky whine, but he shut up by the time they were within earshot. Drew had looked up from his paper, right up at Michael, his expression unreadable.

"Hey." Jesse gifted Drew with a quick kiss on the mouth, and sat down, sliding in alongside.

More slowly, Michael sat down opposite them, eyes averted, wearing his nervous half-smile. "Hello."

Unsmiling, Drew asked, "Where's everybody else? Are they coming?"

"I didn't actually invite them," Jesse said. He ignored Michael's anxious glance, and smiled carefully at Drew.

"Okay," Drew said, unflappable. "Hello, Michael. Nice to see you. What would you like to drink?" and motioned to a waiter with a subtle, commanding gesture. The waiter, who was almost definitely a currently-out-of-work male model, zipped over and gave Drew an eager smile. Drew leveled his gaze at the waiter. "Hendricks, perfect, up, with a twist. For you, Michael?"

Michael shook himself, as if trying to wake up. "Uh, the same?"

"I'd like a raspberry Cosmo—rocks," Jesse purred dangerously, cocking his head, blinking, putting on his well-practiced, cute-kid mischievous smile. By the way the waiter raised his eyebrows, nodded, and rolled away, Jesse hadn't been so much cute as unsettling. Drew stared at him, unblinking, still pushing his lips out; Jesse just widened his eyes back at him.

The situation at the table would be obvious to anyone watching them. Jesse, being the pouty, outraged coquette; Michael like a horny deer in headlights; Drew trying to maintain control, playing Daddy. Oh, well; let them watch. There was nothing good on TV on Saturday nights, anyway.

Under the table, Jesse patted Michael's thigh. Michael jumped, startled. The candle flickered, but miraculously stayed lit. Drew raised an eyebrow, but before he could say anything, Jesse put both hands on the table, cradled his chin on a platform of his hands, and asked, "So how are things going at the office? How's that deal you had goin' down on Wednesday?"

"Quite well, it seems," Drew replied mildly. "Even if he didn't close, I feel like there was some good communication." He paused, and finally his smile appeared: the thoughtful smile, with a hint of rakishness. "And, ah, the client's accountant asked me for my phone number."

Jesse snorted with laughter. Michael said, "You must get that a lot."

"Sometimes," Drew admitted. He and Michael regarded each other across the table. Jesse's eyes flicked back and forth between the two of them, studying, ruminating on their expressions; the shared slight smile, admitting nothing but polite and pointed interest. It had been a while since Jesse had seen Drew look at anyone that way; if he found some other man attractive, either he had no expression at all, or he narrowed his eyes at them, almost as if jealous, trying to figure out what made his look work, assessing his body or his style, then relaxing in satisfaction, never finding anyone his own superior. Michael didn't seem intimidated by Drew's searching gaze; rather, he seemed energized, soaking up the attention like a seedling under sunlight. *Something* was going on, something Drew hadn't seen fit to mention.

Jesse scoffed. "Are you gonna call him?"

The staring contest between Drew and Michael did not waver as Drew calmly replied, "Nah, I don't think so. Not really my type."

"I bet you've got pretty high standards," Michael guessed.

"Yeah, well . . . more like . . . I'm not into . . . that whole Fire Island Pines-wannabe type," Drew said.

"Just the real thing," Jesse added quietly, "he used to go every summer." The returning waiter arrived, bearing a tray of drinks. The waiter lowered his eyelashes at Jesse as he set the pink-hued cocktail in front of him. Jesse smiled back, soft and sweet. The waiter was too professional to really cruise him, but he did arch an acknowledging eyebrow and set the martini glasses before the other two.

"Thank you. I don't really like the real thing, either, which you know," Drew replied, finally turning to look at Jesse. "I had my turn in the circuit; just long enough to get disillusioned about it. I joined in just long enough to get to know the right people. Anyway, how's the show going? Usually by now, someone's complaining about somebody or something." He lifted his glass to his lips and took a soundless sip; Michael mirrored his movements, stifling a startled cough.

"Oh, it's good," Jesse jumped in. "Sets are almost complete, we're just putting final touches on stuff. And everyone's getting along so far; no major temper tantrums or anything." Jesse took a slug of his Cosmo. It was bittersweet and staggeringly strong. At a premium establishment like this, with a patron that looked like Drew, the liquor didn't get watered down. Jesse felt sympathy for Michael; his martini must have kicked like a mule. "So, Monday, I'm back to the ranks of the unemployed."

"Oh, I'm sorry," Michael replied.

"It's cool," Jesse assured him. "I'll pick up some delivery work, or wash dishes somewhere for a little while until the next gig comes along."

"You should be able to find something better," Michael said.

"He doesn't want to," Drew said, dumping martini into his mouth.

Jesse fell silent and took another solid drink.

"I just think . . . with your skills . . . you're a bright guy . . ." Michael shrugged uncomfortably. "You could get a more intellectually-challenging job, I'm sure?"

"Can we change the subject?" Jesse asked, fidgeting with his cocktail napkin.

"Why?" Drew asked coolly. "Don't get uptight, Jess. We're just talking."

"You're being a dick," Jesse said, fixing a stiff smile onto his face. "Don't talk about me like I'm not right here. I hate that. You know I hate that. Why don't you ask Michael about, I dunno, school." Jesse's life decisions made for a dangerous subject, if Drew was feeling vindictive, which Jesse prayed that he wasn't. It was bad for them to go too long without talking; maybe Drew was mad at him, and Jesse had no idea.

"I'm not *in* school anymore," Michael said, lifting his drink thoughtfully. "I don't really want to talk about school, either, Jesse. It gets weird too fast." He glanced over his glasses at Jesse, took another drink, and continued, "Let's just talk about the show, maybe. It's something we're all interested in."

Jesse poured the rest of his Cosmo down his throat as he stood up and moved into the aisle. "I gotta go t'tha bathroom," he muttered, hurrying away as fast as he could go around the thickening crowd of patrons standing around the bar and the other booths.

He didn't actually need to relieve anything except the tension he felt at the table. Instead of going in, he loitered outside the women's room door, pretending to be waiting for someone. He could clearly see the booth from his vantage point, though Drew's back was to him; he was good for a couple of minutes.

At the table, Michael was laughing freely, all tension and nervousness gone, a wide smile on his face, eyes sparkling. Drew sat half sideways, at just enough of an angle that Jesse could see his expression. Drew stared at Michael like he wanted to eat him. Jesse's stomach knotted. Had Drew ever looked at him that way? And if he had, when was the last time? They were so used to each other now, they never had to concern themselves with pursuit, with that first flush of lust and challenge. And it had never been like that between them, anyway. He couldn't blame Drew for wanting something like that. They'd been together for so long. And Michael was so very interesting.

Jesse sighed, shoulders drooping. So this was jealousy. He wasn't used to it. He was never jealous of Drew; he had never had to worry about someone else. He wondered if Drew felt this way about him, whenever Jesse said that he thought someone else was cute. And Jesse had been playing that game with him, all this time, not even caring whether or not it made Drew feel this angry anxiety, assuming that Drew knew that he was the only one, really. But if Drew was truly the only one, why hadn't Jesse admitted that the man he'd kissed the night before, the man he was spending almost every evening with, was Michael Kaminsky?

And what was he going to do about Michael, anyway? It wasn't fair to anybody to lead Michael on like this. He should tell Michael . . . he'd tell Michael . . . *tell him what?*

And what would he say to Drew? *I love you, honey, you're my world, but I need this man.*

He couldn't cut Michael loose, or push him away. He wanted to be what Michael wanted. Drew was just going to have to understand. Which would be a hell of a task, since Jesse himself didn't understand.

Sheepishly, he returned to the booth and slid in next to Drew again, taking a moment to briefly lean his head against Drew's shoulder. He wanted a hug, but there was no need to rub it in. The model-waiter appeared at his elbow again, asking for the next order. Jesse asked for vodka and club soda. As one, Drew and Michael turned their full attention to Jesse, wearing knowing smiles. "So, what're you guys talking about?" Jesse asked, a little defiantly. The Cosmo trickled into his bloodstream, sending a sudden flush of warmth across his skin.

Michael replied, "So far, we've managed to determine that we all love Fleetwood Mac."

"Oh," said Jesse, surprised. "Yeah? Really?"

"Well, Drew asked me what kind of music I like, and he didn't recognize a single one of the bands that I mentioned." Most of Michael's martini was still in the glass.

Drew had only a bit of liquid still floating the curl of lemon peel in his glass, and his face had taken on the rosy sheen that signaled that he was well on his way. "I've heard of Radiohead," he explained, "but I couldn't tell you the name of any of their songs."

"Oh, c'mon, Drew, I play Radiohead all the time. How can you not at least name 'Karma Police'?" Jesse couldn't help smiling a little.

"I'm telling you, I couldn't. Whereas I know 'Gold Dust Woman' by heart." Drew grinned.

That made Jesse laugh. "It's true," he said to Michael. "He always sings along when he hears it. I keep threatening to take him to karaoke." Michael and Drew shared a look of exaggerated disgust and horror, and laughter circulated around the table. Drew gently rubbed the side of Jesse's arm. Suddenly it seemed that the whole room was laughing, relaxed, comfortable.

The out-of-work model inclined his head towards Drew. "Another martini, sir?"

"Please."

"Do you not like martinis?" Michael asked Jesse.

"Not really," he replied, pointing at Michael's mostly-full glass with his pinky. "You don't seem to like 'em, either."

"I'm nursing it."

"Sure," Jesse said, leaning against Drew again. "Watch out; he'll get you drunk. Take advantage of you." He winked at Michael to defuse his words.

Michael just smiled back. "You seem able to take care of yourself," he said.

"Speaking of which, Jesse, you should order some food," Drew pointed out. "I know you didn't eat dinner."

"Did *you*?" Jesse tongued his cocktail straw.

"I had a protein shake . . ."

"Oh, that's not food. You get so skinny when I'm not cooking for you."

"Do you cook?" Michael asked with interest.

"Yeah, my ma taught me," Jesse replied. "I'd love to cook for you sometime. I make a mean frittata."

"I don't think I've ever had frittata, let alone a mean one," said Michael.

"It's really quite gentle and reasonable," Drew chuckled. "Whereas I can't cook to save my life. Protein shakes and toast are about the limits of my expertise. I'm lucky I've been taken care of. How *is* your martini, Michael? I'd hate to think it's gotten warm. Get a fresh cold one, if you like. Please. I insist." Drew waved at the waiter again, and indicated his wishes with a single expressive nod. "You're meant to finish it in three gulps, while the bowl of the glass is still icy on the surface."

"I didn't know that," purred Michael. "It seems I could learn a lot from you."

"Indeed you could," Drew agreed. "And vice versa, I'm sure. What band was that you were telling me was your favorite—IDM?"

"That's not a band; it's a genre. Like, say, banghra, or hair metal, or . . . dubstep . . ." As Drew's forehead furrowed with incomprehension, Michael interrupted himself with rueful, self-conscious laughter. It made Jesse smile to watch him. "It's an initialism. Intelligent dance music. I-D-M. Get it?"

"It can't be that intelligent if I've never heard of it," Drew scoffed. He tossed down the last gulp of his second martini, just as the last sliver of ice melted off the side of his glass and dripped onto the table.

Jesse reached out and touched the water droplet, then reached for his own glass of clear, sparkling liquor and poured a measure down his throat. "It's kind of an old scene," he murmured. "Michael's nostalgic for ten years ago."

"No," Michael cut in defensively, then relaxed as he gave it another thought. "Well, maybe, yeah. It's just the sound of me really learning to enjoy music for the first time. College. Leaving home . . . stuff like that. A new world of existence. A new way of being." As Michael spoke, Jesse just gazed dreamily at him, and even Drew seemed to be drinking in Michael's voice, his words, the naked sincerity of his form of expression. Michael noticed after a moment, and drew back, resettling his mask of cool detachment. "You know, dancing. Being physical with music. It was new to me, anyway."

"No, that's great," Drew quickly assured him. "I understand completely."

"I can't see you dancing," Jesse said.

Michael shrugged a little. "I don't go as often as I did before," he admitted. "I went dancing every single night when I first moved here. I found a couple of good nights within the first few weeks. I couldn't get enough. I don't like the kind of music that usually gets played in clubs. I like music that's more rarified, cold, electronic. I like to add the human element myself."

Jesse couldn't keep himself from giggling, not in derision, but in joy. "Isn't he the best?" he whispered into Drew's ear, too quietly to be overheard over the music. Drew turned to him with a slight nod of acknowledgment.

"Sorry I'm getting all theory-and-practice on you." Michael smiled shyly.

Drew smiled too, all warmth and eye crinkles. Jesse's chest felt warm with joy. "No, it's great. Be yourself. Really."

The waiter appeared once more, and Drew instructed him to bring two more martinis. When they arrived, Michael obediently pushed aside his half-finished one, and took a determined gulp from the new, cold, brimming glass, pulling back with a gasp. Drew gulped his, too, finishing with a satisfied smack of his lips. "Yes, these are better, aren't they? Or maybe just fresher." He focused on Michael again. "So, tell me about your day. Start at the beginning."

Michael laughed. "With breakfast, or before?"

"I want to know what side of the bed you woke on."

"I woke up in the center," said Michael. He took another gulp of martini.

"Were your pajamas tangled, or smooth?"

Michael's face had turned red. "I, ah. Um. I wasn't wearing any."

"Oh, good. I wasn't, either. So. Were you alone?" Drew pressed.

"Drew," Jesse warned, chuckling. "I'm sorry, Michael. He gets nosy when he's drunk."

"I'm not drunk," Drew responded calmly. "If I was, you'd be able to tell."

"Do I have that to look forward to?" Michael asked innocently, arching his eyebrows.

"Probably not," said Drew. "It takes a lot of alcohol to get me drunk."

"That's weird, because Jesse gets drunk like *that*," Michael offered, snapping his fingers. When neither Drew or Jesse laughed, he hastily amended, "I mean, on an empty stomach, that is, I guess . . ."

"Speaking of which."

"I'm not hungry," Jesse protested. He picked up Michael's half-empty, half-warm martini and took a drink. It was like swallowing electric current. "Wow. Plus, if you really cared, you'd order me something when the guy comes around to bring you a new bucket of gin."

Michael let out a sharp, surprised bark of laughter, and dissolved. It was the first time Jesse had seen him really let go. Michael's mouth arched like a recurve bow, and his eyebrows moved away from each other; the proportions of his features became perfect. Jesse wanted to launch himself across the table and kiss him until they both passed out, and he reached beside him and gripped the top of Drew's thigh to steady himself. Drew was laughing too, mostly silently, and shaking his head. "Oh, my God," Michael gasped, waving his hand. "I'm sorry. I just . . . Hello, nice to meet you, I'm Michael Kaminsky."

"Drew Farrow," Drew grinned back.

"And I'm your host, Jesse Muhammad Ali Landon!"

"Really? You can't be serious," Michael said, unsure of whether to laugh.

"It's true," Drew said. "His middle name is Muhammad Ali. It's on his birth certificate and everything. Anyway, you were saying about waking up naked this morning," Drew prompted. Jesse groaned, laughed, tossed back the last of the tepid martini, and slumped in the booth onto Drew's shoulder.

The alcohol hit him all at once, filtering rapidly through his empty stomach to his guts. He tried to participate in the conversation, adding a quip or a joke as it occurred to him, though after a few attempts at this, Drew patted him on the arm and shushed him, half laughing, but only half. At first Jesse was annoyed at having been told to be quiet—if any of these snooty Chelsea gym queens had a problem with his voice or the words he chose to use, they could step up and do it themselves—but when he tried to remember what he had just said, he couldn't. That was fine. He was too ecstatically tipsy to really get upset. Michael gave him the last swallow in his martini glass, maybe just to keep him quiet, and this one went down even more harshly than the first try. It gave Jesse the shudders. He leaned against Drew and closed his eyes, listening to disconnected fragments of Drew and Michael's discussion.

". . .Which was what made me decide to transfer for my doctorate. I just had to get away, and see what else was out there. New York was the obvious choice . . . mentioned that you'd been married before?"

"Yes."

"What happened?"

"It didn't work out. Where do you swim?"

"Just up on 138th . . . been doing yoga for about nine years."

"I bet you're very flexible."

"Ha . . . everyone says that . . ."

"Do they all mean the same thing when they do?"

"Knees behind the ears."

Jesse shifted in his seat and listened more closely. Drew idly stroked the side of Jesse's head. "Handstands? Headstands?"

"Mmm-hmm."

"Mmm."

"Ha ha . . . I get that, too."

"I bet you do. You are so cute."

"I'm too tall to be cute."

"Bullshit. What are you, maybe, six foot three?"

"Six-one. And a half."

"I'm five-nine. Am I too short to be sexy?"

"God, no. Uh—I—I mean—"

Whispered. "I know what you mean."

Tucked in, so close to Drew, Jesse was able to clearly make out the sound of a zipper being slowly undone. It roused him from his stupor, and he glanced down, underneath the lip of the table. Drew's fingers were curled about the tongue of the zipper of his gray trousers, the fly a gaping open V, exposing darkness, but not so much that it wasn't obvious that Drew wore no underwear. Michael stared, mouth open, his eyes closing and opening in movements too slow to be called blinking.

Michael said nothing, and made no move, only looked over the edge of the table, at their hands. The skin on Jesse's back prickled. He let out a long, heavy sigh, and slid his hand into the opening, fingers curling firmly and instinctively around the base of Drew's half-hard cock. If only Jesse could be so bold; if only he could have just opened his jeans last night, and showed Michael the insides, he could have had this. If Michael wasn't going to reach out, and take the prize freely offered, Jesse damn well wasn't going to let it go to waste. Not in a booth, in a twilit bar, in Chelsea.

Drew rolled his shoulders and gave a deep sigh of satisfaction, his hips arching toward Jesse's touch. "Is Jesse too short to be sexy?" Drew asked, his voice a barely audible purr half-hidden in the slinky throb of club music and the chatter of intoxicated others surrounding them.

And yet, Michael had heard. "Never," he murmured, and Jesse felt the syllables through the table, through Michael's belly pressed against it as he leaned slightly forward, his eyes locked onto the shadows where Jesse's hand slowly worked inside Drew's trousers. He clenched, drew upward slightly, pulling loose skin tight, then back down. Drew's groin had been groomed to a sandpapery stubble, not shaven down to the skin, but painstakingly clipped.

Michael looked up and met Jesse's eyes. Jesse smiled back. Drew smiled, too. "Next time, I'd like to see your face when you come," he said, and Michael nodded, slow, hypnotized.

Jesse tried to say, "What do you mean, 'next time'?" but all that came out of him was "Wurrum."

"Come home with us," Drew said.

"I . . ." Michael responded, his voice trailing into a moment's silent hesitation. Then he sat back, taking a deep breath, and a wide grin spread across his face. "No," he decided. "It's late. And I'm really drunk! I should go home."

"No," Jesse protested, sitting up himself. He took his hand back. "Don't go! Currumus."

"No," Michael said again, calm, his eyes steady. "Not tonight. I'm not ready."

Drew carefully zipped his trousers back up, and dipped his chin in a nod of acceptance. "All right," he said. "It's your call."

Jesse felt like throwing a tantrum. Just throwing the table over and screaming, making a scene. Instead, he just sighed and let his shoulders slump. Michael smiled back at him, lovingly, or pityingly, or . . . something. "I'm sorry I'm drunk," Jesse enunciated.

"It's okay," Michael said gently. "You did okay." He turned back to Drew, smiling ruefully. "Thank you for the drinks. It was nice."

"Of course," Drew said, collected and cool. "It was a pleasure."

"Pleasure's mine," Michael said. Some cash was produced, set on the table between damp napkins. "That should cover my first drink, I hope. Thanks for the others . . . Jesse, I'll see you tomorrow. Good night. To you both." With only the slightest intoxicated hitch in his grace, Michael unfolded, stood, and disappeared. Jesse didn't even try to watch him leave.

"So, is it him?" Drew asked.

"Yeah," Jesse sighed, resting his head on Drew's shoulder again. "I really like him. I don't know what to do."

"Don't worry about it tonight," Drew said. He kissed Jesse's hair, just above his ear. "I think you're adorable when you're drunk."

Jesse ran his hand over Drew's now-clothed groin, smiling as he felt the urgent heaviness of Drew's hard dick through the cloth and zipper. "I really ought to eat something," Jesse said. Drew shuddered appreciatively. "Any suggestions?" Jesse asked, raising his head, kissing Drew on the mouth.

Whispered against lips. "Bread and butter at home."

"Mmm, sounds good. Shall we?"

"Let's," Drew said.

They kissed while waiting for the check, and paid. In the taxi home, they sat separated by the length of the back seat, buckled in place, hands on each other's cocks, not looking at each other, but stimulating each other into tumescence. "I really like him, too," Drew said. "Maybe we should play with him."

"Together, or individually?"

"I think we're already doing it individually," Drew remarked.

Jesse narrowed his eyes, but his stroking hand did not slow. "You have some explaining to do, don't you?"

"Breakfast tomorrow. Tell you then. Okay?"

In the apartment, they didn't bother with lights. Jesse took off his clothes in the kitchen, and stood nude at the counter, spackling pale butter onto a stale square of focaccia while Drew kissed him below the waist, groin and buttock and hip. Jesse chewed, wetting the dry mass of bread in his mouth with sips of tepid water, watching Drew gather up some butter on his fingertips, bending forward to touch the kitchen countertop with his forehead. "I wish you had some honey," Jesse sighed, leaning into Drew's buttered touch as his fingers slid inside him. "Put it on . . . the delivery . . . list . . . *ahhhh*! . . . Mmm . . . do you want any of this or I'm gonna eat it all?"

"Bed," Drew said.

In Drew's bedroom the air was drenched in the multicolored hue of streetlight filtered through the paper screens at the windows. In a whisper, Drew begged to be fucked. With more enthusiasm than subtlety, Jesse sucked Drew's cock with his oily mouth until Drew's muted groans became full-throated shouts of pleasure, shouts for Jesse to do what he was told, to give Drew what he asked for. Jesse girded himself in cool latex and warm gel, pushed Drew's thighs up, and out, and slid into Drew's asshole. They rose off the surface of the bed together, moaning, laughing, cursing in release. "So good to be inside you," Jesse hissed, scraping Drew's ribs with his work-ragged fingernails. Drew bucked demandingly against him, muttering, More, more. Jesse jabbed himself deeper and rougher inside, harder than he should, but Drew could always take a lot.

"Give me that sweet hard fucking cock . . . Oh . . ." Drew clutched him, squeezing tight, too tight, then relaxing again. His chest was wet velvet over steel. "I can't come . . . fuck, I'm too drunk. Can you come?" But Jesse was already there, the orgasm darting and sharp, a quick implosion with only the most diffuse, if wonderful, release.

Drew laughed and kissed him on the throat, the chin, and Jesse sighed, half annoyed, half exalted. "Stupid liquor."

"Delicious liquor."

"Answer to, and cause of, all life's problems," Jesse chuckled. He didn't want to pull out of Drew's grasping warmth, but he had to. His clumsy fingers made a mess of the rubber and he had to mop his hands, and the sheets, with a towel from the basket. He put one of Drew's hands on his aching stomach, and Drew obligingly rubbed the layers of muscle under smooth skin. "That was fun," Jesse realized. "I had a good time. Thanks."

"You're welcome. I think it was good. And, y'know?" Drew asked quietly, nibbling Jesse's lower lip. "Michael's done wonders for our sex life. We haven't fucked this regularly in years."

"He's a marital aid," Jesse decided. "Like porn. Or double-headed, eighteen-inch dildos."

He tucked in close, his head pillowed on Drew's warm bicep, Drew's lips against his forehead. "I will always love you best," Jesse whispered, tightening his arms in a hug around Drew's tight waist. Drew didn't answer in kind, but he didn't really need to, having said it himself a thousand times.

5. THANK YOU FOR YOUR SERVICE.

Memorial Day dawned gray, but hot, and stayed that way. Michael did a punishing hour of ashtanga yoga before leaving for the theater. He stopped in at the deli on 84th to grab a bagel with egg and tomato cream cheese, and when the man behind the counter asked him if he wanted to throw in a coffee for another dollar, Michael considered taking him up on it. But then he remembered Jesse's coffee, and politely declined, lowering his eyes as if protecting a secret. The counter man was not moved. "Your loss," he shrugged.

"Not really," Michael replied with a grin. "Thank you."

He ate as he walked with an unhurried step toward the subway stop, hiding his smile behind large bites of the bagel. The food felt great in his stomach, even if it would have been better if he'd been able to wash it down with hot coffee. Still, it was better to wait, and get what he really wanted, even if it slightly compromised the total experience. He thought, too late, that he should have brought one for Jesse, too, and they could eat bagels and drink coffee together. He nodded to himself, vowing to make sure he did so tomorrow.

Even considering the leaden sky and the sticky tang of smog in the air, walking along Manhattan streets listening to Fleetwood Mac on headphones, heading towards Jesse and his coffee, was almost unbearably joyous.

He arrived early, even by his own standards, but he wasn't the first one there; Laurence LaPonte and three of the actors occupied the completed stage set, in position for the start of act three, and LaPonte pointed out movements on the stage floor with a red laser pointer.

"Swing around like this, in a half-circle. Jenna, I want to see you do it; you keep on coming in too tight right here. You walk right out of your light and you can't keep doing it."

"Hello," Michael said, waving. LaPonte and the actors looked up at him, but their faces were set and tense, not so much unfriendly as too anxious and preoccupied to justify responding.

"It looks better this way, though," Jenna, the star of the show, protested, lifting her dirty-haired ponytail off the back of her neck. She was the draw of the play, having played the slutty ingenue in some sub-network TV show that spring. But when she wasn't called upon to look like luscious jailbait, she tended to be gray-faced with hangover, clad in sloppy old jeans and a stained tank top. Still, she was professional and competent, and she'd get asses in seats. "I have to walk faster to make the mark in time with the music. Can't the light follow me?"

"No, Jenna, sweetheart, it can't."

"Maybe it could," Michael suggested.

"Michael," LaPonte said with a mirthless smile, not looking at him, "please shut the fuck up when I'm directing."

"Sorry," Michael muttered, and slouched over to his booth at the back of the house. There was no coffee. Jesse wasn't there today. He wouldn't be back again. Michael pinched himself for forgetting.

Other crew members trickled in, all of them early. Michael checked and rechecked all of the light board's connections, then stood there watching LaPonte running the actors through their marks, over and over again, playing the play's "soundtrack" through a CD boom box sitting on the edge of the stage. The show was as tightly choreographed as a musical, just without any dancing. The lights would provide all the artful motion. Michael wished he could light the actors as they went through their marks, then chuckled to himself when he realized that was exactly what he'd be doing all day, as soon as everybody showed up.

The first tech rehearsal had happened yesterday, that joyless, draggy day when everybody seemed to be hung over and everything took forever. All that day he had struggled against intense drowsiness, paying the price for staying up almost the whole of Saturday night. He'd roamed from club to club, never finding anyone he wanted to go home with, finally retreating, frustrated and baffled. He had lain in bed long after the sun came up, physically comfortable but unable to fall asleep, wondering what the hell was wrong with him.

But everything had become clear last night.

At the end of the day, with the set finished and the crew signing out on their final times, Jesse had approached him and they went outside together without speaking. Jesse walked his bike down the sidewalk, swinging his helmet by its chinstrap. Before Michael was going to beg off from their usual drink, Jesse said, "See you tomorrow, okay," and stretched up to kiss him on the mouth. He followed it with a warm, affectionate hug, but Michael was too startled to try to hug back. By the time he got it together, Jesse had let go, shoved his helmet on, and coasted down the street, side-straddling the bike for a hundred yards before gracefully swinging his other leg over.

That moment played over and over in his mind all evening–not the kiss, as sweet as that had been, that soft burst of breath against his lips as Jesse exhaled into his stretch–but the one-sided ride, the balletic sweep of the leg, the play of muscles against the seat of Jesse's jeans as he pressed for speed. At home alone, Michael had sat in lotus pose, meditating, trying to let the memory slip away into the tide of thoughts. Eventually, after the ache in his legs had long since become a soothing background noise, the memory had been replaced with a truth so basic and all-encompassing that it was no wonder he hadn't seen it. He hadn't found anybody he wanted to hook up with on Saturday night's forced march because none of them was enough like Jesse. None of them was him. None of them was Drew, either, no matter how handsome, how well-groomed, how brilliantly bleached the smile or thick the forearm.

Then, in the shower, he had stroked himself carefully, self-lovingly, to shattering orgasm, stepping forward out of the water to rub his come between his hands, thumbs and forefingers playing against each other with wonder at its heavy texture and coolness. Come. Yes, that stuff, that nasty stuff; he loved it so much, even if he was meant to hate it, to see it as a disgusting, dangerous waste product. He let himself play with it until it was dry, then he rinsed off and produced some more. *One for you. And—ah!—one for you. My men. Oh, dammit, to hell with it, to hell with me. I love them.* He had fallen asleep holding the card with Drew Farrow's number on it in one hand and the phone in the other.

He was so fucked. So seriously fucked.

Now his phone rang. The caller ID read **Jesse**. Michael turned away from the stage and answered. "Jesse, hi."

"Hi, do you miss me already?"

"Terribly," Michael confessed. "How are you today?"

"I'm pretty good," Jesse said. "Got a lot of sleep. Needed it."

"Me, too."

"Boring Sunday night. Went out to dinner, took a shower, went to bed."

"Did you go anyplace good?" Michael couldn't help asking.

Jesse shook his head. "No," he admitted. "I didn't really like it. It's kinda Drew's scene. I just went to keep him company."

"Well . . . I guess that's good."

"Poor Michael," Jesse said softly.

Michael sharpened his voice. "Don't ever let me hear you say that again. You do *not* feel sorry for me."

"No," Jesse said quickly. "Of course not."

"Good."

"I missed you," Jesse said.

"You saw me yesterday."

"I missed you last night, I mean." Jesse laughed a little. "I miss our evenings."

"Meet me for lunch," Michael said.

"That's just what I was gonna suggest." Jesse laughed again. "Meet me at the burrito place at the end of the block. Noon work okay?"

"Make it one."

"Got it. See you there."

To Michael's surprise, Jesse didn't look any different today, now that he was unemployed. He still wore a threadbare old rock band T-shirt — Genesis, this time — paint-stained jeans, sneakers. He met Michael with a kiss. "Before we get some food, I've got something I want to play for you. C'mon, upstairs."

Michael followed Jesse to the upper floor of the restaurant, where almost no one ever sat; they were regulars enough that their presence wasn't challenged. Jesse sat down in one of the chairs and pulled out his phone. "Drew left a voicemail for me this morning before he went out on his run. I listened to the beginning of it, but that's it; I want to listen to it with you." Jesse poked at the phone. "He does this sometimes, leaves me dirty stories and stuff. He hasn't done it in a long time and I was starting to think he wasn't into it anymore. But . . . anyway, listen." He set it to play on speakerphone, and sat back in the chair. Still standing, Michael let his eyes drift to the ceiling, sinking into the husky cadences of Drew's voice, his mind filtering out the tinny half-echo of electronic static.

"Hey, Jesse. I hope you have a good day today. I just wanted to tell you what's been up." A sigh, but not a regretful one. "A disclosure. Feel free to share this with Michael, if you like. So. A couple of days ago . . ."

Michael glanced down at Jesse, who was biting his lip, listening with intense concentration.

"After you left to go to work, I was tidying up the kitchen, and I got a call from Denisse."

"His ex-wife," Jesse amended helpfully. Michael nodded.

"She's doing all right. She says hello, and hello from the kids. You should call them once in a while, before they get old enough to start having attitude. Because believe me, when they're teenagers, they will change." Drew chuckled knowingly. "So, after that, I got more thoughtful than I felt like being. So, of course, I go to the gym, work on my arms and back. I did a bit too much weight, you know? More than I need right now, but damn, it just felt really good."

Just barely audible, but more so than had been detectable when they were drinking at L'ête, Michael could hear a faint lisp in Drew's voice. It was not an affectation; it was too subtle for that. It dragged against Michael's mind like a slightly ragged fingernail against velvet.

"When I was on my way to the locker room, I saw . . . this guy."

"Uh huh," Jesse murmured, rolling his eyes. "Here we go."

"I've never seen him there before, and I'm in there often enough that I know pretty much every face. Every body. I would have remembered seeing him before. Six foot, probably two hundred flat, pale strawberry blond. You know, the type whose eyebrows disappear? And with a fucking ridiculous body. Arms. Pecs. Legs." Drew's voice, nearly groaning. "Nice ripped and defined core, without any of it being too overt. Like he uses it all. Built like a fucking Navy SEAL. A little bit of curly, swear-to-God golden hair on his chest. Kind of . . . rosy nips . . ." Michael looked at Jesse, who gave a dubious frown followed by an uncertain smile. But Drew went on, "Rose-petal pink, just starting to brown at the edges, nice thick pecs that stick out. The ones you can't miss."

"Fuck," Michael whispered. Jesse lifted a silencing finger to smiling lips.

"The other thing that got me was he was really pale. Fair, fair skin. And his face and his neck and shoulders were so freckled that he almost looked like he had a tan from a distance. And light blue eyes. Blond eyelashes. Incredible. He looked about my age, I'm guessing. And he was cruising the hell out of me. I'm in the locker room stripping, and taking off my stinky shoes, and he's like, 'Hey, you have great lats. What's your bench?' and I just look him up and down. And he takes off his clothes, too, and underneath the T-shirt his skin, because it's so transparent and he'd been working so hard, had all turned . . . hot . . . red. That just kind of did it, you know?

"We shower and check each other out. He's got his dick in his hand, not spending too much time on it—y'know, we're in public— but definitely enough to really show it to me. And just like I'd thought, it's immense, uncut, and red as a beet. So I show him mine. By now his eyes are glittering, and I'm having to decide if I just want to wave a hard-on around like a flag, or try somehow to keep it down. I compromise by getting out of the shower and wrapping one of the big towels around my waist, and it's heavy enough to hide the evidence. And that Aryan farm boy freak is right on my tail, and he's not doing too well at hiding that monster between his legs. I head to the handicapped stall on the near end of the locker room–there's one on either end—and Blondie follows me in.

"And he asks me for my name. I say, 'No names.' I put my hand on his arm—I wanted to see if his biceps were as hard as they looked—and they were even more so. Arms like carved wood. He's finally starting to cool down a bit. And that's when I notice, real subtle and small on one shoulder, a tattoo of the eagle on the USN banner. Yes, indeed—a sailor. Holy shit. It's Fleet Week; how could I forget?"

Jesse began to laugh, though he quickly restrained himself and fell silent again. Michael shook his head and let out a quick chuckle himself. If he hadn't, he would have moaned. His penis ached, tumescent against his inseam. He thought about going over to where Jesse sat, and pressing his erection against Jesse's back, or maybe the back of his neck. Against his face. Michael shuddered, and brought his focus back to Drew's disembodied voice.

"He felt up my arms, too. I grabbed one of his sailor nipples and gave it a nice hard wrench. He liked that a lot. He tried to kiss me after that, and I told him no kissing, either. And he got a little pissed off then, and was like, What's wrong with you? Got herpes? So I told him, 'I've got someone,' and grab his cock, and put one of his hands on mine. Thank God. He finally stopped complaining. Big, big dick. Nine inches easy. Louisville Slugger. Uncut, doesn't trim, like some kind of savage, out there on that ship with all those men for months. I'd have hairy balls, too. I really do wish I could have kissed him. He smelled amazing. You've never smelled a freshly washed, uncut dick — or, I dunno, have you? Anyway, it's wonderful, that musk. I huffed it while I was massaging his dick. We had to go slow because we couldn't even use spit for lube; it all comes down to technique, when that happens. You don't have to jerk it to pleasure it. I didn't. He knew what he was doing, too, more or less, probably just copying what I did; I didn't care. It was more than good enough to get me off quick. He thought I'd be done when I was done, but he doesn't know how I operate. I kept it up — sliding the foreskin back and forth with pre-come dripping all down his dick — until he shot his load all over my legs. Thick and ropy; he'd been holding it in a long time. And he moaned, too, and I was ready to stick my fist in his mouth to quiet him down. But on the other hand, heh, I've got you, you sexy fucking bastard." Drew's voice sighed again, long, with a hitch in it. He didn't moan, but the restraint, the quiet perfection of his orgasm, struck Michael to the depths of his belly. "And, of course, when we walked out of the stall, there was a guy in a wheelchair rolling up to use it, and if I thought Blondie could turn red before, it was nothing compared to how hard he blushed over that. Grown man. It's like, oh well, welcome to New York, have a wonderful Fleet Week.

"Anyway," Drew concluded, "that's my disclosure. I hope you'll share one with me sometime soon. Have a great day. I love you."

Jesse snapped the phone closed. "Well," he said, and snickered.

"Oh my *God*."

"That's Drew Farrow for you."

"And you say he does this all the time?"

"Not so much these days," Jesse said. "But that's the thing; we can fool around with other people, but no fluid exchange. And we have to tell each other and be honest about it. And explain why we wanted it. And since we have to do that, why not make it hot?"

"Do you leave him obscene voicemails?" Michael asked.

"Yeah," Jesse said. "In fact, I started it." He grinned. "I don't always tell him a story, though; sometimes I just have one-man phone sex. C'mon, let's get a burrito." When Jesse stood up, the tent in his jeans stuck out like the proverbial sore thumb, and made Michael feel better about his own response.

Before he ordered, though, Michael took a quick visit to the restroom where he verified that he had, indeed, come in his pants. Not too much, easily dabbed clean with a paper towel.

Smiling, Jesse was seated at the counter when Michael returned. "That was hot," Michael said. "Thanks for sharing."

"My pleasure," Jesse replied, winking. "Hungry?"

"Absolutely."

They munched on their vegetarian burritos for a few minutes without speaking. "I have an idea," said Michael. "Do you want to come get a drink with me uptown tonight?"

Jesse stared at him for a moment, pleasantly astonished. He broke into his own crooked smile. "Sure, I'd love to," he said.

"Okay. Meet me at the subway stop on Second and Houston at eight, and we can go together."

The evening sky was striped putty-pink and black, the clouds overhead breaking up at last, and a cool, fresh breeze eddied in the spaces between buildings. The downtown crowds were just starting to emerge, either already drunk from a day's fueled relaxation, or perky and refreshed and ready to enjoy the last evening of the long weekend. From somewhere unseen, a trumpet slowly played Taps, then played it again, as though it had gone on all day and would continue till midnight. "Nice night," Jesse mentioned, walking his bike along the sidewalk.

"It is." They went down the stairs to the station, swiped metro cards, and stood on the platform with the bike still between them. On the train itself, neither spoke, but calmly watched one another with subtle smiles on their faces.

They disembarked at 86th and Lex, and Jesse cheerfully hauled his bike up the three flights of stairs to the street. Uptown was much calmer than the merry chaos of Houston Street; there were people out, winding in and out of bars and restaurants, but the sidewalks were far from busy. They legged the bike along 86th towards Second, winding around the puddled evidence of the afternoon's rain. "So you live all the way up here, huh?" Jesse asked.

"I'm by 90th. I used to live up at the Towers when I was a student, but I got my own place a little further downtown in February. I thought about living in Harlem, but I couldn't find a place. This one's fine, though, at least for right now. And . . . this is the place."

Michael indicated, with a sweep of his arm, a sprawling, ragged-edged corner pub. He walked right in, as confident and comfortable as Jesse had ever seen him, and settled into an open booth. Jesse locked his bike to a rack already housing three other bikes, and came in, settling his helmet on the seat next to him. Already a busty, tattooed waitress was getting an order from Michael, and dropping well-worn paper menus on the table. Jesse asked for a whiskey, and examined the menu's selection of general pub food. "Do you come here often?" he asked.

"I've been a couple of times. It's nice."

"It's quiet." Conversation buzzed in counterpoint to some kind of electronic music that Jesse didn't recognize. It was a nice change from the usual gay bar soundtrack of radio-friendly divas and pop princesses fallen into squalor. "They play your kind of music."

"That does help," Michael admitted.

When the waitress returned with their drinks, Jesse ordered french fries, unable to think of what else he'd want. While Michael ordered a grilled cheese sandwich, Jesse excused himself to go to the men's room. In the small, harshly lit space, he sent a text message to Drew: **having drinks w M. may be out late. dont wait up. love u.** He silenced his phone and tucked it back into a pocket of his jeans.

Back at the table, they clinked their glasses. "To the future," Michael said, and drank.

Jesse drank, too, and grimaced the pungent liquor down. "Yeah," he said. "I try not to think about it."

"Why?"

"I dunno. The future. It's too huge."

"Oh, c'mon, Jesse."

Jesse drank again. "I just, you know," he mumbled. "I find that if I don't make plans, then things seem to turn out better."

"You can't spend the rest of your life that way," Michael said. Jesse groaned worriedly at that, and Michael laughed. "It's nonsense, Jesse. You can't worry about it. You just figure out what you want to do, and then plan to do it, and then work towards it. It tends to work out."

"Yeah. Okay." Jesse tried laughing too. "Thanks. Good to hear."

"I've got your back," Michael offered. "Don't let Drew intimidate you."

Jesse mused on that for a while, sipping the whiskey, but even this shot seemed to evaporate as soon as he touched it to his lips. He shoved some fries into his mouth while he watched Michael devour his sandwich, hot threads of cheese pulled thin by his teeth. Jesse put some fries onto Michael's plate, and Michael ate them, too. He tore off a quarter of the sandwich, and put it on Jesse's plate. Although Jesse's appetite had been blunted by the liquor, he ate the cooling square of cheese, bread, and butter. It was so deliciously different from the dinner he'd eaten with Drew last night.

Drew had taken him to one of the most expensive and glamorous restaurants in the city. Unfortunately, the only thing on the menu that had even vaguely appealed to Jesse was an artichoke raviolini, gorgeously presented and distressingly tiny, with weird curls of fennel on top that he'd shoved to the edge of his plate with his fork. Drew had a great time, and Jesse counted no less than six people who had come to their table to say hello to Drew and thank him for some financial something or other. None of them took more than the slightest notice of Jesse, slumped in his seat and toying with the fennel curls, while Drew beamed and shone, blessing the room with the pearlescent glory of his dentist's-office-calendar perfect teeth. In that moment, Jesse loved Drew, but didn't admire him, or even like him particularly much; Jesse didn't want to be there, and suspected that Drew's offer of a nice meal out had only been a pretense for Drew to go someplace swanky and show off. Six people! Fennel on artichoke raviolini! It was so stupid. Lemon zest would have made sense, but . . . ugh.

"What did you eat last night?" Jesse asked Michael.

Michael quirked his eyebrows in surprise at the question, but answered gamely, "I, ah, had a salad. With pears and goat cheese and weird pecan pralines on it."

Jesse quirked a smile. "Was it good?"

"Yeah, it was tasty. I mostly just wanted to get the evening over with. Notes, you know, with the director. Great way to ruin my appetite."

"I totally know what you mean," Jesse muttered.

"What's the matter?" Michael asked, a little sharply. "Sick of me already?"

"No," Jesse amended hastily, and sweetened it with a smile. "No way. I'm glad to be here. I'm glad to be here. With you."

"Sorry." Michael rolled his eyes, chuckling. "Now who's the paranoid one?"

"Seriously." Jesse laughed and shook his head, and ate one last fry. He didn't want any more drinks; the whiskey lit him up inside, as though he had a low-burning candle in his belly. Any more liquor would just put it out.

"Michael?" he asked softly. "Can I follow you home?"

With a slow, calm nod, Michael replied, "Sure. It's just a few blocks away." As if he'd been expecting it.

"Cool," said Jesse. He thought there'd be a bit more drama, some excitement at the broaching this boundary, but maybe this was better. No threats, no promises. Just a quick peek into Michael's life. And his bed. It'd be fine. Whatever happened, happened.

They split the bill, and walked a few blocks uptown to a brownstone building, opposite a fenced park, with a tortilla shop and a jeweler on the ground floor. Michael opened a nondescript, unlabeled door next to the tortilla shop and unclipped keys from the interior of his briefcase. Along the wall rows of mailboxes bristled with junk mail. Jesse examined the small lobby. It was a poor place for a spontaneous hookup, but not a bad place for a passionate goodbye kiss. Jesse had seen much worse; there was no trash on the floor, even if it needed a quick sweeping, and the only graffiti was a series of scratches into the grayish paint and a mailing label sporting an ornate, indecipherable glyph. He loved going into new places in New York; like a human face, each was different beyond a general set of characteristics. He locked his bike to a protruding electrical pipe which, judging by the nicks on its painted surface, had been used as a bike rack before.

Michael opened another door to a stairwell, and they mounted all four flights to the top. Jesse trailed a few steps behind, watching the muscles clench and release in Michael's buttocks as he climbed. Michael took out keys in front of the door farthest along the hall, and let them in.

He immediately hit a switch along the wall, shocking the room into light. "So, um, this is it," he said.

Jesse stepped in, made sure the door was shut behind him, and then turned to Michael, looping his fingers behind Michael's neck and drawing his head down to meet his lips. Michael drew in a sharp, surprised breath, but matched Jesse's mouth, parting his lips and admitting Jesse's tongue. Jesse wrapped his arms around Michael and held him close, raising one leg up to enfold Michael against his pelvis, moaning faintly in sudden urgency.

Michael drew back, breaking the kiss and creating a wet, sticky sound that made Jesse's balls twang. "Hey, there, hey," Michael murmured, taking a deep breath and shuddering it out. His glasses hung askew, pushed sideways across his nose.

"What's up?" Jesse asked with a faint laugh. He let go and stepped back. "Sorry. I just had to." He shook his head and rolled his eyes up to the ceiling, to the far-too-bright square lens on the overhead lightbulb. "I'm sorry . . ."

"Shut up," Michael said softly. Jesse sighed, and couldn't look at him, glancing around the apartment instead. The medium-sized studio was sparely furnished with a low bed and a nightstand made of metal tubing, a light table with neatly stacked sheets of drafting paper and pencils carefully aligned in a box, a very small desk entirely occupied by a large flat-screen computer monitor, a single chair pushed against the wall, a bookshelf stuffed with textbooks, and a bureau in a doorless closet. There were no decorations on the walls, and no mirror, and the rug was a flat square of dark blue and beige stripes.

"Can I get you a glass of water?" Michael asked. "That's pretty much all I have, unless you want a glass of skim milk."

"Yuck," said Jesse. "I don't drink milk. Water. Yeah, thanks."

"I have an orange if you want it."

Jesse snickered. "No. Water is fine." He sat on the bed and watched Michael walk over to the kitchen space, just as neat and even less lived-in, and said, "I'd think you'd have nicer lighting in here."

"Oh, I do," said Michael, returning with two unmatched glasses and setting them down on the nightstand. Bending down, he flipped switches someplace Jesse couldn't see, and the perimeters of the room slowly illuminated with a beautiful azure-blue glow from a rope light so fine Jesse would never have seen it. Michael turned off the overhead light, awoke his computer, and typed quickly on the keyboard. The rope light began to softly change color, shading into lavender, then a rich, dark plum. "Have you ever heard of the Knife?"

"Whoa . . . wow. . . What?"

Now the apartment was a magical place. It didn't need art on the walls; the secret illumination transformed the space into a realm of dreams, each of the color settings reminiscent of a different environment. This purple was royalty, exotica, Arabian nights, and the magenta that followed was passion and glamor; the pale pink, cherry blossoms in a longed-for spring. "So . . . fucking cool . . ."

From hidden speakers, a faintly tribal beat of electronic drums made Jesse's heart beat faster. And then Michael was on the bed beside him, lifting one of the glasses of water to his lips, taking a swallow, setting the glass back down, catching the copper glow of an orange sunset in the water. Michael took off his glasses and set them on the nightstand. "This is my favorite band right now," he said.

"It's great," said Jesse. He'd never heard this music before, and yet it felt like he'd always known it. A quiet, processed female voice murmured dark secrets, synthesizer notes as cool as the rain-sweetened breeze he had felt earlier when he had been outside.

Michael reached out and stroked the side of Jesse's face. Jesse felt like he was smiling with every cell of his being. He reached down and pulled the hem of his T-shirt over his head. Michael's eyebrows went up in mild surprise and approval. "I want to see your body," Jesse said, unlacing his boots and pulling them off, shedding socks, returning to unzip his jeans.

With a slight nod, Michael bent down to unlace his brown Docs.

Jesse waited, patiently naked, and watched Michael disrobe. He was thin, but not as skinny as his gray, slightly baggy button-up shirt made him look. His pale skin was lightly furred all over with glistening black hair, thicker in the hollow between his pectorals, spreading out like a phoenix across his upper chest and surrounding his small, perfect light brown nipples. Michael's hairy legs went on and on, but nude, his odd proportions made perfect sense – the long torso matched with the narrow dish of his pelvis, and lean, gleaming muscle moving smoothly along with the beat of the music. "Fuck, they make me want to dance," he chuckled. "Do you dance? Do you want to come out with me sometime?"

"Totally," said Jesse.

Under pale cotton boxer shorts, a different spread of thick, shiny black hair framed a wrinkled curve of flesh. To take the underwear off, Michael had to spread his legs slightly, his testicles dangling against his inner thigh, smooth eggs in a shadowed pouch of skin. Jesse couldn't help sighing eagerly, and his head began to ache with tension. "You should probably touch me," Jesse muttered. "Touch me and then kiss me."

Michael hadn't been looking at him, not really, keeping his eyes modestly elsewhere while he undressed. Jesse reached out to him and took his face between his hands, forcing him to make eye contact, and then angled Michael's skull downward, watching the way his face transformed from a kind of casual calm to an intense, almost troubled frown of concentration. Jesse could feel himself getting hard, becoming erect, the cool air of the room on his nuts and the underside of his cock. He took one of Michael's big hands in one of his small ones, and placed it on his genitals. "Touch," Jesse commanded, and lifted his face to brush his lips against Michael's.

Michael consumed his mouth. There was no hesitation or gentleness. His fingers roughly grasped Jesse's dick, and he groaned deeply, thrusting his tongue towards Jesse's throat. Jesse arched himself toward Michael, bumping their bellies together, his knee glancing off Michael's, the pain cascading across his closed eyelids in a white streak like lightning. He tried to whine, "Ow," but it was lost, buried in the kiss.

Jesse edged Michael's legs apart with the hurt knee, and reached out for his own reward. Michael's cock was harder than it had looked, or it had gotten harder in the last few seconds; the core of the tissue was thick and rigid in a sheath of more supple flesh. Jesse's own dick left a wet trail across Michael's belly. They lay side by side, both trying to take the initiative to get on top, but defeated by the urges of the other. Jesse was strong, but there was no way he could get the best of Michael's spider limbs and well-formed core muscles. Michael was just bigger, that was all.

Win by surrendering — a tactic Jesse knew well. He turned over, face down against the bed, and pushed his butt upward, against Michael's stomach. Michael moaned out loud at last, a true sound of lust; he sounded like an animal, like a sunning lion's groan, the room filled with the straw-yellow light of the veldt. He grasped Jesse's ass cheeks with his hands, squeezing roughly, then gently. "Oh, my God. You have the most beautiful ass I've ever seen."

Jesse laughed quietly, and fucked the bedspread a little. "Drew's is better."

Michael sighed. "Mmmm," he groaned. "Okay, we should—"

While he was distracted with that train of thought, Jesse turned over again, and pushed Michael onto his back. He slithered quickly downward, smacking a kiss onto Michael's flat belly, then grabbed a fistful of penis and slid it into his mouth. Michael bucked underneath him, startled, crying out, "Oh!"

"Sssh," said Jesse, stroking down Michael's torso. "Relax."

"You're not supposed to —"

"Quiet," said Jesse. He looked up into Michael's eyes, and

nodded. "It's cool," he added. "Really. Just let me . . . fuck, I just want your balls in my mouth so much right now." He lifted Michael's cock, thickening and hardening in his fingers, and licked a stripe along the side, and another across the top. Goose pimples spread across Michael's skin so dramatically that the prickle of raised hairs tickled Jesse's arms. "Let me suck this cock for you."

"Oh, my God," Michael said again, but he relaxed, spreading his thighs, then tightening them on Jesse's shoulders.

Jesse hadn't had a penis other than Drew's in his mouth since he was eighteen, in college, in Wisconsin. And the dick on that skinny skater boy had put paid to the concept that all black men were well-hung; it had been a salty bonbon that barely filled out his mouth. Michael's dick was long and narrow, and tasted of clean sweat and soap and fabric dust. He licked around the rim of the head, flicked the bottom of his tongue across the urethral divot, tucked as much of tip as he could into his cheek, and sucked. Michael writhed, hissing between his teeth, his fingers sliding up underneath Jesse's overgrown flop of hair. When Jesse let his eyelids raise a bit, the light had gone back to sky blue, and Michael was arched against the surface of the bed, mouth open in a silent cry.

Jesse wasn't a fan of silence, so he groaned for Michael, and sucked harder. A broken gasp emerged from Michael's lips. Jesse moved his head back and forth, up and down, cradling Michael's cock with his tongue, applying no suction, only slippage, letting saliva flood his mouth so that the slick sound of it joined the music. It made Jesse's balls ache even more. He could finally taste Michael's pre-come; there wasn't a lot of it, but the flavor was intense, seasoned with semen. Jesse slid down the cock as far as he could, pausing to calm his throat so that he wouldn't gag; there'd be time for that. Not yet. Michael had gone silent again, clenching the bedspread between his fingers.

"Let me have it," Jesse whispered, and kissed Michael's balls, stroking the wet length of penis with his hand. Was he fully erect? Could it go farther?

"No . . . no . . . oh, God, please . . ."

Jesse just laughed at him, and went down again, sucking now, bobbing his mouth faster, jacking firmly at the base of the organ. Michael bent one knee, opening himself out more, and Jesse paused for just long enough to get some of the excess spit onto his fingers and thumb. With cock firmly planted back into his cheek, he dug into the hair-shaded crevice between Michael's buttocks.

"Oh, God, no!" Michael moaned eagerly.

Jesse wanted to tell him to shut up, but his mouth was so full, and his curious, determined fingers found the hidden crenellations of anal skin. His fingers had gone dry in their exploration, but his thumb remained cool, wet, and slick; he pushed in, slow and firm, the way it should be done. Michael's asshole quickly clenched shut, then relaxed again, allowing him passage. "Oh, God," Jesse echoed, the words obliterated by his mouthful, eyes rolling behind clenched lids as he imagined what a cock like this would feel like inside him. It wasn't too thick — Drew had won the fattest cock contest in Jesse's life — but the length! Seven inches? Eight? It would tear him up, deep inside where no one had ever gone. Jesse's own cock leaked sopping wetness across his stomach and thighs, leaving a sticky slick on the corner of the bed, on Michael's ankle. Jesse captured Michael's foot between his thighs and rubbed his balls against it, tightened his spine, dragging his cock against the rough edge of the sole. He laughed, mouth full. *I am fucking this guy's foot. Yeah, this is real.*

"Christ." Michael actually pulled Jesse's hair, and pushed him off his cock, his own hand taking the place of Jesse's. Jesse angled back and watched, Michael's narrow fingers pulling and pushing until a white blob of come appeared suddenly on the urethra. Then a thick, creamy jet arced out and hit Jesse's chin and neck. Jesse laughed delightedly, and added his hand to Michael's, jacking faster, squeezing out more come, these jets less forceful, mostly just running down over their hands. "Jesus. Fuck," Michael gasped. "Oh, God, I'm sorry, I didn't . . . I didn't mean to come . . ."

Jesse couldn't care less about that. "You can make it up to me," he said, wiping his chin, rubbing the semen into his chest, onto his steel-hard nipples. He crawled on his knees over to Michael, and tried to drop his balls onto Michael's mouth, but by now his balls were so tight and urgent they didn't want to drop. Michael looked alarmed, his face flushed red and eyes glazed, but he didn't resist when Jesse instead bent forward and slid his dick between Michael's lips. To Jesse's immense delight, Michael moaned eagerly, and opened his mouth wider, wide enough so that Jesse's cock slipped in and out with ease. "Yes!" Jesse groaned, letting his cock slip out entirely, then back in again, over and over. Michael's mouth flooded with saliva; Jesse let his cock trail out and slap against Michael's chin, his cheeks, wetting his face. "Oh, yes, that's right," Jesse sighed, half-singing, letting his syllables purl out, fucking Michael's hot, sweet, open mouth in time with the music. Michael grasped Jesse's hips and held him still, and moved his head instead, slurping avidly on Jesse's nearly vertical erection.

Jesse felt dizzy; he pulled away and lay back, and Michael lay over him, upside down, the musky scent of sweat and come and a lightly violated asshole filling Jesse's senses. Jesse wanted to lick the spilled come off Michael's balls, off his still-lengthy and half-hard cock, but he knew that would be going too far. They didn't know each other that well yet. God, he hoped. He wanted to taste all of Michael.

Instantly, he was there. The light was green, a deep Kentucky bluegrass green, and his cock was still in Michael's mouth; Jesse didn't want to tell him to stop or move, but it wouldn't be fair; it wouldn't be right. Jesse grabbed his dick and pulled from between Michael's lips, and turned half over, his own load spurting harmlessly against the damp bedspread. He moaned from deep within his belly, convulsing and kicking, eyes rolling back, his consciousness knocked sideways into senseless ecstasy. He spoke in tongues for a moment, trying to say a thousand things in a single breath.

When he came down, Michael lay beside him, watching reverently. As the green light shaded back into royal blue, Michael's irises changed from chocolate-brown to black. His face glistened damply, his lips swollen into wet crimson pillows. Jesse curled up into him, arms enfolding him, clutching him tightly; in this moment, Jesse always needed to embrace, to feel warm again, to connect himself back to the world. Michael wrapped his long arms around Jesse and held him close to his chest and shoulder, kissing hair, eyebrows, cheeks, lips. Michael's mouth was full of the taste of Jesse's pre-come, luscious, naughty, and private. Jesse hummed along with the music, and stroked the soft patch of hair at the base of Michael's spine. Michael touched the tip of his tongue to Jesse's palate, and followed it with the tiniest, sweetest lip-kiss, and a chuckle.

I think I might be in love.

Michael took a deep breath. "Time for you to go," he said.

"Hmm?!" Jesse responded.

His answer was a slow, wide smile. "You should go home and

get some sleep," he said. "I've got an early call tomorrow. And don't you have to go find a new job?"

Jesse grunted in confusion and protest. "Hey! . . . Really?" He blinked. "You're kicking me out?"

Michael nodded, and stroked Jesse's hair, so pleased, getting off on the control. "You gotta go," he said. "I have to change the sheets and get to sleep. I've got to go swimming in the morning."

"Dude." Jesse sat up and shook his head, sighing. "Un-be-fucking-lievable," he muttered, Brooklyn accent suddenly descending onto his voice. "Fine." He got up and wiped himself clean with a crumpled section of bedspread, since Michael was just going to change it anyway; he was suddenly seized with the urge to piss all over Michael's bed. Instead he found his shorts, and dragged them on, then his socks, then stood there letting Michael get a good look at him.

"That was wonderful," Michael said softly, sincerely.

"Uh-huh. I'm glad you think so."

"You can stay over sometime," Michael added, "just not tonight. I'm sorry." He didn't look sorry; he looked satisfied and horribly sexy. His softened cock had returned to its curved, modest state, half-hidden under a dense thicket of pubic hair.

"Are you ever gonna get your eyebrows done?" Jesse blurted, so that he wouldn't get emotional, or vicious, and just jump on Michael and start fucking him until he had no choice except to let Jesse stay.

Michael laughed quietly. "Yeah," he said. "I'll get 'em done this week. Am I too hairy?"

"God, no," Jesse said, his voice breaking faintly. So much for not getting emotional. He turned away, and picked up his shirt and jeans. "You're . . . perfect. I'm—I'm—"

"I know," Michael interrupted. "You don't have to say it."

"You don't know what I was about to say," Jesse muttered.

"I want to fuck you," Michael said.

"I want to fuck *you*."

Michael nodded, and sighed, almost sadly. "I'll bring you . . . my test results," he said haltingly. "We can't just . . . But if it's really all right?"

Jesse nodded back, and met his eyes. "It's really all right," he said. "And thanks."

A diffident shrug. "Sure," Michael said. "Are you gonna tell Drew?"

"Of course I am," said Jesse clearly. "I love him. This won't jeopardize that." He pulled on shirt, jeans, boots, and finally drank from his glass of water, rinsing the sticky tang of mucus down his throat. *That's that; we're joined now, for better or for worse.* And yet, he didn't feel uneasy about that; he wanted more, no matter what it took. He had never wanted anything so much in his life.

Jesse bent over the bed and pressed his lips to Michael's, smoothing Michael's hair back from the widow's peak, and drawing a line connecting his thick eyebrows. Michael smiled, eyes shining. "See you real soon," he said. "Maybe this weekend. Maybe I can come see your place."

"Uh, we'll see," Jesse said, smiling despite himself. "Maybe." He added one last kiss, and tore himself away before he required another one, and another. He put on his bike helmet, paused in the doorway, and waved goodbye, so that he wouldn't have to say it.

6. HE'S GOT IT PRETTY BAD FOR YOU.

The rainy Tuesday had receded to a humid memory, and Wednesday dawned cloudless. Drew and Jesse ate breakfast out in the back garden of the house. The small, narrow yard was well-kept, with perennials, stones, and slabs of Moroccan mosaic tile instead of grass, shaded with arches of ivy and wisteria, and fragrant with the last notes of blooming jasmine.

Jesse had specifically gotten up early to have breakfast, since he knew they wouldn't see each other again until the next morning, and quickly threw together a meal of toast, honey, boiled eggs, and freshly prepared, angrily hot mustard. "The Brooklyn Half-Marathon is in six weeks," Jesse reminded him. "Time for you to start getting skinny."

"Yeah, I know," Drew sighed, and slid a single slice of toast and two eggs onto his plate, stirring half a spoonful of honey into his green tea. He hated green tea, but it seemed to help strip off pounds. "I've got ten pounds that I can lose. I'd like to take twenty, but I'd be eating muscle if I did. At least I had a Kobe burger and fries for lunch yesterday."

"Oh yeah? How was that?" Jesse stacked slabs of butter on his toast, slathered it with honey, folded it in half, and stuffed it into his mouth. He grinned impishly at Drew, finishing the butter taco in two bites, and proceeded to construct another one of the same.

"Full of meat," Drew said, sipping his tea. Jesse curled his lip in distaste. He cleared his throat. "I think Michael's got it pretty bad for you."

"I know," Jesse said, a little smug. "I like him. He's fun to play with."

"I'm taking him to dinner tonight," Drew mentioned. "To Franca Norris."

Jesse glared. "What? You asshole. You're taking *him* to Franca Norris? I'm the foodie here!"

"Yeah, but," Drew said, smug himself now, "you have to go to that cartoon with your friend Charlie."

"It's an animated *feature film*. And it's only screening for one night. If I want to see it, this is it." Jesse groaned in annoyance. "I'm the one who *told* you about Franca Norris. I used to wash dishes for that bitch."

"I actually read about the opening online. It sounds amazing. I'm lucky to get a table. And you did say that her family meals were phenomenal."

"Money talks, bullshit walks, and Drew Farrow just kinda *ambles*." Jesse wiggled his fingers in the air. "God, I hate you so much."

"Don't be jealous," Drew said mildly, spreading mustard on the pliable surface of an egg. "If I like it, I'll take you next. Maybe I'll take all three of us."

Jesse regarded Drew with a half-suspicious grin. "When are you gonna get in his pants?"

"Sounds like it's pretty nice there."

"It is. Eight inches, and fucking furious."

"I saw him first!" Drew glared playfully, then his face softened into thoughtfulness. "Honey, please tell me. Are you okay? With this?"

After a moment's consideration, Jesse nodded. "I think so," he said. "Are you?"

"Would you stop, if I wasn't?"

Slowly, Jesse shook his head. "I don't know," he admitted. "I'm very . . . interested in him. I feel for him. Have feelings. Y'know? But, at the same time—it's weird—the way I feel about *you* hasn't changed. Not at all. Isn't that weird? It's not supposed to work like that, right?"

Drew shrugged. "I don't know how it's supposed to work," he admitted, the corners of his mouth turned down. "Wait, were you *trying* to feel differently towards me?"

"No," Jesse retorted indignantly, then he admitted, "Maybe. A little? Y'know, I just . . . I'll never *not* love you. You're the world to me. It's just—it's scary sometimes." He glanced sharply at Drew. "I wasn't looking for a reason to leave you," Jesse clarified. "That's not it. I'm not really sure how to say it."

"You were a little bored," Drew murmured. "It's been ten years."

"Yeah. It's normal. You feel it, too. But not *bored*, Drew. That's not it. You just . . . wanna . . ." Descending into mute gestures, Jesse let out his breath in a long, untangling sigh. "I just, I never felt like this. Not even about you. You're two different people. I don't feel the same way about him as I do about you."

"I'm not stopping you, Jesse."

"And I'm not stopping *you*," Jesse countered, raising his chin defiantly. "So, no problem, right?" Drew just shrugged and finished his toast. Jesse sighed, unsatisfied, but having brought the subject out into the open at all had unraveled something tense inside him. He tossed his hair off his forehead, crossed his arms, and stuck his lower lip out. "Franca Norris. Whatever."

"Don't pout; your face'll get stuck like that. You look stupid enough as it is."

"Your momma's stupid," Jesse muttered.

"*Your* momma." Drew tossed a crust at his head.

"Don't come at me, *cugino*. I kick your ass."

"Yep," Drew said, nodding. "I imagine you will."

Jesse smiled at him. "I love you, though."

Drew wouldn't meet his eyes. "I'll bring you a doggie bag."

"Don't eat too much tonight; you'll get jowls," Jesse said, picking up the breakfast tray and walking back inside before Drew could lose his resolve and grab another piece of toast.

Jesse had been friends with Charlie Brownstein since his first year at New York City College. Two odd outcasts from their previous realities, with Jesse an orphaned freshman year dropout and Charlie a refugee from Bronx Science, forced to get his GED after a graffiti arrest. In those days, Charlie was a wide-eyed, red-haired Jewish kid trying to become a b-boy or at least get some credibility in the tagging scene, and Jesse was a skinny, druggy skate punk who was crashing with his rich cousin. They were random gay kids trying to put their lives back together without the help of any matrix of friendship to use as support, and they gravitated towards each other, first in class, then outside of it.

Charlie definitely looked different now, looked a lot more like someone nearly thirty than Jesse did. He wore a nice corduroy jacket over a yellow vintage shirt and Levis, rimless glasses and some kind of rare sneakers, and his thinning russet hair had been clipped short. Jesse still looked, and dressed, pretty much the same as he had when he was eighteen. Charlie never judged, though, and they loped into the movie theater together, chattering excitedly about different animation studios and new releases of old favorites.

Paprika was as colorful, psychedelic, and imaginative as they had heard. After the film, they strolled around the neighborhood in search of frozen margarita slushies. Charlie tapped out a cigarette, and offered one to Jesse. Jesse grimaced and shook his head. "I quit, man. Remember?" he said.

"Oh," said Charlie, slipping the cigarette back into place. "That's right, I forgot."

"I quit a while ago, actually," Jesse confessed. "I just used to take 'em if you offered 'em."

"Ah, well. Sorry for contributing to your delinquency." Charlie lit his own. "So, dude, tell me what's up? You haven't given me an update in months. Don't make me bust my guilt powers on you; you know they're lethal."

"Yeah, I know. Sorry, bubbe," Jesse chuckled. "*Your* new guy sounds nice. What's his name again?"

"Eugene. He's a little uptight sometimes, but just so sexy. I mean, if you like looking at fabric swatches. Which, fortunately, I do. We go button shopping. God, are we a cliché?" Charlie laughed. "He does rugby, too, though. There *is* a butch bone in his body. But anyway, we've only gone on a couple of dates and a couple of sleepovers. But tell me what's going on with you. Over at House Drama, two doors down from the ghost of Montgomery Clift."

"You said it. Seriously, get this. I was building sets at the Lauren Doe for another one of Drew's shows, and I met—*we* met this guy. It's been kind of complicated ever since then."

"What? Are you serious?" Charlie halted. "The kissing cousins now have a shared boyfriend?"

"I really wish you wouldn't say it like that," Jesse replied, laughing a little.

"But that's how you . . ." Charlie's expression shrank to a worried frown. "Really? Are you sure that's a good idea?"

"Hell, no," Jesse said. "I don't know what the fuck. But when do I ever, huh?"

"No, that's what worries me," Charlie said. "I worry about you. All of it; I worry."

Jesse rolled his eyes. "You're a Jew; it's your job."

"And you're Italian, so your job is to do really stupid, overblown emotional shit? But, oh, you're also Irish, so yeah, *stupid,* overblown emotional shit, while you're blackout drunk. Am I right? Tell me if I'm anywhere near." Charlie stared at Jesse, who just shuffled his feet. "Jesus, Mary, and Joseph," Charlie swore, adding a very fake, very bad Irish accent for emphasis. "I thought Drew was supposed to be taking care of you."

"I'm sick of being taken care of," Jesse snapped. "I'm sick of being worried about."

"Do something smart, then," Charlie said quietly. He offered Jesse the cigarette again, and Jesse rolled his eyes and took it. "Here you go; that's a start. Do something *yourself.* Jesus, you can't even cheat on him without him having to get involved. You know? That drives me crazy. I'm really glad you, like, found each other, or whatever, and your post-abusive familial relationship isn't the greatest, but it's not a deal breaker. But the fact that he never lets you have anything of your own?"

"He *does* let me," Jesse replied. "I just . . . I really love him. I need him. I dunno. I doubt myself." He smiled wanly, eyes watery in the glint of the cigarette's glow. "I'm sorry it grosses you out."

"It doesn't gross me out," Charlie said. He put his hand over Jesse's. "Honey. You *know* that by now. But—I'm *your* friend. Not his. And I think you don't need him anymore."

"No," Jesse shook his head. "You don't understand."

"He's holding you back."

"From what?" Jesse shrugged. "A great future? I got it pretty nice right now, in case you hadn't noticed."

"You got it so nice, you're going to go wash dishes for five dollars an hour? But it doesn't matter, because you get to live in a house that's practically on the historic register? It's nice, but it's not *yours*." He fixed Jesse with an exasperated stare. "Dude . . . I just hope you know what you're doing."

"But I'm the cute dumb one, remember?" Jesse said, exhaling a translucent stream of smoke out toward the street. "Now, c'mon, are we gonna get 'ritas? Or, ooh, maybe ice cream. Isn't there an ice cream store around here somewhere?"

"Yeah, it's called the bodega, and you can get a popsicle for seventy-five cents. No, the place is right over there, on the corner. They're open. They're serving." Charlie draped an arm around Jesse's shoulders and gave him a squeeze. "And dammit, Butterfly, I just want the best for you. Okay? I'm not trying to step on your dick. I just care. You know you can call me any time."

"I know, Chuck B," Jesse replied, handing Charlie the half-smoked cigarette, waving his hand, indicating that he didn't want any more of it. "Thanks. I'll be okay."

"Not that I'd hesitate to body-swap with you for a weekend," Charlie added. "That *house*."

Franca Norris was this year's celebrity chef phenomenon. Her eponymous new restaurant supposedly turned out some hybrid crossbreed of French provincial and local-farmed New York heartland, or some other kind of clever synthesis attempting to stand out. For the eleven days the place had been open, food critics had been turning themselves inside out trying to find fault, and hadn't yet succeeded. The restaurant itself was almost forbiddingly modern and minimalist, with lots of hammered steel, bare concrete flooring, and unvarnished wood. A single white orchid stared blankly over each table. Drew found the décor boring, but Michael's eyes drank in all of the elegant pretense, searching for the sources of the hidden, overly-bright lighting. Drew wanted to point out that a place like Franca Norris was designed for people to be seen in, and after the hype of the opening weeks had died down, the intensity of the lighting would follow, but decided that he'd just let Michael have his fun.

Michael wore a nice black jacket and suit trousers with a plain blue T-shirt, hair spiked up a bit, all just rumpled enough to give him the air of an aspiring artist, especially with the evening's growth of stubble. Drew resisted the urge to kiss him in greeting. Instead, he just nodded and smiled, and let him walk ahead behind the maitre d', as if the table reservation had been his. Whether he knew it or not, he was making Drew look good.

As soon as he sat down, Michael said, "This is kind of amazing. I understand now why Jesse's so jealous."

"Oh, was he whining to you?" Drew chuckled. "It's his own fault. I mean, I understand the drive to see a rare film as much as the next guy, but c'mon, it's a cartoon."

"It's *anime*," Michael corrected. "And some of it's very beautiful."

They paused to allow the server to tell them the night's specials and promise to send over the sommelier. "I know the proper name for it," Drew replied airily, perusing the wine list again. "I've seen *Akira*. And I stand my ground. I don't care if it's an exquisite art form, there's no way I could sit in a theater and watch something like that for two hours, beautiful or not. Sometimes I'd rather not go to the art museum." He shook the wine menu, as if it were a newspaper he was trying to straighten. "And I happen to *own* art, if you're thinking I'm some kind of philistine."

"Well, you own the art that you like," Michael said helpfully.

Drew almost shook the single-sheet wine list again, but after a deep breath, he just set it down. "Do you mind starting with a white? Or would you rather a cocktail?"

"Oh, wine's good," Michael replied. "I've had a lot of hard alcohol lately." He smiled. "You might even have something to do with that."

"I always think of it as something that happens, when you're putting on a show," Drew parried. "You've got to turn to the spirits to help you deal with the stress of production."

Michael slowly shook his head. "My God, are you a show-off," he said.

The wine steward came by, held up the bottle, poured some out into Drew's glass. "Hello, Mr. Farrow," he said. At Drew's inquiring look, he added, "You used to come to the Leaf Collection? You were everyone's favorite customer."

"Oh, yes. Chris, isn't it? Yeah. Nice to see you. Glad you're doing so well; this is the place to be." Drew tipped him fifty bucks, subtly angling his head as if at an auction with the promise of more to come, if deserved. Chris bowed his head as well, in understanding. He poured glasses full of pale straw-colored liquid, and disappeared.

"You seem to know everybody," Michael said quietly.

"Lucky guess. Seventy-five percent chance the guy's name is Chris. Why is everybody around me pouting?" Drew threw up his hands. "You're acting like babies!"

"If you'd stop being everybody's everything, maybe people wouldn't expect so much from you."

Startled, Drew could only laugh. "Everybody's everything," he echoed. He grinned. "Am I your everything?"

Michael rolled his eyes and sighed. "Of course not," Michael replied. "But you . . . I mean . . . in a way, *you're my boss*. Your financing is making this show happen. Your money is in my paycheck. I worry that this is improper."

"It would be, if this were a date. It's a continuation of a business meeting. Or, if you'd like to think about it another way, two friends at dinner." Drew smiled.

Michael looked away. "And . . . you're Jesse's partner." The grimace became a smile, but it was equally pained.

"I am his partner, but," Drew said, "Jesse is Jesse. He does what he wants. I never once *told* him to do anything he didn't want to do, except go to school. And he wanted that, anyway, at least at first. I just let him know that there was somebody else in the world who cared that he did."

"That shapes a person," Michael said simply. "It helps them become a good person, when they might not have been."

Drew shook his head firmly. "No," he said. "You still don't know him at all, do you? *Jesse is Jesse.*" He pointed the words out into his palm. "He was going to be a good person no matter what happened. It's inside him. He's decent. He always has been. He helped *me* become a better person." He laughed. "I'm a selfish bastard, I'm sure you've noticed. It's gotten me far in this world. I want *everything*." He laughed again, and sipped some wine. Michael's eyes were wide, listening. "Inside I'm still the same spoiled three-year-old who needs *all* of his toys in his bassinet *all* the time, where I can see 'em, and if anybody else tries to touch them, I bite. I'll hurt *myself* to get what I want. That's how I can run marathons."

"Are you gonna . . . bite me for touching Jesse?" Michael asked. A smile fought its way onto his lips.

Drew chuckled. "You wish," he replied. "Drink your wine."

Michael conceded with a laugh, and raised his glass. "Okay."

Drew drained his too, and like magic Chris appeared at his elbow to top him up. "I'm sure it's not news to you that Jesse hasn't had the easiest time of it in life."

"He mentioned that he lost both his parents suddenly."

"Yes." Drew nodded. "Yeah, it was awful. I didn't really know them . . . not really, at all. My side of that family had nothing to do with his. I only found out about his parents were like, later. His father . . . my uncle, I guess . . . my mother's brother . . . drank too much. Apparently he was like Jesse, one of those types of people who get drunk almost instantly, and claimed not to remember what he did when he was trashed. Who knows what the truth was. He seemed to be a very disappointed man, and I'm sure you know how disappointment can poison someone. He wanted to be a boxer. Hence Jesse's middle name." He saw Michael nodding. "That was his dream, and it went wrong. All of his dreams went wrong. And he needed to blame it on everybody else around him. Couldn't keep a job, terrorized his poor wife, and he didn't want Jesse in the first place. *That* will shape a man, growing up with that knowledge that you were a regrettable mistake."

Michael shuddered. "I'm sure," he said.

"I don't know about you, but at least my parents wanted me." Drew glanced at Michael expectantly, and after a brief hesitation, Michael agreed with a nod. "Jesse's mother was a nice enough woman, I guess, but she didn't know what she was doing. Too young, language issues, got nailed by the wrong guy, got knocked up. But good Catholics marry their baby mamas, no matter how much you can't stand them. Jesse loved his mom, though, and she was good to him. I guess." Drew sighed and looked into the depths of his wine. "I didn't know her. It must have been so hard for her. I really can only imagine. You know? I grew up thinking I had it rough because I had parents that wouldn't buy me a car until I had my driver's license. Not a permit; the real thing." Drew laughed and shrugged. "I was a moron. I barely ever gave a thought to anybody but myself, but even so, I didn't really know myself. I couldn't. I couldn't let myself. I thought that one fact, that I was a queer, would wreck everything. I had a secret that I couldn't even acknowledge. Jesse's different. He's stronger and smarter and braver than I am. He's always known himself and made no apologies for it. I had to make some lives utterly miserable before I could get there."

"Must be nice," Michael murmured.

"Hm?"

". . . Having someone to cook for you now and then." He smiled slyly.

Drew laughed, the tension broken, the confession, if not complete, at least begun. "Heh. Yeah." Perhaps there was a chance that they could truly connect.

For the second time in as many days, they ate opposite each other, not speaking more than impressed murmurs over the food. "If this is a ten, where on the scale would Jesse's cooking fall?" Michael asked puckishly as plates were cleared, and dessert menus refused.

"Something like a four. Maybe five. Six, on my favorites."

"I'm impressed."

"He cooks maybe twice a week. If you ask me, he could use some practice."

"You may have to play the husband card," Michael mused. "Chain him to the stove."

"What a beautiful idea," Drew said wistfully. "If you get his legs, I can fasten the padlock."

"Done deal." Michael relaxed in his chair, stretching out his long legs under the table. His ankle brushed Drew's, and to Drew's surprise, Michael didn't edge away, but maintained the contact of cloth on cloth. His eyes were unreadable behind the glare-smudged lenses of his glasses, and the ambiguity sent stirrings of warmth through Drew's groin. He rubbed his ankle against Michael's, and again Michael didn't move away, but smiled instead. Michael was curious, and that was more than half the battle of having something real.

Drew smiled back. "Want to head back to my place for a nightcap? There's a nearly empty bottle of Hendricks that should be put out of its misery."

"I'd love to," Michael agreed, eyes bright, without hesitation. "I'd love to see where you live."

Drew hailed a taxi for the eleven-block ride home. Within minutes, the two of them climbed out onto the dim yellow nighttime lights along 61st Street, and glanced up at the unassuming gray-brown façade of the four-story townhouse. Drew beamed at it. "This one's mine, all mine."

"You *own* this?" Michael asked, still able to be astonished.

"Yes, I do," Drew said proudly. He punched in a security code and swung the door open. "After you."

He flicked on the vestibule's overhead light. Standing at the foot of the stairs leading up to Drew's residence, Michael breathed, "Wow . . ."

"Been ages since you saw a staircase, huh?"

It got a laugh. "Not one like this. It's really nicely designed. No way was it like this originally, was it?" Michael gazed up at the Calder-inspired chandelier that sent moving beams of white-gold light along the cherry wood steps, yellow-bamboo-colored carpeting, ivory walls, and black picture frames.

Drew shook his head. "It was renovated back in the sixties, by somebody with decent taste, thank God. That chandelier, for example. I did a little more redecorating when I bought it." Drew began mounting the stairs. "That was seven years ago. I got it just in time, for three-five, before the property market got ridiculous. Such a stroke of luck. I waited for a while to get onto this block . . ." He got nearly to the top before he realized that Michael had stopped halfway, and was staring at the large silver-gelatin prints mounted on the wall. "Oh, yeah. You like those?"

"Yeah," Michael said. "Wow. You've got 'em all, don't you? Marlon Brando, James Dean, Cary Grant—wow, Harry Belafonte! He was *really* hot! And is this . . . Gregory Peck?" Michael let his fingers trail over the malachite name tags on the picture frames.

Drew walked down to join him, and gazed lovingly at his photo print collection. It had been a long time since he'd really noticed them; they'd just become another feature of the hall, something to pass on the way home. Some of them had cost him fifty thousand dollars. "Yep. I started this collection just before I moved here. They really fit beautifully there, don't they?"

"Montgomery Clift," Michael said in a low voice. "God. He was gorgeous."

"I know," Drew said reverently. "He used to live on this block, you know; a few doors down. I've been a fan all my life. It's a little silly, but I've always thought that Jesse resembled him a little bit."

Michael clearly didn't see a resemblance. "But this guy looks just like you. Who is that? Tony Curtis?"

Drew laughed. "Yeah. I got that one because, yeah, Jesse said I look like him. Which is complete bullshit, but pretty flattering all the same. Have you never seen a Tony Curtis film? You've never seen *Some Like It Hot*? Great movie. We should watch it sometime."

"You look a lot more like Tony Curtis than Jesse looks like Montgomery Clift."

"It's a good photo," Drew shrugged. "It's a good collection."

Michael smiled whimsically. "I'd have never guessed you were so obsessed with old movie stars."

"I wouldn't say obsessed, but it's definitely been a lifelong interest. Which, again, should have tipped me off to understanding what I was." Drew chuckled. "I like that glamor. I grew up on these old movies, on TV in the afternoons, in revival houses. I never envied the movie star lifestyle or anything; I was interested in them as men.

As symbols, but also as living men. Wondering what their skin felt like; how looked while they fucked . . . Can you imagine? Fucking Montgomery Clift? Did he like it? He had to have. It killed him. Indirectly, but . . ." He trailed off, and waved upstairs. "C'mon, let's kill that Hendricks. Don't worry, there's not a lot left."

He led Michael through the kitchen, pointing out the half-bathroom, and into the living room with its off-white walls, dark red Kroll sofas, flat-screen TV, and the David Hockney exhibition poster he'd picked up on a whim at Christie's the week after signing on the house. "Have a seat," Drew said. "What'll you have that has gin in it?"

"Oh, I don't know," Michael said, examining the poster. "Just make something. I trust you."

"That's a dangerous thing to say," Drew replied. He returned with two tumblers, stacked with clear ice. "On the rocks. Nothing fancy whatsoever. I like it with a slice of cucumber under the ice, but . . ." He shrugged, and chimed the rim of his glass against Michael's. "Enjoy."

"Thank you." Michael sipped. "Mmm. Somehow I thought I didn't like gin. I learn such wonderful things from you."

Drew looked him up and down. His shoulders were barely relaxed, his posture stiff as he almost perched on the edge of the sofa. Drew wondered if he should put on some music, but he didn't want to pause any more than he already had. "Put your drink down for a second," he commanded. "Take off your jacket. It's warm in here." He watched the movements of Michael's arms and chest, and took off his own blazer, draping it over the square red ottoman. "Take your shoes off."

"Jesse kinda looks more like Richard Gere," Michael mused.

"He's gonna hate that you said that," Drew chuckled, sliding out of his loafers, and edging his shoes and Michael's polished brogues together. "Sit back. Relax." He sat down beside Michael and watched closely. Michael was utterly still, so much that Drew couldn't detect his breathing. "Are you afraid of me?"

"No."

"Are you afraid of what might happen?"

Michael met his gaze, and Drew could finally see straight through the glasses at Michael's cool brown eyes. "Not really. Not right now."

Drew moved in closer. "I'm gonna kiss you," he murmured.

He expected a protest, or even an escape. Instead, Michael smiled, pulled his glasses off, and stretched over, pressing their lips together with a faint laugh.

Drew let the kiss stay closed-mouthed, experimental, and chaste. It was Michael's tongue that broached the barrier, seeking the edges of Drew's teeth. Drew grasped the back of Michael's head and held him still, lashing Michael's mouth, licking the sweetness from his palate. Michael grasped back, but his fingers slid onto Drew's shoulders, shoulder blades, hands encircling Drew's upper arms as he sighed audibly. Through the thin fabric of Drew's shirt, Michael's fingertips were cool, pointed, and precise. Drew pressed his urgent erection against Michael's leg, sucking his bottom lip.

Their seated positions softened into Michael half-lying against the cushion, Drew crouched with one knee on the floor and the other questing between Michael's thighs. There wasn't enough room on the narrow seat for them to lie side by side, but Drew actually enjoyed his precarious position, the way it made his heart race in his throat. They could fall apart at any time. His fingertips traced Michael's chest until he found the tight nubs of nipple, rolling them, twisting them in the silky T-shirt fabric until Michael swiped his hands away. Drew responded by shoving the hem of the shirt up over Michael's belly, trailing his fingers through the path of hair leading away from the recess of his navel, all the while shimmying his tongue around Michael's mouth.

Michael reached behind him and retrieved his drink, and sipped out of it while Drew broke away from his mouth, trading it for kisses on Michael's stomach, around the subtle curves of his chest, rubbing his cheek against the body hair. He was aware that he was worshipping Michael's body while Michael calmly enjoyed his cocktail and arched against him, accepting this turn of events as if he had expected it. The nightcap had little to do with drinks, and everything to do with Drew's hunger to taste Michael's skin. Soap and salt and — perhaps Drew's imagination but — a faint tang of semen. Michael's navel was somehow immaculate, a miniature fur cup, enfolding a rich scent of skin and laundry. Drew smelled his own cologne, a custom blend of lavender, cedar, and musk, rising from the pulse points in his own groin, and his own pheromone signature rising from his balls and armpits. He sighed and felt hot, cheekbone resting on a lattice of Michael's ribs.

Momentarily, Drew stopped what he was doing and sat up, reaching for his own drink. Michael watched him, misty-eyed, his posture now thoroughly relaxed. "Do you want more?" Drew asked, carefully letting a drop of condensation land on Michael's bare belly.

He barely even twitched, but a massive, naughty smile grew on his face. "Yes," he said.

"What kind of 'more'?"

"Get on top of me," Michael said. "And kiss me some more."

They fit that way, Drew crouched over Michael's long body, one knee balanced on the edge of the couch, the other wedged between the couch's back and the firm, uncompromising muscle of Michael's buttock. Drew dipped kisses onto Michael's face, his ears and neck, and even the chest, pressing his lips and breath against the T-shirt, pushing it up almost onto his shoulders. "Need me to take this off?" Drew asked.

Michael tensed. "No, no, leave it on. Clothes on."

"It doesn't have to be," Drew panted. "It's all right—"

Michael gasped faintly. "I – I – To be honest, I really need a shower first. And I'm way too full. And —"

"Okay, I get it. Just say you don't want to fuck."

"But I *do*—"

"Just not right now." Drew straightened up, and sat on his heels, knees protesting. He poured the drink down his suddenly dry and scratchy throat. He needed a glass of water, but the ice at the bottom of the glass would have to do for now. "God, you are frustrating. What is it, midnight? You don't need a shower; you're clean as a whistle. Fuck it. It's time for me to go to sleep, anyway."

"So I should go, huh?" Michael grabbed the edges of the couch, and slid back to a sitting position, his legs sliding across Drew's. He didn't look even slightly regretful, even if his trousers sported a railroad spike.

"I'll call you a car." Drew didn't want to get up. His blood surged with anger. This state of mind was one of Jesse's favorites, and it was so hard for Jesse to irritate him quite like this, after all this time.

He knew all of Jesse's games. But this . . . "But before I do, show me your dick. I really do have to look at it."

Michael eyed him strangely. "You're kidding."

"I'm not," Drew said coldly. "I need to see it. Right now. I know you know what I mean."

"Are you gonna show me yours?" Michael seemed intrigued, his kiss-blushed lips drawn into a curving red smirk.

"No," Drew decided. "You can see it later, maybe. If we can go further one of these days. Which I hope is sooner rather than later."

"You seem awfully sure of yourself." Michael was nearly purring.

"I am," Drew said. "I know you're just as curious as I am. If not more. You know I have something that you want. And that 'something' isn't Jesse. You can imagine what I must be like . . . You're always such a good guy. So restrained. You know you won't have to be that way with me. You know I'm willing to do everything you've ever imagined. You know I won't fuck around; I won't play games. Unless, of course, that's what you want."

It was Michael's turn to gulp desperately at his drink, and Drew sat patiently, chewing ice, ignoring the ache in his knees. At last, Michael unfastened the waistband of his trousers, tugged down the zipper, and peeled black ribbed underwear down from his waist. All at once, his penis popped forward, its length reddened and the skin stretched shiny. Just the cock, not the balls, which remained safely hidden underneath the elastic waistband. Michael's cock, long and narrow like the rest of his body, with a thick red circumcised head, glistening like a Roma tomato, visibly trembled as it throbbed. Drew's finger itched to reach out and draw the elastic away from Michael's balls; instead he used that finger to idly stroke the wet sides of his tumbler. His own cock jumped impatiently in his pants. "That would feel really good inside me," Drew muttered. "I'd like to touch it, but I didn't get permission."

"You want my permission?" Michael almost laughed. "Is that what you're about?"

"I'm about respect. I think respect is what's going to make this all work."

"Do you have a plan or something?" Michael tugged his

underwear back into place, grimacing slightly as his penis had to jostle for room in his flat-front trousers.

"No, not exactly. But I think you've presented some interesting possibilities."

"I better go," Michael said breathlessly.

"Yes, you'd better." Drew stood, and picked up the phone resting on the end table. While he was waiting for the car service line to pick up, Michael sprawled on the couch, gingerly handling his genitals through the barrier of cloth. His brow knit, as though it hurt. Drew smiled. "Hi, I need a pickup. Yes, from my home. Right away, please. Thank you." He ended the call with a press of his thumb on a button, put the phone down, reached down, and stroked Michael's hair. "Can't you imagine sucking my cock, Michael? I'd love to see you crawl across the room, right up to me, and put my dick in your mouth. I think about that all the time. Ever since I first saw you. I just pictured you in all kinds of situations. Permission? Heh. Yeah, I want your permission, all right. But until I get it . . . until I know you want it, and you're ready . . . go home and do some yoga until you can suck your own cock."

"You are such an asshole," Michael muttered, pressing his face against Drew's palm.

Drew slid two fingers between Michael's lips, and Michael shuddered and sucked them hard, finishing with a nip from his teeth. "I tend to get what I want," Drew said, lightly slapping him on the cheek. Michael faintly growled, and Drew smiled in satisfaction. "And I want you. Yeah, there's really no need to be nice with you."

"Fuck you." Michael nuzzled the palm that had struck him. Drew's cock jumped again.

"I know. Stand up, you prick tease."

Michael smoothly rose to his feet like a flag unfurling. "I'm leaving." He kissed Drew again, his lips sharp and desperate, their scruffy chins and upper lips scraping past each other. Drew half-hoped he'd end up with beard burn, just for the sensual memory, but broke away from the kiss knowing that the unshaven, chapped-skin look didn't quite cut it at Morrow.

"You'll be back," he said.

Michael rested his arms on Drew's shoulders, and drew him in close, almost in a hug, but less personable; he was only testing their heights against each other, and finding that Drew's brow met him in the nose. "I'm too tall," he muttered.

"You're perfect," Drew growled. Michael's boner poked right into the most sensitive spot of Drew's lower belly, his heart on Drew's throat. "Put me up against the wall and ram that cock up my ass. Fuck me like you'd fuck a woman's pussy. *Think about it.*"

Michael's hands cupped Drew's buttocks, pressing his fingertips together to form a heart shape, flexing them again to squeeze. Drew pressed his own erection against Michael's groin, high on the hipbone, and groaned under his breath.

The phone chimed in Drew's hand, breaking their shared reverie. "That's the car," Drew said. "I have an account, so don't worry about it."

"You have this sugar daddy thing down pat, don't you?" Michael retrieved his jacket and double-checked his fly. "You should know that doesn't work on me. I've got what I need."

"No, you don't," Drew sneered, and brought the empty glasses to the kitchen. Michael passed by him and down the stairs without a goodbye or any other acknowledgment, but it wasn't really necessary. There was nothing more to say to each other that night.

But once he'd rinsed the glasses and set them on a towel on the counter, Drew went to his bedroom to see Jesse stretched across the bed, a pillow bent around his head, deeply asleep. Drew sat beside him and sighed, lightly stroking Jesse's hair, wishing he'd been awake. Since he wasn't, Drew went to his closet to masturbate, touching his own body with his fingertips like he used to do, aiming his ejaculation at the mirror, and sitting for a while, the fire inside him banked, watching the spunk drip down his reflection.

7. OPENING NIGHT.

Jesse opened his eyes to a clear, blue-tinted late morning, the air perfumed with lilacs and cut grass, and a yeasty tang of baking bread from the restaurant at the end of the block. It was pleasant to be alone in the bed, stretching out his limbs to occupy as much of it as he could reach. After a brief hot shower, he wrapped himself in a bathrobe and sat cross-legged on the bed, booting up his laptop, hoping to hear back from the bike delivery job he'd applied for last night. He barely had a browser window open when he heard footsteps coming from upstairs.

He thought that Drew had already left for work, but there he stood in black suit trousers and a plain white T-shirt, hair still damp. He must have been in his office upstairs. "Oh, good, you're awake. Come make me breakfast," he said.

Jesse groaned reluctantly but nodded, muttering, "Okay, let me check my email first."

"If you must." Drew waited. There was no email from the Italian deli, just a bunch of spam and a supportive note from Charlie. Sighing, Jesse put on a T-shirt and cotton boxer shorts, and followed Drew to the almost painfully sunlit kitchen.

Drew stood and stared out the windows with his arms clasped behind his back. Jesse ground coffee and sliced bread, calling over his shoulder, "What else do we have?"

"A few things," Drew said. "I stopped by the corner store on my way back from the park. Some dates, some O.J., yogurt, oh yeah, and a mango? I dunno, it looked good but I have no idea what to do with it."

"Yeah, okay." Jesse blew out his breath impatiently, tossed the bread into the toaster oven, and held out his hand. "Just give it to me. Want me to show you?"

"No, no, you got it." Drew went back to his "titan of industry" pose in front of the window.

"I call the last egg."

Drew chuckled. "Knock yourself out."

"How was your time this morning?"

"Two hours," Drew replied, "ten and a half miles. Not bad. I wasn't pushing myself very hard."

Jesse poured a demitasse cup of black coffee for Drew, and pulled the toast out of the oven. He picked up a nice sharp knife, and scored the skin on the mango. "Well, you seem to be in good health and good spirits. So what's up? What do you want to talk about?"

"I'm sure you know," Drew said.

"Mebbe I don't," Jesse grunted.

"Michael?"

"Oh yeah." Jesse dug the point of the knife into the fruit. "What about him?"

"I'm . . ." Drew's voice wavered with regret or disbelief. "I *really* want him."

"Join the club," said Jesse. Then, feeling strange, he turned back toward the counter and poured his own coffee. "I mean, I *know* you want him."

"It's not just sexual," Drew elaborated. "I want to spend time with him. Know more about him."

"Do you want him to know more about *you*?" Jesse asked.

When he turned to face Drew, the older man looked pained and confused. "Yes," he said, sounding surprised at himself. "I feel like . . . he'll understand."

"*I* understand," Jesse pointed out.

Drew waved his hand impatiently. "Yes, yes. I know you do. Maybe . . . maybe I'm just greedy. You want him; *I* want him, too. But it's more than that. I don't want *him* to get one up over on *you*. I don't want to do that to you. But I want him." His eyes reflected back the white gleam from the teacup, and for a moment he looked almost religious. Or, at least, like a very hot televangelist. "But I want you to get him, too."

A long, silent moment surrounded them, a simultaneous plunge into introspection, neither one meeting the other's eyes. Drew broke first, shaking his head and taking a deep breath. "You know?" he commented reflexively, shrugging his shoulders just to bring them back to life.

"It's funny," Jesse said, his fingers lightly splayed on the security of the knife, loosening the mango so that it split neatly from its pit into thick orange cubes. He always felt better with a tool in his hand: a chef's knife, a drill, a wrench. He could exact a concrete change; he left his mark on the world. "I feel pretty much the same way. About him. Because I want him to know me, too. And I feel like he'll understand. And yeah, I know *you* get it, but this is different."

"And what kind of thing do you want for me and him?" Drew asked.

Jesse could only shrug and smile. "I want you to be satisfied by him," he said. "But we have to figure out what we want him to know. Are you gonna tell him about us?" He never had to elaborate on what he meant when he referred to *us*. "And do you think he'll really understand? Or is it just wishful thinking? Some people freak the fuck out. Hell, Charlie freaked out when he first learned. He's still kind of weirded out."

"Charlie's a nice Jewish kid; of course he freaked out. But c'mon. It shouldn't be a big deal. We're adults. We're rational. Right? Besides, it's not as though we're going to *breed*."

"Maybe we just shouldn't tell him," Jesse suggested.

"Well, I haven't. But how long do you think we could keep it a secret? I mean, if he really wanted to snoop, it wouldn't be hard to find out. Google exists. It's right there. Mary and Joey Landon, and their little sister Amelia, and these are their kids."

"I don't feel like keeping it a secret. We haven't got anything to be ashamed of. It's not—well. Heh. Maybe this is why we haven't tried this before. This shit is complicated."

Standing, they ate from the kitchen countertops, Jesse adding elements as he remembered them; a bowl of raw almonds, two spoons for the pint of Greek yogurt, frying the egg and sliding its crisp white and liquid yolk onto a piece of toast, salting and peppering it, and feeding Drew a piece before he remembered that he wasn't going to share. "It's important to talk about it," Jesse sighed. "It's just another closet. Do *not* be ashamed."

"Michael—he's gotten into me somehow," Drew said, picking up a slab of mango and letting it slide down his throat with only the barest of chews to release the juices. "Even his cock-teasing little ways. Usually getting denied like that would turn me right off, but this time it just made me hotter—"

"I thought it was 'just dinner,'" Jesse murmured, grinning. "It's never 'just dinner' with you, is it?"

"Mmm." Drew put his arms around Jesse's shoulders and kissed his ear. "It gave me some kind of respect for him," he continued. "That he could want it that much, and just walk out the door. Like he could take it or leave it, as long as he knew I wanted him. Like that's all he needed to know. Ridiculous self-control. Or maybe it just seems that way to me. I'm so jealous of you." He shook his head, and held his cheek against Jesse's. "Of both of you. What's between you two seems so . . . pure. And fresh. Natural. And right. You just move right past the hang-ups." He sighed heavily. "I feel like shouldn't come between you. But I want to. But I'm not giving *you* up."

"You know you can have him if you want," Jesse sighed. "It'd be totally easy for you."

"Yeah, I know," Drew replied with a shrug. "And I do want. Men need variety as much as they need love. It's just a fact."

"Okay, now *I'll* be honest," Jesse frowned. "That hurts a little bit."

"Oh, no, Jesse, you're getting me wrong."

"I mean, shit. I feel like *I'm* standing between *you* guys."

"But you're not. You can't keep me from getting what I want. You couldn't cock-block me if you wanted to." Drew hugged Jesse tighter as the younger man's muscles tensed in frustration. "No, no, no. It's not like that, either. You're my partner. You're my best beloved. I believe in *us,* baby. I'm not going anywhere. Besides, he's obsessed with *you.*"

"Drew—"

Drew kissed Jesse's ear, and his voice lilted softer. "Besides, of course I want to fuck his sexy ass, but it could be a bad idea while he's still working for me. He wouldn't sue me, would he? You'd better not turn him down. He might get mad and tell people I made him show me his wee-wee."

Jesse gave in to the hug with a resigned smile. "The thought of you and him fucking gets me really hot," he admitted, laughing. "Do you know what I mean?"

Drew released Jesse from the embrace, stepped away, and chewed some dates, washing them down with the last swallow of his coffee. He shook his head, but said aloud, "Yeah." For a long moment, he gazed into Jesse's eyes, as if looking for a solution, for absolution, but Jesse could only shrug. Drew sighed and turned away. "It's almost eleven. I gotta get to work," he said. "Another lunch meeting. That Indianapolis deal is getting close to final, and I've got to be on a conference call at noon. I'm working until I'm done with those details tonight, and it might be eleven or midnight, so don't worry about dinner. And we're going out tomorrow night after the show, right?"

"Opening night," Jesse agreed. "The big show."

Drew kissed him gently on the mouth. "See you later, boo," he said. "And please, get a haircut."

"Wish me luck getting this job, okay?"

"You'll get it if you want it," Drew said vaguely, eyes already half-focused, already mentally in the Morrow offices.

Jesse cleared up the kitchen—Drew's housekeeping service would be around in the afternoon, but Jesse hated leaving a mess for them—and returned to laptop, his email, his bank account.

He didn't have a lot of money available. Grandma Landon had left Jesse a decent inheritance, but so much of it had already been spent on his parents' funeral and fulfilling their extensive debts. After he'd dropped out of college the first time, his trust had been amended to provide him with only five hundred dollars a month until he turned thirty or got a master's degree, whichever came first. Gran was a stickler for education. Right now, he had thirty bucks in his wallet to last him until the weekend, when he'd get his last check from *Viridian*. There was just barely enough left in his account to get his bike tuned up.

Drew made sure he didn't go hungry or homeless, but everything else was up to him. He really needed to get a job as soon as possible; a week without earnings wasn't something he was prepared to face, not with all this other stuff going on. Work, hard physical effort in exchange for pay, helped keep his mind occupied, or at least pleasantly blank. He didn't go to therapy anymore—that was something Drew had paid for, until Jesse told him to stop—but he had gotten enough guidance and techniques to know that working hard, as much and as often as possible, was easily the best thing for his mind. He didn't have night terrors anymore; the burn scars on his arms were fading; the break-bump on his nose was more handsome than askew; he didn't smoke tobacco, except on special occasions. And only rarely these days did he drink too much and talk a stranger's ear off trying to explain his middle name.

He had gotten distracted looking at the website for the bar where the opening night party was to be held when an electronic tone, his text message notification, chirped through the air, startling him. Jesse dug out the phone from yesterday's pockets.

It was Michael. **just thinking about you.**

Jesse punched in letters as quickly as he could on the phone's tiny keypad. **Oh hi just talking abt u a bit ago**

The reply came almost immediately. **With D?**

Fraid so ;) only good things I promise

Couldn't sleep last night. Too anxious after dinner etc. Hope you're not mad at me.

Abt Drew? No its cool. Yr sexy 2gether

Glad you think so. Hard to be round him. I'm always afraid I'm staring.

Jesse's face creased into a smile. **U should go ahead and fuck him. Hes not gonna stop hitting on you. He likes to fuck.**

This reply took a little longer to arrive. **Good to know. So am I officially dating you both right now?**

Jesse thought for a moment before responding. **I like u, we see** each other when we want to. D likes u and im ok w that. No big deal lets just keep it simple right now ok?

I feel guilty.

Don't. Jesse shook his head, suddenly not wanting to moderate this right now. Gotta go take bike to shop & get haircut. C u soon, its all good xx

1000 kisses to you! See you tomorrow night, good luck with the Genova delivery job!

Nice of *someone* to remember. Jesse put the phone away, put on his black jeans and sneakers. "A thousand kisses," he repeated aloud to himself, smiling. "A thousand and one."

Hours later, Michael was the first person Jesse texted to announce that he'd gotten the job and started tomorrow. Neither Michael nor Drew replied to the news until Jesse was already asleep, each too absorbed in his own work.

For his opening night sartorial statement, Drew decided on a mix of subtle and showy: a sage-and-white striped Miu Miu collared shirt, cuffs linked with little amber smoked Lucite cubes that went with nearly everything, drapey charcoal Valentino pants, and a pair of lighter gray vintage Stacy Adams "town boots" that were more handsome than comfortable on his running-blasted feet. His dogs might have been tough as hell, but the first few weeks of serious retraining still left their mark. He could pull it off, though; he'd be sitting all night, and the look was perfect.

He never really dressed for Jesse; that kid liked him best naked, or in an old T-shirt and those ancient Wrangler jeans so worn in the seat that the pockets were only shadows. But he liked to look good on his behalf anyway, especially on important occasions like tonight. And then there was Michael's mind to blow, not to mention the impression he could make on the other off-off Broadway theater investors.

The first person he saw that he knew when he arrived at the theater was Elaine Gold, who had also kicked in fifteen grand for the show. Catching sight of Drew, she swept over and breezed air kisses past his cheeks. "Once again," she drawled, "it's time to look at the results of the finger-painting class."

Drew embraced her wiry, whiskey-colored shoulders with a genuine smile. "I've heard reports that they're quite nice this time. Maybe we've got a new Picasso in our midst?"

"Hope springs eternal," she replied. "I tell you, though, if we don't get a hit play pretty soon, I'm taking my business elsewhere. I could be snorkeling in Madagascar instead of this."

"You look lovely."

"So do you. As usual. Have you had plastic surgery?" She grinned impishly, and lit a cigarette. Around them, ticket buyers meandered into the lobby of the theater, most of them with the sort of glazed expression that meant that they were seeing this show only because they loved Jenna Margolis and hoped that she'd be in a state of undress similar to what she favored on her TV show.

Drew laughed. "Not yet," he said. "I'm hoping that I swing toward the 'distinguished' side of my genetic family tree. My dad didn't look too bad, all the way into his seventies." A slight exaggeration; Alistair Farrow had been sixty-nine when the last in a series of strokes that had taken sight, mobility, and finally sense wiped him out for good. But even then, he'd been damned handsome: a silver-haired, black-eyed, catatonic phantom. *That'll be me*, Drew thought. *Lord, take my bladder control, but leave my looks.*

"You men have it so easy," Elaine said, her gestures painting curlicues through smoke. "First of all, you have those eyelashes—"

Before Drew could bear witness to the usual tirade, he excused himself and went ahead into the entrance of the Lauren Doe.

In the time that it took for his ticket to be torn, Elaine Gold had caught up with him again. "Hey, not so fast, handsome. Might I sit with you?" she asked, elbowing in front of someone else, plucking two programs from an usher.

"Of course, Elaine," Drew soothed. "Shall we?" He held out his elbow for her to grasp, steadying her on her immensely high heels as they progressed into the house. He made a beeline straight for his preferred seat—third row, right side aisle—and sent Elaine in first.

She settled her handkerchief dress around her. "The middle's still open. Why do you always want to sit here?"

"For luck," he lied smoothly. He sat there so that Jesse always knew where to look into the crowd to find him. When Jesse was with him, he would sit where Elaine now sat, at arm's reach to the left, and they could hold hands.

This was how they had sat on their first date, not knowing it was a date, *From Here to Eternity* at the Cinema Village. Drew had seen it more than fifty times already in his life, and so he watched Jesse watch it, wide liquid eyes drinking in the drama and male bonding and sexual tension, sighing at the sad parts, gulping at the sexy ones. Jesse had been sixteen then, Drew twenty-eight, his divorce papers barely filed, still unaware of the dimensions of emotion he felt for his unfortunate, previously unknown Brooklyn cousin.

Elaine handed Drew one of the programs, and perused the other. "So, where's Jesse tonight?" she asked. "Didn't he work on the sets?"

Drew confessed, "Yeah; he just started a new job today. He'll be here at intermission. Might have to stand at the back."

"Good for him," Elaine hummed pleasantly. "I'm glad he doesn't just sponge off you, even if you'd secretly like him to."

Drew couldn't help laughing. "No, no, he's his own man. I wish he'd go back to school, but . . . Landons are nothing if not stubborn."

"Speaking of which, how's your mother?"

"She's fine," Drew said with practiced smoothness. He had no idea, really, except that no one had called him to report that she had died or broken a hip on one of her shopping jaunts in Lisbon. Last he'd heard, in a conversation they'd had at Christmas, she was still hale enough to take a train on her own when she got bored with her stone house in the center of the sleepy coast town that had given Drew's father his name. "She keeps busy."

"That's for the best—oh, here we go," Elaine whispered excitedly. "Let's watch a show." The room went completely dark, punctuated by the red light of Exit signs. Out of the darkness came a resonant male voice, repeatedly intoning a single phrase.

"Romance—adventure. Adventure—romance. You never know where they will lead you. Every day is a choice. What's behind the door?"

Soon, offset by a few syllables, another voice joined it, then a third, then several, the phrase becoming a round, then an audio blur. Simultaneously, the eyes of the audience lifted just above the edge of the backdrop, trying to determine the source of a multitude of tiny, dancing lights. Drew just sat back and smiled, his heart swelling with pride. He thought, *Of course he's good.*

At intermission the house lights returned a warm, impersonal illumination to the benumbed audience. Drew and Elaine rose and joined the stream of patrons headed to the lobby. "Ladies," Elaine excused herself, parting from him and making a beeline toward the restrooms. Drew gave a finger-wave that she never saw; his hand was immediately seized by Avi Mueller, one of the Nightlight Theater's board of trustees, barking in his ear, "Farrow! This show is dull as dishwater, all except for the lighting. That's spectacular. Who thought it'd be a good idea to hoard Jenna Margolis until the end of the second act? That's who we're all here to see, isn't it?"

Drew gazed with longing at the table where glasses of wine and champagne were being proffered, but had to quench his own thirst with a bottle of water; he was saving his alcohol calories for the after-party. He didn't want to agree that the play was boring in case critics were eavesdropping, so he spoke warmly about Michael's lighting design. "Innovative, isn't it? Makes the stage seem infinite. This is a very cerebral show."

"I'd like to see more of Jenna Margolis's infinte rack. Heh! Heh! It's going to waste! Am I right? Any way you can give some notes to the director, Farrow?"

"I'm not sure that he'd like to change tack this late in the production," Drew vouchsafed, gulping water while he had a chance, glad he'd dressed lightly. The lobby was stifling and the fabric under his arms itched. And the damn town boots were like leather vices on his swollen, blistered phalanges. He hoped Jesse would show up soon and save him.

"Drew, I'd like you to meet—"

"This is Carl Hiatton, of Ramer, Yolen, and Mars. Any chance you know each other from Princeton? He was class of '89."

"I'm afraid I don't. Drew Farrow. Pleased to meet you."

"I'm looking to do secure some share of Pfizer but I need projections on their new statin. Could you have one of your guys call me? My card."

"I *am* head of client services at Morrow. Here's *my* card. Give me a call on Monday and we'll get something set up. Lunch?"

"Cipriani's, two o'clock?"

"Mr. Farrow, I'd like you to meet—"

"Yes, perfect. See you then. Drew Farrow. It's a pleasure."

"He's a producer for this play."

"Executive producer," Drew demurred. "I only came up with the money." It brought a round of amused, unctuous laughter and knowing nods. Drew envied Jesse so badly he could taste it. Jesse would just laugh at these people. He didn't have to kiss ass like this. But Drew had to admit, he was just so incredibly *good* at it.

"So what do *you* think of the show?"

"I'm glad to see a sold-out house," Drew said with a grin. "I'm optimistic I'll make my money back." There wasn't a chance. Drew had known that going in. He'd have never invested if he wasn't comfortable with losing it all. But that's what his father's money was for; Alistair had hated the theater, hated theater people, thought they should all get real jobs.

Figured they were all faggots and fairies.

"It's giving me motion sickness, all that whirling. I can't tell where the floor is! And I wish there was more of Jenna. But that black fellow—what's his name? He's got a great voice."

"Tolo Edigewe," Drew said. "And yes, he does. Great casting. He's done some radio. . . ."

"Does his character even have a name, though? Isn't that a little racist?"

The water bottle was now empty. "I, uh, couldn't speak to that. The program lists him as 'The Barker'; it's all in the O. Henry original. The playwright's around here somewhere. Suppose you can ask her?"

At the flickering of the lobby lights, Drew broke into a

practiced grin. "Oh, it's time," he said to the group of people surrounding him. "Thank you all for coming, I appreciate it. . . ." He caught sight of Elaine's ridiculous dress and all but ran to rejoin her.

Getting back into the performance space was an even slower process than getting out. As the audience crammed the aisle, Drew was tempted to take out his cell phone and text Jesse, asking where he was. Or text Michael, for that matter. He wondered what the tall man was up to backstage. He hadn't done theater since high school, and didn't remember what the lighting crew did at intermissions. Maybe Michael knew Jesse's whereabouts.

Drew checked his phone. An hour ago, Jesse had texted **Running late; harsh first day.** Drew set his jaw and returned to his seat, angling his knees toward the empty seat next to him.

At the lighting consoles, Michael stared hungrily out at the house, watching Drew Farrow enter and sit. He looked irritated. It was far too sexy, and Michael leaned against the board, his entire body aching with lust, listening to the stage manager's voice commanding quietly, "FX two, lobby three and five, intermission end signal."

"I'll be with you soon," Michael whispered, too quietly to be picked up by his headset microphone.

He lowered the house lights until everything was dark again, the faces of the crowd a blushing, monochromatic red illuminated only by the exit signs. The seat to Drew's left was empty. Shouldn't Jesse be there? Michael took a deep breath and held it, rerouting energy from his cock to his brain and his hand. The next few cues were critical. This was the moment of truth, the instant where he truly showed the world what he could do. He couldn't worry about the two of them, or one of them there, the other mysteriously absent.

"Sound, playback in four, three, two, mark. FX two, cue eighteen, at four, three, two, mark. FX one, cue forty-two. Five, four, three, two, mark."

Instead of the "Tinkerbell illusion" lights that signaled the start of the play, the stage returned to the gloomy, murky, green-gray full illumination of the "tenement interior" where Jenna's character,

"Marilyn," spread her legs over the back of a visibly threadbare couch, hair hidden underneath a ratty wig. It was meant to symbolize a kind of impossibly sexy, perhaps heroin-fueled poverty, and the character "Rudy" came into spot focus (cue twenty-one), on his knees, bent in desperate supplication in front of her. "Marilyn" roused herself gradually (cue forty-three, a peachy LED spot from the ceiling, focused tightly on her face), and broke into a brilliant smile. Before getting the job on the TV show, Jenna Margolis had done some toothpaste commercials, and for good reason.

"Please, tell me you're all right," "Rudy" breathed. He was too quiet, but Michael wasn't in charge of sound; he could maybe give Matt a note tonight.

A mutter in Michael's headset: "Shit. FX, cue twenty-three, already."

From his peripheral vision, Michael saw a blinking red light on the auxiliary board that shouldn't have been there. A ground loop, the red light a circuit overload warning. Michael had had to reset the dimmers on his own board after this afternoon's notes. He thought the ground loop had been closed after lunch. That connection had been fine throughout the first half of the show. Had he knocked it loose . . .?

"FX two, cue twenty-three, where is it?" The stage manager's voice was taut.

Grimacing, Michael re-grounded the auxiliary. On stage, just as "Rudy" was crossing stage left to leave "Marilyn," all six major fills lit up far too brightly for a moment before Michael could bring them back down to their correct setting. The music playback continued, heedless, a new ominous tone rising; but now the cues were off, and Michael's programmed effects along with them. The audience shifted uncomfortably in their seats. *Trainwreck. Skipped a groove. Keep going, keep going, you idiot.*

Jenna popped up like a jack-in-the-box. "What's up?" she chirped, too loudly, and the audience laughed.

The stage manager whispered furiously, "FX, what the fuck?"

"It's fine, I fixed it," Michael said.

"It's not fine—fuck, look at her."

Jenna had let the neckline of her dress slip down, exposing a few more inches of her famous cleavage. Matt hesitated, confused, and the music galloped along without him. "Back to your mark!" Jenna merrily yelled, and the audience rocked with laughter.

"Fuck," the stage manager said. "Kendrick, can you do anything?"

"Not without stopping," Kendrick replied mournfully.

Matt scrambled off stage left, and Jenna rose off the couch like the Bride of Frankenstein. "Thank God," she declared. "I was wondering if he'd ever leave." She was a million miles off script, and loving every minute of it. "Are we starting again or what? Lights? Mommy?"

Michael let his breath out in a staggered groan, and triedtrying to hit his cues faster in an attempt to catch up with the music playback, but so much of the lighting design had been programmed and automated because he didn't have six hands to do it all live. The audience was a mess, audibly rattling their programs and food wrappers and empty bottles and whatnot. They were lost. Jenna was doing God knew what, jumping back and forth between circles of spotlight.

"Stop the show?" Michael murmured into his headset mike.

"No, no, it's too late," the stage manager said heavily. "Nobody's leavingWe gotta keep going; it'll take too long for me to find the mark again. Just do the best you can. By the clock, FX two, Tolo's entrance; cue thirty, mark."

"FX two. . . check," Michael sighed.

The rest of Act Three was like improv comedy in a disco. Act Four went off without a technical hitch, with every cue and every note in sync, but Jenna couldn't stop corpsing, breaking down into laughter and taking Matt along with her. The stoic Tolo just performed his lines as if nothing had ever gone wrong, but his jaw was clenched so tightly that a muscle visibly jumped in it. Lights down, at the end, was greeted with watery applause. The cast returned to the stage for a single perfunctory curtain call, bowing together, then fleeing backstage. Michael brought the house lights back up, then crumpled over his board, his breath shaky. "It's okay," he said to himself. "These things happen."

He wondered if anyone else would feel that way. *Pooraka; rechaka.* He wouldn't let this destroy him.

Backstage was ugly. Matt ranted at Jenna; Jenna ranted at Ashleigh for designing such a stupid, uncomfortable dress for the first act; Ashleigh shoved costumes at Marnie and ranted at Dol for putting too much makeup on Matt and making him look like "a Palm Beach gigolo." When Michael entered the space, everyone fell silent and stared at him. Shaking off the cold, sinking nausea in his guts, he shrugged and rolled his eyes, walking to the refrigerator and taking out two bottles of water. He took a deep breath and turned back to the company, holding his head high. "Good job, everybody," he said.

"God, shut *up*," said the stage manager, brushing past him.

"Good job, Mike," Tolo replied stoically, slapping him hard on the shoulder.

"You too, Tolo," Michael replied, deciding not to correct him to let the hated nickname slide this time. "You were awesome." He even exchanged a fist bump and a sharp warrior's nod with Tolo. Tolo was a pro; he'd make sure the show would go on. And wasn't that what Michael had done? There was nothing to be ashamed of, no reason not to take pride in what had gone smoothly with the performance. Right?

Jenna, wearing just her panties, artificially enhanced D-cups thrust forward like gun turrets, stormed off to the dressing room in a huff, waving her hand behind her and snorting, "What-*ever*."

Matt crossed his arms and sighed, "Coke whore . . ." It almost broke the tension, making half the people around him laugh, but the most senior members of the crew all looked like they'd just swallowed a pill that wasn't quite going down. Michael shrugged again, and went back out to the wings. He still had work to do.

"Michael!"

Jesse's hair was shorter, neater. He looked older, more handsome, and Michael was so grateful to see him that his legs wobbled. Jesse smiled. "Dude," he said.

"Did you see it?" Michael asked tightly. He held out one of the bottles of water.

"I snuck in just after intermission," he said, accepting the water, and taking a long swig. "Thanks." Michael continued packing up his equipment, shutting down the hard drive with all the programming on it. "What the fuck happened?" Jesse asked.

"The board broke at the top of Act Three and I botched, like, five cues in a row. I fixed it, but Jenna Margolis was like a dog in a sausage shop and just went on a goof-off rampage. So now everybody's pissed off at me. And Jenna." Michael twisted his mouth. "It would have been nice if you'd actually showed up on time."

"Oh, c'mon, I had to go home and change. I saw the best parts."

"I guess," Michael said. "Shit happens. I just feel like an ass. I should have checked it before we got started tonight."

"Ounce of prevention." Jesse shrugged. "Me too. I was up on Seventy-first, and my chain just kind of fell off into the street. I spilled hot lasagna all over my pants. It sucked; had to go back, get a new one, pay for the one I wrecked. Stupid bike; I just got it tuned up! SoAnyway, basically, I didn't get paid at all for, like, nine miles of riding. God. I need a drink so bad."

"I think we all do. Do you want to head over there nto the party now, or try to catch up with Drew . . .?"

"Dude, let's just go. I wanna get *out* of here. I can *smell* the hostility."

They fled out the side exit, the one that led to the back of the prop storage building. On the dark landing that led to Fourth Street, Michael grabbed Jesse's shoulder before he could hit the press-bar on the door. He bent his head, Jesse arched up, and their lips met, hungry but seeking to impart comfort, aided with tongue and teeth and water-cooled breath.

Michael pulled away again before Jesse's hands could go searching for an erection around the front of his jeans. "Let's go meet Drew," he reminded Jesse, and with an understanding, indulgent chuckle, Jesse opened the door.

There wasn't a free taxi to be seen, and Jesse had his bike anyway, so they walked. Michael had never been so grateful for nine long blocks in his life. He and Jesse didn't talk about what happened during the day, but they stepped so closely together that they kept colliding gently, inspiring increasingly obsequious apologies.

"Excuse me."

"Sorry, cupcake!"

"Oh, do forgive *me*, sir!"

"The fault is mine alone."

"Oh dear me, so clumsy! So deeply, profoundly sorry . . ."

"The humility oozes from my pores. I will cut off my testicles at once, and burn them with caustics."

Long before they reached Angels & Kings, they had descended into hysterically freeing, cleansing laughter.

The establishment was a large one, two full floors, the downstairs packed with Friday night notables and the upstairs divided into three private rooms for parties such as theirs. Jesse and Michael told the bouncer that they were with the *Viridian* company, and the bouncer actually asked to check their IDs against his guest list. Jesse was aghast, but Michael took it in stride, scooting Jesse ahead of him before Jesse could explode at the bouncer. "What the fuck?" he spluttered.

"It's because of Jenna. Look."

Completely blocking the staircase to the upper story, Jenna Margolis stood at the center of a thick crush of people and digital phone camera flashes, posing in a metallic red skintight mini dress in a snakeskin pattern, and high-heeled gladiator sandals. She paused occasionally in her rapid-fire responses to a reporter's questions to flash her famous teeth. Jesse and Michael blinked bemusedly at the scene, as there was no way they'd be able to get upstairs with *that* going on. Jesse loudly applauded when Jenna ordered, "Let's go on in." Michael burst out laughing again, and the lowest of Jenna's entourage glared at him. They let themselves be borne along in the wake of the crowd, up to the door on the right, only to have the arm of an enormously muscular, monstrously tall man slam down across the doorway.

"This room is for Ms. Margolis's party only," growled the bodyguard.

Jesse snapped, "We are *with*—"

"No, you're not." The bodyguard smirked down at Jesse. "*You're* over there." He pointed at the main private room. Its doors were open, a hand-written sign that read *Viridian* taped to the wall next to the entrance. "Ms. Margolis will send an invitation to the next room if she wants to provide entry for you, and at this time, I've received no such invitation. Enjoy your night, gentlemen."

"The fuck—!" Jesse spat, red-faced, too furious for coherence. "Fuckin'—Look, dude—"

"C'mon, it's not worth it," Michael said, again taking Jesse's shoulder and half-shoving him in front. "Easy, tiger. Stick to the plan. Copious amounts of alcohol. What're you having? It's on me."

The small room was already populated with all of the producers. Michael made his way up to the cash bar, joining them on the rail. He'd lost Jesse, who was accepting a squishy-looking bear hug from someone he didn't recognize. Michael sighed and slumped his shoulders. It wasn't *his* world; maybe after tonight, it never would be. God, he hated mistakes.

"Michael."

It was Drew Farrow. He'd been hidden behind Tolo and his harem, all of whom were taller than he was. "What're you drinking? I got it," Drew offered. "The tab's open."

"You don't have to do that," Michael protested.

"I'm covering most of the drinks here tonight." Drew grinned at him. "It's all part of the producing game, and," he said, winking a little, "everybody here needs a drink."

"Definitely true," Michael admitted, momentarily curling his lip. "I appreciate it. Gin and tonic for me. Whiskey for Jesse."

"Oh, did he finally show up?" Drew asked, nodding at the harried bartender. "Woodford, neat. Make it a double. Jesse deserves a nice bourbon tonight, I figure. Hendricks okay for you?"

"I'd prefer Sapphire, if that's okay." Michael grimaced apologetically.

Drew crinkled the corners of his eyes and patted Michael on the arm. "You're a fool, but okay. Where is the kid, anyway? Didn't see him back at the Doe."

Michael nodded across the room in Jesse's general direction. "He's talking to . . . somebody."

The happy glow he'd worn on the walk over had evaporated, and now he hugged himself and glanced uneasily around the room. No one had spoken to him, and the ones who met his gaze merely arched their eyebrows and wrinkled their nostrils like he still had a Goodwill price tag on his shirt. It made Michael far too conscious of the fact that he smelled like sweat and backstage dust, that he was taller than almost everyone else in the room, that he wore glasses, that he was a skinny, hairy, nancy-boy. He took a solid swig from his cocktail, inhaled a deep breath, and stood up as tall as he could, straightening his glasses, and nonchalantly tossing his head, silent reciting to himself, *Yeah, I'm a big, queer, nerd freak, and proud of it, and fuck you.* He was sick of being looked down upon; he'd had too much of it already. He was in New York now.

Drew grinned at him, as if he'd read Michael's mind, and headed toward Jesse, leaving Michael to carry all three cocktails. When he watched Drew give Jesse a quick, brisk embrace, and Jesse's mouth quirk in a comforted half smile. It was almost as good as getting a hug himself.

He had a sudden, vicious desire to watch them kiss.

Not a peck, either. A tongue-sloppy, consuming, ravenous kiss that swept drinks off the table and generated gasps of shock from everyone else in the room. It wasn't fair that they couldn't just do that. Hadn't they paid their dues by now? Hadn't they pledged their commitment to one another? Why should they have to be denied a moment of public passion, just because they were both men? Besides, these were theater people; it wasn't as if they had never seen two people of the same sex kiss before, even passionately. It vexed Michael so much that he slurped the top from one of the cocktails at random, only belatedly realizing that it was Jesse's whiskey.

He wound his way over to them, and handed Jesse his drink. "Thank you, you're a saint." Jesse sighed and inhaled the double shot in one swallow. "They got anything to eat here? I don't know about you, but I'm starving."

Drew tried to look over the heads of the crowd. "Should be hors d'oeuvres on the table. C'mon, let's sit down. Look, Ashleigh has her computer. She's checking to see if reviews have been posted yet. The turnaround's so fast these days."

At the long table next to the window with a view of Second Avenue, Michael sat at the end to one side of Jesse, Drew on the other. Ashleigh, the costume designer, sat next to Elaine Gold, who accepted a pour of champagne from a waiter. Somehow Jesse had found a champagne flute, too, and elegantly held it up. "Hey, Elaine," he said, scooping up a handful of cheese pastry puffs.

"Good evening, Jesse," she replied, sipping from the rim of her glass and leaning toward the glow of Ashleigh's laptop monitor. "Did you happen to see the show?"

"Only the good parts," Jesse replied with his mouth full, already grasping for the plate of stuffed mushrooms. Michael widened his eyes at Jesse, and Jesse pouted defiantly.

"This is Michael Kaminsky," Drew interjected. "You haven't met him before, have you? Lighting design."

Michael shook Elaine's proffered pinky. "Pleasure," he said, sweeping the platter of mushrooms away from Jesse before he ate them all. Jesse gave him the finger.

"All mine. Beautiful work on the lights, by the way. I was pleasantly surprised." She didn't look up at him, absorbed in the computer screen. Michael quickly speared three mushrooms on a toothpick and consumed them, washing the mouthful down with gin.

Drew exchanged a glance with Michael, then they both looked at Jesse. Jesse set down the champagne glass, squirming under the scrutiny. "So where were you?" Drew murmured, voice carefully pitched so that no one outside of the three of them could hear. "What happened?"

"Bike chain," Jesse replied, downing the champagne. "Dropped a delivery, had to go back. Hot lasagna down my pants. By the way, I'm okay; not too burnt."

"Any time you want to stop dealing with that crap and work indoors, the world waits with bated breath. What do you think, Michael?" Drew asked, holding up his own glass for a toast. "To work. Keeps us out of trouble."

"Here's to 'fuck you,'" Jesse replied, clinking his glass against Drew's, then Michael's.

"The page is loading!" Ashleigh suddenly shouted. "*New York Mag*'s website just refreshed!" Their corner of the table disappeared under a swarm of partygoers.

"Ahem! '*Viridian*, Lauren Doe Theater." Ashleigh read aloud. "'A peculiar remake of the classic O. Henry story *The Green Door* is another one of those examples of ambition outstripping ability and . . .'" She had to swallow before she could go on. "'. . . and humanity. And talent.' Ouch. Oh, man. 'With a highly anticipated debut from

Trailer Hitch hottie Jenna Margolis, the work has nothing truly new to say and no particularly clever way to say it. The music is pretentious, attempting a Radiohead-flavored avant-garde electronic modernity—'"

"It's *Sakamoto*, you fuckwit!" shouted Kendrick from behind Ashleigh's shoulder.

"'The play descended into a kind of slapstick chaos which, if intentional, should put Margolis right in line to star in *Scary Movie 6,* coming soon to DVD cutout bins at a Costco near you.'" The costumer sighed miserably. "I can't go on. Does anyone else want to read it?"

The room filled with agonized groans and sharply spit profanity. "'About as essential as high school theater.' Fuck this dude!"

"They said something nice about your dress—oh, wait. Sorry."

"He was nice to Tolo, anyway."

Drew sighed and shook his head. Elaine Gold raised her hands, tossed down the last of her glass of wine, and declared, "Well, fuck me for a *schlimazel*. I'm outta here. If I leave now I can still catch *Project Runway*."

Michael watched the gauze of her dress shimmer as she set down her glass and swept elegantly out of the room. As others crowded around the computer, reading the first review for themselves, the groans grew quieter and quieter, until the only sounds of the party came from the music on the sound system and the clink of glass behind the bar.

Jesse stood up and quietly began surveying the hors d'oeuvres, setting some onto a napkin and putting others directly into his mouth. Michael felt awful, but he was too hungry to care much. When Jesse returned and sat down, he set the high-piled plate of food between them. They ate in silence.

"So, who do we have to thank for these sterling notices?" The stage manager, Kate, stood up and approached Michael from behind. "Who was the source of the fuckup that wrecked our opening night? Well, gee whillikers, they were even nice enough to point out 'ambition that outstrips ability.' And who here fits that bill?" Michael chewed sullenly on a particularly brittle slice of bruschetta. When Kate raised her voice, he flinched so hard he nearly choked. "I do believe that would be our lighting designer! Am I correct? Am I correct in assuming that it was a lighting error that made the dominoes fall?"

"It sure as fuck wasn't my fault," Kendrick broke in. "The music's been programmed. It played. It's a *playback*."

"Fuck you," Michael muttered.

"What? What was that?" Kate held her hand up to her ear. "This was *your* error, and you fucking know it. Why didn't you listen to me a month ago and try to simplify?"

"Because this is the lighting I did," Michael protested. "It worked fine. Even *you* said it worked fine. This was just a mistake."

"Yeah, that's the one thing we can agree on," Kate hissed. "It was a *mistake* to do something that can't be corrected as needed. You knew this could happen!"

"That's why we rehearsed," Michael insisted. "And it was fine. And I *corrected* the problem."

"It was not fine. You were too busy fantasizing about Chachi here, and you got sloppy. You fucked up. And now we're all fucked!"

"Ms. Wells?" Drew stood up and faced her, his voice all cool warning. "Let me tell you something."

Kate was only an inch or so shorter than Drew, but she visibly recoiled and paled, as though her blood was being slowly drained. Michael couldn't be sure, but it looked like Kendrick was hiding behind her.

"The lighting design is not the issue. The lighting design is, in fact, the best thing about this show. It certainly isn't its above-the-line star. And, dare I say, it isn't the stage management, either. You've done a perfectly fine job, yes, but what you do has no bearing on whether or not the show is special or unique. Michael's lighting design does that. It is the *only* thing that does that. We all know that. Come on, we're adults. We've seen plays. This is not the best play ever written or produced for the stage, but I'll be damned if it's not the most visually-striking show I've seen in a long time. So, okay, our show's star is a bitch, but at least she kept the audience in their seats. It's your responsibility to make sure the actors are where they are supposed to be, and doing what they're supposed to do. If anyone's at fault here, Ms. Wells, you have to accept your part in it. A simple performance error in the lighting had no business getting out of hand like that." Drew paused to take a sip from his tumbler of gin. "And

Kendrick, you are no Sakamoto, or whoever it is you're trying to imitate. If it *was* Sakamoto, maybe audiences would attend just to hear his music. You're not there yet, and if you don't learn to dance a little faster, you never will be."

He took another deep breath, and said, "You two—come with me. Out into the hall. We'll continue this in private. Like professionals, huh?" Before he departed, he patted Michael's shoulder, a firm and manly pat, for the public. It felt good, and Michael couldn't hide his triumphant smile behind another bruschetta.

"Should have done it in writing," Ashleigh murmured.

Someone turned the music up a little louder, though it didn't quite disguise the sheepishness that now filled the room. Michael looked at Jesse, wondering why he hadn't said anything, but Jesse was too busy working his way through the hors d'oeuvres and would not return Michael's gaze.

Drew, Kate, and Kendrick shortly returned to the room, Kendrick wearing an embarrassed half-smile, Kate stony and silent, and the natural curve of Drew's lips sternly flattened. He went to the bar and loudly announced, "Another round for the company!" A woman laughed about something, glasses clinked, and the party resumed, albeit with a certain black-humored vigor.

"C'mon," Drew said, "let's go sit at one of the tables back there." He pointed to the left of the bar, into a shadowy nook where a few neatly arranged chair legs attested that no one else had yet discovered the area. "Get you another drink, Michael?"

"Yes, please."

Michael walked ahead of Jesse to the back table. The thumping bass beats coming from the room where Jenna Margolis's private affair raged were louder than anything else. Drew joined them, sitting heavily. "Well, that sucks," he sighed.

"I'm sorry about all that," Michael said.

"Is it helpful? Being sorry?" Drew asked mildly, and shrugged. "Hmm. Well, we could look at this two ways: One, you just opened my bank vault, withdrew forty-five thousand dollars, and wiped it on your ass. Or . . ." He shook his head, mouth thinning again. "I wasn't going to make it back, anyway. And also, fuck you, dear Papa."

"I did it right earlier," Michael pointed out. "Rehearsals were fine. I missed one detail. Today, after lunch. One detail."

"And the house of cards fell down." Drew looked over at Michael and smiled. "It was a house of cards. It was a beautiful, complex house of cards."

Michael squirmed. "I shouldn't have designed it that way," he said.

"Just do better next time. If it worked once, it'll work again."

"It was my mistake," Michael said.

"Michael, stop it. Don't go there." Warningly, Drew raised one finger. "Just do your job, do it right, and learn from this. Focus."

"Yes, sir," Michael murmured. And it felt so right that only after a minute of silence had passed that Michael realized that he'd said it, and that Drew simply accepted it as his due.

But Jesse rolled his eyes, lips pursed impatiently, toying with his empty champagne flute. He rolled it between his deft, pointed fingers. "You okay?" Drew asked him.

"Yeah," Jesse said, shrugging. "I didn't get run over. I got the bike fixed. It was a first day."

"Have you two been distracting each other?" Drew asked, his voice an amused purr.

Michael was the one who dug up the courage to speak. "Probably."

"Maybe you think about each other too much?"

"No," Jesse put in.

"I just want him," Michael whispered. "I can't stop thinking about it."

They both heard, and watched him, appraising him in the low illumination of the room. "What would help with that?" Drew asked.

The three fell silent, examining each other, gathering details, Drew immobile and expectant. Michael shrugged fractionally, and confessed, "I don't know." At that, Jesse gave a silent laugh, and shook his head. "What?" Michael retorted. He blushed furiously, staring instead at the ceiling. "I mean . . . besides the obvious."

"The obvious, huh?" Drew grinned. "Jess? What do you think? How could you become less distracted?"

Infuriatingly, Jesse leaned over and murmured something in Drew's ear. Michael rolled his eyes and cleared his second drink. Drew spoke up, and his voice was so casual, so noncommittal, one might imagine that he couldn't care less about the response he received.

"Are you ready to come home with us?"

Michael took a deep breath, straightened his glasses, and looked away for a moment, just long enough to completely orient himself in his new reality, where there were new rules. Or no rules. There was nothing to hold him back from becoming manifesting the person that he was.he knew he could be. When he looked up, Jesse smiled hopefully, and that was all he needed.

"Sure. Sounds like fun."

8. PLUMS.

After a quick examination of the front door, Michael found a call buzzer neatly camouflaged behind a brushed brass panel, its lower right corner engraved with the address and the initials ALF. "Andrew L. Farrow," Michael whispered to himself, sliding the panel aside. "What's it all about, Alfie . . .?" He gave the exposed button a brief tap.

A tinny voice replied. "Michael?"

Michael flinched in surprise, and croaked, "It's me."

He had almost turned back half a dozen times on the subway ride from Angels & Kings, fighting down all of the excuses that loomed in his mind. *Bad idea. Do you really want to see them together? Bad idea. You're on his payroll. Bad idea. He could be a serial killer, and Jesse his victim procurer. Bad idea. You're drunk.* Nonetheless, in defiance of his insecurity, he had ended up here.

"Come on up." The intercom's distortion did nothing to disguise the lazy pleasure in Drew's voice. There was no buzzer, only the muted click of the door unlocking.

Michael stood in the foyer and stared up at the chandelier, marveling at the mid-century modernist construction of the fixture, dotted with amber-colored bulbs. He could get used to the lemon-cedar scent of the antechamber. The entrance to Drew's house was easily the size of his entire apartment, and Michael imagined bringing a sleeping bag next time, just bunking down on the bench next to the steep staircase. But he'd never be content down here when what he wanted was upstairs.

He meandered up the stairs and through the kitchen, spotless but for crumpled cellophane on one of the counters, the plastic torn free from a charming-looking basket half-full of various fruits, packages of crackers, and tiny jars of jam. His ears pricked to the sound of muted voices and even quieter music, and his legs moved, drawing him toward it as though he were being slowly reeled in.

The lights in the living room burned low, not as dim as in the foyer, but not at full intensity. Lamps, rather than overheads. The air held the spicy funk of burning cannabis and some kind of incense. Near the center of the room, Drew sat in a straight-backed chair, Jesse nestled comfortably on the floor at his feet. Both men were stripped down to underwear, Drew caramel-tan all over, Jesse's arms and face and neck browned and the rest of him creamy olive-pale. Undressed, Drew's musculature was heavier than it appeared when he was clothed, with thick biceps and shoulders and striated thigh muscles. Drew's feet were hidden in a dark blue plastic bucket, its surface glistening with condensation, parked on a multicolored rag rug in front of the chair.

For a long time, Michael could only stare, and Drew and Jesse both looked at him and calmly smiled as if nothing could be more ordinary. "Hey," Jesse said, slurping from the top of a soda can. He set it down, picked up a slim white cylinder, and began stuffing one end of it with olive buds from a tiny plastic baggie. "You want a drink? Or some pot?"

"Uh... water," Michael stammered. "Water would be great."

Jesse flicked the flame of a lighter over one end of the cylinder, and slowly exhaled a thin stream of smoke. Michael hadn't seen a one-hitter in so long he'd almost forgotten what they looked like. Sophomore year at CMU, at a party he hadn't been invited to, but had trailed along to after a straight guy he was sweet on. Intoxicants weren't his thing back then; he figured beer and bong hits were for kids who weren't serious about their studies. Later he'd understood, even if to this day, he still hadn't developed a taste for beer. He hadn't smoked marijuana since spring break, months before, when he was still a student. He hoped he wouldn't have a bad reaction.

"I got it," Jesse said, setting down the pipe, and scrambling to his feet. He paused at Michael's side, rubbed his hand gently across Michael's stomach. "You want ice?" he asked, and when Michael shook his head, continued toward the kitchen.

"Glad you made it okay," Drew said. "I was wondering. I stayed a while after you, and I still beat you here."

"Yeah, I made it. Train got delayed at Thirty-Fourth Street. You know how it goes. Um." Maybe he didn't. Drew Farrow did not ride the subway. Michael approached, glancing dubiously at the bucket, wondering if he should try to ignore it.

Drew sheepishly laughed. "Ice. My feet are a mess. I sacrificed comfort for style this evening."

"May I see?" Michael asked softly. Drew hummed assent, and lifted one dripping foot from the ice water. The skin, a patchwork of grays and purples and spidery blues, stretched over weirdly distorted, splayed bones, the ball of the foot nearly flattened, toes spread wide like rolled putty. The water had reduced the blisters to soggy, colorless rosettes. The nail on the big toe was shrunken and black; the pinky toenail was all but gone. Michael grimaced. "What the fuck," he breathed, half reverent, half sickened. He tingled all over at the grotesque sight. "How'd you do that to yourself?"

"Running," Drew explained, returning the foot to its ice bath. "Eleven miles today. I'm starting to train for the Brooklyn Half-Marathon, and it's always damaging for the first few weeks. It used to be worse. My feet are much more structurally sound than they used to be. Tougher. And yeah, in case you're wondering, it hurts. But not as much as you might think."

"Do you run a lot of marathons?"

"At least two a year," Drew replied. "But the race is just an excuse."

Michael fell silent for a moment, letting the thought sink in. "I didn't know you smoked pot," Michael said, searching for something less profound, less intimate to talk about. He hadn't known Jesse did, either, though that made a little more sense.

"I don't," Drew said. "I can't, not with running. I don't really like it that much anyway." A lazy grin spread over his face and he quirked his eyebrows, adding, "Not that I have a problem with a little contact high. Go on, you can look. My feet. It's okay. It's a freak show; it's fun."

Drawing a rug from the stack half-hidden on the far side of the brick red rectangular sofa, Michael sat on the floor beside the chair and stared down into the depths of the bucket, fascinated by the way the ice pieces obscured the shape, but not the color, of Drew's feet. Drew's hand settled on the back of Michael's head, stroking idly, curiously, through his hair. Michael shivered at the touch, but didn't pull away. He wanted it to go on and on.

Before he could give in to his urge to plunge his hand into the ice and grasp one of Drew's feet, Jesse returned with a thick glass tumbler of water. "Didja hit that weed yet?" he asked. He spoke in his normal tone of voice, too loud for the soft atmosphere. He bent at the knees and settled the water glass onto Michael's rug, then flopped back into his previous position, closer to Drew than Michael was, head lolling against Drew's knee. His eyes were clouded by a reddish haze; he'd been at itsmoking a whilesince before Michael arrived.

"Not yet," Michael said, picking up the metal cylinder and the lighter. Drew didn't lift his hand from Michael's head, but he put the other hand on Jesse and played with his hair in the same way. Jesse gazed at Michael over the hillocks of Drew's knees, smiling happily, seemingly pleased to be sharing. Michael smiled back and shrugged, feeling foolish, and lit the pipe.

Warm, dense smoke punched his lungs. Startled, he exhaled hard, thick clouds tangling themselves in the hairs on Drew's leg. He coughed until he couldn't see. Jesse laughed. "Whoa! Careful there, Snoop," he teased, handing Michael the glass of water.

Gratefully, Michael swallowed half of it. "Jesus," he spluttered, and kept coughing. Drew thumped him between the shoulder blades. He was extremely, abruptly high. "Whoa. Wow, that's strong."

"Sorry, I should have warned you to draw carefully. You okay?" Jesse's eyes widened in concern, and Michael nodded, vainly trying to gulp saliva onto his raw throat.

"Go get Michael a little something to eat," Drew advised. "Maybe cut up one of those pieces of fruit?"

"Yeah, it's good. It's from Georgia," Jesse said, scrambling up again.

Michael had no idea what he was talking about. "I'm—really

high," he tried to explain.

"That's okay," offered Drew mildly. "Just relax. You put on a show tonight; time for you to take it easy. Do you see, on the couch, a white towel?" he directed. Michael nodded. "Think you could bring that over here? I think the dogs've been on ice long enough."

Again, Michael wasn't sure of Drew's meaning, but he could get the towel. "Oh, your feet," he said, coming back and sitting down on the floor again. He breathed deeply, forcing his brain to get its language centers back on line. His body felt marvelous though, fuzzy and heavy, like the thick, nubby towel, a blanket of terrycloth as long as Drew's legs. "I like . . . your shorts," Michael said.

"Thanks," Drew said, chuckling. He spread his legs a little, showing off the bulge of his genitals. Even through the pot smoke, Michael could smell the specific perfume of cock and balls; not sweaty, not dirty, just *strong* and *there*. Right there. "They're pretty comfortable."

Do it, Michael said to himself. *Bite him.* Instead, he broke down laughing, grinning. "I lit a show tonight," he repeated, voice lilting in disbelief. "My first Broadway show. And it bombed. You should be pissed at me."

"Oh, I am," Drew said pleasantly, a smile on his face and a drowsy, hungry look in his eyes.

Jesse returned, this time carrying a shallow wooden bowl. "Let's eat this plum," he said cheerfully.

Drew reached into the bowl and retrieved a pink-gold slice. Michael followed suit, chewing and swallowing the silky, wet fruit pulp, the tart shock of plum skin. Immediately his throat felt better, his mind overwhelmed by the flavor of the plum. "It's so sweet and sour; it tastes like wine," he said.

"When you care enough to send the very best," Drew quipped.

"Who sent you the fruit basket?" Michael gripped two slices, precariously sliding against each other, between thumb and forefinger.

Drew and Jesse traded a heavily significant glance, and both looked back at Michael. Michael chewed innocently. "Jess, would you get the towel ready?" Drew said.

Sucking the end of his thumb, Jesse picked up the heavy cotton from Michael's lap, and Drew lifted his dripping feet out of the bucket and onto the towel. Jesse skillfully wrapped Drew's feet, briefly binding them tight, momentarily letting the tension in the air unravel. Michael slid the bucket and rug out of their way. Jesse set the towel in its place, and Drew propped his feet onto it.

"Thanks," Jesse said. "Hey, do you want to rub the pain cream on 'em? It's pretty sensual. You kinda bring 'em back to life."

"Okay," Michael agreed, smiling shyly. Was he so obvious? Or could Jesse just tell?

Jesse handed him an unmarked tube of ointment. "Make sure you rub well between the second and third toes," he directed. "You'll feel a callus there."

"This cream actually hardens calluses," Drew added. "Nice stuff. I get it custom-made. Heard about it years ago from a session bass player who swore by it." The cream spurted out as thick as mud, but rapidly became slippery between Michael's palms. "A couple of weeks of this, and I can walk on broken glass."

"Awesome," Michael breathed. Next, he could touch Drew with his slick, tingling hands. He closed his eyes for a moment to manage the profundity of the moment.

Jesse giggled and Michael glared at him, wondering if he was being laughed at. Jesse just winked and held out a slice of plum towards Michael. Michael first grasped Drew's left foot between his hands, then accepted the offering, letting himself be fed. Jesse's fingers were warm and honey-sweet, and it seemed rude not to suck them just a little bit. In Michael's hands, Drew's feet were the texture of wet beef jerky, and hardly seemed human at all.

Drew sighed, a long, groaning animal sound. His tongue quickly swiped his lips. "Jesse, can I . . .?" His voice begged quietly, breathlessly.

Somehow understanding, Jesse slid some plum into Drew's mouth, and followed it with a quick kiss. Drew's feet were wood and bowstring under Michael's fingers, the skin worn as smooth as a stone. The rise curving around the sole of his foot was one massive callus, the stiff skin becoming resilient as the cream worked its way in. The flesh, colder than the water Michael had been served, resisted the urge to warm for so long that he began to worry. Then, as sudden as a sun breaknrise, the blood rushed up to meet his palms, Drew's pallid skin flushing red. "That's good," Drew said. "That's real good. You're done. Now make sure you wash your hands before you touch your face, or anything else. That stuff's got capsaicin in it."

Michael had never heard the word pronounced before, but he recognized the chemical's tingly effects on his hands. "Okay," he said again, carefully rising without using his hands to balance himself.

"Bathroom is through the bedroom, out the hall, and up the steps," Drew said. "In fact—would you like to take a shower?"

"Huh?" asked Michael.

Jesse snickered at him again, but now that Michael could see his grinning face, he knew that the sound was affectionate, or at least involuntary. The whites of Jesse's eyes were blazed, his smile sloppy and crooked. "Jess, would you please show Michael to the bathroom?" Drew requested.

"Mmm-hmm," Jesse agreed, trying to stand up, too, and slipping on a loose edge of rug. The bucket sloshed. Thrashing, he managed to catch his balance, laughed, and shook his head. "Whoa! Okay, lesson learned. I am not slick. And I am still drunk. C'mon. Follow me."

Michael obediently followed, watching the twitching globes of Jesse's ass cheeks, neatly outlined in a pair of thin gray briefs. "You have a beautiful back," Michael said, mounting the three steps that led to another level, another room, at least the size of the living room they'd just left. This room was furnished in dark blues and tarnished brass and copper, a huge square bed at the center. Two walls were windows, shaded by tall single-panel rice paper screens printed along the top edge with tiny East Asian characters in a language Michael didn't recognize. A single large artwork occupied each of the other two walls: a massive photo of a deserted, sun-dappled European street and, under glass, a long, ragged-edged brown sheet of paper, inscribed with small rows of numbers. "This is an incredible room!" He stared at the numbers, trying to make sense of them.

"He's got taste, that's for sure."

"What is this?"

"He'll have to explain to you what the scroll is; I've got no idea. Something super old and Portuguese. I think it's astronomy or alchemy of something. That photo's from Lisbon, too. Gifts from his dad. C'mon."

"What's the language on the window screens?" Michael asked.

Jesse stood in a new doorway, eyes shining and playful. "It's Malay. C'mere, stoned boy. Give me a kiss."

Michael walked to him, bent his head, and let his tongue flick against Jesse's, which felt and tasted like nothing so much as a hot, sweet slice of plum. Pursing his lips, Jesse put his hand against Michael's shirt front. "You're still wearing your Sparky tee," he remarked. His hand seemed to burn through the fabric and spray paint, as if he gave off radiation. Gamma rays, something to break his tissues apart, stamp his bones forever. "Take it off."

"Are you going to take a shower with me?" Michael asked, unhesitatingly twisting the shirt off over his head, releasing an intense pong of dried anxiety sweat.

Jesse shook his head. "I already took mine," he said. "Drew decided he was clean enough. But you . . ."

With a deep breath, his voice trailed off and he stood aside, allowing Michael to gape anew at the master bathroom. Again, it was nearly the size of his entire apartment, with a slick white tile floor and walls, sparkling black granite shower stall, a separate matching raised bathtub a few steps away, seemingly big enough for even Michael to fit his entire body in it. "Okay, yeah, this place is ginormous," Michael breathed.

Jesse reached forward, grasping Michael's waistband, and unbuckled his simple black mesh belt.

Chuckling, Jesse yanked Michael's pants down from the sides, stripping his underwear with them. It was sticky, and clung to his balls and inner thighs. Hardly hesitating, Jesse cradled Michael's aching testicles, gently pulling the fabric away from the skin, using the other hand to lift Michael's penis out of the way. "What I would do," Jesse said, his attention absorbed by the semi-erect state of Michael's cock, "is maybe rub one out in the shower. Unless that makes you sleepy." He let go of Michael, and smiled. "We want to play all night."

"That's . . . what this is?" Michael asked plaintively, eager for confirmation.

"Of course it is," Jesse said, rolling his eyes impatiently. "I'd get down on my knees and suck you off, but I know how you are about being dirty. So wash it off. And clean it out, if you need to." He angled his head toward the toilet in its own half-closet, its companion bidet sitting beside it like a helpful younger brother. "Michael," Jesse added more gently, stroking the back of his hand against Michael's cheek. "Cut it out with the shy damsel routine. You know we want you. So hurry up." He left and shut the door behind him.

Michael spent a few minutes sitting on the toilet, wondering if anything needed to happen, but his bowels were unresponsive. He'd barely eaten in days. Compared to Drew, his naked body would look scrawny, hairy, pale-skinned. He wasn't golden-sleek and graceful like Jesse, either. But they had invited Michael over, got him high, and fed him plums. It had to be okay.

He soaped and scrubbed himself all over under hot water, then turned the tap to its coldest setting until he was shivering and his erection shrunk down to nothing. His nipples were sharply erect, stiff and red. Stepping out from the black granite stall, he picked out an immense rust-colored towel, the duskier twin of the towel used to wrap Drew's feet, from a warming rack on the far wall. He scrubbed himself dry and tied the towel around his waist, calming and centering his breath.

The bedroom's lights had dimmed, the music become even more ambient, and Drew lay on top of Jesse on the bed. Michael took off his steam-opaqued glasses and squinted. No, that was Jesse on top of Drew, and back again, wrestling and rolling back and forth, limbs clenched, hands slapping against each other's bodies, teeth gleaming as they laughed. "What's this?" Drew panted, a hand slipping between Jesse's thighs. "What's this you got here?"

"It's m'dick. Ow! Bitch. I'll fuck you in your ear," Jesse grunted.

"In my *rear*? You want to try it?"

"In your *ear*, asshole!" Laughing. Biting Drew's bicep.

"In my rear, asshole?"

Michael quietly set his glasses down on the surface of an antique, copper-hued desk.

"Shut *up*," Jesse shot back. At once, they both looked up at Michael. Jesse broke into a grin. "Hey, he's back!"

"I didn't think I took too long," Michael protested, stepping cautiously closer. Naked, now. Both of them were naked, cocks wobbling between their legs, thickening, bobbing up taller each moment.

"Then why am I bored?" Jesse inquired. His arm shot out as fast as a cobra striking, grabbing one end of Michael's towel and yanking it. Michael had the choice to either let himself fall forward or slip backward onto his ass. Just in time, he raised his arms and relaxed his legs, and let himself fall towards them.

He landed on a blanket of bones and hair, muscle and breath and scent. Jesse's pelvis and Drew's collarbone met his ribs, his sternum. Before he could catch his bearings, Drew's fingers were in his mouth, his wrist grabbed and yanked, a knee shoving his own knees apart. It was like the fantasy of a rugby scrum, of being on the bottom of a sacking on the football field, buried under a sudden tide of boys, unable to yell or resist, every blooming bruise divine. He shoved with his free hand against someone's chest—Drew's—and felt the velvety hairs on Jesse's ass against his shoulder. Drew's fingers popped free from Michael's mouth, and Drew let himself be shoved, rolling away, a hand coming up to rub against his nipple, still hard, but warmer now.

Jesse, behind Michael, grasped his wrists and pulled his arms behind his back. "You clean?" he asked pleasantly.

"You smell good." Drew kissed Michael's chest and neck.

"More or less clean," Michael sighed. "Oof! You guys play rough!"

"You can take it," Jesse replied, gripping Michael's biceps hard. "You're a big, strong man."

Drew grinned, staring into Michael's eyes, burning away his self-consciousness. He licked his lips and groaned, "I love tall men. There's so much . . . acreage." His fingers plucked at the hair on Michael's chest, twisting some, running his fingers over the skin underneath, circling a nipple and poking its stiff apex. "Love these tits . . ." Drew mumbled, pinching, not too hard. Michael closed his eyes, sighed, and let himself be carried along the stream of sensations, determining the difference between their hands, their touches. Jesse was pointed, cool, direct; Drew, smooth-textured and sure. Michael groaned, arching his back, offering his nipple to Drew's mouth.

Drew's mouth did not close over him, and Michael opened his

eyes inquiringly. All he could see was Drew kneeling, his swelling chest muscles inches away, the auburn-brown hair on his chest thicker and darker over his heart. His pubic hair was as painstakingly groomed as his sideburns, trimmed shadow-close all across; at the center, his thickening penis rose and sank with each breath. "I said I'd show you mine," Drew reminded him, grasping the root of his own shaft, stroking upward, pushing pulsing, dark lifeblood toward the end. "Do you approve?"

Michael tried to swallow, and had to slurp a suddenly runny mouthful of saliva back into his mouth. He gave a few vertical jerks of his chin. Jesse laughed, chewing gently on the side of Michael's neck. "Isn't he delectable?" he purred to Drew. "So sensitive."

"Oh, yes," Drew sighed, "Oh, yes."

He slid both hands down Michael's body, tangling his fingers in Michael's thick, wild, jet-black pubic hair, spreading from hipbone to hipbone. "I'm sorry," Michael struggled to get the words out. "It's a jungle down there—I don't really groom—"

Drew silenced him. "I like it." Smoothly, gracefully, he slid down onto his belly, wrapped his fingers around Michael's cock, and licked it all the way around, as if striping an ice cream cone. Michael remained silent, afraid that if he gave voice to his feelings, he'd break the windows with a scream of joy. Drew reached the curved helmet atop the shaft and slid it between his lips, lightly scraping the underside of Michael's cock with his teeth. He sucked, relaxed, drew back, forward, sucked again. Michael wanted his hands back, but Jesse had them, held securely behind his back, pressed down onto the bed. Jesse sucked Michael's earlobe, releasing it with a quiet moan.

"I know you like it," Drew said. "You're getting harder." He stroked firmly at Michael's dick, and Michael bit his lip. "Why don't you tell me how good it feels? It does feel good, doesn't it? I don't want to make you do anything you don't want to do."

"No, it does," Michael breathed faintly. His balls repositioned themselves in their silk purse, dropping, tightening, the hair tickling their hairy selves. "I'm just. . . . Wow. I've never . . . done this before . . . not with . . . not really." He couldn't talk; his tongue wanted to do other things.

"You'll get the hang of it," Drew said calmly. "Jesse, you want to let him go and join me down here?"

"Happy to," Jesse said, releasing Michael's hands. Michael left them where they were, tight against the bed, restraining himself. Jesse slid around his side, next to one spread leg, climbed over it, spread it even more—Michael breathed into the sudden stretch—and rubbed his face into Michael's groin. "Mmmm, he does smell good," he murmured approvingly.

"I'm gonna suck these balls," Drew murmured.

"Oh, fuck," Michael whispered.

Neither acknowledged Michael's exhortation. They kissed each other between Michael's legs and chose their positions, Jesse high on the cock head, Drew low, face lost in the black pelt. Michael closed his eyes and felt a tear escape from under his eyelid, not caring if it was seen.

Drew gathered Michael's balls into his mouth, both at once, hair and all, and sucked vigorously. Jesse outlined Michael's glans with a precise tongue. Michael stroked both their heads, hysterical laughter breaking from his throat in fits and starts. They paid him no mind, busily licking and sucking, turning him inside out, making his asshole tingle and his nipples and earlobes almost painfully sensitive to the air. Michael pinched one of his own nipples, then the other, as hard as he wanted them done. He rubbed his ears hard, tugging the lobes, and pinched his tits some more, yelping faintly under his breath. Drew let the balls spill wetly out of his mouth, rubbed them against his cheek, breathing hot and heavy against them. Michael's crotch was wet, hot, twitchy, savage, and humid. Michael let out a keening whine, tightly grasping hair—someone's hair, silky and wavy, he wasn't sure whose. "Hey, hey. Chill. You're okay." Jesse, rubbing his scalp. "We're just having some fun. Don't pull so hard unless you're fucking me. Feels good?"

"You fucking know it does," Michael hissed. Jesse chuckled.

"I want specifics," Drew said. He spread the leg closest to him even wider. Michael groaned, and moved it back a few inches. Tonight was not the time to experiment with doing the splits.

"I love it," Michael said. "When you suck my balls . . ." He trailed off into giggles.

"I love to do it," Drew replied cheerfully.

Michael could hear Jesse's fingers on his own cock, fast and dry, and his fingers tightly clenched the bedspread. "Lick them . . ." Michael whispered.

"Like this?" Drew murmured, darting his tongue between the testicles, making Michael groan through gritted teeth. "Lick 'em like this?   Mmm . . . like that?"

"Oh, God . . .!"

"I know what we should do," Jesse suggested, pushing back the tousled fringe of his hair. "Let's go down on Drew, and give him a taste of his own medicine. He could use the extra help. You into that?" When Jesse kissed Michael, Michael tasted his own skin cutting through the sweetness of the plum juice on his palate.

"Okay," Michael gratefully accepted.

"What do you mean, I could use the extra help?" Drew complained, repositioning, scooting back against the massive bed's headboard. It was a simple hyphen of marine blue fabric that Michael realized was suede so fine it looked like raw silk. The headboard was not padded, but the wall behind it was.

"Nothing, honey," Jesse said, arching Drew's left leg and draping it over his back, settling himself right next to Drew's dangling balls and fattening cock shaft. "You're perfectly, endlessly virile."

"That's damn right," Drew grunted. His hand on the back of Michael's head was light, gentle, but insistent. He took his cock in hand and painted Michael's lips with the tip, as if applying lipstick. Michael gasped, a nearly voiceless *ah*, opening his mouth, accepting the flesh. It filled his mouth, and then some. The only way to establish equilibrium inside his mouth, inside his *head*, was to suck. "That's fucking right," Drew sighed. Next to Michael, cheek to cheek, Jesse licked the lower shaft, his mouth smacking out overt, sloppy noises. His saliva smeared onto Michael's chin. "Oh, yeah, that's fucking right. Both of you sucking my cock at once. I hope I'm making your dreams come true, because this is one of *my* dreams coming true. . . ."

"Just the one?" Jesse quipped, and went back to his mouth-work.

"Oh, definitely, just the one," Drew agreed, pulling his penis from Michael's mouth, lightly tapping Michael's cheek with the hard and heavy head, and returning it to Michael's tongue. Michael groaned obscenities with his mouth full. "I've got a dream of sodomizing this boy—" He stroked his fingers through Jesse's hair, making it stand on end. "—on the front steps of City Hall. At noon. Making the whole world watch. Enough. Give it to Jesse. *Give it.*" Drew pulled his cock away from Michael again, and Jesse fell upon it like a starving man on a banquet. Michael had to content himself with Drew's balls, defining their curves with the point of his tongue, half-drunk on the smell, on the sounds created by Jesse's mouth, hums and groans and half-gags and the churning of saliva into froth. "And you too, Michael. I've got dreams about you, too. I want to fuck you. I want to ride your cock until one of us gets hurt. I want Jesse to fuck you until you cry like a little girl who lost her puppy."

"Why?" Michael asked, his cheeks hot.

Drew grinned wickedly "Okay, *you* can fuck Jesse. The crying, though, is not optional."

"Sweet," Jesse said, not missing a beat.

"Quiet, you. Suck it."

"Mmm-hmm."

Michael palmed his own cock, quivery,-achy, its surface chased with blue and purple veins, and dazedly flicked at Drew with his tongue, more often than not missing his target. Jesse had nearly crawled on top of Drew now, plunging his mouth up and down, his neck straining with tension. Michael wanted it back; it was his turn. Between Jesse's legs, his dick surged toward his belly, thrumming and rigid. Michael watched the organ bob for a moment, then reached out and swatted it with his hand.

"Fuck! Oh, Jesus!" Jesse yelped.

Michael laughed anxiously, hoping he hadn't hurt Jesse, his eyes locking onto Jesse's equipment, his heart surging with joy when a few clear drips of fluid leaked from the slitted head.

"Ow," Drew grunted. "You bit me, you little shit." His massive hands grasped Jesse's shoulders, tossed him aside, and rolled him over onto his face before Michael could do more than get out of the way of Jesse's knees and elbows. Jesse mewed an abject apology, ignored by Drew, who raised one of his broad, hard hands and brought it down on Jesse's buttocks. Michael watched, benumbed with desire and still fairly stoned, wondering if this was the moment when the kinky abuse scenarios began. Jesse didn't cry out in pain; instead, he writhed and moaned, exhaling a deep, blissful sigh. "You distractible little bitch," Drew said, spanking the other cheek, grabbing them both, squishing them together, parting the hemispheres, exposing the long, dark, hair-lined crevice, the winking eye of the anus, the straining ligament between Jesse's balls. Without hesitation, Drew shoved his mouth into the valley, moaning, slurping, licking.

"Oh my God," Michael whispered, his nerves on fire. This was something he'd never seen, never experienced, was always repulsed by, fascinated and horrified by. Drew muttered and wiped his mouth on his shoulder, leaving a trail of gleaming saliva on himself. It was too much. "I'll be right back," Michael said shakily, rising from the surface of the bed, the solidity of the floor surreal. "Need a drink."

"Don't be long," Drew said.

"Don't leave me alone here with this crazy person," Jesse added, earning himself another spank.

Michael teetered out of the room, down the short flight of stairs to the living room, and sat on the chair, lifting his barely-drunk glass of water to his dry lips. He'd forgotten how dehydrating sex was, how freaky the whole business could get. He needed a moment to breathe and think. He wondered if he'd ever let someone do that to him . . . or if he'd ever do it to someone else. It was an awful thing, with no nice names for it. *Analingus* was an awkward neologism; *eating ass* wasn't quite accurate either. Oral-anal contact. It was a bad, bad, stupid, dangerous, disgusting thing. A delicious, wrong thing. From the bedroom he heard Jesse cry out, "Oh, *God*, it feels so *good*!" and his cock jumped hard, pumping out its own pearl of pre-come, cloudy with stored ejaculate.

He drank the water, thinking back to the first time he'd ever encountered the idea, how it almost made him gag. So many things had changed, so many perspectives, including gagging itself. He had never had his balls sucked, either, and now he knew with an absolute certainty that it was amazing, that he loved it.

He examined the damp rag rug with the bucket of melting ice on it, and, reflexively glancing around first to be sure he wouldn't be caught, lowered himself silently down onto his hands and knees, and, like an animal, sipped some of the water out of the bucket.

The flavor was dusty-sweet.

He went to the kitchen sink, running water through the filter attached to the tap, fingers in the stream, waiting for the water to run cold. He glanced again at the partially deconstructed fruit basket, this time seeing a cream-colored notecard propped between crackers. With his dry hand, Michael pulled the card free and examined it. Handwritten, a hasty feminine cursive.

Andy + Jess—

Break a leg on opening night—sorry I have to miss it! Best wishes and love always to my amazing nephews— back in town by the 6th, you owe me lunch

Your adoring aunt, Amelia

"Really," Michael said to himself, glancing toward the bedroom, mind spinning with possible connections. He filled the glass.

New rules, or no rules.

Michael returned to the bedroom, chewing his lower lip. He wasn't sure what to say, or whether to say anything. When he saw them, though, his concerns became irrelevant. Together, on the bed, they made a delightful sight. They were beautiful, adoring, gazing into each other's eyes, stroking each other in wonder. He couldn't leave. He'd come too far. He needed them, whatever they were; whatever was between them was just an additional intimacy, a secret, a stimulant. Drew and Jesse, Jesse and Drew. And him. He wanted to be like them, shameless and effortless and together and free.

He stood in the doorway and whispered inaudibly, "I love you."

Jesse sprawled on the bed like he'd fallen out of an airplane and landed that way, limbs quivering and twisted. He looked at Michael like he was receiving a holy visitation. Drew, sitting up, took the glass of water. "Thanks," he said, gulping some down.

"Aww," Michael sighed, tingling with irony, "now it's all contaminated."

Drew stared in disbelief for a moment, then shook his head and laughed. "Be that as it may." He handed the glass to Jesse, and Jesse drank heedlessly. Michael's skin tingled. There was never anything to be afraid of.

"He looks so hot without his glasses," Jesse said.

"He looks hot with 'em." With an impatient sigh Drew asked,

"Why are you just standing there? Get over here and suck my cock. And do it right this time." He softened it with a wink.

Michael almost wished he hadn't. What he really wanted was one of those skin-cracking spanks that had made Jesse's pale ass cheek turn rosy pink. Still, his skin craved the warmth, the contact, the no-sense of this. "Yes," he said, "Okay," wondering if he should add *sir* or *master*. He didn't want either. He didn't need to be asked nicely, but he would never call anyone "master," not even Drew Farrow. He sure did sound good, though, being stern like that.

Michael settled back onto the bed, on his belly, and slid between Drew's legs again, unhesitatingly filling his no longer dry mouth with the thick contours of Drew's cock. It wasn't as long as Michael's, but it was probably twice as wide, with a thick rim of coronal tissue around the head and a plump, flexible frenulum that returned again and again to the soft trough in the center of Michael's tongue. Drew laughed lazily, stroking Michael's hair and shoulders.

"That's good," he murmured. "That's good; that's better. Like you want it." His hips rose, pushing the glans deeper into Michael's mouth. "You know you want it. Show me."

Jesse let out an incoherent moan, and as if he'd just been the one commanded (had he?), he slid himself over onto Michael's back, balancing his weight on his fists, on either side of Michael's ribcage, and shoved his erection through the hair at the base of Michael's spine. Michael lifted his head in surprise, and—delight of delights—Drew lightly slapped him on the cheek. "Pay attention while I fuck your mouth," Drew muttered.

Michael couldn't help laughing. "You're such an asshole," he said.

"Stop talking." Drew pushed his dick back into Michael's mouth, and Michael sucked as hard as he could. "You love it anyway."

I tolerate it, Michael thought, caressing the clenched curve of Drew's buttock, the tender skin at the groin, and Drew's breath escaped in a shudder. *No, I love it. I fucking love it. I love this. I'm having fun.* He had never thought of sex as fun before; it was a cruel, necessary urge, trying to corral his messy emotions for long enough to get his dick wet and shoot a load. *Don't fall in love, don't look into their eyes, don't give yourself over.* So many rules. With Drew—with them both—it was far too late. He reached behind him, stroked Jesse's side, and Jesse slid their hands together, fingers gripping tight as Jesse fucked Michael's skin.

"Feels so good . . ." Jesse whispered. "So good . . ." His penis was as hard as a roll of silver dollars, like a knife handle, its tip wet, leaving slug trails through the hair on Michael's back, on his ass. "You are the best friction fuck. Yes. Yes."

"You want to fuck that ass, Jesse?" Drew growled. Michael sighed, struggling for his breath.

"*Unh*! Just wanna *fuck*!" Jesse momentarily hugged Michael's ribcage, his waist, kissed him between the shoulder blades. His face was wet, his crotch wetter, his cock finding its way between Michael's buttocks and arching back and forth there.

"You want your ass fucked, Michael?" Drew asked, holding Michael's head tightly onto him. Michael longed for so much that he couldn't *want* anything in the moment. This moment was so intense, so overwhelming, his mind out of itself, on a hazy plane of existence he had only approached until now. He couldn't reply; his mouth was full of hot, surging flesh.

"I want *my* ass fucked," Jesse muttered through gritted teeth.

"Come here, greedy. Don't whine." Drew's voice, plainly affectionate though thickened and husky with lust, purred into Michael's mouth. He withdrew his cock, dripping with saliva. Michael sighed in relief to have that thick meat removed from his tonsils for a moment; he had been holding his breath so that he wouldn't choke. Michael rolled aside, throwing an arm over his eyes, but careful to not completely obscure his view. He wanted to see this, even more than he'd welcome a fuck himself. He could watch, memorize, remember on a long, cold, lonely night. Jesse kissed Michael's hand before letting it go.

Still sitting up, Drew tore a wrapper, rolled on a condom so transparent that Michael could still see the veins on Drew's cock, squirted on thick, clear lubricant, and pulled Jesse close, all in a series of smooth, rapid movements. "It's time." Jesse spread his legs and climbed, shifting his hips, settling, their hands working together behind Jesse's swinging sack. Michael cursed himself for lying at the wrong angle to witness the moment of penetration, and yet, was grateful; the sight probably would have made him come instantly.

"Uh." Jesse hissed.

"Yes?"

"*Uh*, oh, yes," Jesse said, joined to Drew at the groin like puzzle pieces sliding together, his knees coming down to meet the surface of the bed. "*Uh!*"

"Oh my God," Michael said starkly. Drew had been taken to the hilt within seconds. He couldn't even imagine the levels of control Jesse would have to have, control and familiarity, the ability to relax an ordinarily tight series of muscles in such a short time. Michael lay dazed from the intensity of his desire to try it out, to see if Jesse could take him in so smoothly, so eagerly. What it would feel like.

Drew smiled at him, glassy-eyed. Jesse's hands splayed on Drew's shoulder and hip, holding still, eyes closed, breathing slow as if meditating. "Get closer," Drew whispered. "Touch. Do whatever you want. Oh. . . . Poor Michael . . . don't get left out—" Drew suddenly caught his breath, though Jesse hadn't moved, and his voice continued, rising in ecstasy. "You need your cock sucked, don't you?" Michael nodded jerkily in reply. Jesse's hips moved sinuously back and forth, and Drew started babbling and sweating. "I want you to get off, I want you to—" Drew's voice broke off as Jesse rose, fell, rose again, faster, scooping his hips forward. His hips inscribed figure-eights on Drew's pelvis. "I want you to be satisfied. I want us to—Oh, fuck. Ahhhh. You need that, you deserve it . . . God, *Jesse*! Michael, I can't wait 'til you can fuck this ass! It's incredible!"

You've loved it a long time, Michael thought. *And now you're going to share. Good God. Your aunt, Amelia! Does she know? Who knows this? How can this have happened?*

"Come here," Jesse sighed to Michael, his temples streaming sweat, hair in a crazed corona of spikes. "In front of me. We can make this work. Scooch down," he added, stroking Drew's shoulder, grasping his hand, shoving his tongue into Drew's mouth, across his chin. Still joined, Drew slid his hips down the bed, head away from the headboard, enough space for Michael to fit. Shoving the pillows aside, Drew lay back, Jesse atop him, crouched forward. "Gimme," Jesse said, extending his tongue. "Cock in my mouth. C'mon."

Michael moved slightly up onto his knees so that his cock could reach Jesse's mouth, and moved again to slide it deeper inside. Under Jesse, Drew arched his hips, and Jesse moaned around his mouthful, drooling, saliva dripping from the corners of his mouth and landing on Drew's chest and neck.

"Fuck his face," Drew whispered, eyes rolling up under his lids, raising his hips. "With me. Like this." He took Michael's hand and squeezed it, and raised his hips again, and Michael, groaning, mind spinning, moved his own hips forward.

Jesse's eyes crossed, his hand spread against Michael's stomach. Holding him back, then releasing him, incorporating the rhythm. Directing. He wanted Michael to alternate: his thrust, then Drew's. Michael wanted to close his eyes, to concentrate, but he couldn't break his gaze away from the two of them. Their faces were similar, so similar, eyes nearly the same shade of green-brown, jaw lines the same, noses much the same except that the bridge of Jesse's was crooked from having been broken. Their voices sounded in perfect harmony, Drew's moans and Jesse's desperate, spit-soggy whines. Good God, it was true.

"This is how we fuck him," Drew said.

He broke the rhythm to slam into Jesse from underneath, hard and fast, fingers digging deeply into the pale skin of Jesse's hips. Jesse whined desperately, mouth full, his head bobbing, trying to keep the pace, to slow back down to the perfect rhythm so briefly established. It couldn't be brought back; too much lust swirled in the air. Every man for himself. The rhythm shredded. Michael heard himself moaning, pitching higher and higher, in time not with Jesse's mouth on him, but Drew's cock punching into Jesse.

Jesse's throat—Michael's cock had made it to the incredibly hot soft tissue of his palate—seized around the head, and pushed Michael's meat away, past molars and incisors and lips and tongue. Jesse coughed almost as hard as Michael had on his pipe hit, spattering Drew with spit. Jesse's mouth hung open and he gave a surprised grunt of completion, his limbs and neck jerking. His cock, purpled and crooked, riding the sweat-slick space between his belly and Drew's, sent out three quick jets of semen, running together in a puddle in Drew's navel.

"Oh, Jesus," Michael said helplessly. A white flashbulb of orgasm blotted out his senses for a second—less than a second—and when he could see again, his long, narrow dick was shooting a thick rope of come right at Jesse's face. Jesse was too dazed to dodge, and the spunk hit him on the side of the mouth, dripping across his cheek.

Another jet, even more powerful, shot towards Jesse's shoulder.

"Ha, ha . . . icing for the cupcake," Drew breathed, and laughed.

"Fuck," Jesse blurted. "Fuck me." Not a directive; a general expression of helplessness.

Michael put his hand to his mouth. "Jesse, I'm sorry. I keep—"

Jesse laughed too, harder, freely, released. "Shush." He wiped the semen off his face, and rubbed it into his chest, onto Drew's chest. Michael helped, finger painted Drew with mixed come, his own and Jesse's. Drew kept thrusting, unencumbered now, Jesse blissfully laughing in response to Drew's rising, increasingly urgent moans. "C'mon, baby," Jesse murmured, pinching Drew's nipples roughly. "Come inside me, come deep inside me. . . . Do it. Yeah? Yeah. Oh, *yeah.*"

Drew abruptly slammed a fist down onto the bed beside him, his spine curving, eyes clenched shut, abdominal muscles leaping into definition. "Ah, *fuck!*"

"Yes, right?" Jesse murmured. "Yeah. Isn't that good? Doesn't it just feel so fucking good?"

"Mmmm," Drew groaned, eyelids fluttering. "Oh, God."

Grinning, quivering, Michael lay beside Drew, face-up like him, soaking in Drew's orgasm through the vibrations of his limbs against the bed. When Jesse disengaged himself, climbing off, Michael just rolled over, on top of Drew, kissed his reddened cheeks, kissed away the semen staining his chest. Drew lay completely still for a while, one hand clamped over the spent condom, accepting Michael's affection. Jesse kissed the back of Michael's head, so Michael turned to him, meeting mouths. He knew that Drew had probably kissed Jesse with his contaminated mouth. Right now, it didn't matter, not in this pile of sticky bliss. It was, in fact, perfect. He kissed Drew on the lips, too. Everything was all right.

After returning the kiss, Drew turned his face away and said, "Move." Obligingly, Michael and Jesse moved aside, and Drew separated himself from the pile, sitting up and stripping the rubber from his penis. He held it up and looked it over. "It's almost a shame to throw out this good come," he mused, "what with all this fluid play happening here tonight."

"Gross," Jesse said, wrinkling his nose, tucking himself in close to Michael. Michael wrapped Jesse in his arms and held him close, kissing him, savoring his heartbeat. He agreed with them both. Drew discarded the condom in something underneath the bed and rejoined them, arms winding around them, hands holding, nuzzling, legs weaving themselves together.

"You know what?" Jesse said eventually. "I have got to pee."

"If you must," Michael agreed sadly. Drew kissed Michael between the eyebrows.

"I'll get us a clean towel." Jesse unfolded himself and stood up, angling one hip to stretch his lower back and pelvis. "Entertain each other for a bit. I won't be long."

Michael and Drew watched him pad naked to the bathroom, noting the fading red slap marks on his hips and ass, then turned their attentions back to each other. Drew ran his fingers through Michael's damp pubic mane. "Did you like that?" he asked.

"That was the most amazing experience of my whole life," Michael confessed.

Drew grinned. "Good," he said. "There's more where that came from. We can do this amazing thing whenever we want."

"And it's okay with Jesse?" Michael asked, circling Drew's nipples with a fingertip, following with his tongue. The flavor and scent of semen flooded his mouth, and he licked carefully, methodically, trying to taste it all.

"He's been begging for it," Drew replied. "He wants you, but he wants me, too. I feel the same way. I like you both together. You communicate so instinctively, even if . . ." Drew chuckled. "Sometimes it seems like you don't get it. And sometimes, you seem to get it exactly."

"I'm just responding," Michael defended himself. "I'm just learning. I don't know what I'm doing, I just . . . try to do the right things."

"Don't be so anxious." Drew stroked Michael's cheek with the back of his hand, and Michael leaned into the touch like an eager cat. They kissed again, and Michael felt more relaxed, more attuned, than he had in years. Or ever, really. He had never felt so wanted.

But, despite the directive, Michael couldn't relax completely yet. "I have to ask you something," he said. When Drew's only reply was a quirk of his eyebrows, Michael continued softly, "I saw, in the kitchen . . . on the fruit basket. From your aunt, Amelia."

Drew smiled, his expression flickering between chagrin and amusement. "Mmm," he acknowledged.

"What are you and Jesse?" Michael murmured. "You're related, aren't you?"

Drew gave a single, subtle nod.

"How?" He stroked Drew's back, firmly, lovingly, letting him know that he wasn't afraid or angry.

"We're cousins," Drew said.

"How close?"

The chagrin crept back into Drew's expression, this time mixed with apprehension. "My mom," he explained slowly, "and his dad were brother and sister. I'm Andrew James Landon Farrow. He's Jesse James Muhammad Ali Landon. And it was just . . . never like that.we were related." His body, still lying calmly next to Michael's, was suddenly tense, ready for a change.

"Okay," Michael said, still gently caressing Drew's back. "Explain how it was."

"I didn't know him growing up," Drew said. "I barely knew he existed. He *didn't* know I existed. We met when he was sixteen. I was twenty-eight." He looked away thoughtfully. "I pretty much fell in love with him right away. I tried not to admit it to myself for as long as I could. I mean, he was a kid, for one thing. He was too young, he was messed up, he needed a friend more than anything else. But . . . he felt for me, too. He wanted me. And he needed me, and I needed him. He doesn't feel like family, except that he does, but it's something we made for ourselves, not something imposed on us by . . . well." He sighed, still not meeting Michael's eyes. "It's kind of fucked up. I won't lie to you. We do have to be careful about who knows what. Some people know us as cousins; some people know us as a couple. Very few know us as both. We're really just two people, lucky enough to find each other. If it makes any difference, *he* seduced *me*."

"I can see that," Michael replied, still rubbing Drew's back. "But, yeah. It is kind of fucked up. Yeah. But . . . it's okay. I know what it's like to live with a secret, to be horrified by what you love and what you want. I'm the last person who should judge you."

Drew lightly kissed him. "As long as it doesn't drive you away," he said.

"No," Michael said, shaking his head, kissing him back. "I'm not going anywhere. And I won't tell."

When they looked up, Jesse was back with a towel over his wrist, a glass of water in one hand and the pipe in the other. "You guys look so beautiful together," he smiled, sitting down beside Michael. "Like a panther and a wolf, making out."

"Have you ever considered the fact that you might just listen to a little too much heavy metal?" Drew mused, rising up on one elbow and taking the towel. He roughly scrubbed the drying semen out of his chest hair.

"Clean water for Michael," Jesse declared, ignoring him. "But first . . ." He lit the pipe and took a draw from it, bent over, pressed his lips against Michael's, and exhaled the smoke into Michael's mouth. Michael inhaled and held the smoke, letting it trickle, spent, from between his lips.

Drew waved the smoke away from his face. "Michael, do you like ass?" he asked conversationally.

"I suppose so," Michael replied, furrowing his forehead.

"Do you like to fuck it, or do you like yours fucked?"

"I guess . . ." Michael shook his head, slurping his water. "I like them both?" He blushed.

"Do you like having your ass played with? I feel kind of bad that I stole your fuck." Drew grabbed a pillow and bunched it under his head.

"It's not the kind of thing you can steal," Michael said. "It was kind of nice to watch. It's been a long time since I watched."

"Can I play in your ass?" Jesse asked.

"Umm . . ." Michael put the water down on the bedside table, next to the tube of lubricant. "Sure." He was far from tired, far from satisfied, and with this new knowledge, felt restless all over again.

Jesse beamed. "Awesome. Oh, yay! I've been so looking forward to this. So . . . lie on your side, one knee up. . . ."

"He's very good at this," Drew said. "He'll make you come again, even if you think you can't."

"I know a thing or two about a thing or two," Jesse said. He chuckled. "I'll use a glove, if that makes you more comfortable."

"Uh . . . yeah, I guess . . ." Michael positioned himself as he'd been told, and Drew commenced kissing the curves of his ribs and waist and hips. His lips, surrounded by rapidly roughening sandpaper stubble, tickled deliciously. Jesse's gloved fingers were chilly on Michael's buttocks, and he couldn't help flinching. Jesse's response was a sound slap on the ass. Michael yelped, then groaned with delight.

"I think we've found something he likes," Drew mused. "You two have that in common."

"Relax, Michael," Jesse murmured. "Really relax."

Plastic-encased fingertips probed the surface of Michael's anus then, lubed slippery, worked their way inside. It was barely erotic, despite the eager, salacious look on Drew's face, until Jesse grasped Michael's buttock and pulled it aside, spreading him wide. Then he spit, and pushed it in with his fingers, and suddenly sex was all it was about.

"Oh my God," Michael moaned, exhaling long and slow, then abruptly gasping, "Oh!"

"Look at me," Drew said. His dark-hazel eyes had become predatory and intense, but it gave Michael something to focus on while Jesse thrust and wiggled two fingers into his asshole. "Are you sad that I didn't fuck you?" Drew asked, stroking himself. His penis, though softened, still dangled heavy and dark and thick. "You think you could take this cock?"

"I definitely wanna try," Michael slurred, half hypnotized.

"Really? I wonder. Are you brave enough? Are you strong enough? What do you think? I think that tonight, you weren't ready. You were scared."

"I didn't know who you were," Michael protested. "I didn't know   what . . . or how . . ."

"Of course you know who we are," Jesse put in, kissing Michael's buttock, then slapping and spreading it again, inserting his fingers up to the knuckle. "Flex on me. Yeah, like that. You knew what you wanted."

"He knows a little more now," Drew admitted. "Somebody's kind of a snoop, isn't he?"

"Blame the card in the fruit basket," Michael gasped. "Not me."

Jesse made an impatient noise. "Whatever," he said. He gently added another finger, using the tip of his middle finger to stroke Michael's prostate. Michael groaned helplessly. Three fingers already. Maybe he was more ready than he had ever thought. "I see you haven't left," Jesse added.

"No—no—you're amazing," Michael protested.

"He loves you," Drew said.

"Uh-huh," Jesse replied calmly, fingers in and out and in deeper. "And I love him."

To Michael's surprise, that made Drew smile, a warm, generous, open smile. "Good," he said. He crawled down the bed, pressed his face into Michael's groin, dangling his cock inches from Michael's face. Michael didn't strain up to meet it, but now and then, the tip brushed against his cheek, his upper lip, allowing him to flick out his tongue and touch it, taste the trace of latex and sperm on its skin.

Somehow, he fell into the music: a lazy, snaky, vintage funk groove, instrumental, alto sax and congas and marimba, almost sleazy and yet not quite. It was a perfect reflection of the physical sensations he experienced. Jesse murmured something incomprehensible, spread his fingers, and spit again, right into him this time. Michael felt the warm saliva drip inside him. Jesse could see into him, could taste the inside of him if he wanted to, could offer him up to receive any cock or finger or object he wished. "Harder," Michael begged. "Harder. Faster." Drew's soft cock filled his mouth before he could say any more, and Jesse's fingers filled his anus, thrusting in just deep enough to hit his locus of hypersensitivity every other time, drawing the pleasure out, making Michael long for those occasional shocks of bliss.

"Ah! That!" he cried out, suddenly, reaching behind him, grabbing Jesse's wrist, keeping his hand in place buried inside, all of it but the thumb, pressing down on his perineum. Surrendering to the quivering electricity chasing itself around his groin, seeking release, Michael grabbed his cock and jerked the head against his palm until he had a handful of sticky milk and honey. "My God, yes," he mumbled. "My God, yes. *Ah*. Ah—ah—*ahhh*."

"That's it," Drew replied, "I told you he could do it. Jesse's good."

"I trained with the best," Jesse said.

Michael smiled into the bedspread. He had never doubted it. Now he felt drained in the most wonderful way, like the moments after a fever breaks and the overflowing wellspring of peace and relief almost makes the previous hours of suffering worth going through.

Jesse drew his hand out and sighed, yawning expansively. "I'm sleepy," he said plainly. He snapped the glove off, and it went to the same secret chamber underneath the bed. Michael was too tired and content to care about the specifics. Jesse handed him the damp, rust-colored towel Michael had earlier been wearing as a sarong, settled down into Michael's arms, and curled up, holding him close. Michael chuckled; Jesse really was greedy.

"You're both done," Drew remarked. He got up and fetched a light knitted blanket from the other room (Was that a closet? It was immense.) and draped it over them. "Nap time."

The bedroom lights dimmed all the way to total darkness. Drew tucked himself on Jesse's other side, containing him, fingertips on Michael's thigh. Almost immediately Jesse began snoring, quietly, charmingly, like a puppy. Drew poked him until he rolled over a bit, still holding on to Michael, and the snoring stopped. "He always snores when he smokes weed," Drew explained. "Don't let him roll over onto his back or he'll keep you awake all night. That's why I made him stop smoking cigarettes. I need sleep sometimes."

"I don't think a concrete cutter could keep me awake," Michael murmured. "I think you took care of any insomnia I might have."

"You're lucky," Drew said. "I'd have loved to come again. No way, though, not after the way I drank tonight. We're fortunate to get one."

"I hope it was a good one," Michael said.

"Incredible," Drew replied, fingers circling on Michael's

shoulder.

"You're not upset about the show?"

Drew rolled his eyes, their surfaces gleaming in the dim glow coming through the paper screens. "No point in getting upset," he said. "It is what it is. I've lost more money before, and I didn't even get the satisfaction of seeing a show out of it. It's okay; I'm not in that business to make money. I want to nurture talent. Like yours."

"Thanks for the chance," Michael murmured.

Drew kissed the back of Jesse's head. "I can't reach you without disturbing him," he said. "Can you feel it when I do that?"

"The kiss? Yeah."

"Good." He pressed another kiss onto Jesse, who stirred, but didn't wake. Michael hugged the small, slight, scarred body in his arms. When Drew's voice rose again, it took Michael by surprise. "*Are you in love with him?*"

Michael's eyes opened, but there was nothing in particular to see in the dark, only Jesse's serious, relaxed, sleeping face. What could he say? He was already in it, and in Drew's bed. "Yeah," Michael said softly. "As far as I understand it. Is that okay with you?"

"Yes," Drew whispered. "It's okay."

9. SIDEWAYS.

The sound of a toilet flushing yanked Jesse awake, though he was muddle-headed and achy enough for the interruption of his sleep to physically hurt. He groaned and rolled over, flinging out one arm, but grasped only a cool, squishy pillow to hold against his face as a comforting shield. It was almost enough, but the quiet tugging sounds of Drew tying his running shoes made Jesse realize that he was now alone in bed.

Jesse opened one eye at Drew. He didn't want to notice, but the glowing hands of the clock on the bookshelf pointed at five – almost five – and eleven. "Where's Michael?" he mumbled.

In the indigo shadows of the light before dawn, Drew was a glowing avatar of white T-shirt and silvery shorts. "He was gone when I woke up," Drew replied, voice low, respecting the quiet. By the tone of his voice, he was just as drowsy.

"Don't run," Jesse yawned, closing his eyes. "It's Saturday. Come back to bed."

"Not today, Jess," Drew said. "I've got golf today. Get some sleep."

Jesse turned his face away and pressed the pillow more firmly into his face. That hadn't changed, anyway. He didn't know why he'd even bothered to ask. "Fuck you, you're stupid," he mumbled. As he sank back into sleep, Jesse replayed the memories of Michael's cock, Michael's orgasmic grimace, the prickly, soft hair on Michael's ass that he'd fucked, the way Michael had sucked the plums off his fingers.

It was nearly the same time when Michael made it home. At least it was before dawn. He needed to be in bed before the sun came up and the world became ordinary again. He couldn't take the return of that world yet. He couldn't stomach the idea of waking up in their bed and having to either smile and pretend that this was so normal, so mundane, or worse, to wake to awkwardness and remorse.

Back in Drew's bed, he had actually passed out for a little while. He couldn't help it, tipsy, drained of every tension, drenched in pot smoke and armpit sweat and the harmonic rhythm of their breaths. He would not think in terms of love, no matter how freely they flung the word around. It couldn't mean anything, and he shouldn't have said it himself. He had gotten up silently, refusing himself a sight of them sleeping together, telling himself it was too dark to see anything. He found his clothes without trouble and put them on in the living room, sliding into his shoes while standing on a rug. Slipping through the faintly humming kitchen, he kept his eyes trained away from the remains of the gift basket. He couldn't stomach that, either. He needed sleep in his own bed before any of this could have happened.

The subway had taken a long time to come and a longer time to get uptown. His eyes felt like crumpled cellophane, his face weighted into a miserable, bitter frown, eyes half-lidded against the flashing semi-nothingness through the windows. He'd made his way up endless stairs and out onto the street, the sky the color of lapis lazuli, the city beginning to wake. He walked the last few blocks as fast as he could, feeling like a ghoul desperate to elude the sun.

He made it, just barely. In his apartment, which now seemed cramped and cluttered, he toed off his shoes and hit play on an ambient music mix on his computer, volume low on the external speakers. The music continued humming as the image on the monitor switched to a pattern of circuitry, and finally winked itself off. He undressed in bed, tossing out garments as he removed them, yawning viciously, jaw cracking. His lips were dry. He should have gotten a kiss before he left. But then . . . he might have met Jesse's eyes, or Drew's, and had to explain, justify his presence. His absence. His existence and his excuses.

He tried to locate the lip balm on his bedside table, but fell asleep before he could do more than reach for it.

When he woke again, deeply refreshed, he lay in bed for a long while, chin resting on his crossed forearms, pensively appreciative of the bright sunlight hiding behind the blinds. He thought of the kisses he wanted, rubbing his dry lips, against the hair on his arms.

As morning exercise, Michael performed sun salutations in an actual beam of sunlight, a rare seasonal treat given the position of his window and the buildings surrounding his own. His muscles and tendons responded eagerly, and he was soon brimming with strength and resilience. He promised himself a swim later, during the heat of the day, before he made his way to the theater and *Viridian*'s second night, and sometime in there, a good solid spank session to the memories of last night.

A small splash of dread and anxiety washed over him. What had he done? How was he supposed to look Jesse in the eye the day after a night of filth and glory like that? But how could he *not*? Dealing with Jesse again after they'd lightly fooled around. . . . Well, that was different. That was playful and casual. Last night, though— that was the opposite of casual. It amazed him to remember the depravity, the weed-hazy descent, the eager slurping of Drew's tongue on Jesse's asshole. . . . Even the memory was too intense for him to handle. He'd now seen the way Jesse fucked, the way his balls dipped and bounced against Drew's thighs, heard his desperate choked moans as he took all the cock he could. He had looked into Drew's eyes as he fucked Jesse, and seen a smoldering message in those eyes. But now, Michael was unsure of how to interpret it.

Cousins.

He still couldn't approach *that* in his mind. First, he needed to resume his normal life. The yoga had helped, but it wasn't quite enough. Michael put the kettle on to make green tea and sat in front of his computer, keying up a terminal window to check his email. At the top of the list were a few dull administrative ones from school, a message from his bank, a digest from the Ninja Tune mailing list. Below that, their timestamps all from late last night, were a dozen messages from unfamiliar email addresses. *Great lighting design! Amazing design on* Viridian*! Best thing about the show.* He recognized one address, that of his photonics professor at CCNY, the one with whom he'd had screaming arguments about aesthetics versus funding.

Michael opened the message and read it, his head slowly tilting to one side.

Great design work. I'm impressed. You were wasted on academics.

"Wow," Michael murmured. His face ached, and he had to rub against it with the palm of his hand before he realized that he was grinning. "I actually did it."

Michael read through several more of the positive emails, taking a moment to reply in thanks to every one. Puffed with altruism and pride, he went back to his neglected task of preparing tea. He was supposed to be of calm mind while doing this, but he kept breaking into song. " *'I'm in love with your brother—what's his name?* '" he purled, off-key, whisking matcha into a little bowl and dousing the powder with boiling water. " *'I thought I'd come by to see him again . . . I thought I'd come by.* '"

When the tea was ready to drink, Michael sat up on his knees on his yoga mat, bold in his nakedness, soaking in the sun on his belly and thighs. He held up the tea in tribute. He told himself that it was to the sun, but he knew it was to himself. He deserved to celebrate himself. He raised the tea bowl to gulp down the hot, bitter, perfumed fluid and take its energy into himself.

He barely had the rim to his lips before his phone rang. Startled, he burnt his mouth on the bowl's interior, and a gasp of surprise hurled hot tea down his windpipe. "*Spllpf . . .! Fuck!* Shit! Ahh! Fuck!" He had to stand up and bend over, coughing, head between his legs, for the fluid to work its way out of his trachea. On the fifth ring, just before the call would automatically go to voicemail, he managed to snatch the phone from the bedside table—beside the lip balm, he saw now—and answered it without looking at it. "Michael Kaminsky," he snapped.

"Sweetheart, it's Mary? Your mother? I haven't heard from you lately. Your father and I miss you very much. He wants me to tell you hello from him; he's taking a little nap right now. And I know that he's as curious as I am about that play you were going to work on? What's it called again? *Meridian?*"

Michael clamped his fingers across his forehead, and dug into his temples with the fingertips. He waited for several seconds, making sure she wasn't going to talk again, before answering in a voice that sounded like a flooded carburetor. "It's—ahem—*Viridian*, Mother."

"Oh, yes, that's right. How is it going? Have you made some new friends?"

He laughed sharply, belatedly reining himself back in. "Yes, Mother. I have. The play opened last night, no major problems. Nothing I couldn't handle."

"That's lovely, Michael. Please send me a program for my scrapbook. Mrs. Ohlmeyer will be so jealous. We're both very proud of you. Well, you sound healthy. Are you doing all right? Are you going to Mass?"

"I don't go to church anymore, Mother. You know that."

"Mm-hmm," she responded, making it clear that she wasn't listening. "I'm glad to hear that you're still doing all right on your own. Your father and I are getting along fine on our own, too, though of course, it'd be easier if you were here."

"No—" Michael started to say, then cut himself off and sighed. "Yes, I know. I'm sorry. I need to do this, though. I'll make sure you don't want for anything, but I can't be there. There's so much more that I need. Didn't you ever—"

His mother continued, hardly pausing for breath. "I planted some strawberries, but I can't seem to get them to thrive. The blackberries, needless to say, have gone absolutely wild. Your father can't seem to control them. That nice neighbor boy, Edward—You remember Edward, don't you?— He comes by once in a while with his tools, but he can only do so much . . . ."

"Of course I remember Edward," Michael replied dully. Would never forget. Edward and the baseball player's butt in his tight jeans, ten years out of style, football jersey, thick, rough blond hair. Edward, who Michael had tutored for three weeks, until Edward held him down and shoved his smelly dick into Michael's mouth, and like an idiot, Michael had sucked it and was grateful and felt his life would change. Edward who had scratched the word "pansy" into the paint on Michael's locker on the first day of senior year, and so Michael had to see it every day. Everyone had to see him standing next to it every day, and so it became his name. "Is he still an asshole?"

"Now, Michael, never use that kind of language. I am your

mother and he is helpful. He's got a family of his own now, and they just live across the way, with his mother. I used to sit for baby Kalisha, before the problems started with my health. Please, just do this one thing for me, would you? Go to Mass and light a devotional to me and to your father. It would mean so much, and it may lift your spirit to go to confession. Just once, just for me. Would you, please?"

"Mom, please—"

"It's not as though you haven't got anything to confess."

He held the phone at arm's length and shouted at it. "I'll send you a program from the show," he declared, "but right now, I gotta run. I'm going out for lunch. Love to Dad, 'bye now." He flung the phone away from him, the plastic handset bouncing across the surface of his bed and hitting the wall.

Returning to his yoga mat, Michael positioned himself in a lotus and forced his breathing to return to his control, blinking away the prickle of tears under his eyelids, exhaling the urge to scream, returning himself to a closed system, armored, protected. In the back of his mind, some other part of him said, *Forgive me, Father, for I have sinned . . . and how swift and spiteful your retribution!*

After his usual Saturday massage and grooming had been completed, Drew climbed into the back seat of a maroon Lexus sedan, one of the Morrow company cars. It had been dispatched to ferry him all the way out to West Nyack to play golf with the CFO. "*Dobre utra,* Vaydm," Drew said to the driver, buckling up and slipping his shoes off.

"Good morning, Mr. Farrow," replied the driver. He was a tow-headed, constantly smiling Ukrainian who once drove international diplomats to and from the airport in Kiev. He was delighted to have an American job that paid ten times as much for half the driving and substantially less personal risk. His English wasn't very extensive, and Drew had only mistakenly tried to cruise him once, which Vadym had discreetly ignored. Vadym was one of Drew's preferred drivers because he didn't attempt conversation, allowing Drew much-needed time alone with his files or his thoughts.

This morning Drew had no files to review, and he spent the trip glancing uneasily at his reflection in the window. He wasn't surprised that fatigue showed on his face. Even after a ten-mile run and two huge cups of green tea, he had fallen asleep once on the massage table and again while his hair was being cut. He'd gotten maybe three hours of sleep the night before, watching Jesse and Michael facing each other, gently trading kisses, then swiftly melting into sleep. Eventually Michael had turned over, turned away, and only then had Drew been able to fall asleep himself.

In the back of the Lexus, Drew sipped bittersweet green juice, now and then holding the glass bottle against his tingling cheeks, glad to be alone and insulated in the muffled white noise that passed for silence. He thought about texting Michael but hesitated, examining their relationship, trying to decide if such a thing was appropriate. He paid Michael. Michael was a pleasant distraction from the everyday. Michael was in love with Jesse. Michael's lust for Jesse made Drew want to fuck Jesse, but Michael also, to test them against each other, to put them in their place, force them to make up their minds about him and each other. Michael was a spice, an irritant interpreted as pleasurable.

Drew lay his hand flat on his thigh and tightened his jaw. The first thought Jesse had had when he woke up was "Where's Michael?" Not "Come back to bed and kiss me," or "Breakfast?" or "I loved sharing you." Only "Where's Michael," the elusive object of desire, already gone when the quiet alarm on Drew's Blackberry woke him at 4:45. And Jesse's curse had cut deep enough to linger. Drew sighed irritably. That stupid play was costing him more than money.

The Lexus wound its way onto the luxurious grounds of the golf club, and paused on the asphalt drive that stretched in front of the palatial clubhouse. "*Spasiba*," Drew thanked Vaydm, slipped his loafers back on.

Chuck Levine, the chief financial officer of Morrow Claymore Advisors and Drew's immediate superior, sat in a soft leather chair in one of the clubhouse's bars. "Afternoon," Levine said, his attention focused on his Blackberry. The gray-haired executive's voice was dry and distant. "Hungry?"

"Definitely," Drew replied. "I'm thinking a steak sandwich."

"Lobster risotto for me. Too hot for red meat today."

"You're probably right," Drew assented, relaxing his face into a genuine smile in case Levine looked up. "But the stomach wants what it wants."

Drew was an indifferent golf player, only as competent as he needed to be. He had never enjoyed the sport, though he had played in high school at his father's insistence. *You don't have to be good,* Alistair had pointed out, *but you better know how to play if you're going to get anywhere in the boardroom.* His father had been right, of course. He was right about everything regarding business. That was his game of choice. He was a gifted tactician, and had endless stamina. Drew had inherited the stamina, but he could never come close to matching his father in the area of sports. He'd just pushed himself to be good enough to play, or he'd have almost never seen his father at all.

"Nice shot, Farrow," Levine said. "You're on the green. Another round of drinks? That Pimm's Cup you were having looked pretty good."

"I like that idea."

Drew neatly sank his shot, Levine following, and they waited in the shade for their drinks to arrive. "I was corresponding with Richards and Iommi just before you arrived," Levine said, wiping his brow with a handkerchief. "The Indianapolis deal is all but inked."

"That's excellent news."

"I need you to go to Indianapolis and make sure they've got the right pens."

Drew couldn't stop the scowl that stretched his lips thin. "But—sir," he protested.

"Uh-oh. When you call me 'sir,' I get scared. What's the problem, Farrow?" Levine accepted a tankard of Pimm's Cup and raised his eyebrows.

"It just seems a little—excessive, doesn't ito send a managing executive to finalize a deal that . . . I don't know, why don't we send Dolores Velez on that? She's been doing great work, and jockeying for an opportunity to make a splash."

"I don't want Velez on this," Levine said. "Sure, she's good, but she's good in town, with paperwork. She's more of an administrator, as I see it. We need her here to get the tax strategy prepared for this year's 4Q."

"What about Sorsky?" Drew knew he was starting to sound whiny, but the idea of going to Indianapolis was about as appealing as brushing his teeth with water from the toilet. "Sorsky's a great client services liaison."

"Farrow, I'm surprised at you," Levine replied mildly. "I should think you'd be all over this gig. This really needs a personal touch. These guys have mostly dealt with you. Now, I've made my decision. What's with the long face? It's only ten days for eight million in billing." Levine handed his drink to his caddy and fixed Drew with the full intensity of his we're-not-really-equals stare. "What's up with you? You got something more important to do? A new girlfriend, maybe? Huh? I know how demanding they can be when they've just fallen for you."

The Pimm's now tasted like cucumber acid, like the vegetal chemical peel that the spa facialist liked to put on him when he tried to scour away the hint of wrinkles and worry lines. Drew passed off his drink as well, turning away and grimacing out of Levine's sight. Levine knew that Drew was divorced, and had remained unmarried, but that was as far as it went. He didn't know anything substantial about Drew's personal life; almost no one at Morrow did. Bert Sorsky had a strong suspicion that his boss might be more inclined towards men than women, even going so far as to expressly say to Drew that he had no problem with it. Even to that, Drew had only replied, "That's very open-minded of you." He walked on hot coals every time he entered that office. Every time he met someone he knew from work, when Jesse was with him, the coals crackled and glowed and threatened to burn through the ground and pitch him into anthracite darkness. He introduced Jesse as his cousin or, if Jesse had been demonstrative in their presence, merely as his friend, his housemate. He couldn't risk anyone knowing more. He couldn't risk his position at Morrow, or Denisse, or Lake and Monty. Imagine if Lake and Monty's teachers knew about Jesse.

Even Michael had run off, too, after all.

"Yeah, nothing like that," Drew said finally, shrugging. "It's just . . . Indianapolis." He made a face.

"You don't know shit about it," Levine replied, laughing.

Friendly, unsuspecting. "You're Upper East Side, through and through. It'll be good for you, take you out of your comfort zone. I don't send you on too many business trips; maybe I should send you more."

"Sure," Drew grinned, following along, "I'm sure that'd be fine."

"You never know, you might meet the love of your life there. Or at least a nice waitress with a great set of tits. Or both! I met my wife on a business trip, you know." Levine gave Drew a friendly slap on the shoulder before getting back into the golf cart.

Drew could barely process that quick, manly gesture of connection and support, a rarity from the ordinarily brusque Levine. He sat in the back of the absurd little vehicle and let his eyes unfocus until he saw only a vivid green blur passing by, his thoughts focused inward. He had to leave town, and leave Jesse and Michael together. So much could happen in ten days. He might come back from Indiana to find the house empty, and the two boys run away together. Jesse might fuck something up and drive Michael away altogether. Or Michael could just come to his senses and decide he wanted nothing more to do with a couple of incestuous alcoholics. There was nothing Drew could do about it. There never had been.

He kept the smile fixed on his face and ordered a double scotch on the rocks.

Cell phone use was expressly discouraged on the links at this club. By the time they made it to the eighteenth hole, Drew didn't feel like calling Jesse, and had mostly forgotten that he had anything to say to him. He did think about calling Michael, sending him a text, telling him about Indianapolis, asking him if they'd see each other when Drew returned.

Enervated by the alcohol, Drew decided against it. It'd be better to talk it over in person, where they could be near each other. If he could look into Michael's eyes, be within reach of him, just touch him one more time . . . maybe it'd be enough so that Michael wouldn't just forget him, since Jesse was going to be right there, the whole time.

There had to be *something* he could do.

+

Now and then Jesse woke from his slumber, got up for a drink of water or a pee, and stumbled back to bed and to sleep. He shut out the brightness of the bedroom, catching summer sunlight through walls of window glass, with a pillow over his eyes. In an ecstasy of rest and naughtiness, he lost track of how many times this happened.

He repeated this until almost noon, when his brain finally refused any more sleep. He took a leisurely shower in Drew's black marble bathroom, washing away slug trails of semen and a night's shared sweat, humming to himself, stroking himself off with a soapy hand. His dick and his butthole ached. He felt divinely accomplished.

Two at a time. He'd had both his lovers, learning each other through him, with his body a conduit. Two cocks in his body at once, for the first time in his life, in perfect and beautiful rhythm, even if only for a few careful moments before lust and longing shook it apart. He wanted to do it again, switch it up, with Drew in the middle, maybe. He didn't think Michael was ready for that yet, although with his instincts, his rigidly controlled longing, he might teach both Drew and Jesse a thing or two. Jesse sighed and smiled, rolling his thumb around the soft but responsive tip of his penis, pretending it was Michael's tongue, the splash of water on his shoulders becoming Drew's arms around him, the whisper of the spigot Drew's voice in his ear.

Drew had left a note on the kitchen table: *Golf w/ Levine*. Drew played golf with his boss regularly, if not often. The experience always left Drew prickly, snappish, and oftentimes possessed of an intense, almost medicinal need to get blind drunk. Jesse understood this state and didn't judge it, but he didn't feel like dealing with it today. He had a delivery shift scheduled, starting at two, and he would probably come home feeling pretty much like Drew would, if he didn't just start drinking before he went home.

But maybe not today. It was a beautiful day, and Jesse felt fantastic already. He decided that he would default to happiness.

With buttered toast and a pear, Jesse sat down at the table in the kitchen nook, got his phone, and called Michael.

Michael picked up on the first ring, while Jesse's mouth was still full of pear. "Michael Kaminsky." He sounded grumpy.

"Hey, girl, it's me."

"Don't call me that," Michael snapped harshly. "Don't you *ever* call me that."

"Whoa, calm down." Jesse barked an embarrassed laugh. Silence on Michael's end, maybe an aggrieved sigh. "Sorry. Just fuckin' with you. I was just gonna say you sounded like the Batman . . ." More silence. Jesse cleared his throat. How could he be unhappy after last night? Was he hungover? "So, um, how's it going?"

"It's—fine."

"You don't sound fine."

"Hasn't been the greatest day so far." Michael bit off his words. He had never sounded so sarcastic.

Jesse countered with softness. "Really? I'm sorry. What's the matter?" When he got no reply, he pressed on, "Were you looking at the reviews?"

"No." Michael sighed exasperatedly. "It's fine. I don't care." Again, silence.

"Oh," said Jesse again, just to take advantage of the connection. He hated sitting on the phone with nobody saying anything. It seemed like such a waste. "Um. Well, I was just calling to say hi, and, um . . ."

"Thanks, Jesse. I've got to go. I'm sorry."

"Well, okay, see you later, maybe . . .?"

"Sure," said Michael. "See you. Goodbye." He hung up.

"Whatever the fuck that was," Jesse whispered to himself, closing the slim case of his phone and setting it down beside him. A dull pain spread throughout his chest, settling into a cold knot in his stomach. His face stung, as if he'd been slapped. "Fuck you, too," he said aloud, wishing Michael could hear it. "*Girlfriend.* Giant faggot. Pansy pink fucking queer. *Girl.* Fucking bitch."

The fragrant remainder of the juicy pear disgusted him. He put it in the fridge, stood at the sink, and gargled water to wash the sweet, mealy taste from his mouth. So okay, that was that. Michael didn't like him anymore. Simple. It shouldn't have been a surprise. Jesse would have to survive that, just as he'd survived everything else that had happened to him. Stone-faced, he pulled on some cycling clothes and shoes, secured his helmet, and got his bike from the locked back deck, escaping out into the sunshine.

Genova had changed a bit since Jesse had last worked there. Now he had to wear a uniform shirt, for one thing, and they had increased their delivery radius by two miles. None of the people who used to pedal for them still worked there; turnover was constant. Jesse filled out new paperwork, glancing occasionally at the other delivery riders, and a delivery van driver, assessing their morale. The driver was a silent Guatemalan man, the rider a peroxide-platinum blonde punk chick with bone spirals in her stretched earlobes. The driver looked dazed and glassy, the punk pissed-off. Jesse nabbed the items on his first pick list, double-checked his toe clips, and rode off, eager to be away from that vibe.

He was out of shape. Even if he biked a lot even when he wasn't working delivery, it was nothing like the combination of speed and strategy necessary when trying to service dozens of neighborhoods while towing a cart behind him. By his first break, he was so tired he laid on the sidewalk in the shade, flicking drops of water at his own face. The punk chick gave him one of her gel nutrient packs, reminding him to drink more water and eat almonds, and somehow the second half of the day was easier.

By his lunch break, Jesse felt that he was back in the swing of things. Adrenaline was sufficient to keep him going for the next few hours, he could take the subway home, and then soak his aching body in an Epsom salt bath before going to sleep. His last delivery before the break took him well downtown into the East Village, on Third. Jesse double-checked the time on his phone. The theater, only a few blocks away, would be a hub of activity; twenty minutes to showtime, twenty-five to curtain. Jesse sat still on his bike, one foot on the ground, thinking it over for sixty full seconds before he set the pedals in motion again with nearly numb legs, the blocks between that alley and the theater skimming away underneath him.

Back stage door was open as usual. Inside the theater, the atmosphere was quiet and strained, no joking or raised voices, everyone on polite best behavior. Jesse felt disoriented. Everything really *had* changed last night.

"Hey, what are you doing here? You don't work here anymore." Kat, the stage manager, put her hands on her hips, blocking his progress.

"I just need to holla at Michael right quick," Jesse replied mildly. He put his hands gently on her shoulders, and just as gently moved her out of the way.

"Watch it, asshole!"

"Just, like, two minutes," Jesse said, holding up two fingers, but not really looking at her. He kept walking until he reached the lighting board.

At the sight of Michael, closing the plastic cover of the DMX console and reattaching the power cables, Jesse's throat swelled with confused emotion. Michael looked amazing—an active sex life did wonders for his skin—and yet so tense, eyes not glazed with excitement, but dull and glassy as if trying to dissociate. Even the headset he wore looked good. "Hey," Jesse announced to him, just loud enough to be heard. "Came by to see you for a minute."

Michael glanced up at him and nodded. "Hello," he said, calmly, coldly, as if Jesse was just anybody.

Jesse didn't want to betray the effects of the ripping ache in his torso, so he just nodded back. "You okay?" he asked neutrally.

"Fine," Michael replied. He didn't respond to Jesse's dead tone. "You maybe shouldn't be here."

"I had a minute," Jesse said casually. "Just wanted to come ask you, what's your fucking problem?"

"No problem," said Michael, smooth, unruffled. "I'm fine."

"I'm okay, too, thanks for asking," Jesse said. Michael only nodded. "So . . . that's it, huh? You're just done?"

"Who said that?" Michael asked, the corners of his mouth rising.

"You're not acting like—"

Raising his hand, Michael interrupted, "No, I'm *not* acting 'like.'"

"It's just—I kinda dig you, okay?" Jesse said hoarsely.

"Yeah, I know," Michael said, nodding to someone upstage and turning to the console. Michael checked his audio and fixed Jesse with a pitying look. Contemptuous or not, Jesse couldn't tell, but it was definitely superior. Sometimes Drew looked at Jesse that way, and it could drive Jesse into violent frenzies of rage. He couldn't just go off on Michael though, not right now, not here, not after last night. *Last night!* Jesse felt a tiny muscle in his face involuntarily tighten, but he met Michael's gaze, unblinking.

Again, Michael didn't intimidate. "Later," he said. "Okay? I've got to do this show. Curtain's in seven minutes."

"That's fine," Jesse said calmly. "Call me later."

"When there's time. Not today." Michael rolled his eyes a little. "I like you, too," he said grudgingly. "Just—go away right now."

"We've already forgotten how to talk to each other," Jesse remarked.

Michael grimaced suddenly, as if he had tasted something bitter. Like a bug in a salad. "Jesus, Jesse. Step back. You're a basket case."

"Yeah," Jesse admitted. "Yeah, I kind of am. Sorry. I got emotions an' shit." He shrugged. "Anyway, call me, okay? When you're okay. Ready to talk, or whatever." He walked backwards, babbling, with set movers herding him towards the back door and shoving him out of it. The door swung closed and locked behind him.

As he wolfed down two tofu burritos, Jesse flicked off a quick text message to Charlie. **Had best sex ever and fell apart in front of new guy in same 24 hrs. I need a 40 and 12 hrs sleep. Love, your friendly local fuckup. Back to work.**

+

After the sun had finally set, the sky cooled to darkness, Drew bent over his laptop.

He sat up in bed, sprawling more than anything else, legs open and belly skin rumpled, wearing his glasses and cotton boxers, his hair disheveled. For a few hours, he had skimmed through an Indianapolis local newspaper's online edition, mining for facts he could convert to small talk next week. Jesse was in the TV room, probably passed out. He had come home a little before nine, clutching a beer bottle in a paper sack, snapped, "Leave me alone, don't wanna talk about it," and retreated into the bath. Drew didn't want to talk, either, so he ignored his cousin, left him to groan and hiss in the bath, and later, to slump on the couch in front of the TV. He'd regret sleeping on the couch instead of in bed, but that was for Jesse to figure out.

At a corner of Drew's laptop screen, his instant messenger program's icon turned green and flashed eagerly. Launching the application, Drew didn't recognize the user name trying to contact him: **ventolin**. Could be someone who dredged up Drew's user ID from last year's fun but ultimately disappointing week experimenting with text sex with strangers on Gay.com. He wasn't going to meet up with any tricks in real life, so what was the point?

Hello?

Hi. It's Michael.

Drew laughed quietly, grinning with the jolt of pleasure he got when he saw Michael's name. **Hey,** he typed back. **I was just getting bored with the computer. Guess I'm not anymore!**

I'll take that as a compliment.

How are you? Missed you this morning.

Sorry, had to go. Got overwhelmed. Needed my own pillow.

Understandable. Drew scratched his trimmed armpit hair and yawned. **What's up?**

Can't sleep. I feel bad. I think I was shitty to Jesse today.

Oh? He probably deserved it, ha ha.

Is he crazy, seriously? I can't tell if he's like a borderline personality or what.

Drew rolled his eyes. **No more psycho than anybody, just unfiltered. What'd he do this time?**

He just called me at a bad time today. I had just gotten off the phone with my mother. She's like a travel agent for guilt trips.

Sounds stressful.

I haven't come out to her yet. I know, it's dumb.

Drew smiled sadly and hesitated for a full minute before replying, **I'm not out to my mother, either. I tried once but she really just doesn't want to know.**

So she doesn't know about you and J???

Double ditto doesn't want to know. Don't want her to, either. None of her business.

Wow, Michael typed. **Anyway J came by the theater just before curtain and was acting all emo, super needy. It was weird. And gross.**

Drew sighed. **Yeah, well. He doesn't like to take 'slow down' for an answer. He did the same thing with me. Guess he really likes you. I don't blame him.**

The online conversation lapsed for a few agonizingly long minutes. Drew almost began to chew one of his fingernails, quickly substituting the cap end of his cheap fountain pen. He took it upon himself to write, **I can think of other ways to pass the time, since neither of us is sleeping.**

Like what?

So innocent. Or at least, pretending to be, and that was just as good. Drew slipped his hand through the waistband of his boxers and felt himself up. He wasn't hard in the slightest, but even the thought of anything sexual involving Michael sent a warm flush of blood to his skin. **Do you have a webcam? You could take a picture and send it to me. Bend over in front of it, click click.**

Michael again didn't reply for a long time, giving Drew an opportunity to stroke himself vigorously and with purpose. He imagined Michael disrobing, touching himself in a similar way, perhaps getting into position with his dark and hairy asshole pointed towards the computer monitor. When Drew saw the subtle flash of a new message, it seemed to hold a sharp erotic charge.

Then he read it. **I'm sorry, I really need to go to sleep now. I don't have an external webcam, but if you like, I'll get one for next time. I miss you, take care.**

"What?" Drew whispered incredulously, typing **wait!** "Are you serious?"

Michael had already logged off. Scowling, Drew typed, **You are the biggest, most infuriating cock tease in the world. I hope you have a wet dream tonight and end up with your own cum up your nose.** He hit return with vigor, sneering at the return message **ventolin is offline**. Still, there was a chance that Michael would see it next time he logged in. Drew thought to find his phone and call up the twerp, just to give him a piece of his mind, but his phone was all the way on the other side of the bedroom and his legs were too stiff to want to move.

Sighing, groaning with annoyance, Drew instead clicked on the bookmark for his current favorite porn website, the one that seemed to specialize in smooth-fleshed twink boys who often looked like Jesse, often contorted into somewhat painful-looking poses, their faces scored with strain. There was another version of the site with similar models, but their expressions were blank or calmly joyous, eyes imploring the camera, *I need you*. This site was in a Slavic language he didn't speak. It was perfect.

10. SPA DAY.

From a distance, Michael's vertical posture and preternatural stillness suggested a statue more than a living man, or even a mannequin. The modern mannequin posed at least a little, enough to show off the movement and drape of its clothing. Not Michael. He stood on the sidewalk at the address Drew had given him that morning, white earbuds snugly tucked into his neat pink ears, wearing a checked cotton shirt and lean black jeans, arms relaxed at his sides, as upright and unmoving as a lamppost. Drew was impressed by the strength necessary to hold so still. It must have been the yoga.

Drew strolled up from behind. "Hey, gorgeous."

All at once, the unmoving pillar unfurled like a stop-motion film of a lily bursting into bloom. Michael's limbs and face flickered into movement. "Oh! Hey! Hi!" he replied, grinning hugely, lowering his gaze. "How are you?" His face was unshaven. It was a good look for him.

"Glad to see you," Drew said.

Michael beamed. "I'm glad to see you, too," he said. "I'm feeling kind of weird, standing out here on the street." He glanced nervously around at the tall buildings surrounding them, the relatively spotless gutters and sparsely populated noontime sidewalks, as if he expected the wealth police to spring upon the interloper at any minute. It was curious; Jesse never had that look, and *he* had reason to. "I can't believe there's a bath house in *this* neighborhood," he remarked in disbelief.

Drew chuckled. "It's a day spa, not a bath house. I stopped doing the baths a long time ago."

"Oh, really?" Michael's tone was light and teasing. "I should think you'd be really good at it."

Drew shrugged. "I got sick of being good at cruising," he replied, walking down the block toward their destination. "It's not a very healthy scene. At least, not the way I was doing it. But I do like a massage and a sauna now and again, and I'm taking a day off."

"I thought you said you have to make sure you're back in the office by two," Michael said.

"Oh, yeah. I mean a day off from running."

"I didn't think you could take days off."

"No, you have to. You break down otherwise. It's too bad, although I would *like* to run every day. I used to, at first."

"What do you mean, at first? Like, when you were a toddler?" Michael snickered.

Drew raised his eyebrows. "You're quippy today," he remarked.

"I'm in a good mood."

"I'm glad. I ran track in high school, but I didn't start running seriously until about eleven years ago. I did it to get sober, actually."

"Meeting Jesse didn't help?"

"Oh, God, no. Not at first, anyway. Besides, running's lot more fun than AA."

"You're far from sober," Michael pointed out. "Should I be worried?"

"Nah, I'm all right. I just had to stop for a while—stop everything. Sex, drugs, alcohol, work, until I could learn some limits. Running will teach you limits, that's for sure. It worked; I'm not dead. In fact, I'm in the best shape of my life. And I don't drink *alone* anymore." Drew smiled. It was only slightly a lie. "That's the difference."

"Hmm," said Michael distantly. "It's true, you are in good shape. Pretty much all over."

"Thanks. So are you." Chuckling, Drew led the way into a

nearly undetectable side street, the stone and brick buildings fringed with ivy and awnings. "I think you're the first one I've, ah, brought over here. To this place."

"Make a trick feel special, wouldja." Michael's voice was nonchalant, but his eyes roamed over every detail of the little dead end half-street, from the blue sky overhead to the very clean sidewalks, and he kept his hands tucked deep into the pockets of his jeans, as if he kept the fact of Jesse hidden there.

"Just thought I'd show you a good time. Someplace where we could be alone. Together, for a little while."

"Somehow you always manage show me a good time," Michael said with a smile.

The entrance to Gullfoss, or whatever the spa was called this week, was located at the corner of the block, occupying the entire green space between massive old stone buildings. Without signage or number, it could be identified only by landmarks: A splotch of red paint on the sidewalk one paving stone before the half-street; the sculpture of a leaping dolphin, painted in chipped and chewy-looking red, barely visible behind a tangle of Japanese maple, ivy, and wrought iron. Drew punched a six-digit code into the lock on the front gate and let them into the mossy grounds. Michael immediately mounted the slate steps that led up to the house, but Drew pointed down the hill and said, "This way, sweetheart."

If anything visibly impressed Michael, it was this odd little wooded area, quiet in the center of midtown Manhattan, a peculiar maze of lichen and stone and phlox that only appeared to grow wild. An assortment of plants drenched the air with oxygen, and hidden sprinklers kept the air almost unpleasantly moist. A long, pitched-roofed house emerged gradually from the leaves. The exterior itself was low-slung, made of mossy, dark wood, hardly the height of a standard house. Most of Gullfoss was actually underground, built into the hill, its front wall carefully built around ancient-looking, gnarled tree roots. "This is crazy," Michael murmured.

Drew smiled. "It's a folly. Nobody can afford to keep the place running for long, so it's constantly changing hands. The remarkable thing about it is, nobody ever changes it. The only people who even know about it are the ones who've been brought here."

"So—it's *very* exclusive," Michael determined.

"Male only," Drew said. "Very, very, *very* high-end. Currently it's owned by one of my clients, and before that, it was owned by another, different one of my clients. Essentially it passes from hand to hand."

"Hmm."

"And the identity of these clients is one of my most critical professional secrets. Unknown even to my superiors. This is actually, professionally, none of their business. I just happen to be a member."

"And how is this not a bath house?" Michael tilted his head, blinking innocently.

"You're cute," Drew quipped. "I think I'll keep you." Michael only barely reacted to that statement. His eyes became momentarily vague, but just as quickly sharpened and focused again. "Follow my lead."

Walking into the semidarkness of the building, Drew had a momentary, dizzying pang of conflicted lust and guilt. That very morning, he'd woken up ferociously horny but done nothing about it, not even in the shower, not even touching the warm, unconscious figure of Jesse in the bed beside him. Like he was saving himself. Like he was planning all of this. Wasn't he? Why couldn't he just admit this to himself? He wasn't doing anything wrong. Planning a crime was not a crime.

What he planned, what he hoped, wasn't a *crime*, either. He wasn't doing anything wrong. He wasn't cheating on Jesse. This was not that. And he wasn't stealing from Jesse, either. Drew wasn't sure what this was, with Michael. But he wanted more of it; he wanted to play this game. It was more fun than he'd had in years.

He and Jesse hadn't spoken since Saturday morning. The younger man occupied his life now either sleeping or off somewhere on his bike. Drew had no idea what Jesse's hours were, or how much he was being paid; the only evidence that Jesse was even telling the truth about having the job were the half-dozen bags of food in the fridge and on the counters with the Genova logo imprinted on them, and how heavily Jesse slept. Drew had informed Jesse of the business trip by text, and received no reply. He shoved the twinge of worry down to the back closet in his mind. He wouldn't force Jesse to communicate, and for the moment, Drew had other things on his mind. *He can take care of himself,* Drew reminded himself. *He's almost thirty years old. It's time for him to manage complex issues on his own. And Michael. . . . Ah, Michael. He's with me right now.*

In the cedar and bamboo changing room, Michael and Drew shed their street clothes and exchanged them for identical short, black silk robes, chosen from neat shelves marked by size. At first Michael was hesitant about disrobing in front of Drew, but when Drew stripped down to nudity without hesitation, the younger man took off his glasses and began to undress. Drew watched him, smiling encouragingly. Michael said, hastily pulling on the robe, "Sorry. I don't know why I'm nervous. There's nobody here but us."

"Nobody here but us," said Drew, reaching out, casually grasping Michael's bare penis in his hand. Michael flinched in surprise, but did nothing to stop him.

"You just have such beautiful skin." He tentatively reached into Drew's robe and touched his dick in return, but not in such a way that he seemed like he wanted to. "Is this the kind of place where—"

"Of course it is," Drew said. "I wouldn't bring you here otherwise."

Michael removed his hand with a shaky laugh. . "And here I was thinking that you were just so perceptive and generous, springing for a massage, but all you want is a nooner."

Stepping closer, locking eyes with Michael, Drew put his hand back where it had been. Michael's cock was soft and cool to the touch. Drew wanted to soothe and warm it in his mouth. Instead, he withdrew his hand. "No, we *are* actually having massages," he corrected, softening his gaze. "A chance to just relax together and forget for a little while. This isn't just a fuck palace. I'm just saying it could be."

"I've always wanted to be a nooner," said Michael wistfully.

"Tie your robe," Drew said, chuckling. He stroked the fur on Michael's chest. "We can keep talking on the tables."

In one of the cozy massage rooms, Drew lay face-down on a padded table and his usual masseuse, a calm-faced young southeast Asian woman, discreetly tugged his robe up and tucked it around his buttocks. Michael sat in a reclining chair and another masseuse, a sixty-year-old Icelandic lady who had given Drew some of the best therapeutic massages he'd ever had, pulled up a stool next to him, making sure that she didn't interfere with their line of sight to each other. Drew closed his eyes, listening to the sound of oil being poured into and rubbed briskly between feminine hands, his body tensing in pleasurable anticipation.

As he felt the touch of hands on his feet, Drew sighed in satisfaction and continued talking as if he and Michael were the only ones in the room. "So, I'm going to be in Indianapolis on business from Wednesday through Tuesday."

"Uh, cool?" Michael gulped faintly, his right arm lost in the blur of rapidly rubbing hands.

"Not really. I'm not particularly excited about going," Drew added. "I've never been there before, I'm not particularly interested in the city, and to be honest, I don't really want to be away from *you* right now."

"Really?" Michael breathed, his voice pitched faintly higher. Drew couldn't help chuckling at his nervousness.

"Have you not had a massage before?"

"No. I mean, I have, but . . ." The Icelander pummeled Michael's flushed skin with her fingertips, and he laughed. "This is pretty intense."

"Not too hard?"

"Somehow, no."

"Good." Drew smiled at him. "I'll be quiet so you can concentrate."

"Right," Michael agreed, sighing, taking slow, deep breaths. His muscles slackened visibly and his posture became a sprawl, his thighs parting a bit, gapping the hem of his robe. Drew couldn't see underneath, but he studied the shadow, the surface of the silk on Michael's lap, alert for any sign of arousal.

The massages were brief, but powerful. Drew's thighs felt chemically tenderized, and his legs threatened to buckle under him when he first tried to stand up. Despite the Asian woman's slight form, her fingers were like steel cables. "Now we take a quick shower and do thirty minutes of sauna," Drew directed, nodding to the masseurs as they left the room. "Or, as close to thirty minutes as we can stand. Usually I can do all thirty, but it's okay if you can't. If you get too hot, go back to the shower and stand under the cold water for a while—"

"Yeah, I know how to do sauna," Michael said, adding under his breath, "It's not like *I've* never been to the baths."

"Well, it's not *quite* the same."

Michael's eyes sparkled. "I'm sorry, Drew, but this is totally a bath house. It's just . . ." He followed closely behind Drew as he headed to the slate-tiled showers. A skylight promised bright blue skies outdoors. "...super nice. And discreet, and private. And expensive, I'm sure. You like that, huh?"

"'Course I do," Drew admitted, shedding his robe and turning on the water.

"Have you ever run into one of your colleagues here?" Michael took off his robe too, neatly hanging it on an available hook instead of just tossing it on the ground the way Drew had. His red, oil-slick, arms contrasted starkly with his pale torso.

"No," Drew said. "They don't really know about it. To them, this is just one of my solo projects. The previous owner needed to sell it in a hurry, so I secured a new buyer, and helped *him* restructure its financing. It was a win all the way around."

"You like to win," Michael said, turning his face into the water.

"*You* like to figure things out," was Drew's rejoinder.

"Is that okay with you?"

"I love it," Drew replied. "I love your brain."

Michael laughed. "Thanks, I guess." He ran a hand over his wet hair, blinking at Drew from under the spray. "Can I—can I wash your back?" he murmured.

"Of course," said Drew.

Cool soap, warmed in Michael's massive palms, worked quickly into lather, slicked over Drew's shoulder blades, arms, again the back. It went up and over his neck, down his side, never touching sensitive belly, to his chest, buttocks, throat. "You're amazing to touch," Michael murmured. "I could just—touch you all day."

"Like that? Driving me crazy? You just have no idea how hot you are, do you?" Drew reached behind him and seized one of Michael's soaped hands, rinsing it under the water, then sucking two fingers into his mouth. Michael gasped so gorgeously, so sincerely, that Drew turned to face him and pushed him against the wall between shower spigots, sliding one of his quivering thighs between Michael's. "Do you get off on being a giant cock tease?" Michael gave no resistance, and Drew's pulse began to pound in his ears. "Tall, handsome man like you," Drew muttered, pinching Michael's left nipple. "You should know better by now."

"I do—I mean, I—" Michael's voice cut off in another gasp. "I just—I don't know what I'm doing."

"Yes, you do," Drew muttered. He reached down. Michael's erection sprang up to meet Drew's hand, bouncing off his palm. He did not wrap his fingers around it and pull the skin back, tight over the head, slide his fist down to the balls. "You're playing with me. It's a dominance game. You won't win. But c'mon." Instead, he took hold of Michael's hand. "Let's get in the sauna."

Michael gave a quiet groan of protest, but he let himself be led.

Drew didn't bother putting his robe back on, only tossing a towel over his shoulder and, otherwise naked, walked down the curved hallway toward the sauna stalls. These were less private, but he and Michael saw no one. Drew opened the door, met by an unyielding wall of dry, cedar-scented heat. He sat on his towel on the bench and patted the space next to him.

"Hot," Michael murmured as he sat. Drew gently stroked his shoulder, but kept the touch brief.

"Relax," Drew whispered, closing his eyes. "Let it happen."

"I know . . ."

They lapsed into silence, broken only by the occasional dizzy, sensual moan. After some endless, heat-stilled minutes, Drew reached into the wooden bucket on the floor and dashed a few ounces of water onto the hot stones, releasing a choking blast of superheated steam. Michael groaned, slowly shaking his head, rivulets of sweat pouring off his temples. "Sit down here, where it's a little less unbearable," Drew suggested. Michael clumsily repositioned himself on the rubber-matted floor. Drew gently kneaded the muscles of Michael's shoulders with his hands until Michael relaxed even more, mouth open, slumping back into Drew's grasp. "If you want," Drew murmured, "I can strike you with the *vihta*. It feels awesome."

"What the—? No," Michael refused, his voice childish and petulant. "Don't beat me."

Drew laughed. "It's just birch twigs."

"I know that," Michael replied, "and I don't care."

"Maybe at home?" Drew leaned down and kissed the wet shell of Michael's ear.

Michael reached up and threaded his fingers through Drew's hair. "Maybe I'll smack *you* with the *vihta.*"

"But *I'd* be into it," said Drew.

Their mouths found each other, sideways, clumsy, slick and salty with too much sweat. Drew pulled back, wiped his hands over his face, and went in for more, tongue sliding between Michael's lips. His mouth was cool and sweet inside. "But not now," Drew breathed into him. "In fact, I'd like to go take a few minutes to cool off outside with you, if you'd like to join me."

"Shower?"

"No," Drew said. "Just to cool off. Shower later. There's a private room. Want to?"

Without speaking, Michael gazed up and smiled, and stood up from where he sat. This time Michael held out his hand, and Drew took it.

In the tiny cool-down room, the only furniture was a simple, narrow, low wooden bench. Michael climbed up and stood on it, affording Drew almost perfect access to his long, bobbing, half-hard cock. Drew patiently wiped the streams of sweat trickling down Michael's thighs, slid both hands into his mouth to suck at the perspiration, now mostly free of salt but retaining its essential mineral flavor. Drew wrapped both spit- and sweat-wet hands around the length of Michael's cock, enfolding it entirely, and slid them down a fraction of an inch, exposing the moist, bright pink glans. Drew flicked his tongue at the urethral slit, making sure Michael could see it. Michael sucked his breath through his teeth as sharply as if he had just cut himself, and his cock twitched hard.

"Yeah," Drew purred, Michael's cock hardening instantly in his grasp. He moved his fisted hands in opposite directions until the sweat coating his skin went dry, then took both hands away, slicked his right palm with as much saliva as he could produce, and began firmly pumping Michael's cock.

Michael grimaced and bit his lip, his long thighs quivering.

"You know," he breathed, "I'm not going to be satisfied with just a handjob."

"I know," Drew replied. He kissed the straining crown of Michael's cock, but didn't use his tongue this time. "This is foreplay."

"I don't *need* foreplay."

"But," Drew pointed out, "you like it. Don't you?" Instead of licking his palm, Drew spit into it, and continued.

"Oh, fuck," Michael whispered, squeezing his eyes tightly shut.

Drew smiled to himself. *I've still got it,* he thought.

"Yeah, I do," Michael continued, his voice shaking. "I'm—I'm almost not used to it, y'know? I'm not used to being *wanted* like this. Having the time taken. I'm not used to being *seduced.*"

"That's the cool thing about me," Drew murmured. "I'll never stop seducing you, even when I have you." He fell silent, his smile fading away, realizing that he hadn't bothered to seduce Jesse in . . . well, he never *did* seduce Jesse. They had grown together, like two beech trees planted too close, their trunks fusing into one from separate root stocks. He played with Jesse, sure. By now, they were well-practiced experts at deferred desire and the explosive, grateful relief when the wanting was finally satisfied. Drew had never seduced anyone in his life, not like this. And he was enjoying himself. He was the man he wanted to be, watching Michael dissolve at the touch of his lips. He wanted to torment Michael into a frenzy of lust, to make Michael come until he passed out. He wanted to make rose-petals-and-candlelight love to Michael. He wanted Michael to be happy and in love.

Drew quickly shook his head, blinking away a threatening prickle at the corners of his eyes. It had been a long time since he had nearly wept with gratitude and joy, but this was not the time or place to give in to it. Not before Michael was truly his. He was so close, but as nervous and prone to flight as an animal in the wild. Drew had to stay strong and in control, drawing him out, guiding him. Michael *needed* that. He needed . . .

"I need you to fuck me," Michael whispered.

Perfect, thought Drew.

"We haven't much time," he replied airily, looking up. Michael's dark eyes, open now, fixed Drew with a near-glare of diamond-sharp want.

"I don't need much," he said.

"Oh, yeah?" Drew challenged. He spit onto the forefingers of his left hand and reached behind Michael's hip, letting his cheek rest against Michael's hard, flat belly. Half the spit had dried already by the time Drew slid the fingers down between Michael's ass cheeks, and his fingers were far too dry to be gentle on their way inside. Michael hissed through his teeth again. His dry asshole flexed at his touch, but there was no affording the fingers access. "That's what I thought," Drew added. "I got no lube, I'm sorry. You're just gonna have to wait for the deluxe edition."

Michael relaxed. "Dammit," he said, pouting.

"But you can come, if you want to," Drew said, and spit in his right hand again. "I want to make you come. Do you want to come for me?"

"Yes . . ." Michael arched against him, a hand on Drew's shoulder, then both, clutching him close. Drew opened his mouth and let the tip of Michael's cock smack against his tongue with every jerking stroke of his hand, alternating the motion between hard, brief sucks of what fit quickly into his mouth, humming low in his throat, caressing the curve of Michael's ass. The movement was impossible to resist, one of Drew's favorites from the days when he did this in the bathhouses, and needed to get a man off fast. It worked on Michael as predicted. Within a minute, he was grunting, voice half-swallowed by lust, "Yes—oh! *Fuck*. Oh, yeah. Ohhh, *yeah*." Drew closed his mouth and turned his face. A thinjet of semen arced out and struck his chin, but mostly the come dribbled down over his hands, onto his chest and Michael's thick black pubic hair.

"I love it," Drew said. He wiped his face with his fingers, resisting the urge to lick them, and instead wiping the issue onto Michael's furred belly and chest, leaving a glistening trail around a nipple.

Michael watched him with dismayed interest. "That always happens," he murmured. "It kinda goes . . ." He curled his tongue and made rude spurting noises. When Drew laughed, Michael grinned his beautiful grin. "It *does*! Always ends up on—on somebody's face."

He didn't say Jesse's name, but he didn't have to; his expression said it all, momentarily dreamy, suddenly clouded with guilt and longing. Drew nuzzled Michael's thigh, a low groan rumbling in his throat, comforting wordlessly, the last traces of Michael's come tangled in the hairs smudging his skin. Drew, too, wished that Jesse was there, bright-eyed and lasciviously willing, eager to lick the semen off, there to hug Michael, to be the next in line.

But at the moment, there was only the two of them. Drew looked away and said briskly, "So—back to the shower for you. It's later than I thought. But I'm good. You good?" His own cock was full and sensitive, craving touch, but his senses told him that, again, this was not the time.

"Yeah, guess so," Michael admitted, sheepish again. He grabbed one of the clean towels stacked underneath the wooden bench, wiped himself down, draped his midsection, and left the cool-down room by himself. Drew chose a towel for himself, and went to the locker room.

He quickly rinsed his hands, retrieved his phone, and sent a text message to Jesse.

Spending time with M this evening, but should be home by 8 or 9.

The response took no more than a minute to arrive. **cool have fun b safe. tell him to call me.**

"Huh," Drew said. Somehow he'd expected at least some token resistance, some whining at least. He typed in the reply, **OK love you.** He hesitated before sending the message, adding, **Will be thinking of you.** He didn't wait for a response.

Drew joined Michael in the shower a few minutes later. Michael looked almost surprised to see him, his body hair frosted with soap lather. "Hey," Drew said, stepping under the same shower spigot. "How 'bout I come over tonight and we finish what we started?" He examined Michael's body appraisingly, stroking a hand through the lather on his belly. "Promise I won't waste your time with too much foreplay."

Michael's cock twitched, as if in reply. "But . . ." he stammered. "But what about Jesse?"

"Don't worry about him," Drew said reassuringly. "He actually said it was okay, so I'm going to assume it is. See you at six-thirty. Get clean."

Drew only needed the barest rinse, and turned and walked away with an extra sway in his hips, showing off his own ass. As much as he would have loved to look over his shoulder at Michael's expression, he kept himself on the path back to the locker room, back to his underwear and his Prada suit and mirror-shined bespoke shoes, and the tooth of the comb pulled back through his hair to create the perfect, "effortless" side part.

For once, his briefcase didn't feel like a prison in which he carried himself around; for once, he wasn't sorry to hail a taxi and return to the Financial District. He practically danced over the gutters and swung himself into his desk chair as if he were in a musical. His colleagues might have been staring at him, but he didn't care. The stiff, heavy weight of the erection in his shorts was like a gift, like the best birthday present in the world.

Michael sat next to his window, sipping ice water, watching East Ninetieth Street through a gap in the blinds. The air conditioner hummed and paused with a thunk of inner machinery. In the gap of sound, the apartment was as silent as it ever got, even in the middle of the night. Traffic swished by on the street below. Garbage cans rattled, and car horns bleated in the distance. Michael could hear his own breathing, deep and steady, drawing in relaxation. It was important, essential for relaxation. Drew Farrow was coming by to have sex, with Jesse's full permission.

Michael hadn't settled for Drew's word for it. After leaving the magic spa, he sent Jesse a text: **Hi is it OK if the lunch date picks up again at dinner?**

His response was immediate. Yep its ok. it's funny that you're both asking me like I'm authority. I'm too busy & tired to care right now anyway, working a ton, good for me to just work & be solitary

I just miss you, want you to be OK.

I'm ok! I miss u too. srsly I don't mind. have friday off, maybe hang out then?

Michael sure as hell didn't have Friday off, but after curtains, his night was his own. **Sure, maybe get a drink. Stay in touch.**

He got up to refresh the ice in his glass, and started a playlist of ambient music on his computer. When he sat at the window again he felt looser, almost drowsy, as the tension dissipated from his neck and back. Whatever would happen, would; he was ready to accept it. Or, he hoped he was, anyway. He just wasn't sure what to expect. Drew was like no one else he'd ever met, and there was no real way to prepare himself.

Down on the street, a black town car stopped at his corner and, after a brief pause, Drew stepped out of it, still wearing his workday's suit but without the tie. Michael chuffed a laugh to himself. So he'd come straight from the office. Michael imagined Drew at work, surreptitiously stroking his erection through his trouser pocket, making plans.

The downstairs door buzzer sounded through the speaker grille next to Michael's door. He stood up and pressed his finger against the button, holding it there for thirty seconds, long enough for Drew to come through the front door and the door that led upstairs to the apartments, then released it with a sigh and another deep breath. This was happening now. No second thoughts.

Michael opened his apartment door and leaned against the frame. Drew stepped through the door to the hallway stairs, his stride rapid and firm, with purpose. Drew looked him up and down, then brushed past him without speaking.

Michael barely had time to close the door behind him before Drew grabbed him by the collar of his thin T-shirt and pulled him down for what was less a kiss than a vicious thrust of tongue into mouth. Michael held on, pulling the hem of Drew's shirt from his waistband, pushing the suit jacket off his shoulders.

Surprising Michael, Drew pushed him away and busied himself draping his jacket over Michael's desk chair, unbuttoning his white dress shirt, shaking it out and draping it in turn. "Hello," Michael said.

"Hello," Drew replied. He wore no belt with his slacks. The waistband latch slid open, and Drew stepped neatly out of his trousers. Underneath, his sky-blue briefs held a thick shadow of bent cock and heavy balls. Michael dropped his eyes to Drew's socks—dark blue knitted silk with scattered yellow squares, matching the tie that he had been wearing before. When Drew spoke again, Michael gave a near-flinch of surprise. "Take off your clothes, unless you want me to do it."

"Oh—yeah." Michael pulled his T-shirt off, still eyeing Drew's feet with great interest. "Can I take off your socks?" he asked.

Drew smiled indulgently. "Sure," he said. He sat on the edge of Michael's bed and daintily pointed his toes. "You really like my feet, huh?"

"They're so fucked up," Michael confessed, giddy and fascinated. The sock peeled off, foot damp with sweat, revealing the scar-whorled skin and rocklike muscle. Perhaps he really *had* once walked on broken glass. "It's fascinating. It's . . . erotic."

"Suck it," Drew commanded, pointing his big toe.

"Oh, God," Michael moaned softly, "I can't—"

"I said, suck it. Just the one toe. I know you want to. Go on."

Michael took a deep breath, tentatively brushed invisible silk lint from the toenail, and took the extremity into his mouth. He tasted sharp, glorious salt, a faint trace of Gullfoss's lavender soap. He pulled away, trembling, and asked, "Um, do you want anything to drink? Or eat? It's dinnertime."

Drew shook his head and pulled his briefs off, tossing them neatly into the seat of the chair. "All I want is you."

"Okay."

"Come here." Drew reached out for Michael, pulling him down onto the bed beside him, hands roving all over Michael's body, stroking and poking and grasping everything from his armpits to the backs of his knees, closing over his throat for a brief thrilling second only to release him and instead clench roughly in his hair. Michael moaned and brought their open mouths together, slid closer until their cocks touched. Drew's was rigid, the very tip of it moist, testicles hanging down to touch Michael's. Michael didn't just want to suck a toe; he wanted to suck all of him. If he could have put Drew's entire body into his mouth, he would.

Michael didn't notice that he had opened his legs wide until Drew clamped them closed, rough hands on his knees. Pulling his hair again, Drew pushed Michael's skull away, down, towards the pillows, towards the surface of the bed. Michael joyfully figured it out; Drew wanted him face-down. He rolled onto his belly, bent his knees, and raised his hips, ass to the air.

Drew slapped his buttocks hard. Michael groaned and clenched his fists in his bedspread. Drew's hands grasped and spread Michael's ass cheeks. "What've you been up to since last I saw you?" Drew asked conversationally, kneading the gluteal muscles and then slapping them again. "Were you fingering yourself?"

"I—I—" Michael gulped, and gripped his own cock in his hand. "I washed. Real well."

"Excellent," Drew said. One hand went exploring, winding through the hair lining Michael's ass, surrounding his anus. A finger circled, outside. Michael gripped himself harder.

"I have a little toy."

"Yes? Smart." Drew kissed both buttocks on their sensitive inner edges, kissed Michael's asshole, and began to lick it with big, wet swipes.

"Oh . . . oh my *God.* You can't—you shouldn't—"

"Relax." Drew took one of Michael's hands and closed it around Michael's cock. Michael gripped his cock, trying to divide his attention so that he could bear the sweetness of the sensation of Drew's warm tongue brushing back and forth against him, Drew's lips nibbling at him, the tongue turning firm and pointed and trying to push its way inside. Though it couldn't, Drew didn't seem discouraged; he returned to his side-to-side lick, adding vertical motion for good measure.

Michael's eyes rolled back into his head. "I didn't know—! Oh, man, that feels. . ."

"No foreplay," Drew said, lips and tongue still pressed, vibrating, against his anus. "This is actual sex."

"I'll say!" said Michael, lapsing into giddy laughter. Ridiculous. He sounded like a bright-eyed farm boy, but everything felt too good for him to be embarrassed or ashamed. He reached behind him with his free hand, balancing himself on his shoulders, and pulled his buttocks open wider.

"Yeah, that's right," Drew murmured, humming, adding to the already excruciating sensation. "Show me how much you want it." Michael's hand on his own cock overflowed with a sudden welling of pre-come. He reached behind himself again, smudging it onto his asshole. Drew moaned with approval, and licked it up.

"Filthy!" Michael whispered in scandalized delight.

"Just the way you like it," Drew said. "You're a twisted little freak, and I'm so glad I found you."

Michael laughed. "I'm not little," he pointed out.

"No, no; huh," Drew acknowledged. "Here, c'mere. Why don't you put that dick in my mouth for a minute, let me see what I can do?" Rather than turning Michael over again, Drew lay down on his back and slid between Michael's thighs, slurping at his hanging balls, licking at the sensitive underside of the penis and clasping the head in his mouth.

"Does that . . . taste *good*?" Michael moaned. Drew nodded, mouth full. Michael's voice changed. No more of the gee-whiz hick, and no more of the breathy, insincere protests. These words came from deep in his throat, gravely and rough. A shiver traveled over Drew's skin; Michael felt the hairs rise against him. "*Feels* good. Yeah . . . ahhh. . . . Ah, man, you're gonna make me come."

"You won't come," Drew said, flicking his tongue sharply against the tiny knot of sensitive flesh at the base of the head of Michael's cock. Michael whimpered desperately, grabbing the base of his cock to make sure it didn't explode and end all of this far, far too soon. Drew batted Michael's hand away and rubbed his cheek, his forehead, his chin against the now-slick cock head. "You came earlier today, which means you've got some more time to play. Unless you're one of those multi-orgasmic freaks who can just come and come and come. Which would be beautiful."

"I'm not," Michael admitted. "I'm not. I wish."

"So, you could come all over my face and still fill up my ass? Yeah, I know what you're thinking."

"Fucking filthy!" Michael laughed. Drew just moaned again, and kept licking and stroking his face all over Michael's cock, all over his balls. But not sucking, Michael realized. Michael wanted him to, but he also didn't want that. He didn't want this to end. Calming himself, he reached toward the windowsill and brought his water glass to his lips.

Drew slid out from under Michael and stood up, walking nude

and muscular into Michael's kitchen. He helped himself to a glass of water from the tap and brought it back to bed. Michael beamed at him when he returned, but Drew shook his head. "Don't turn over," he said. "I'm not done yet."

"You'd better not be."

Drew grinned, his eyes sparkling. "I like you," he enthused.

"I like you, too," Michael said, setting his water down, resettling himself on his belly. "I'd like you to continue."

"Say it," Drew said, sinking down onto the bed behind him.

"Keep going."

"And what am I doing?" Drew kneaded Michael's ass some more, adding another smack, and another, until the skin tingled.

"Playing with my ass," Michael said quietly, shy and unsure.

"Eating your ass," Drew corrected, stroking and pinching his own nipples, the change in Michael's voice having its intended effect. "Say it."

"Keep eating my ass."

"Say please."

"Please," Michael grumbled, ending on a moan. Drew's tongue had finally breached him, and a thick finger followed. "Please eat my asshole out! Please!"

"There you go," Drew murmured. He thrust his finger in. "Oh, yes," he said, voice low and thick, as if it were happening to him. Michael's cock began to ache. "Oh, *yes*. Oh, like that. Yes. Umm. You need me to fuck you. Isn't that right?"

Without having to be told, without removing his inserted finger, Drew picked up the bottle of lube that sat at the edge of the desk. Smoothly, a newly lubricated finger slid into Michael alongside the one that was already there. Drew was using two hands to do this. Michael's cock began to ache in earnest. *Everything* made sense; this was what he wanted, and always had. "Oh, fuck, yeah," Michael gasped.

"That's right," Drew soothed. The first finger withdrew, and the slick finger worked into him, past the outer ring, past the inner, tighter ring. More lube, and a second finger from the same hand was inside him, twisting and quirking, learning how he felt. "I don't know how you like it," Drew murmured, kissing Michael's lower back, leaving a damp imprint from his lips. When Michael remembered where those lips had been, his cock tried to rise out through his back. It had to settle for standing up rigidly against his belly. He had never been so hard before in his life; he was being manipulated inside, milked, an internal massage as skilled and as knowledgeable about every hot spot inside him as if Drew had studied a chart. "Hard? Rough? Fast? Slow and wet? Can you tell me?"

"I like to fuck," Michael panted. "I like all of it." He sucked in his breath. Drew pulled out and pushed in again, thicker now, the twisting coming from his wrist. Three fingers, maybe four. Michael's head danced full of white static. "Hard," he finally decided. "And slow. At first. Let me really think about what I've done."

"It's what you've done, and not what I'm doing to you?" Drew mused. "Interesting. The nice thing is, you can take a nice big cock. Which is good, because that's what I've got."

"I know," Michael breathed. Somewhere, Michael heard the quiet ripping of a condom wrapper. He wasn't sure how it was possible with Drew's hand half inside him, and the air conditioner falling quiet again, and the world all in a tumble.

"And that's what you want inside you?"

Michael nodded. "Hard," he said. "And slow."

"At first. Okay, got it. I got it." Drew chuckled. "Pushy bottom."

"I'm always pushy when I'm on the bottom."

"Oh, really?" Slow pulses of the digits inside him, a fingertip stroking electric sparks against his prostate. Behind his closed eyelids, Michael watched a liquid light show of unnamed colors, interrupted by lightning.

"What are you like when you're on the bottom?" Michael gasped, trying to rub himself against his bedspread, but also not do it. He'd been sorry doing that before, rubbing himself literally raw, back in the days when men like Drew were a fantasy so absurd he slapped himself. "I bet you're the pushiest bottom on Earth."

"That's why I have to be kept in line," Drew replied. "I need firm control. Tremendous discipline from without, if it can't come from within."

"Handcuffs? Leg chains? The iron maiden?" Michael joked.

"A ball gag and a good, solid pop to the face if I act up," Drew said. He didn't sound like he was kidding. Michael made no reply, no sound at all, but he arched his back and shuddered with the effort of holding himself together.

I will be that for you, he vowed. *Anything for you. I'll treat you like a naughty slave because . . .* Even his thoughts stalled for a moment before he allowed himself to proceed. Why else was he here? Why else was he in New York, if not to learn how to be honest with himself? To let go, and be the person he was, instead of what he was expected to be? To be true to every part of himself, to speak every desire, at least to himself?

Because I bet Jesse can't do that. Not like you want. Not like you think you need. And maybe you do. I'll beat you like a mouthy whore, bitch, if it makes you come. If it makes you love me.

"Please," Michael whispered. When he was younger, he would have come already; his dick would be battered and bruised from trying to fuck a bedspread that did not and would not ever fuck him back. He drew his knees up to his stomach, back curved over, almost the crane yoga asana but with his feet and knees anchored below him. His spine tingled eagerly. "Do it hard. And slow. Make me feel it."

Drew groaned with pleasure, and once again grasped and parted Michael's buttocks, spreading him wide. This time, though, he spit directly inside Michael; Michael promptly got the shakes, his calculated yoga calm shattered, exactly to Drew's advantage. Drew positioned the head of his cock, let it rub for a few strokes, and then pushed firmly inside.

It made him groan again, but with effort. Michael groaned too, grimacing. The stretch, as it always was, was just too much. Crazy and reckless and man-was-not-meant-to-do-this. He concentrated as hard as he could, not on the burn of his stretched anal skin, but on the hot weight of Drew's cock inside him, deep in there, seemingly embedded in his guts. Actually, it *was* embedded in his—

"Oh my fuck, you're so fucking tight," Drew muttered.

"I am your fuck, aren't I?" Michael gasped back. He regained his balance and, with a deep breath, re-anchored his knees and his feet and his hands, spread flat on the bed, on the already damp and stained bedspread. His dick had spilled and dripped a streaky fluid, almost come but not quite, a livid and half-clear streak on the dark canvas. "Do it."

Drew grunted and pulled out altogether. Once again, he spit into Michael's hot, waiting hole. "Like this?" he said, and thrust in, as requested, slow and hard—and deep, all the way deep, Drew's balls coming to rest against Michael's perineum.

"Yes." Michael whined and grit his teeth. Again the withdrawal, the spit, and the long, slow, swordlike thrust into his interior. "Yes."

"Ah. You take it well." Drew rested, holding himself there, deep, still enough that Michael could feel the cock trying to jump inside him. But he was too tight around it. He let his internal muscles relax, tightening the channel even further, making Drew emit a staggered moan.

"I want it," Michael said darkly.

"Yes, keep talking to me like that. Love your deep voice. You're a man and I'll fuck you like a man."

"Do it. Harder."

Drew slid back, only a bit, then in, hard. "Like that?"

"Yes. Faster."

"Just as hard? You gonna take it?" Drew combed his fingers through Michael's hair, grasped a handful, pulled sharply.

"Yes, fucker. Just do it."

Drew laughed and smacked Michael's ass, hard this time. His previous swats had only been play. If Michael's muscles hadn't already been taut and desperate, or if Drew had hit him somewhere other than his ass, it would have seriously hurt. In the face, it would have made him bleed. Michael gritted his teeth hard so that he wouldn't bite his tongue. "Fuck you," said Drew, both a defiant response and a statement of purpose. His next thrust was met halfway by Michael's eager hips.

"Fuck *you*," Michael groaned.

"Yes," Drew purred. "Exactly. Show me what you got."

He knew what he was doing, that Drew Farrow. He increased speed, stabbing lightly, adding odd little twists and sharp distractions on the rest of Michael's skin, pinches and slaps and twists and rough bites along his spine. Only when Michael lost control, mouth open to release his moans, hips bucking back, did Drew do as he'd promised—fast, hard, and deep, plunging into Michael's unresisting asshole, holding Michael's hips steady. He was driving and he meant Michael to know it. He even pushed Michael's head down, utterly wrecking his asana, but making his hips rise even higher, pushing against the bed with his feet, forcing Drew to rise with him until both men stood on their feet, Michael on the bed, bent over at forty-five degrees, and Drew's feet on the floor. "Oh, Jesus," Drew shouted. "You take it so good!"

Without warning or permission Michael's body reacted, flooding him with a rush of orgasmic energy. He cried out senselessly, incomprehensibly, his dick all but leaping out of his hand. That pesky first jet of semen hit the underside of his chin, and the rest spurted out against his belly, running down the incline towards his face. He let it happen. He couldn't stop it. "Oh, shit," Drew said, almost conversationally, still steadily fucking him. It sounded like he was going to laugh. "It's on *your* face this time." Michael didn't mind; the absurdity was all part of the bliss.

Drew didn't laugh, though. His breath hitched, and he moaned half in his throat and half in his mouth, a wordless litany of ecstasy and disappointment. His whole body jerked hard and he lost his grip on Michael's hips, which was all that had been keeping Michael from face-planting onto the surface of the bed. Michael didn't fall down alone; Drew's weight followed him, collapsing in a painful tangle of limbs and bones and ribs and hips, still grinding hard until it just didn't work anymore.

Michael disengaged himself just enough so that he could lie on his back, thighs in the wet spot, but Drew clung to him, shuddering terribly, moaning a litany of "Oh, God, oh, fuck." The condom slid off and smeared them both with come. They were both covered in it now.

It was perfect. The air conditioner clicked off again. It was still dusk outside, still hot. That was reality. Michael was glad it was out there, and not in here.

"I think you broke me," Drew whispered, relaxing at last.

Michael chuckled lazily. He couldn't remember the last time he'd been so content. Except for that wet spot on the bed, and the spunk on his torso and legs, and the condom sticking to him. Oh, cold reality . . . "Be right back," he decided, sitting up, stripping the rubber off his leg, and heading to the bathroom. When he glanced back, Drew was writhing on the bed, still moaning quietly, or maybe humming something to himself. He was flushed and shaking and glistening with exertion. Michael smiled and hugged himself.

Presently he returned to Drew's side, folding over the bedspread to cover the wet part and handing Drew a glass of iced herbal tea and a wet towel. "Here you go," Michael said softly, stroking Drew's hair. "I guess I *did* wreck you." Drew opened his eyes and sighed gratefully, wiping his mouth, belly, crotch. Michael kissed him on the lips. "Sorry," he said smugly.

"What kinda tea is this?" Drew asked fuzzily, taking a sip and then setting it down.

"Lemon mint," Michael said.

"Would you . . . hold me, please?"

So Michael did, their arms wrapped around each other, heads together, heartbeats slowing to a drowsy pace. Michael kissed Drew's forehead and held his hands. "You're beautiful, Andrew," he whispered. In response, Drew smiled faintly, eyes closed, not drifting away so much as dropping beneath the surface of an inexorable wave.

ii. HOW DREW DOES THINGS.

Drew rolled over with a grunt and a cough, shaken by a too-vivid dream of his father drowning, and forced his eyes open.

The room was dark and hot. His sweat-slick hands slid across his face and down his thighs. On the bed, beside him, the lean curve of Michael's side rose and fell. Eyes peacefully closed, he slept deeply, unconcerned and unheeding. The panicked shouting Drew could have sworn he'd been doing must have been part of the dream.

He groaned, shook his head, got out of bed, and stood up, trying to orient himself. He would have sworn he'd just closed his eyes for a moment, but it had been daylight then. Blue, red and white light flickered faintly from behind closed blinds. He peered out to the street. Two police cruisers had converged at the corner of Second Avenue, where a car was propped awkwardly on the sidewalk. The sirens that had awoken him finally stopped.

He blearily fumbled his Blackberry from the inside pocket of his jacket. He squinted in disbelief at the minuscule screen, but the stark numbers at the top corner only changed from 2:43 to 2:44.

"Oh, *shit*," Drew whispered.

He was dressed, shod, and down on the street in seconds, operating through pure reflex. There seemed to be a lot of police. Drew jogged away from the scene, toward the sounds of traffic. East 90th wasn't exactly hopping at this time of night, but he was able to flag down a taxi with little trouble, despite his half-buttoned shirt and psychotic-looking bed head. The light of the Blackberry worked as a signal no cab driver could ignore. Drew slumped into the back seat, sighing out his address, wiping more perspiration from his face.

His hands smelled like sweat, asshole, and come. Like *fucking*. Now that he was awake and away, Drew couldn't help smiling and chuckling, even as he rolled his eyes and sighed with remorse that he'd passed out, across town, in somebody else's bed. After having fucked that someone. Someone who wasn't Jesse. For the first time in almost a decade.

Michael. *They'd fucked.* He had fucked Michael. Hard. Good Lord.

It had been ages since he'd come home at three in the morning, disoriented, half smug and half horrified, knowing that he'd had sex—real, penetrative, intimate, sloppy, dick-in-major-body-cavity sex that he wasn't supposed to have—and was now, by the skin of his unbrushed teeth, escaping the scene of the crime. The taxi ride of shame. It had been years since the last time, and nothing had changed. Except everything. Except that now he was coming home to Jesse with the taste of sin in his mouth.

This had never happened once he was truly *with* Jesse. He had never fled from Jesse's bed, nor had he ever had to run back to him with the memory of some other fuck rocking in his mind. Jesse *was* the sin. No other desire had even come close. But this—!

Oh, Michael. . . . . .God, that's so good. . . . . .Take it. You feel that? Take that. Take all of it.

Drew crept silently into his house, the foyer arching dark and silent, the stairs' carpet muffling his steps. A dim amber glow spilled from the open bedroom door, produced by one of the bedside lamps. On the bed, Jesse lay sprawled, naked, face down, glistening with sweat, the sheets tangled between his legs. His hair spread in a dark fan on the pillow. A paperback book mirrored him, open pages-down on the bedside table.

After a moment of silent aesthetic appreciation, Drew picked up the pillows that had scattered to the floor, righted the book, tucked a loose red ticket into place between the pages. He hit the lights and sat yawning on the edge of the bed as he shed his sweaty clothes.

When Drew tugged the sheets clear of Jesse's legs and lay beside him, Jesse roused, turning his face against the pillow. He kept his eyes closed. "Drew?" Jesse murmured.

Drew kissed him. "I'm sorry I'm home so late," he whispered, stroking Jesse's hair. He drew the wrinkled bedsheets over their bodies.

"That's okay," Jesse said, closing his eyes again, cuddling into Drew, resting his head against Drew's shoulder and laying an arm across Drew's chest. Drew shifted to accommodate. Instantly they assumed their usual falling-asleep position, Drew's body bracketing Jesse's, their bodies limbs finding their vague but assigned divots in the mattress. Jesse smelled of shampoo and soap, mingling with his fresh sweat. Showered, but already sweating again; it was a young, innocent smell.

"I came really hard," Drew said softly, hugging his boy, rubbing thumbs across Jesse's stiff nipples. "And I fell asleep. Just . . . passed out."

"You didn't even notice, did you?" Jesse sighed. His hand curled around Drew's.

"No," Drew replied, kissing Jesse's moist forehead. "Notice what, honey?"

Jesse murmured, "The money," and almost immediately began to snore softly.

It took Drew a while longer to relax. He forced himself to focus on the present moment. The perfectly cool temperature, the comforting bed, and sweet Jesse in his arms, so cute with his sleep-talking nonsense. The kid really was working too hard these days.

But, inevitably, Drew's thoughts drifted back to Michael. His sounds, his scents, his hunger. *Michael.* The thick hair on his arms; the strength of his pulse; the sensitive wet tip of his cock; the dense, tight heat inside his asshole, as if no one had ever been so deep inside him before.

Jesse smiled and sighed in his sleep, as if he'd read Drew's mind and agreed.

But Jesse had already *had* Michael. Drew wanted to know what it had been like—not to be told, but to *know*. How could his little boy handle all the man that Michael was? All that hunger? How could Jesse have withstood it?

True, though, they hadn't fucked. Drew had gotten to that checkpoint first. It didn't make sense. What were they waiting for?

Why was Jesse not more upset that Drew was getting some of that now, too? Why wasn't Jesse awake and demanding details, cooling him with recriminations? How could he possibly be so tired that he didn't want to know?

Drew sighed, wondering if he could relax faster if he turned his back to Jesse. Instead, he fell quickly back into sleep.

‡

In the morning, after Drew returned from a running the Central Park perimeter loop to find, Jesse remained in bed just as he was left, eyes closed and breathing slowly in sleep. Stripping off sweat-soaked clothes and shoes, Drew smiled tiredly at the heap of boy tangled in his sheets, and headed towards the shower.

When he emerged, cleansed and shaved, the bed was empty. It was just past seven-thirty, the bedroom still shadowed and dim. Sounds of quiet activity emerged from the kitchen. Curious, Drew got dressed and padded towards the sounds as he buttoned his shirt.

Moving slowly, clearly still more than half asleep, Jesse was setting the kitchen table. He set the table for one, with expertly coiled cloth napkin, juice glasses, main plate, egg cup, the South Seas fork, spoon, butter spreader. He glanced up at Drew, and gave a suggestion of a nod. "Toast, soft-boiled, sardines, coffee on its way," Jesse said. "Let me know if you want cultured butter; I picked some up yesterday."

"Uh, thanks, yeah," remarked Drew with surprise, sliding obediently into the chair. "Hmm! I haven't seen the South Seas set in ages. I forgot we had it. Was it in the attic?"

With a quick and practiced hand, Jesse plated the food, and set down a beautifully prepared cappuccino sprinkled with cocoa powder and nutmeg. He said nothing, and did not look at Drew.

Drew sighed heavily. "What is it?," he grunted.

Jesse stood a few steps away, his posture very erect and straight, eyes cold. He seemed completely awake now. "You really *didn't* notice, did you?" he asked.

Drew loaded his buttered toast with the fish, quickly sauteed in some kind of oil, sprinkled with dill and some other green herb. "Notice what?" he asked with his mouth full. Jesse made the most delicious meals when he was angry.

Jesse grabbed something from the kitchen counter and smacked it down in front of Drew. A handful of money slowly bloomed from a ball, ones and fives and twenties. "So what's that?" Drew asked, his hands feeding food into his mouth without conscious effort. He sipped his coffee. Of course, it was perfect as well.

"Take it," Jesse said tightly. "It's my all tips from the last three days. Two hundred and ninety-two dollars. It's rent."

"I don't want that," Drew said, scoffing.

"It's not enough?"

Drew sighed heavily and took a few more bites of toast to fortify himself. All the cells in his body seemed to moan in pleasure from it; he just couldn't stop. Perfect toast, perfect butter, perfect with the sardines. Drew's breakfast when he was a boy, back then, his nemesis when all he'd wanted was Cookie Crisp or at least pancakes, like normal kids on TV ate. Now, as an adult, his favorite breakfast, and Jesse prepared it flawlessly. "C'mon, Jess, we dealt with this ages ago. You live here because it makes sense. You keep the money you make. I don't need it."

"You've never needed it," Jesse put in.

"No, I never have," Drew admitted. "And I definitely don't want it." He scooted out from the table a bit, and patted his lap. "C'mere."

Jesse ignored the summons, shaking his head. "I worked my fucking ass off," he declared. "That's my tips. I'm lucky they hired me back."

"Yeah," said Drew, shrugging helplessly. "Since you're in the habit of quitting without notice. Look, I don't need your money and I don't want it. *You* earned it; it's yours. Do whatever you want with it."

"I *want* to give it to you. Please. Let me feel like I'm doing something. I'm just—" Jesse tightened his lips, looking away, combing his hand through his hair. "I'm just—fucking tired—and sick of feeling—*beholden* to you."

Drew scrubbed his hands over his face to keep himself from blurting out, *This again?* "You are, dammit. Like I am to you? Like me, owing you my life?"

"You know what I'm talking about. I mean, look at this." Jesse pointed at random corners of the kitchen, then at his comparatively sad little pile of money. "This is the best I can do."

"No, it's not, and you know it. Jess . . ." Drew hastily shoved the rest of the food into his mouth, and gestured emptily while he chewed. "Look, honey, I appreciate the breakfast, you didn't need to do that. But I've got to hustle and get going. I'm leaving work at three today and I've got a lot of shit to figure out at the office before the trip."

"Yeah, okay, I get it," Jesse said.

Drew gritted his teeth. "I'm not trying to diminish what's bothering you. I'm not. I just can't address it right now. That's fair, right? Why don't we have dinner at home tonight. And if we need to talk about something, let's do it in a relaxed atmosphere instead of you being half asleep, and obviously not getting enough to eat these days—"

"Thanks, Mom."

"—Then we can do it then. Listen to you. It's ridiculous. You're not even close to being rational. And you really should shave. You're starting to look like a Mexican meth dealer. When do you get off work? I'll call in delivery. Chinese sound good?"

"I can bring dinner home. 'S kinda what I do."

"I know you can. But don't. We'll eat something else. There's other food besides Italian."

Jesse shook his head grudgingly. "All right," he said, false lightness in his voice. "I'll be home at eight. Is that okay?"

"Sure. Thanks. Love you." Drew quickly kissed him on the temple, and hurried back to his bedroom to get shoes on. On his way out, he had to go through the kitchen, and ignore Jesse, sitting there at the table, arms hanging loosely at his sides, his mouth turned down grimly. Drew shook off the urge to kiss him again, hoisted his briefcase, and got on with his normal life.

Drew didn't do as much business travel as he'd once done. He'd had gone out of town no more than twice a year for the last three years, and not at all since the trip to Lisbon in February. He felt both anxious and relieved to leave the Morrow offices even temporarily. There, he could act almost completely on instinct: his corner office with a tease of a river view; the unused espresso machine in the kitchenette; the executives' men's room where he had, more than once, rubbed an unwanted and troublesome erection into a few seconds' bliss. This morning, Drew had hoped to get a few moment's privacy to do just that (if he concentrated on it, he could still smell Michael on his hands). Instead he spent four hours on a conference call with the anxious Indianapolis investors, and went straight from there to a debriefing with Levine and a green-juice protein smoothie instead of lunch. His back ached whenever he stood up, and Levine called him out for being fuzzy-minded and distracted.

At three o'clock, stepping into the elevator, the Bluetooth headset in his breast pocket was still hot from his ear. He pictured it glowing with frustrated, dammed-up calls. Drew set his jaw and stared straight ahead, brows low, wearing; his *don't talk to me* look. No one did. He would not let this company own him. He would dance for its pleasure, clean its kills, and donate his sperm to its sewer pipes, but when he was leaving for the day, he was done.

Back home, he did a handful of crunches to loosen his back and hips, bandaged the bleeding blisters on his heels, and took a long, cool shower. Michael's smell had finally vanished from his fingertips. Drew wished that he'd taken some kind of talisman from the man—a pillowcase, a T-shirt, a towel, something that held his scent—when he'd had a chance.

Still naked, he sent a text to Michael. **You're amazing.**

There was no reply by the time Drew was dry, and Drew shrugged and plugged his phone in to charge in case there was one later.

Drew put on the bottoms of his cobalt-blue Armani linen pajamas, a plain white T-shirt, and sandals, and ordered dim sum delivery. He ordered everything he liked: roast duck buns, soup dumplings, Grand Marnier prawns, rice steamed in banana leaf. When the order arrived, he sat down in the foyer and ate before he tried to go back upstairs. By the time he returned to the kitchen, he was so drowsy that he tucked the other takeout cartons and bowls into the microwave, set his alarm clock to give him an hour, and fell into a dead-solid sleep on his unmade bed.

On waking from his nap, Drew put the delivery order on a folding table in his bedroom, and turned on the lights in his closet, which was half the size of the bedroom. Originally a his-and-hers shared closet, the entire space had been taken over by Drew's clothes and shoes.

He hauled suitcases, garment bags, and toiletry bags from the shelves, shook them out, and zipped them all open to air out. The bags released a dusty, grape-must smell of Portuguese air. The scent reminded Drew of his father, of the trips that they'd taken there, when his mother insisted on accompanying her husband on his business trips there, and often, bringing Drew with them. At first, Drew had thought his father hated business trips; in actuality, Alistair Farrow just hated when his wife and kid went with him. His father lived to travel, actually, was in his element in a new place with a product to sell (those fucking sardines). That he'd settled in New York was only due to the fact that New York was the center of the business world, and as good a base of operations as any. The Portuguese businesses had only been a springboard to launch Drew's father into the larger world, and now, the remains of these companies were only the excuse to return to Portugal now and again. Drew wanted to understand it, relate to it, feel that part of that country was within him. But as a kid he was bored and lonely in Lisbon, and as an adult, he was too much like his father— despite the longing for romance and identity, it was only a place to do business. It made no difference whatsoever that his mother now lived there, never to return.

I'm going to Indianapolis, he reminded himself. *Dad's dead. He doesn't matter anymore.*

Drew sat down to rest his legs, and checked his Blackberry for messages. There were plenty from work, but none from Michael. Drew snapped a quick picture of himself, probably from a bad angle, but hopefully charming anyway. He sent it to Michael's email address, in case his phone couldn't receive data messages.

He had pulled all of his lightweight suits from the closet by the time Jesse arrived at a quarter to eight. He smelled of the street, of oregano and tomatoes, of the greasy sweat on his tousled hair. "Hey, I got bounced early," Jesse said. "I got us some wine."

"Thanks," Drew replied, and opened his arms expectantly. Jesse embraced and kissed him, but not enthusiastically, and Drew turned away to stare at the assortment of suits. "Food's on the table in the bedroom."

"Great, I'm starving." Jesse rifled through the boxes. "Okay. Is there anything here that doesn't contain meat?"

"Sure there is. There's gotta be."

"It's dim sum, Drew. And it's not from Chong Foy, so even the vegetables are probably cooked in pork fat. God damn it!"

Drew took a deep breath. "Rice in banana leaf. That's gotta be safe. There's plain rice, too. Go on; it's not gonna hurt you. You're not *allergic* to meat."

"That's not what it's about, and you know it. I don't want to eat dead animals, Drew. I can't believe that you didn't remember that. Always order dim sum from Chong Foy. We've been over this."

"Look, I was hungry," Drew snapped, "and Evergreen was on my speed dial. Sorry, okay? I'm sorry. Jesus fucking Christ, Jesse, I didn't do it on purpose. I'm tired today. I've got a lot on my mind."

"I know you do," Jesse sighed, slumping onto a padded bench along one of the mirrored walls of the closet. "I'm sorry. I'm hungry, too. I'll get a plate."

Jaw clenched, Drew kept his back to Jesse, but he could still see Jesse's reflection in the mirror; his head hung low, as if he was tired or depressed. "Eat out of the carton. It's fine."

Jesse morosely picked up chopsticks. "Good thing I ate some cake before I left work," he mused.

"So it would seem. Would you mind pouring the wine?"

"Don't mind at all," Jesse said, sounding much happier. "I know *I* need a drink."

Both of them finished a glass before speaking again. Drew handed his empty glass back to Jesse, clearing his throat. "Weather forecast for Indianapolis says clear and sunny all week, highs in the low eighties. I don't know how much time I'll be spending outside; probably not a lot. So, a dark color?"

"I'm thinking," Jesse opined, poking at the banana l-leaf rice, "that one, and that striped one there."

"Seersucker? Jesse, no. I don't want to seem like I'm making fun of them."

"It just looks casual," Jesse shrugged, handing Drew his refilled glass. "I dunno. Got anything in a lighter blue?"

"I'm leaning towards this Westwood three-piece. I can strip down to the vest and a shirt for after hours, keep my tie on."

"That sounds good," Jesse said. "So, that one, and the dark gray one, and maybe a pair of jeans? Do you want to seem ultra- New York, or do you want to be on their level?"

Drew smiled. Jesse really had no idea what he was talking about. He was back of the house kitchen staff, a bike messenger, a constructio dogsbody; he knew nothing about the nuances of business dress code. "What, do you figure they're going to take me out horseback riding?"

Jesse frowned, and curled an arm around his own bike-jersey-clad torso. "I don't know. They might. Maybe be prepared? You never pack light, mister. Just bring a bunch of shit. Whatever. You don't need my help; this is your jam. I don't even know the labels of any of this crap."

"None of it's crap," said Drew. "I don't buy *crap*. I don't wear *crap*."

"Do you need help picking out your panties?" Jesse asked, poker-faced. "Or your girdle? And, ooh, a corsage. I'm thinking a nice orchid; nothing too showy."

Drew sighed, zipping the dark-khaki Westwood suit into a garment bag. "So, okay. Do you want to tell me what's on your mind?"

Jesse wasn't even looking at him anymore. He gulped down his second glass of wine and poured himself a third. "Sure. Did you have a good time last night?"

"Yes," Drew murmured. "I did. Did you talk to Michael today?"

"No," Jesse replied distantly.

"Really?" asked Drew.

"Really." Jesse met his gaze, holding it steady as he poured himself another glass of wine, finishing off the bottle.

"Oh. Okay." Drew set placed the suit he would wear tomorrow on his flight onto the hanger on the back of the closet door. "Are you two not speaking?"

"We're in kind of a holding pattern," Jesse replied coolly. "Probably because he wants to concentrate on you."

"If he did, I appreciate it. It means something to me. He means something." Drew's throat tightened suddenly, and he sipped desperately at his own somehow-empty glass. "Last night, I thought I was doing the right thing by coming home as soon as I could."

"Don't worry on my account," Jesse said.

"That's the thing, though—I do." Drew sat on his bed and gave Jesse his full attention. "I was hoping you'd be okay with it."

"I am okay with it, okay?" Jesse suddenly stood and grabbed Drew's empty glass. "What I'm not okay with is you acting like a fucking entitled asshole who's is all sad because everybody's not continually obsessed with you and what you think and what you feel. Maybe other people are too busy thinking and feeling their own shit."

"Jess—!" Drew laughed shortly. "You know, I could say the same thing about you."

"Look, you don't need me for this. I don't really give a crap what you wear. I'm fucking tired; I'm going to bed. Good night." Jesse took off with the empty glasses. Momentarily the sound of angry washing came from the kitchen, the tinkle of the glasses placed in the drying rack.

After a moment's stunned pause, Drew followed. "There's a dishwasher, Jesse," he pointed out.

"Yeah—me!"

"What the hell is up with you? What's with the class warfare all of a sudden? You act like I never do shit, when you have no idea how hard my job can be. It's not sitting around smoking cigars and plotting."

Jesse smirked. "I work pretty hard, too," he said.

"You couldn't handle my job."

Jesse's eyes widened warningly, his face suddenly very red. "I don't *want* that job," he snarled, "or anything even vaguely like it. Oh, but there you go again. Just because I work with my sweat and I don't pull down seven figures a year, I couldn't *handle* your job."

Drew rolled his eyes. "It looks to me like you can't even handle falling in love without flipping out."

"Did Michael say something to you?"

"Yeah," Drew answered. "He did. It wasn't so complimentary, either."

"Oh, yeah?" Jesse's voice wavered. His face slowly drained of color as Drew continued.

"He was pretty bothered by your behavior, you know. I'm not surprised he'd put you on hold for a little while. I'd have done the same thing. Oh, in fact, I remember, I kinda *did*." Drew raised his eyebrows for emphasis, and picked up another bottle of wine from the counter. "You've been known to come on pretty strong."

Jesse stared into space. He said quietly, "Once upon a time, I could at least count on being hot enough to keep you interested. I wonder when that stopped."

"What the—? What is this passive-aggressive bullshit?" Drew snapped. "You're starting to piss me off, so I'd advise you to tell me, flat out, what your actual problem is. You want me to tell you you're hot? Okay, you're hot. You're real pretty, Jesse Landon. In fact it's almost disgusting, just how gorgeous you are. And if you've got a problem with Michael, you need to take it up with him. Not me."

Jesse held himself so tightly the veins stood up in his forearms, his eyes closed, shoulders hunched. "Flat out. Okay. I'm afraid you're going to leave me. For him." He took a deep breath. "And I'm starting to think maybe you should. Maybe it's time we quit all this. It's not healthy, you know. It's been ten years of this weird quasi-thing we've got going on. And to the outside world, I'm not even your cousin; I'm just a weird twink who struck it rich and now doesn't even have to work for a living. Just sit around and look pretty and not ask any questions and make the coffee and ride your dick. You lucked out, too, but you can always do better. Somebody with a brain. Somebody going places. Somebody you don't have to hide."

Underneath, Drew had known that this was the answer, but he was still shocked into silence. Jesse, in full misery now, added,

"You've always been ashamed of me. And I don't blame you. We should never have . . ."

Shaking his head in disbelief, Drew left the wine bottle corked. "Oh, well, *that* is just bullshit," he said. "If you want to leave me, leave. I don't know where you think you'd go, but I'm not stopping you. That's the thing, Jesse; I've never stopped you from doing whatever you wanted to do. Okay? And oh, have I ever wanted to. Yeah, it's true in a way; you're not what I'd like you to be. But you won't get there by starving yourself and throwing money at me. No, three hundred bucks doesn't impress me. *Sorry*. And now you're moping because suddenly *you're* not the center of the universe. Think about *that*. Get over it. We're all fucking damaged." He clasped his hands over his face, astonished he'd say such a thing aloud, but then he nodded to himself, and gave Jesse a solid stare, regardless of whether or not Jesse would meet his eyes. When there still came no response, Drew said, "I've gotta finish."

Jesse had been right on one score, anyway; Drew really didn't need any help packing. He stacked clothes into his suitcases, breathing slowly and calmly, wishing he had thought to put on some music so that the house wouldn't feel so silent. Any minute, he thought he'd hear the door close, and Jesse leaving, but it never happened.

Once Drew had packed to his satisfaction, he took the last of the dim sum to the kitchen and put it in the refrigerator. Jesse still stood there, leaning against the counter, as if he hadn't moved over the last hour. But there were crumbs of cheese and bread on the counter.

"Are you coming to bed?" Drew asked softly.

Still no reply.

"Jess? C'mon," Drew said. "Don't schiz out." Finally, Jesse looked at him, his thin face a pattern of misery. "Would you come to bed?" Drew begged. "Please? I'm leaving tomorrow. I'll be gone for ten days. In fucking Indianapolis. Please let me hold you before I have to do that. Lie down. I'll give you a back rub."

With a sigh, Jesse went to the bedroom, to the bed. Drew sank down beside him, reaching out, stroking Jesse's dark, disheveled hair. Touch made all the difference. For the first time that day, Jesse's knotted shoulders relaxed.

"I love you," Drew whispered. "I don't want to leave you. Not now. Not ever." Jesse turned his head into the petting, savoring it, but not responding more than that. Drew took Jesse's hands in his, nuzzling and kissing them. Slowly, inexorably, Jesse brought the hands to his own mouth.

Drew toed off his sandals and quickly stripped himself naked, then pulled the garments from Jesse's body. They lay side by side on the bed, kissing, rubbing noses, kissing each other's hands, only gradually bringing their bodies together.

"Those things you said hurt," Drew said. "They hurt me, and they hurt you."

"I know," Jesse murmured.

"I have never for a moment been ashamed of you. Sometimes I think you're being silly, or lame, but shame? Never comes into it. I'm proud of you," Drew insisted. "I've always been proud of you. Be proud of me?" He tapped Jesse's still-unshaven chin. "I could make a lot more money if I wasn't such a nice guy."

That made Jesse smile. He let his eyelashes flicker against Drew's cheek, and kissed his lips a little more. "You're not *that* nice," Jesse said.

"You know," Drew said thoughtfully, "if you want to hook up with Michael while I'm gone, I just want you to know that it's okay with me."

Jesse scoffed, rolling his eyes. "Oh, thank you, Sister Andrew," he drawled. "For the indulgence."

"I'm serious," Drew insisted.

"I honestly wasn't planning on it," Jesse said. "I honestly don't even know if he likes me anymore."

"Ask him, then," Drew suggested. "It's just life, Jesse. It's not that important if he doesn't know what he could have if he wanted it." He gave one of Jesse's buttocks a meaningful squeeze. "Stop being so dainty about it. Just go get 'em."

To Drew's surprise, Jesse turned his back, but pulled Drew's arms around him. "Get some sleep," he said. "You're traveling tomorrow. And I biked forty-two miles today. I need rest."

Drew nibbled on the back of his neck. "But what about your hotness? I'm interested in it."

"You'd have to fuck my unconscious body. And I don't

consent to that."

Very soon, Jesse fell asleep. Drew gently disentangled himself, got up, and checked his Blackberry. Still no reply from Michael. Drew grimaced, and went back to bed, holding keeping his own worry private.

12. CHARLIE AND OLIVE OIL.

The next day Drew left before Jesse woke up, and then, late to work, Jesse forgot to check his phone until four in the afternoon. While Jesse had pedaled madly around Manhattan, trailing a wave reeking of tomato sauce and garlic, Drew had called three times and left messages twice.

"Hey, I'm here. I've got meetings pretty much immediately, but I'll call you back later. Don't work too hard. Love you."

"Hey, it's me again. Answer your phone. You're lucky I'm not more paranoid. Anyway, taking a break before dinner. This place I'm staying is like the Harvard Club, but way less cruisy. I should make sure to check all the men's rooms for glory holes. Ladies' rooms, too, I'm sure. This is Indiana, after all. So, uh, call me back when you get a chance." His voice became suddenly snappish, sarcastic, clipped. *"I don't know if you're still mad at me or what. I don't even know what I did. I can't fix it. I'm sorry. Go get your hair cut. Buy a new bike. Get your dick sucked, or something, I don't know. I love you, shithead. Bye."*

When Jesse called back, it went straight to voicemail. He frowned at the recording, in which Drew's voice sounded like the voiceover in an expensive car ad. When it was time for him to speak, he mumbled, "Hey, it's me. Glad you're okay. Um . . . I'm not horny and the bike I have is just fine. I'm not mad. And I'm not insane. I just gotta think about shit. And I haven't. I'm scared, okay?" He sighed and rubbed his forehead. "You should go get *your* dick sucked; it's clearly on your mind. It's fine. Rules out the window. Do whatever you want. Later."

He got home just after ten. Too early. He was physically exhausted, but being back in the house brought back all the hopelessly tangled, overwhelming thoughts he had been able to suppress while on his bike, when there was only the work, the streets, balance and speed.

Uncorking a bottle of *tinta roriz* that Drew had been hoarding all year, he took it up all the stairs in the house, outside, and up the tiny service ladder to get onto the roof. There was a pleasant illusion of privacy, out there with the antennas and tar paper and dry leaves, open to the sky, but still hemmed in by taller buildings on the end of the block. Anyone else on a nearby roof could have seen him, but for now, he was all alone under the sky.

The rich, dark wine burbled through the bottle's throat and into his. It was good enough that he forced himself to slow down and taste it. Drew probably wouldn't be upset that Jesse drank it, though of course he'd be horrified at Jesse drinking straight from the bottle. Drew, Drew, Drew. . . The man who joked that he'd be fine on a desert island as long as he had cloth napkins.

I didn't think I'd miss him so much, Jesse thought. *It's only been a day. But it feels so wrong to be in this house without him. It's unhealthy. The two of us, alone together, with all this space around us. It's ridiculous. A whole fucking town house. How could we fill it? With furnishings? We're like a city with only two inhabitants, but now I'm the last man on Earth. No wonder I feel so fucking empty; part of me is missing.*

But it's not just that. Something else is bugging me, something fundamental. My worst fears coming true. I could never be everything to him. I needed something else. Drew did, too, and I always knew he would. We tried. We worked as hard as we could to be enough for each other. His gifts to me, mine to him. He has given me so much. My life. A sense of family, out of nothing. He is my best friend. Maybe I should just be happy with that.

I should give him Michael. That would be the best gift I could ever give him. Walk away and let them be together.

Jesse sighed and stared at the dark, starless sky. *It makes sense. More sense than me and Drew. I should leave. Go back to Brooklyn, back to the neighborhood. Become my own man, not a kept boy, a freeloading loser of a parasite cousin. I don't need much. I've got skills and I still know people. I'd be okay without him. And it's not like*

I'd be gone gone; we'd only be separated by a river . . . and a whole set of social circumstances.

We could still maybe see each other once in a while, even if it would never be enough. . .

He almost choked on his next slug from the bottle. *Oh, fuck, why am I trying to bullshit myself? I need to see him every day. That's why I fucking live with him. Look at me, sitting on a Midtown roof and drinking a seventy-dollar bottle of wine like it's a Pepsi. I don't know how to do this.*

Michael. I miss him. He's done something to me.

I have to do what's right and give him up. Michael's a real scientist. Going places. Drew won't get bored with him. They'll be happy together. Good together. Different. Better and healthier than me and Drew's mess.

Fuck! I have to be alone again!

Now, dude. Sack up. Get it over with.

He sent Drew a text. **I can never not love you. I'm sorry. But I'll do the right thing.**

Taking another solid swallow from the bottle, Jesse thumbed Michael's number and pressed the call button.

"Hello, Jesse." Michael sounded cautious, but not surprised. He paused for a moment and added, "What's up?"

"Hey," Jesse said. "Nothin'. Drinkin'." A moment of silence fell between them like a brick. Desperate to shove the dead space away, Jesse blurted, "Say something nice to me."

"Huh! Okay." Michael laughed softly. It sounded like he was in bed—a fuller cadence of his baritone voice, chest relaxed. Jesse rubbed his fingers over his suddenly aching forehead. Michael continued, "Well, the weather is nice, which of course you know. Oh, and I just got a multi-gigabyte file of Frankie Knuckles remixes from this woman I know in Spain. Did you know that Frankie Knuckles is actually his real name? I just found that out today. Um, what else? I dunno!" He laughed again. "I'm not sure what to say. I just got home a few minutes ago. I'm tired."

"How was the show tonight?"

"The usual. Fine. Tourists."

"Yeah," Jesse replied knowingly. If only out-of-towners were coming to the show, it was a bad sign. "Hey, um, I had an idea," he said. He gripped the neck of the wine bottle and took a deep breath. "Are you busy tomorrow at lunchtime?"

"No," Michael said. "Have to be at the theater at five, like usual. You want to meet for lunch?"

"Actually, I thought . . . I'd like to come over to your place, and make something for you."

"Oh," said Michael in surprise. "Wow. Um . . . sure! That sounds great."

"Really?" Jesse responded. Yes, it could actually be that easy. The weight he felt was imaginary. "Cool. Okay if I get there at one? Or would closer to noon be better?"

"Depending on what you're making, one sounds fine."

"Nothing too complicated. Just pasta. Do you have a problem with . . ." He ad-libbed a combination of ingredients. "Almonds, mushrooms, asiago cheese, dried tomatoes, or fresh rosemary?"

"Wow, no. None whatsoever. You're a real chef!"

"I cook a little, yeah. And do you have a five-quart pot? I'll bring everything else I need."

"I have a pot I use to boil pasta in. Not sure how big it is, but it's big enough, I'm sure. That's really nice. I'm a little overwhelmed. No one's ever made me lunch before. And I'd love to see you."

"Good." Jesse couldn't help smiling. "It's been too long," he added.

"I know," Michael said gently, regretfully. Quickly he added, "I'll see you at one tomorrow. Bye."

"Okay. Bye."

Back indoors, Jesse unfolded a blanket and lay on the couch in front of the TV, watching ballet on the PBS station. He kept the phone beside him but fell asleep. Hours later, the sound of an incoming text woke him. It was from Drew.

What the hell are you talking about? What did you do?

Jesse deleted it without replying, and went back to sleep.

At ten minutes to one, Michael's door buzzer sounded. He rolled his office chair to the wall and held the open button down with the side of his hand, then moved back in front of his computer and turned his music down. Since he'd woken up, he had been doing yoga asanas and discussing, in traded emails, Frankie Knuckles tracks with the woman in Spain. All his limbs were buzzing with dancy enthusiasm. He felt positively high.

Jesse opened the door and edged in sideways. "I'm here." His flushed face and arm muscles glistened with fresh sweat. He had visibly lost weight since Michael had last seen him, and yet he seemed *more*—higher cheekbones, thick wind-ruffled hair, lips plump and red, eyes gleaming with adrenaline, brown skin. Slung over both shoulders, his delivery panniers bulged as if he had brought half the grocery section of the deli with him.

Michael grinned at him, hands up to his mouth, resisting the urge to knock Jesse to the floor and kiss him. "Here you are," he replied, savoring the words in his mouth. He added quietly, "Looking *so* good."

In the kitchen, Jesse set down the panniers and began unloading. "I might have gone a bit overboard, but I figure you can use this stuff anyway," he said. The food items kept coming—doubled lengths of supple, fresh pasta; fistfuls of rosemary; a paper bag filled with intriguing-smelling mushrooms; smoked cherry tomatoes in a jar; a papery head of garlic; a bag of whole raw almonds; a wax paper-wrapped hunk of dry white cheese the size of Michael's palm. "Maybe just a *little* overboard, but whatever; that's how I roll." He held up the last items with obvious pride. "A little sherry finishing salt, and some olive oil."

"That's, like, a gallon," Michael teased.

"No, it's not," Jesse scoffed. He set the bottle on the counter, next to the dish-drying rack. "It's a liter and a half. That's not that much. It's really good oil, too; fresh, not that rancid stuff you get at the grocery store."

"I've never had finishing salt," Michael said, staring at the pile of artisan ingredients on his tiny kitchen's scant counter. This was enough food for a week, maybe even two.

"Oh, I'm sure you have," Jesse replied. "I'm almost positive you got some at Franca Norris. That bitch *love* her a finishing salt—"

"Look at all that. You really shouldn't have."

"But I did. I just got it from work. You can use it." Jesse rearranged the food on the counter, his cycling shirt soaked at the back of the neck and armpits, drops trickling down from his temples. Not once since he had come through the door had Jesse made eye contact. Michael frowned, narrowing his eyes.

"Why go to all this trouble just for lunch?" Michael asked.

"It's no trouble," Jesse said lightly. He placed the pasta pot under the kitchen tap to fill with water. "I actually haven't cooked for a while and I just brought what I thought I'd want. Those are dried wild porcini mushrooms, by the way. If you don't wanna eat 'em, I can just use the soaking water, but we really should eat 'em because they're expensive. And good," he added.

Michael took a deep, centering breath before replying in a mild voice, "I said I was okay with them." He stood up and moved behind Jesse, close enough to touch. When Jesse turned off the water, Michael reached out and caressed some of the sweat pooling in the curve between Jesse's neck and shoulder. "So... what's it all about? Hmm? Why are you in such a hurry? Are you going to show off your mad culinary skills for me?"

Jesse didn't startle. He had anticipated the touch, somehow. Michael glanced up to see his own reflection, faint but unmistakable, in the window over the sink, and Jesse's eyes watching him. Michael drew the cotton curtain across the window, blocking the reflection, and returned his hand to Jesse's back, caressing around his shoulder blade. "I'm just gonna make a little pasta," Jesse said, but his voice had changed, gone softer, a little breathier.

"Don't you want to take a shower first?"

"I just wanna get the water on. I—Just—" He fell silent, his breathing suddenly heavy.

"C'mon. Why are you really here?" Michael whispered in Jesse's ear, palm against the dampness of Jesse's skin-tight jersey. "Be honest with me." The spongy fabric was moist and cool. Michael reached across Jesse's chest to find the front zipper, pulling it down. "You can't wait a minute to start cooking? Are we in a hurry? What is it, really?" He tugged the hem out, up, over. Jesse raised his arms to be let free. His armpits smelled of garlic, hormones, deodorant. Michael briefly rubbed his cheek against Jesse's stretched triceps, not burying his face in the armpit hair as he most wanted to do, but indulging himself in a deep breath of Jesse's scent. "What's the matter? I thought you were here to have fun."

Michael embraced him again, licking the side of his neck with long swipes intended to taste the sweat, almost to clean it off, like one animal grooming another. "I'm. . . ." Jesse began, voice trailing off into a deep sigh as Michael gently rolled his hardening nipples between his fingers. "Okay. Oh, that feels good. Okay. Um. Hang on." He half-turned, holding up his hands against Michael's chest, pushing him slightly away. He tried to make eye contact, but his eyes had gone heavy-lidded, and he closed them again, his expression pained and uncertain. Fearless, Michael gazed down at Jesse, moistening his lips for the inevitable kiss. "I'm . . . gonna . . . let you go," Jesse said tentatively.

At first not quite understanding, Michael smirked, then returned to his lazy grin. "No, you're not." He returned his touch to Jesse's nipples, rolling them between his fingers again, his grip tightening. Goose pimples spread across Jesse's chest. He was feeling the music too, his head nodding slightly to the beat. In another situation, Michael would have made him dance, but that was only Michael's second-favorite thing to do to music.

"Yes, I am. I really think—I think it's time to—step aside, you know?" Jesse turned to face Michael, a hand skimming down Michael's worn black T-shirt. Instead of stroking Michael's arm, he wrapped his fingers around it, holding on to him. "Don't worry, it's over if you want it to be. You can go. I know you want to."

"I don't think so," Michael murmured. He bent his head, nuzzling the curve of Jesse's neck where he had licked. "I don't want to *go* anywhere. I don't think you even believe that yourself. You can see how much I want you. And I trust you enough to show you."

"You are messing with my head," Jesse muttered, digging his fingertips in. "You blow me off, you talk shit about me . . . and then you say things like that. I don't know you think what we're doing."

"We're *dating*, Jesse. I guess. As far as I know. I think that's what it is. It's confusing, isn't it?" He shook his head. "And I never talked shit about you."

"Oh, but you did, though," Jesse insisted. "Drew wouldn't lie to me about that. He doesn't have it in him. No, he and I have talked about a few things, and so, y'know. . . ." Jesse frowned at the ceiling as he searched for the right word, then sighed, dropped his gaze, and wrapped his arms across his chest. "I thought it would be a nice way to end things."

Michael stepped back, his eyes flicking quickly across Jesse's face, combing the features for detail. "Why do you say it like it's *my* choice?"

"'Cause it is." Jesse tightened his arms around himself. He was a portrait of misery almost laughable in its perfection. It remained at the stage where Michael wanted to take his picture, so he could cherish this beautiful visual forever. "It's not my relationship anymore."

Michael wanted to reach out to Jesse, hold him, comfort him, tell him how gorgeous and ridiculous he was. Instead, he stood even taller and narrowed his eyes. If Jesse was afraid of being coddled, Michael would make sure he didn't engage in it, even if it seemed like the most perfect thing to do. "And *you* don't get a say in the matter?" Michael asked incredulously.

"I do. I did. That was my—offer." Jesse rolled his eyes desperately. "You don't have to see me anymore if you don't want to."

"I don't accept your *ever-so-kind* offer. Thanks all the same. We're seeing each other, and I'm kind of crazy about you, so that's that." Michael smiled pleasantly at Jesse's expression of frustrated dismay seeing an unmistakeable hint of private joy underneath. "So, thanks for the breakup lunch that's not a breakup lunch. Let's just have a regular lunch."

Softly, Jesse said, "Okay."

Michael reached past Jesse and picked up the bottle of pale straw-colored oil. "So this is good stuff, huh?" He unscrewed the top, sniffed the neck, then poured a measure into the palm of his hand. It smelled sharp and felt somehow more liquid in texture than other oil. He dipped his tongue into it.

"Hey!" Jesse protested. "Would you be careful with that? Do

you know how much that costs?" He took the bottle from Michael's grasp.

Michael blinked at Jesse; he had sounded genuinely upset. "I can pay you back," he said, shrugging innocently.

Jesse rolled his eyes in dismay, arms spread, hands wagging in frustration. "No, no. I don't want you to pay me. I just . . . want you to—be careful—oh, shit!"

The bottle slipped from his hand. Michael reflexively tried to grab for it, but it slid easily away, bouncing on the kitchen rug and landing on the linoleum. With a cheerful gurgle, oil pooled on the floor. "Oh, no way!" Jesse groaned like he'd been punched in the stomach. "Fuck."

Michael clapped his hands to his mouth in horror, but the motion also slapped his handful of oil onto his face, all over his glasses, up his nose, over his lips. "Fuck!" he echoed, laughing helplessly, bending down to right the bottle before its entire contents was lost. "Oh, wow," he said, setting the bottle in the sink next to the full pot of water. "Oh, well."

"Oh, God," Jesse whispered, staring at the puddle on the floor. "Even at wholesale."

"I'm so sorry." Fighting down laughter, Michael licked the oil from his lips. Its flavor was vegetal, almost floral, but peppery. The delicious slickness made his mouth tingle. "Mmm, that *is* good."

Jesse finally looked him in the eye. "Well . . . let's not waste it. Take off your clothes."

"Whoa. Okay. I thought you'd be—Never mind." Carefully setting his glasses in the sink, Michael stripped and tossed the shed clothes at his bed. Carefully, he lowered himself to his knees onto the oil-splashed linoleum, swept his hands across the floor, and began rubbing the oil onto his chest and belly. He smiled up at Jesse. "If you're sure."

All the tension in Jesse's shoulders dissolved. "This is not going the way I planned," he protested weakly, toeing off shoes, standing on one leg and then the other to remove his damp socks. He tugged down his bike shorts and underwear in one movement. "But hey."

Michael's hand slicked across Jesse's skin, unhesitatingly

sliding between Jesse's thighs. "So whatever you're trying to do, not now, okay?" Michael said. "Not today. Not tomorrow, either." Oily balls, oily perineum, oily groin. Jesse gasped and bit his lip. Michael's large palm lifted the thickening shaft of Jesse's cock. "You want me," Michael whispered, kissing the head. "And I want you . . . so ridiculously much."

"Michael," Jesse murmured thickly, stroking Michael's hair. "Why do you want to make this so hard?"

"I'd love to make it hard," Michael chuckled, oiling him up, licking him clean and dry, oiling him again. "And it's Friday, and everything is ridiculous. Now, just let me. . . ." He widened his mouth until he could fit everything in: cock, balls, all of Jesse on Michael's tongue, rapidly growing until Michael had to let go before his teeth left.

Jesse groaned. "Ohhh, you're really—not such a shy boy anymore, are you?"

Michael tongued Jesse's balls, his freshly oiled fingers crawling across Jesse's hips and buttocks, slowly working towards the center with both hands. "I missed you," Michael murmured, spreading him apart, greasing his crease, "so much. I have fucked your brains out in my subconscious every single day."

"You should have called me." Jesse slowly lowered himself down to Michael's level and kissed his mouth. Michael turned Jesse around, knees slick on the linoleum, and rubbed his oiled chest against Jesse's back, holding him. Almost effortlessly, his cock slid between Jesse's buttocks, the head seeking entry. Shockingly, delightfully, Jesse fumbled with his own hands, helping. The head of Michael's cock slid against his asshole, burning hot, but not inside; it felt too good, just where he was. He held Jesse for a moment, dropping kisses on his shoulders, stroking Jesse's tightening balls.

He rubbed his cock between Jesse's buttocks, his slick hands taking turns jerking Jesse's dick until he whimpered. They lost balance and purchase on the slick linoleum, sliding, collapsing together with a splash. The oil coated their bodies, their faces. Michael slid his fingers inside Jesse; Jesse returned the favor, creating a rising chorus of harmonic groans as they lay side by side, Jesse's arm improbably twisted behind him. Too soon, he had to take his hand back in an attempt to steady himself against the slippery floor. Michael pressed

Jesse's shoulders down and arched against his ass, watching the reddened head of his penis emerging from the gleaming, pale-golden mounds of Jesse's ass cheeks. Soon, thanks to the sight of his own cock, urgency built, crested, and snapped inside Michael. He felt like screaming in triumph and frustration. But he only gasped when he came, spurting thick, white curlicues of semen against the soft patch of hair at Jesse's tailbone. He grasped Jesse tightly around the waist, holding him still against his own shaking, and underneath them, Jesse's own semen jetted four times onto the floor. "Oh, fuck," Jesse whispered. "Oh, *fuck*."

Michael settled himself back onto his heels, wiped oil and come off the floor, and rubbed the mixture onto his face. Jesse let out a bark of disbelieving laughter. "Oh my *God*! You are so fucking sick."

"Best skin conditioner in the world," Michael replied, grinning. He wedged his face between Jesse's legs, licking the drooping comma of Jesse's cock, tasting the last drops clinging to the head. With spunky, sticky cheeks, hands, and lips, he anointed the holy points of Jesse's body. "We'll both be gorgeous."

"You're already gorgeous," Jesse breathed.

Michael slid his tongue into Jesse's mouth, exchanging one flavor for another. "Oh, I'm crazy about you," he whispered into Jesse's mouth. "You are so cared for. I *care* for you. Don't waste time with worry. Okay?" He held out his hand, waiting for Jesse to take it. "Ready for your shower, now that we're both covered in really expensive, extra-virgin sex grease?"

Grudgingly, Jesse laid his hand on top of Michael's. "Okay. You win."

"We *both* win." Carefully, Michael stood up, and bracing himself against the kitchen counter, and helped Jesse to his feet. Somehow the oil hadn't really gone past the small rectangle of tile that defined the kitchen area, and the carpet had been spared. All the oil had ended up on their bodies.

"You're such a freak," Jesse remarked lovingly. "Reminds me of the way I used to be." His grin frayed at the edges. Michael gave him a comforting hug, and a kiss on the ear for good measure, and finally, at long last, Jesse gazed at him and smiled.

Under the hot water and steam, they kissed more than they

washed, shampooing each other's hair and scrubbing each other with fingernails. When they finally emerged, Michael threw brown paper bags and their damp bath towels over the oil slick on the kitchen linoleum. Standing on that more secure surface, Jesse sliced some of the cheese into thin matchsticks, opened the jar of tomatoes, and poured the bag of raw almonds into a bowl. He brought the food to where Michael sat, naked and expectant, on his bed.

"Lunch," said Jesse. "See?"

"You're not going to make the pasta?" Michael asked, popping almonds into his mouth.

"Without olive oil, it's not gonna be the same."

"So, maybe come by tomorrow night and make it for me?" Michael prompted. "With the mushrooms and everything? Bring a new bottle; I'll pay for it." Without his glasses on, he couldn't make out the minutiae of Jesse's expression, but he seemed to wear an embarrassed smile. "So why are you trying to dump me? Did Drew ask you to do that?"

"No," Jesse said quietly. "I don't know. I'm just really . . . unhappy."

"Are you unhappy right now?" Michael asked. When Jesse shook his head no, Michael persisted. "Are you unhappy with me? Do I make you unhappy?"

"No, no. I'm not unhappy; that's the thing. I think I *was* unhappy. I just didn't know it. And I'd been unhappy in the same way for so long I didn't really know what to do when that changed. I don't know. I've never had to go through this before. I don't know what I'm doing."

"You're unhappy with Drew," Michael surmised. "Hey, there's oil in these tomatoes. Could that be enough?"

"No! No. I mean I'm not unhappy with Drew. Drew's fine; he's perfect. Look, I'll cook for you some other time," said Jesse. "Nothing—this whole thing—" He groaned in exasperation. "Nothing has worked out. I had this whole plan for how today was gonna go and none of it came through. Do you *want* the pasta? I can make it."

"I'm okay," Michael said reassuringly. "But—answer me."

"I love Drew," Jesse said. "I love him so much. But he makes me want to kick through a window. He makes me feel like shit. Well, no, he doesn't. Not on purpose, I don't think. Maybe I am. Unhappy with him, I mean. I shouldn't be. Everything's great."

Michael shook his head. "I don't have my glasses on, but you look really fucking depressed for someone who says everything's 'great.'"

"I'm not depressed," Jesse claimed. He broke into a big, bright smile. "I'm happy right now. I'm happy you still like me."

"Of course I do! Look, Drew's not even in town right now," said Michael. "Let's just forget about him for a little while." He used the side of his foot to stroke one of Jesse's taut calves. "Relax. Be here with me for a while." He rolled his eyes a little and added, "We'll deal with him later. Okay? I'm right here. You don't have to deal with it by yourself anymore."

"It's okay, I got it," Jesse insisted. "I mean, I can handle it. With or without you."

"Probably easier *with* me," Michael said airily, and fed Jesse the biggest slice of cheese. "You don't have to fix everything right now. You can just . . . hang out with your clothes off for a couple of hours. When you're ready to leave, you can leave. But you can even stay here tonight, if you want to. Your house is pretty big. It's probably not fun to be there all by yourself. You want to stay here?"

Jesse just smiled. "You just want somebody to help you clean up that mess."

"I think I like mess," Michael said.

FRI JUN 9 22:40 from Drew Farrow

Nice to get your call earlier. You shouldn't work so hard. You don't need to.

FRI JUN 9 22:46 from Drew Farrow

I don't mean anything by that, in case you're wondering. Your paranoia is contagious. Just throwing some protectiveness your way. You home yet?

FRI JUN 9 23:10 from Drew Farrow

You're either asleep, riding, or out getting your dick sucked. I would choose asleep. On the other hand, getting head is what you ought to be doing.

FRI JUN 9 23:27 from Drew Farrow

Staying at Columbia Club. Old, Natl Reg site, dark wood, etc., lousy with Republicans. Nice sheets, passable food. I'm bored. I almost had a moment during one of the meetings with the Indy group's advisors earlier. I got a Look. He also gave me a card for someplace in town to "check out" if I find the club's gym facility to be "limited." He didn't seem to be cruising me, which is good because I wouldn't. Probably. Maybe later this week if I go out of my mind. Sleep tight, am thinking of you.

FRI JUN 9 23:48 from Drew Farrow

I'm going to check out the place. Club Indianapolis. Sounds shitty but I've done worse. Worth a drink or two just to stretch my legs. Jeans, Versace T, see how it goes.

SAT JUN 10 00:53 from Drew Farrow

I got picked up on the way. Two guys in an Escalade. Youngish, both have dark hair. They have candy. Looking up!

SAT JUN 10 00:59 from Drew Farrow

Going to Deke's place on way to club. Deke younger, Joe older. I could use a drink. It's hot here even after dark. They are impressed I'm from NYC. I plan to close my eyes and imagine it's you two.

SAT JUN 10 02:13 from Drew Farrow

On a run to get better shit. That stuff was more stepped on than a weight watchers scale. Hate Deke's; empty and tacky. He's in computers but clueless about living. Not even a rug. I blew him anyway because of course. He couldn't come. Also nothing to drink but beer. I want to go home now.

SAT JUN 10 03:10 from Drew Farrow

If you get this, please call me back and tell me to stop it and get the fuck out of here. I have a headache and a limp dick and I don't want anything going in my ass.

SAT JUN 10 03:15 from Drew Farrow

This is bullshit. Leaving.

SAT JUN 10 03:18 from Drew Farrow

Don't pick up a guy just to go home and play video games. What the fuck kind of shit is that supposed to be? Are you adults? Yeah, yeah, thanks for the blow, but I pretty much paid to replace it with ten times the quality and fuck, I've just been had. I been had. I been had. I have been had. I have bean head. Oh yeah, there was a reason why I stopped in the first place, and it wasn't for you, butterfly.

SAT JUN 10 04:01 from Drew Farrow

All-night bar, tiny, sixth floor, three chairs. Secret clubhouse within the clubhouse like the ones at Yale Club. We should go back there. I ran into Anschutz from earlier, the one who gave me the card, up drinking coffee. Went back to his room, he made me herbal tea and gave me a valium. One user always recognizes another. I must have looked bad, all sweaty, grinding my teeth. Like a sad old used-up club whore. He asked me if I wanted to have him do some NA shit, but I got away and now I'm in my room. In bed. I turned up the AC and now I wish I hadn't because the bed is painfully cold.

SAT JUN 10 08:55 from Jesse Landon

Dirty D, it's not my job to keep you clean. That's your job. No more yayo, not with strangers in dildomobiles. It's dangerous and you know it. you need to get your freak on, pick something that won't wreck your palate. I haven't even made gelato yet.

SAT JUN 10 08:59 from Jesse Landon

Miss you too. Don't be an asshole. Day at a time.

SAT JUN 10 09:48 from Drew Farrow

Developed by Norman Lear. Breakfast is terrible. This OJ tastes like they scraped up old dried Fanta and reconstituted it. I will lie back and think of Barney Greengrass.

SAT JUN 10 19:21 from Drew Farrow

If I have to go to a breakfast meeting tomorrow, I am going out tonight. Hold the yayo. Two martinis, three if they're good. Best or only decent club in town apparently. The weekend doorman tipped me off. Intriguing haircut. Apparently there are

queens all over the place in this town. Why don't they leave?

SUN JUN 11 02:38 from Drew Farrow

Every mary in the place had a turn wetting me down one way or the other. In taxi still dripping wet. Had perfect amount to drink. Blackout back room listening to fucking, jerking off, baptized in piss. No names, no touching, no faces. Fun but not as great as I remember. Thinking of M licking me clean, licking other mens cum off my feet. Are you two in touch? Call him, don't be scared. Please suck his cock for me.

SUN JUN 11 02:50 from Drew Farrow

I officially hate it here.

SUN JUN 11 10:53 from Drew Farrow

Overslept. Puked. Barbed wire in my head. Praying for death. Anschutz for the save; said last night's flank steak salad might have been bad. I hope he has another valley of the dolls for Old Miss Andy. Horseback riding? Have to keep telling myself "seven-figure deal." Please be having fun back home. Someone should.

SUN JUN 11 22:45 from Jesse Landon

I AM having fun. Thank you. Mackenzie Phillips says hi.

SUN JUN 11 22:46 from Michael Kaminsky

Check your email. Jesse body-groomed me. I can show you the extent of it. NSFW! I look IMMENSE. Don't tell Jesse I showed you. It'll be our secret. I know you.

A week later, a town car dropped Drew off in front of his house on East Sixty-First Street. Resisting the urge to drop to his knees and kiss the pavement in gratitude, Drew did allow himself to glance two doors down and whisper to himself, "Monty, I'm home."

When Drew dragged himself upstairs to the second floor and the kitchen, he saw a note clipped to the refrigerator with the magnet shaped like a pinup girl riding a rocket. He leaned against the counter, reading, a slow smile spreading across his face.

Michael and I are meeting at Agra for dinner at ten. Meet us and eat non-American food. There's a strawberry agua fresca in the fridge for you. Have that first, take a shower, put on something sexy, then come on down! Love, Butterfly

Drew followed the directions to the letter, changing from his sweaty travel clothes to a loose cotton Oxford shirt, dark red linen trousers, and soft leather moccasins, leaving his hair disheveled and his face unshaven. Downing the agua fresca was like drinking the essence of life itself. The restaurant was two blocks away, up Lexington, and he did the walk in a daze, eagerly drinking in the sights of his neighborhood in the fading red light of the warm day.

Located on the second floor of a very residential-looking house, Agra was actually a lush little Indian restaurant with excellent ambiance and a good view from one of the tables by the window. On his first visit there five years ago, the same week as they had moved into the new house, Jesse had decided on a favorite table. Tonight there he sat, wearing a satisfied, almost smug smile. Michael sat next to him. They looked to be almost finished with a bottle of wine, and had not yet been served food.

Drew stood at the entrance, half-hidden behind a beaded curtain, and studied them. They matched in more ways than one, both wearing plain white Hanes T-shirts and blue jeans, their hair the same shiny shade of not-quite-black, heads tilted in the same direction, legs crossed the same way, hands linked between their laps. Despite the difference in height, they looked almost similar enough to be brothers, grinning the same way, so taken with each other that they didn't even have to look at each other anymore. Drew felt something twist inside him, envy and jealousy and desire and sentimentality fighting for the top spot. Half of him wanted to rush toward them, flip the table, yell at them to cut it out and stop being so perfect; the other half wanted to quietly leave them to it, let them be in love, just shimmer away. They didn't need him.

But then Jesse looked up and caught his eye, and broke into a smile so pure and radiant that it was humbling. "'Ey, *cugino*!" Jesse yelled, noisy, outré. He waved his arm frantically. "We were waiting for you!" Michael looked up too, also smiling, but less overjoyed than calm. Satisfied. Relaxed and contented. An *all's right with the world* smile. Drew sighed heavily, letting the weight of everything roll off him, smiled back, and went to them.

Both men rose from the table and gave Drew hugs and kisses on the mouth. "Welcome home," Jesse said.

"I'm glad to see you survived," Michael added.

"Just barely," Drew chuckled. "Let's get some pappadums so I can erase the memory of iceberg wedge salads from my palate."

"Oh, poor baby!" Jesse replied. He poured the remaining wine into a waiting glass and handed it to Drew. "Don't you worry, arugula and mesclun are here to make it all better. Well, not *here*. Do they eat salad in India?"

"Who cares," Michael put in, lifting a menu and adjusting his glasses. "As long as there's sag paneer, I don't care. I'm so sick of pasta. No offense, Jay."

"None taken," Jesse replied.

"'Jay'?" Drew inquired, blinking indignantly. He didn't like it. "Am I gonna be 'Dee' next?"

"No, silly," Jesse said. "You'd be 'A.'"

"Alf," Michael put in.

Drew groaned theatrically. "Don't remind me. I was in high school in the eighties."

Jesse stroked Drew's leg with his ankle. "Valedictorian," he reminded Drew. "Captain of the football team. Class president. Debate champion?"

"And mathlete," Drew added grudgingly, his face flushing.

"I was a mathlete," Michael mentioned, deadpan.

Jesse shrugged. "I sucked dicks for money."

"Jesse." Drew shook his head warningly.

"Oh yeah, also for fun. Annnnd for me. It was the nineties—"

"Quit trying to change the subject," Drew said. "By the way, Michael, there's something actually important I have to tell you. It's not great news, but—"

"I'm fired?" Michael guessed, unbothered, sipping his wine.

Drew sighed. "Not exactly. But. The show closes on Thursday. It was on my voicemail as soon as I got off the plane."

Michael shrugged, but he looked crestfallen just the same.

"That's showbiz, I guess," he admitted. "Tonight we had eleven seats. It's too bad. There's been a big improvement in quality over the last week or so."

"Too late," Drew said. "Those early reviews killed us. Oh well. Nothing ventured, nothing gained. And hey, it's not like nothing good came from it." He looked directly at Michael and smiled slightly, as if weighing all the angles of the idea. "I'm glad," he decided. "It was worth it. We put on a good show. It's about developing talent. And, most importantly, there's always the consolation of throwing a good closing party. There's no real budget for it, but we can do something fun, if someone's got the space."

"How about your place?" Michael suggested guilelessly.

"No," Drew replied quickly. "No. Absolutely not. No parties at my house."

"Why not? What a waste, I'd think."

Drew shook his head. "No, I just—"

"Control," Jesse interrupted. "Everything."

"I like to go home after a party, not have it be there. No, other suggestions are welcome. But not my place."

"You heard the man," Jesse said with a shrug. "Not at his place." Michael rubbed Jesse's arm and patted his hand.

Drew gave them a look. "Our place," he amended.

"I don't give a fuck," Jesse said. "You know better than I do. And it's not *ours*, it's yours. Don't even, let's not go there right now."

"Right," Drew agreed. "Let's not." He examined the menu. "Anyway, what do we want to get? They're going to kick us out in an hour, so be decisive."

Sag paneer, samosas, and a lamb biryani for Drew ended up being more than sufficient. None of them ate very much, and half of the meal was packed up into cartons to take home. During the meal, Drew regaled them with horror stories from Indianapolis so that Jesse and Michael wouldn't have to fill the silence by telling him what they'd been up to all week, alone together, apparently learning how to match and synchronize their movements. Michael had picked up several of Jesse's mannerisms, and also kept reaching out to touch him as if to calm and steady him, though Jesse hadn't seemed so relaxed and mellow in months. And both men were very interested in Drew, asking questions and laughing at the right moments, and touching Drew's legs under the table to an almost annoying degree. It was arousing to be touched that way, but Drew was also bone-tired and wanted to go to bed more than anything else.

At eleven, with the table cleared of empty glasses and stray grains of rice and pea, Drew angled his chair back and gave Michael a smile. "So," Drew said languidly, "where do you want to be tonight? You know there's room in our bed."

With only a polite level of hesitation, Michael smiled back and shook his head. "I'm going to head home. Get some sleep. You two should be alone together tonight," he said. "I'd just complicate things."

Both of them glanced at Jesse, who was looking intently at Drew. "Do you think so?" Drew asked Jesse, reaching across the table. "Just be at home, get some sleep? I'm off for the next four days, so. . . ."

"I work in the morning," Jesse said slowly. "So . . . yeah, just some sleep."

Michael stood and dusted off his lap. "Great," he said. "See you both later this week. Sleep well, okay?" He bent down and kissed Jesse, turned and kissed Drew more slowly, sucking Drew's upper lip momentarily between his teeth before letting go. "Come see the show before it's all packed back up." He gracefully strode away, disappearing beyond the beaded curtain.

Drew and Jesse watched him go, then looked at each other, and Jesse finally took the hand that Drew had extended to him. "Let's go sleep together," he murmured. "I need it."

"I need it, too," Drew replied.

They held hands all the way home. Upstairs, even in the dim half-light, Drew could tell that the bed had remained untouched and unslept in since he'd left. He was too tired, too relieved to be home, to care.

13. *VIRIDIAN* MANIFEST.

For the next few days, Michael found himself with his hands full with a major board failure. And when he wasn't painstakingly rewiring and testing the device, he was scrambling to try to rent, secure, and program backup lighting for the show. There wasn't time to spend with either Jesse or Drew—he had to set an alarm to remind himself to eat—and so he had to make do with exchanging text messages a few times a day.

Michael didn't really mind; he was still worn out and sore after those days in Jesse's voracious presence while Drew had been away. He'd never eaten so much in his life, let alone fucked and come so much, or spent so much time on roofs and fire escapes and in stairwells and ladders that led to them, listening to all of Jesse's stories about those same places, his personal memories of them. Fights and flights and thefts and blowjobs. So much climbing, so much effort, all of it tinged with a fundamental sadness and loneliness.

Michael had been blown away by Jesse's generosity and trust. But he'd missed Drew. And clearly, despite the energy and enthusiasm flowing throughout everything he did, Jesse had seemed a little lost, unmoored, without him.

Michael was glad to hand Jesse back over. There really was work to do.

On Friday evening, ninety minutes before the second-to-last

performance of *Viridian*, Jenna Margolis stood center stage and prudly announced that she had secured a sponsorship from an up-and-coming vodka company to host the closing-night party at Manifest, a club over on Waverly and Sixth. "I work, and it's in my best interests to get another job as soon as possible," she explained, "so these guys are going to fly me back to LA and I'll host another party for them. See? Occasionally my selfishness actually benefits everyone." She winked and chuckled, and Michael enthusiastically joined in the round of applause from the rest of the company. As entitled, single-minded, and superficial as she was, he had gained immense affection for her, as well as admiration for how effortlessly performance came to her. What had at first seemed obnoxious, Michael had come to see as fearless energy. All the same, he'd be glad to see the back of her.

Ducking into the relative quiet of the projection booth, Michael made a phone call. "Drew Farrow," was the response.

"It's Michael."

"Mmmm! What a marvelous thing to hear!"

He couldn't resist snickering. "My God, you make everything sound so dirty."

"When it comes to you, well . . ."

"Jenna got a company to sponsor the closing party. She just announced it."

"Oh, for Pete's sake. I've already hired catering to do it at Laurence's."

Michael suggested, "Could they just serve it at Manifest?"

"Different zoning, different purpose. I don't feel like dealing with the permits. Fine, one more kill fee. The show is now eighty-*four* hundred dollars in the red." For once, Drew didn't sound sexy. "Oh well. It's only money, right?"

"Are my paychecks gonna start bouncing?" Michael asked lightly.

"Ooh, I hope not. No promises, though. Show business."

"I'd really hate to get the union involved."

"That's not actually funny," said Drew.

"Ah. Yeah. Sorry. This whole humor thing is—yeah. Uh, how

are you? In some abstract, non-financial sense?"

It got a laugh. "Fine, good. Too much sleep. Whether I need it or not, I don't like it. Looking forward to going out tomorrow night. Wish you could come to dinner first with us."

"That's okay," Michael said. "We could maybe get dinner late. Like, afterwards."

"After the party?" Drew inquired, as though the idea of anything happening after a party was inconceivable. "Okay, yeah. Well, we'll see."

"I'll be hungry. Um. Hey. I miss you," Michael said, the whole point of him calling in the first place.

"Mmmm, well, I can't wait to taste you again," Drew growled, voice firmly back in seductive cadence. "Come by tonight? Fuck the lights. It's curtains tomorrow; who cares?"

Michael laughed dazedly. "Well, I do," he replied hesitantly. "I know you get to put on a show whenever you feel like it, but these kinds of chances are rare for me." His tone solidified as he went on. "I mean, the critics, the audiences, whatever. I mean, for me to build and operate something that had just been in my mind before? In New York? Jesus . . . Yeah, I care."

"And *that's* why I hired you," Drew said, voice gravelly with satisfaction. "I don't want it to be as unlikely as all that for you anymore. I do get it, you know."

"Yeah."

"I'll see you tomorrow night," Drew said. "Save it for me, okay?"

"Save—? Oh." Michael laughed, his cheek suddenly very hot against the plastic case of his phone. "Sure, I absolutely will," he said, though he could tell that Drew had already disconnected. He sat bemused for a few heartbeats, amazed at Drew's ability to just process him and set him aside so deftly. He returned to work with a smile on his face.

In the morning, his ringtone woke him out of a feverish dream, and he brought the handset to his ear without checking the source of the call. "Hmmm . . . ?"

"Michael, sweetheart?"

"Mom?" He struggled upright and squinted at the clock. "Hey, it's only a little after seven. Everything okay?"

"Well, more or less. I just wanted to be sure and catch you before you got busy for the day."

He muffled his groan of dismay. "Ah, well, yeah. Good call. Today's gonna be—You sure everything's okay out there?"

"I'm hanging in there. Your father is fine."

"Good, I'm glad to hear it. I'm fine, too. But I, uh, I honestly do have to go in a moment." Michael found a stack of paper to rustle. "The show is closing tonight, actually, so I've got a lot to take care of today."

"Oh, is it? Is that good or bad?"

"It's, uh, well, it's a shame you won't get to see it." Yes, with the simulated blow job scene that would probably give her an aneurysm.

"You should have told me. I'd have come. Oh, Michael, you should have told me earlier."

"I didn't know myself until very recently," Michael said. "Sometimes there's practically no notice. I apologize. Next time, I promise you'll have front row tickets, opening night."

"If there even *is* a next time. Does this mean you're going back to school?"

Michael opened the window blinds and stared down at Second Avenue, realizing that he had barely given his next move a single thought. "Not sure at the moment, Mother," he said, "but I do apologize. I really do have to go now. Promise I'll call you tomorrow and we can have a proper conversation, all right? Like, a real talk."

"Remember we're not home from church until noon. I don't think we'll visit with Norma this week so that's no worry. She's had such a hard time of it since Matthew."

"Yes, Mom, I know. Talk to you tomorrow." He clicked the "end" button immediately, then stared at his hand holding the phone. *I did that. It's easier than I thought. Just hang up. No feelings, no fuss.*

It felt wonderful. Erotic, even.

He went for an excellent, if earlier than scheduled swim, ate lunch sitting on a park bench in the sun, and made his way down to the theater, wearing the same calm smile throughout. His original board was fixed, finally, just in time, and working perfectly. He had all the time he wanted to wander around the theater, absorbing and memorizing as much detail as possible.

His mother was right; there was no guarantee that he'd ever be able to do this again. The kinds of things he did weren't necessarily suited to plays or traditional theater structures. The clubs he'd designed for hadn't had opening or closing nights, not like this. They had no cast, no active crew, and only the barest semblance of a director. It was far from the same thing. There was no feeling of company.

But he could probably do without that, honestly. It wasn't a deal breaker. He wasn't so desperate to work in theater, specifically, that it took precedence over all the other things he might want to do. There was so much more he *could* do. It wasn't worth getting attached to this one path.

Viridian's final performance came off as perfectly as could be imagined. Two weeks after opening, everyone had found the rhythm, the groove, and everything was easy. For the first time since he had read the initial script almost a year ago, Michael really appreciated the musicality and spectacle of the show, its overly sensual oddity, and not just the technicalities of making it look the way it should. He caught the eye of the writer, Lavinia Marcus, as she sat in the house. They shared a nod and a smile. All the same, he felt no desire to join the rest of the creatives onstage at curtain call. When the director waved at his booth, he responded with a rippling wave that passed along the lights surrounding the house. The audience, as sparse as they were, gave an enthusiastic cheer at that; a piercing, overarching whistle came from third row, aisle. Michael laughed, seeing Jesse with his fingers to his lips and Drew grinning at him, rubbing his hand across Jesse's back.

Jesse pointed at Michael, his lips forming, emphatically, *You.*

Michael couldn't take his hands off the board to gesture back. Instead he had to content himself with a wink and a smile and getting back to work, lowering the stage lights on the show for the last time and calling up the house lights, stilling the applause, instantly transforming dozens of faces with just a few flicks on the sliders.

He and the grips hustled through the final shutdown as quickly and efficiently as they could, but Michael was still gritting his teeth impatiently by the time he shut the door on the storage space across the alleyway from the theater. The lobby was deserted, and those still left behind were either not going to the party, or were heading there themselves. Michael managed to grab a ride in a cab with the costumers. They skipped out of the vehicle immediately upon arrival, leaving Michael to pay the driver.

The nightclub had been closed to the public, but Michael could hear that things were already raging inside. The lighting and environment were nothing much by his standards, but they weren't actively bad, and a band with two drummers, an accordionist, and a fiddle player stomped out a lively rhythm that reminded him pleasantly of the Pogues. And before he could be distracted even more, he felt his arm gripped and tugged, almost yanking him off his feet.

Jesse shouted in his ear, "I have some molly."

For a moment, Michael just gaped at him. "Really?"

"It's . . . not that rare, dude." Jesse seemed embarrassed. "You want to?"

"Yes," Michael replied. "Fuck yeah."

Jesse grinned. "Awesome! That's right, I forgot you're all about that ac-eeeed!" He wagged his hand to approximate bumping bass.

"Glad you said something now," Michael said. "Otherwise I'd end up face-down in a bucket of margaritas."

"That sounds great," said Jesse.

Eyes sparkling in squares of light reflecting from the mirror ball on the ceiling, Drew smoothly approached, smiling wickedly. "What are you drinking?" he asked Michael, laying his hand on Michael's chest so that he had no need to shout.

"I guess I'm not drinking," Michael confessed.

Drew looked at Jesse. "Oh, really?"

"Fuck you both," said Jesse. "Bring me a shot of DiSaronno."

"Amaretto?" Drew replied. "Fuck *you*." He kissed Jesse on the forehead and slid away.

"Amaretto?" Michael echoed, arching his eyebrow.

"It's so I don't drink too much," said Jesse. "I haven't gotten shitfaced on amaretto since I was ten years old. C'mon, let's go dance. I'll get you set up."

Michael didn't so much dance to this kind of music as he just sort of jumped around and vibrated, but Jesse couldn't do much better, nor did anyone else. The floor was small enough that they were all crammed together, anyway. There was a line five deep at the bar. Jenna sat prominently at one end, actually on the bar, her baby-oiled legs elegantly crossed at the ankle, with an actual spotlight trained on her and everything. The sight made him laugh so hard he doubled over and almost caught one of Jesse's knees to the face. "Too much," he said to himself as he straightened up, dropping his hand onto Jesse's shoulder to steady himself.

"Or not enough?" Jesse replied softly. He seemed to wipe the end of his nose, only to unfurl his tongue and display a tablet, neatly bitten in half, held on the tip.

Michael leaned over and caught Jesse's open mouth with his. With his tongue, Jesse poked the tablet into Michael's cheek, and Michael held his breath until he could draw away and swallow. It was bitter and awful, but at least it was done with. There was no way to tell if anyone had seen that kiss, and it was too late, and it didn't matter anyway who saw or what they thought of it.

He had never been so free.

Drew reappeared and handed Jesse a shot glass, and Michael a bottle of water.

Michael gratefully took a sip, just enough to clear the bitterness from his mouth. Drew, empty-handed, took Jesse's face in his palms and kissed him, hard and insistently, while Michael stared at them. Drew let Jesse go, turned to Michael, and extended his hand. "Dance?"

"I was . . . already . . ." Michael shook himself and shrugged. "Right. Yeah, sure."

Drew's idea of dancing, even to high-velocity Irish folk-punk, was to enfold Michael in his arms and sway a little, cheek to cheek. Admittedly, it did feel nice. "I've got a gram of that white girl," Drew murmured into Michael's ear. "If you want some."

Michael laughed and shook his head. "Are you two trying to get me high?" he murmured back. "Take advantage of me?"

"I shouldn't think you'd need that much persuasion."

Michael grinned, feeling Drew's fingers slide from his waist to his ass and squeeze. "Now you're calling me a slut. You've really got to work on your people skills, Mr. Farrow."

"I'll get right on that," said Drew.

His dexterous fingers settled on Michael's crotch, probing, selecting. Michael quivered as a song ended and the pond of jouncing bodies came to a roaring halt around them. "My people skills tell me that within an hour, you'll be on your knees in the men's room, in front of me with my cock in your mouth," said Drew, eyes glittering intently.

"You get a head start on the coke?" Michael asked breathlessly, looking around for Jesse to step in and save him. But the younger man was at the bar, talking to Jenna Margolis like they were old friends.

Drew shook his head. "Oh no, when I start I don't stop until it's gone. That's why I only got a gram." He smiled. "Drink your water," he said. "I think you'll need to be hydrated."

The band performed one more song and then a DJ took over, filling the room with the high-energy nonsense of Fatboy Slim, which Michael had never enjoyed so much as now. Drew disappeared and Jesse returned to the tune of "Give the Poor Man a Break," his dancing skills better than usual. Perhaps it was just the light. People kept coming by, congratulating Michael. That was probably why Drew had left off palming Michael's cock, as much as he hadn't wanted him to stop. He could almost still feel Drew's hand there, warm, protective, demanding, distracting. *Once I start, I don't stop.*

"Is this shit real?" Michael said in Jesse's ear.

"Real? What are you talking about?" Jesse wiped his eyes, shook his head. "Oh, you mean the molly? Sure. I think."

"Fuck, I hope this isn't just fucking speed, Jesse. That would not be cool."

"You feeling okay?" Jesse asked, hands out, smiling. "I am. This doesn't feel like speed to me."

"Shit." Michael raked nervous fingers through his hair. He had just violated one of his personal rules, taking a drug he wasn't absolutely certain about. But Jesse didn't seem bothered; he wrapped his arm around Michael's shoulders and kissed his cheek.

"I think it's all good," Jesse said reassuringly. "I've never gotten substandard stuff from this chick, and I've been buying from her for years. And, besides, I split it with you. It won't be a strong dose of anything, or we'd feel it by now. Everything's gonna be fine. Do you feel okay?" His hands stayed on Michael, stroking his arms, his chest. "We can go."

"No, I . . . I don't." He tried to laugh at himself. "Forgive me."

"Of course," Jesse said. "There's always that 'oh, crap, I've just taken psychoactive drugs' moment of panic. And now it's over! Yay. It's your night of triumph. Relax. Go tell the DJ to play something better. This is your party." Jesse seemed to be having problems focusing his eyes. He blinked, and tears streamed freely down his face. He tried to wipe them away with the back of his hand. Michael caught the hand, brought it to his lips, sipped the tears from Jesse's fingers, and moved to licking them off Jesse's face. Jesse giggled and hugged him. "I think you're rolling," Jesse laughed. "I'm pretty sure."

"Where's Drew?" Michael asked.

He saw Jesse's cheek twitch, as if his mouth wasn't sure which direction to go. "I think he's in the little girls' room," Jesse replied, "powdering his nose." He smiled grimly. "Could you go be a dear and remind him that cocaine causes erectile dysfunction?"

"Are you okay? What's with your eyes?"

"Nothin', they're fine. It's just something that happens when I'm on something." Jesse waved Michael off. "It's an Italian thing. No, go find him. If he's hitting the blow we need to get him out of here before he runs out, or we might not see him again until next week. That shit. . . . Hey, just do me a favor, okay?" Jesse grimaced. "Motherfucker, harshing my mellow."

It was better to walk away from that drama, Michael thought. The bottle of water that had disappeared into him now wanted to exit, anyway. The path between where he had been standing and the restroom was a minefield of well-wishers, and he was starting to get annoyed by the time he was through them, his jaw aching from smiling. He would need to get some gum or something. . . .

In one of the two stalls, Drew leaned casually against the metal partition as if he were in a particularly gritty downtown modeling shot. "Come on in," he said to Michael, as if he did this every day. Michael took a deep breath and stepped into the stall.

"I actually have to pee," he admitted.

"Be my guest," said Drew, edging aside, away from the toilet bowl.

"Oh my God." Michael rolled his eyes and looked to Heaven. "I really am not sure I can with you staring at me—"

"You'd better," said Drew. He smiled and crinkled his eyes. "I could go run water in the sink, if that would help."

"Ugh. You fucking pervert." Michael sighed and unzipped.

Drew didn't even pretend not to stare. "I know," he whispered.

Michael pictured the parting of the Red Sea in *The Ten Commandments* and managed to let down, bright piss arcing into the bowl. Even it looked a bit epic, the way Michael was seeing and feeling by now.

Rather than continuing to watch, Drew instead rubbed his hand down Michael's back, nuzzling against Michael's neck with a jawline faintly textured with new stubble. "I don't know if I can get into this with you," Michael said warningly.

"You already are," Drew replied, and kissed Michael's cheek.

"Fuck—! Stop it, I'm trying to take a leak." Michael laughed helplessly.

"You're succeeding." Drew laughed too. "Make me stop? Make me."

"How can I do that?"

"You know," said Drew.

"You straight?" Michael asked before he thought better of it.

Drew's expression didn't really change; he raised an eyebrow and seemed to consider Michael more carefully. "Not," he replied, grasping Michael's cock before he could put it away, "exactly."

Michael sighed tightly; the sense of arousal he'd had for a while, and which had been making urination challenging, receded into the general turmoil of every amplified sensation. "You know what I mean," he said.

"The candy remains in my left hip pocket," replied Drew, unruffled. "Untouched. I'd like you to verify that. So you know you can trust me." In the muted light of the men's room Drew's eyes, hooded by winglike lashes, were dark but completely lucid. "You know you can trust me, Michael. Never let it be said that I'm dishonest. Yeah, I've got a lot of things wrong with me, but I'm not dishonest." He shook Michael's cock, just enough, and gently tucked it back into the fold of his briefs. "Everything's under control. Now. Get on your knees."

"I won't," Michael said, lifting his chin, hoping he wasn't grinding his teeth too hard. "I'm not like you."

"You just wish you were." Drew shook his head, still wearing the calm smile. "Go on, check my pocket. Stroke my dick while you're there, since you're too good to bend down for me."

"I'm not too good," Michael murmured. "I just . . . don't want to." There wasn't much room for his hand in Drew's tailored pocket, but he felt and then withdrew a small billfold-shaped envelope. He marveled, as he opened it, that he had never thought of hand-tooled leather wallets for wraps of cocaine, but it made all the sense in the world. There was no real way for him to know if the wrap had already been sampled, but he imagined that it probably wouldn't be intact at all if it had been. "You gonna do this later?"

"Maybe a little," Drew said.

"You sure you want to do that?" Michael slid the envelope back into Drew's pocket, making sure to add the intimate stroke that had been requested.

"Yes," Drew said with a sigh. "At home. And I'd like us to go soon. That's not all I want to do." His eyes fluttered closed, hand trapping Michael's in place. "A whole night, working over two hot young fellows, both rolling balls? What the fuck are we waiting for?"

"Jesse was just . . . concerned," Michael muttered.

"And I love that about him," Drew returned smoothly. "Come on, let's go. Before *he* drinks too much."

If Michael didn't leave here soon, he was going to have too much to drink too. His mouth tasted awful and an intense, obsessive craving for tofu bacon was taking over his thoughts. A tofu bacon and peanut butter sandwich sounded perfect, washed down with one of those vodka-and-Coke cocktails Jesse liked. He was losing his mind, and the DJ put on a remix of "Y.M.C.A." for some reason, and Michael wasn't sure how much more he could take.

Drew appeared, as before, at Michael's elbow from out of nowhere. This time he had recovered Jesse from somewhere in the shadows, and was herding him, his front to Jesse's back, towards Michael, who stood dazedly in the middle of the dance floor. "So fucking high," Jesse shouted, dramatically throwing an arm across Michael's shoulder.

"Don't be so bridge-and-tunnel," Drew said reproachfully. "Michael? We'll get a taxi."

"Are you all fucked up?" Jesse whispered at Michael urgently. When Drew's head was turned, saying good night to one of the co-producers, he added much more soberly, "Is *he* fucked up?"

"No, no, he's square," Michael replied, laughing faintly. Jesse winked at him and turned in Drew's arms, theatrically covering his face, hairline, and ears with kisses. Michael took up his place behind Drew, encouraging the herding, aiming them at the door. As soon as they were outside, Jesse straightened up and seemed entirely in command of his faculties, if not entirely sober. It was much better than Michael felt.

Drew sat in the front seat of the taxi, next to the driver, and allowed Michael and Jesse to slump together in back. Michael really felt that he needed that quiet, warm time when he almost could relax, listening to Jesse's breath and heartbeat, holding hands. Up front, Drew fluently conversed with the Algerian driver in French.

By the time they had all gone inside the house on Sixty-First Street, Michael definitely felt the drug inside him. It wasn't MDMA, most likely. Or at least not purely, probably combined with something else that was similar but less bright, less sharp. He'd taken MDMA enough times, both pure and adulterated, to be aware of the difference. He wasn't sure what it was, but least it wasn't methamphetamine, or PCP, or something else grotesque and jagged. This just made him want to spend the night in a pile of pillows and blankets, curled up with Jesse.

It seemed, though, that Drew had other ideas. "Guest room," he said, setting his keys on the kitchen counter and fussing with something in the cabinet. "Jesse, will you show him?"

"Guest room," Michael said wonderingly. "Of course." He had yet to see the whole house.

"Actually, it was four bedrooms when he bought it," Jesse drawled, taking Michael by the hand and leading him up another flight of stairs behind a door at the side of the kitchen that Michael had never really noticed before. "He knocked one of them out on that floor to expand the kitchen and Drew's bedroom. Up here, that door leads to the office, and that leads to the gym, and this—" Jesse turned the knob on a door painted an incongruous sky blue. "Is a guest room. Or it's my room. Sometimes."

It was dark inside until Jesse turned on one nightlight shaped like the Eiffel Tower, and another one shaped like the Sydney Opera House. There was just a bed—another staggeringly large California king like the one in Drew's room, this one's headboard in what looked like deep violet suede—a plain wooden chair, and a tiny wastebasket. They took up the entire room. A violet curtain hid any existing window. There didn't even seem to be a closet. "Is this where they keep Harry Potter?" Michael quipped, charmed by the cheap, tacky nightlights.

"What?" Jesse asked, clearly uncomprehending, busily stripping off his shirt. "This was a doctor's house, apparently, once upon a time. He saw patients downstairs in what's now just the foyer. It's like, holy shit."

"Holy shit," Michael echoed, staring at Jesse's bare torso, underlit by those two tiny incandescent light bulbs, one very slightly warmer in color than the other. They were staggeringly well-positioned to perfectly outline all of his muscles, bones, tendons, the perfect tight V of his lower abdomen. "I know you're probably hungry all the time, Jesse, but can I just say you look absolutely amazing right now?"

Jesse looked stymied for quite a long while before his face softened into a smile. "Of course you can," he replied. "Just . . . it was freaky. You sounded just like Drew for a minute."

"Oh," said Michael. "Really?"

"Why are you still wearing clothes?" came Drew's voice from the doorway. "Jess, is Miles okay?"

"Yes," Jesse yelled back, and sat on the edge of the bed. "You heard him," he said to Michael.

Michael cocked his head. "Undress me," he suggested. *Sketches of Spain* emanated quietly from a speaker grille by the door.

"Take off your own boots," Jesse qualified. "We're not there yet."

"Would you like to be there?" Michael asked quietly, sitting beside him, remembering the sight of Jesse at Drew's feet.

"I dunno," Jesse said. He ran his finger around the neckline of Michael's shirt, stroking his knuckles against Michael's larynx. "It's a pretty major level of . . . dedication." Moaning from a sudden throb of need, Michael caught Jesse's hand and brought it to his mouth for a kiss, grateful for Jesse's gentleness. Jesse stroked the side of Michael's face, then worked his hands under the hem of Michael's shirt, neatly pulling it off and folding it, retail-style, in the same movement.

"Hey, that's some skill."

"I worked at Abercrombie when I was twenty," Jesse admitted.

"No way."

"And got scouted for modeling on the first day. And then got fired the second day."

"What!"

Jesse laughed, smoothing his hands down Michael's bare torso to the waistband of his jeans. "I needed a job," he replied. "All I did on the first day was fold T-shirts. I was like, fuck *this*. Ended up in a fistfight with the assistant manager—he said some racist shit about the only person working there who was nice to me, this guy Taurean, stuck in the back room because he was black. So I raged out and threw a swing at the manager dude and his stupid ass tried to fight me back. Gave him a split lip. Asshole was lucky I didn't break his nose for him. Then he could be sexy like me." He grinned. "Up," he said, and pulled Michael's jeans down, leaving his underwear in place. "Oh, I thought of something," Jesse added, bending down to the rumpled pile of his own clothes and putting his underwear back on. He put Michael's hand on the warm lump in the ribbed white fabric and placed his own hand on Michael's, clad in dark green. "Yeah," he purred approvingly. "Let's do that."

Drew entered the room then, already quite naked himself, hands full of stuff Michael couldn't make out in the dark without his glasses. He could, however, see that Drew had stopped in his tracks, his eyes flickering wildly as he took in the scene, then focusing squarely on their crotches, their mutual fondling. "Fuck," he breathed.

"Oh," said Jesse languidly, leaning against Michael's shoulder. "You caught us. I hope we're not in trouble."

Michael felt a spurt of wetness in his own shorts.

Back in control of himself, Drew murmured, "Hmmm . . . I don't know. I'll need to determine just how close you two have gotten." He set the stuff down on the floor.

"With your teeth," Michael said softly, hardly believing the words coming from his own mouth.

Jesse's lips twisted, holding back laughter.

Drew wasn't about to be taken out of the scene by Jesse's silliness. "Jesse, lay him down," he said sternly. "Let me see what's going on."

Ceremoniously, Jesse angled Michael back and turned him sideways so that his legs were also on the bed. Without much further ado, Drew bent over him, first smelling Michael's pulse points. Then, inhaling deeply, he took the waistband of the briefs between his bright, even teeth and raised his head just enough to make a gap between waistband and waist. Surprised, Michael sharply sucked his breath as Jesse angled his head and looked down into his underwear.

"There's definitely come in there," said Jesse.

Michael squirmed, his upper lip damp with sweat. Drew grunted contemptuously, dragged the pants down to mid-thigh. "Does it taste like come?" he asked. Between their faces, Michael's stiff cock wobbled like a metronome. They stared at each other for a long time, the gaze unbroken until Drew sniffed, seemingly against a runny nose.

Just as Michael felt the pressure in his penis start to flag, Jesse took it into his mouth, directly, no hands, and the briskness of the act brought Michael back to the edge again. "Oh, God," he burst out, clenching his fists in the bedspread.

"Hmmm," Drew murmured, stroking Michael's forehead with fingertips. "Hang in there. You've got a lot of fucking to do tonight."

"Oh, God," Michael said again with a nervous, delighted laugh.

Jesse sucked deeper, slowly, hands still spread at Michael's sides. Michael realized that he had his own hands, and grabbed one of Jesse's. He slipped and his mouth went way down, far too far. Jesse didn't gag—somehow—but he sprang off and away in alarm. "Oh, fuck, I'm so sorry," Michael gasped.

"Be careful with him," Drew admonished. The gravel in his voice made it clear that he wasn't even slightly upset, certainly less than Jesse was, and Michael reminded himself as hard as he could that this was a scene, that he was engaged in a *scene* now, that Drew really liked it that way. And it was fun; like acting exercises, but the character he was playing was a version of himself. He barely felt a flicker of surprise when Drew gave him a backhanded slap across the face. It wasn't too hard, but the blow was sharp enough to make Michael blink and stare at Drew.

His eyes, those beautiful, huge eyes, in this light, seemed to drink Michael in, all paradoxes of light and heat. "Don't break my toys," Drew warned.

"Shut up, Drew," said Jesse, rubbing his mouth with the back of his hand.

Drew raised his head. "*You* shut up," he replied. For that moment they sounded almost exactly like brothers, with years and decades of saying those things to each other. Michael grimaced, remembering just how close they really were. He rolled over, towards Jesse, but sat up too, refusing to be protective.

"I'm gonna go get a glass of water," he said, swinging his legs over the side and standing up.

As he had hoped, Drew grabbed him by the shoulders and brought him down to the bed again. "Oh, no, no, no," Drew said. "I'm in charge of how much water you get tonight—you better trust me to do that. There is a gallon jug next to the bed and that's it for both of you. *You* don't have to go anywhere." Drew gave Jesse a look and added emphatically, "Everything we need is in here, and please excuse *our* rudeness."

"Just don't call me your toy," Jesse said. "I'll be your come dumpster cock-sucking whore anytime." He ran his hand over the back of Drew's head, and tightened his fingers in Drew's hair, giving

Drew's head a little jerk. "But I'm not a toy." Drew let his breath out slowly, shakily, and his hard cock twitched along his groin. "It's *your* fault," Jesse whispered. He yanked Drew's hair again, invoking a gasp this time. "He was gonna leave. You did that."

Jesse had a sex voice, too.

Michael took his own shorts the rest of the way off. He couldn't resist checking them out, either. He really had ejaculated a bit. "I'm sorry," Michael said, hearing the heavy baritone timbre of his own voice, and it was glorious. "I was saving it. Like you said."

Drew laughed a little, nuzzling Jesse's hand. "How long?"

"Well, all day and night."

"Hmm. You can take some more edging." The older man had relaxed back into control. "Wish I'd thought to tell you to put a ring on it. Well, no time like the present to develop a little control."

"Hey, I know something fun we could do," Jesse put in. "Michael, show us your favorite yoga pose."

Michael thought it over, chuckling, while Jesse and Drew both ran their hands all over him, haloed in the light. "Okay," he decided. "Instead of showing you my very favorite one, which is just sort of lying very still and is not too exciting, I've been working on the screaming pigeon pose. I might not be able to fully do it, but. . . ." Since there was no room on the floor, he had to try it on the bed. Drew and Jesse moved away to give him space, both of them with eager looks on their faces. Michael sat up, then moved up onto his knees, gently tensing and relaxing the muscles of his thighs, and slid one leg out straight behind him while bending the opposite knee and breathing into the stretch. Prana flowed through him like electricity, banking in a joint or muscle and then springing free as he moved, bending the knee at an angle that spread his legs incredibly wide, his balls nearly brushing the surface of the bed. "And then, ah," Michael said aloud, sliding his arm under the bent knee, and reaching toward his hand on the opposite side. He breathed through his frustration. He wasn't in pain, but no way could he actually make the connection yet. Still. "I secretly call it . . . the pretzel pose."

"Jesus," Drew said. "How the fuck do you do that?"

"Expertise," Michael sighed.

"Can I touch your dick?" Jesse asked breathlessly.

"No," Michael said, laughing. "No, please don't. Let me—phew, just move out of this one, and—into—" He disentangled his limbs and lay down on his back, grasping one foot and angling his leg back to open up his hips. "Okay," he said, relaxed. "I can lie here in this for a while, if you want to."

"Your groin," Drew said, "is a work of art."

"Yep," Michael agreed, shivering at Jesse's touch as it slid up and down on his cock, and gasping faintly as Jesse put it back into his mouth. "Eh . . . eh . . . ah, eleven years of practice. And I'm not even particularly good yet."

"I think you're pretty good," Drew said, genuinely impressed.

Jesse, bent over Michael, had his ass in the air, waving it slowly, enticingly, back and forth. Drew reached for Jesse's buttocks, his hand sliding down right between them. Michael couldn't see what he was doing, but it made Jesse moan around his mouthful of flesh, and Michael had to close his eyes to manage the flood of sensation coursing through his body from the intensity of the current pose and the expert suction of Jesse's mouth.

Michael heard Drew sniff, determinedly, purposefully, again.

"Fuck you, hooker," Jesse said, with a soft laugh.

"Oh," Michael sighed before he could stop himself. "Don't do that shit, Drew. I want you to fuck me."

"Don't worry, I plan to. This is just . . ." Drew trailed off in an ecstatic hiss. "Just a fucking cherry on top."

"Drew, put that down and eat his asshole," Jesse growled, as if angry he had to stop what he was doing to speak. Michael wasn't certain but it sounded like Jesse had actually given Drew a kick. "Put your toe in his asshole. You want that, Michael, I know you do. You want him to fuck your asshole with his whole body, don't you?" He returned to hungrily sucking.

"Oh, God," Michael gasped. He couldn't deny it.

"Every time you say that," said Drew. "Every time you think you're talking to God, I keep hearing 'sodomize me, and make it count. I need to be fucked so hard it changes my life.' Why don't you just say that?"

Jesse laughed. "Not *everybody* says that, Drew." They smiled at each other.

"I'm sorry, I really need some water," Michael begged. "Please." He really needed a moment's break or he wasn't just going to come, he was going to have a heart attack. Jesse lifted the jug out of nowhere, took a big swallow himself, then handed the jug to Michael and went back to blowing him, mouth now wetter and cooler. It felt painfully exquisite. So much for a break.

Michael relaxed the stretch just a little, closing his legs but only slightly, and swallowed a dripping gulp of water. Drew followed suit, and right away his mouth, curved, lush, and cooled by the water, was all over Michael's balls and the base of his cock, on the hypersensitive inches not already in Jesse's mouth. Jesse actually pushed Drew away, so Drew set his tongue to wetting Michael's anus and perineum, briskly, without sentiment.

"I can't hold back anymore," Michael pleaded. "I can't."

"Relax, and hang on to that come," Drew ordered, raising his head, firmly grasping and holding the base of Michael's cock. "You're just making it better the longer you hold on. Jesse, stop sucking him off."

"Drew . . . damn it . . ." Michael groaned.

"I'm not," Jesse protested, but without much defiance. His hands did a full sweeping caress of Michael's torso, nipples to pubes, and he kissed Michael's cock like a sweetheart. Then, he slung one arm under the small of his back to make a sort of platform to keep his genitals accessible. Drew added his own efforts, pushing Michael's thighs back and up. One of Michael's thighs ended up over Jesse's shoulders, the other over Drew's. "Fuck, yeah," Jesse muttered. "Open that shit up."

Michael keened wordlessly, dragging his fingernails over two backs. Now they were both licking at his ass, kissing each other, kissing him, sticking spit-slickened fingers into him, both at once. Michael let out a hoarse cry, but Jesse maintained his grip at the base of Michael's cock—or was that Drew's hand?

He was being prepared. With harmonious choreography, as if they'd been practicing for this all their lives, Jesse and Drew prepared him for the fuck.

"Help me," Drew said into Michael's ear. When Michael

opened his eyes, he saw Jesse seated spread-eagled a few inches away, sticking a finger desperately into his own ass, his cock wine-dark and straining. "Stop that, young man," Drew said, grabbing Jesse's violating hand. Drew sucked on the finger and let it go sloppy-wet, let Jesse finger himself once more, then took over the task himself, digit sliding in to the knuckle. To the palm. Insisting, insisting.

"Lube time," Jesse breathed. "Now. Hurry, please. Before I let you rip me up. 'Cos I'm *there*. Holy fuck, am I *there*."

"Yeah," Drew agreed. "It's time." To Michael he said, "Hold this," handing him a plain white jar about the size of his hand. Michael held it on his sternum as Jesse and Drew both scooped out big three-fingered dollops. It seemed rather a lot, until Michael allowed himself to understand why. This was the hard business, and it would go on for a while. Now they both knew what he could take, and they meant to go beyond that.

Drew gently but briskly slotted his sticky fingers between his own buttocks, and Jesse, more slowly and carefully, twisted one finger, then two, into Michael's ass. "Yeah, that looks so good. Put some on your dick," Drew said, voice shuddering, to Michael.

Michael's voice came out unsteadily, too. "Okay . . ." He arched his hips desperately towards Jesse's fingers, wanting them deeper, smudging thick lube onto the side of his cock. "Please . . ."

Drew had put a rubber on already, fingers smoothing gel down over its surface, his lips curved in a determined, unselfconscious sneer. The latex-wrapped end of his cock pushed against and into Michael.

Even with the lube, the stretch burned. The same regretful panic clawed at Michael's instincts. "Too much. Oh, fuck, I can't," Michael groaned.

"I am ignoring you," Drew said coolly, his grip steady, pushing further in. Michael groaned again. Jesse, wide-eyed, echoed him. Drew grunted, "Let me in. Concentrate. It's too late to stop." Drew held Michael down on his side, one hand on Michael's shoulder and the other on Michael's hip, firmly rocking back and forth until he had fucked the head of his cock entirely inside. Too much. Three fingers wide, and more. Too thick. Too much. Michael gritted his teeth hard, choking off further yelps of protest. "That's it. Feel that," Drew said. "You feel that?" Michael's chin jerked slightly, nodding. "Good," Drew said, and pulled out entirely. Michael opened his eyes, ready to protest that he didn't want to stop, not *really*, only to see Drew using his mouth to push a condom onto Jesse's rampant cock. "He's yours. Fuck him brutally," Drew said to him. "Hurt him a little. He really needs it."

And then, Drew used the same oral technique to wrap up Michael's cock. His lips encircled the slippery shaft, his fingers pushing the reinforced end down against Michael's balls.

"And you better fuck *me* hard," Drew said again, smiling. "I really need it."

He pulled Michael's body against his, spreading his own legs, granite-hard thighs around Michael's hips, lowering himself onto Michael's nearly painful erection. He was smoothly supple and open, and Michael easily slid all the way inside.

"Jesus *God*!" Michael exclaimed.

Jesse giggled. "Vatican Three—with a vengeance," he said.

"Hold him," Drew said, chuckling. "Tripping boy. Hold him steady. Give it to him slow. He's tight."

They were tangled, lying on their sides, trying to connect. One of Drew's legs hooked Michael's waist, his belly against Michael's, his thicker chest hair scraping Michael's nipples. Drew's mouth lapped hotly at Michael's neck, but turned away from Michael's breathless, desperate attempt at a kiss. Jesse's hands smoothed over Michael's back, the dip of his waist, his hips, his ass cheeks. Jesse's cock followed the same path Drew's had, slow but inexorable, a single deep sloping in, no burn this time, just the pleasure of the violation.

"Now, this," said Drew. "Ohh, God, yes, this! What I want— yes—*this*!" He lay still, and Jesse lay still, and Michael whimpered, hardly daring to breathe for fear that he would just shatter, explode into a billion pieces, sodden and throbbing in Drew and Jesse's arms.

He savored this moment of peace, chained, locked, linked together.

"Beautiful," Jesse murmured reverently, kissing the back of Michael's neck, his ears. "You're so beautiful. So great. You're doing it."

"Have you—ever done this before?" Michael managed to ask. His thighs and back began to twitch involuntarily.

Jesse shook his head against the back of Michael's neck. Drew smiled against Michael's clavicle. "I did. Just once," he said. He was so still that Michael could feel Drew's pulse, thudding around his cock, and instinct screamed at him to fuck to the rhythm of that pulse. But Jesse's heartbeat was different, and he was fucking Michael just as surely, if not even more so. He could set the pace and Michael would have no choice but to follow. Drew murmured pleasantly, "I was in the middle that time. It was absolutely incredible. I always wanted to do it again, with Jesse—"

"In the middle. Why isn't *he* in the middle?" Michael moaned, sweat stinging his eyes.

When Drew and Jesse both laughed, Michael bit the side of his fist to keep from screaming. There wasn't any pain, just a sense of overwhelming . . . occupancy. So many hearts beating, he didn't know which was his.

"Maybe next time," said Drew.

Michael moaned again, a guttural, bestial, ugly sound, and squirmed between them. The motion of his hips caused him to rock down onto Jesse, and Jesse cried out and fucked back, three swift, hard strokes. Then Michael arched away, deeper into Drew, who clutched him tighter, bucking his ass, begging him for it.

There was nowhere to go, no relief, no escape from the pummeling waves of ecstasy.

Despite Drew's commands, the fucking didn't get a chance to approach brutality in any sense. It was more a slick, sliding, half-melted puddle of flesh joined at Michael's cock and ass, and none of them could seize control. It was all too complicated, too deliciously absurd. They came apart over and over, reconnecting wetly and immediately, twisting and lunging for kisses amongst the three of them. Soon Michael's face and hair were wet with sweat and saliva, his body below the waist a slick amalgamation. There were no words; just sharp cries, groans, shuddering gasps of surprise and grunts of lustful impatience as no one found a rhythm, just a cascading series of reactions to any movement any of them made.

Much later, but far too soon, Drew tensed, whispered "Fuck," and bit down hard on Michael's shoulder. Between their bellies a cool bloom of semen spread. Jesse whined urgently, rubbing his hand into the ejaculate, massaging it into Michael's stomach, hips increasing in urgency, now pounding vigorously into him, finding the rhythm he'd been desperate to establish all along. His fingers laced through the hair on the back of Michael's head and clenched hard.

Drew pulled off and away, rolling over, springing up off the bed onto his feet. Without another word he left the room.

"Oh, Jesse," Michael gasped, tensing, spasming. He had wanted to ask Drew where he was going, but he needed even more to praise Jesse for this, to praise them both. The orgasm was a lance of white quartz through his body from crown to toes, and his ejaculation actually hit the underside of his chin and kept on coming.

"Yes? Yes—yes—Ahhh, me too, baby—Me too—Ahhh, *fuck*." Jesse wrapped his arms around Michael and squeezed him tightly, hips tight against Michael's ass, kissing the back of his neck. Eventually they collapsed, too, but lay in place on the bed, still moaning, the drug lengthening the feeling of post-orgasmic afterglow. Michael's come had gotten everywhere.

"Oh, man," Jesse sighed, "I never want this feeling to end."

"Never say that," Michael teased, smiling. "Just saying it brings it to an end."

"I was just fantasizing out loud."

"This," Michael said, stroking the bite mark on his shoulder, then kissing Jesse's mouth, "is pretty much my fantasy."

"Exactly," said Jesse sleepily.

14. NOBODY EVER LIES ABOUT BEING LONELY.

Drew made instant coffee and brought it to bed where Jesse lay sprawled, not even having bothered to try to sit up. Jesse raised his head to sip from the mug, then lay back, pouting miserably. "I can't walk," he reiterated. "I need to lie still."

"You already said that. Drink up. Might improve things."

"It's just really important to state and be known. Clearly. Fuck, this is awful. Why do we even have instant? Did you buy this? Fucked up that you can't even use the French press."

"I wouldn't trust myself to do it right. You flipped out last time I tried." Drew built a back support out of a stack of pillows and propped himself against the headboard, sucking down the coffee. Skim milk did not enhance it, but that was all there was, and drinking it black was inconceivable. Jesse let out an elaborately mournful groan, and Drew suddenly felt seized with bleak, cold energy.

"So. Where's Michael?" Drew asked.

Jesse opened his eyes, all at once wide awake. "I dunno. He was here where I fell asleep. Did he leave a note? Did you check?"

"I didn't see anything," Drew said mildly.

With a deep breath, Jesse righted himself and finished his coffee in a series of hard, determined gulps. "I'm gonna go take a shower," he announced, clapping down the mug, hard but carefully, and walked with high-headed dignity from the room. Drew yawned, and though tempted to occupy the space Jesse left warm and concave in the blankets, he got up and started in on clearing up the devastation left on the floor of the guest room.

Drew had just stirred up another cup of instant coffee when Jesse came to the kitchen, washed, dressed, his shining hair wet-combed. Drew slumped at the counter sadly, rubbing his finger over the black plate that had held his lines of cocaine. "So you did it all, huh?" Jesse asked, rubbing a towel over the back of his head. "Got up in the night to finish it?"

"What do you think?" Drew muttered. "It was barely a gram."

"Yeah, that's nothin'. I'm surprised you didn't go on a run to get more. You didn't, did you?"

"Wouldn't be your business if I did," said Drew. He squinted, rubbing the bridge of his nose, weighing whether or not to take it back.

There wasn't going to be a chance. "Wow." Jesse laughed shortly, humorlessly, filling a glass of water from the tap. "Okay."

Drew narrowed his eyes.

"Did you sleep at all? You look pretty rough," Jesse continued, giving him a thin, twisted smile. "I dunno, I've never done that much blow. Doesn't it keep you awake? You get all strung out and fucked up?"

Drew glared back. "So, are you going to make breakfast?"

Jesse slowly and calmly drank the water, then slammed the glass in the sink hard enough for shards to fly out onto the counter and the floor. "No, asshole, I'm not gonna make you fucking *breakfast*. I'm gonna *go* get *myself* a decent coffee. Have someone else make it for *me* for a motherfucking change. You–! You are just the fucking limit."

Drew startled at the sound of the breaking glass, and cursed himself for not having more control over his reflexes. It took everything he had not to start crying. He walked after Jesse, into the hall and down the stairs to the foyer. Jesse did not slow his pace, yanking open the free-standing wardrobe where he kept his skateboard.

Drew caught Jesse's arm as he opened the front door. "Hey, hey, now. You could at least bring me something back."

Jesse closed his eyes, voice cold and rigid. "I could, but I don't feel like it. Order in. There's a whole under-society of people employed to do just that."

It felt to Drew like being punched right in his congested face. "Fine," Drew said, opening his hand, releasing his grip on Jesse's bicep, stepping back, holding up both hands in surrender. Jesse stepped back, too, and walked out onto the sidewalk, not bothering to close the door behind him.

Drew went back inside and slammed the door, walked up three flights to the gym on the top floor , and got onto the elliptical machine. He turned it to its second-highest resistance and stomped the mechanism into action. It wasn't as good as a run outside, but Jesse had totally spoiled Drew's desire to go out. It would have felt like copying, like some form of apology, a concession. Drew was perfectly capable of hard exercise without leaving the house.

His original plan was to only do the elliptical until Jesse came back, but after an hour, Drew simply had to climb off and lie down for a few minutes. His stubbornness egged him on toward free weights. A second hour of activity left his arms and shoulders feeling like overcooked spaghetti, but did not induce Jesse's return.

After another lie-down, Drew took a cold shower, then put on a T-shirt and linen drawstring trousers, remaining barefoot since he had no intention of leaving home. The workout had restored his appetite, but he certainly didn't feel like cooking. He settled on making himself a protein shake from a powdered mix. They were out of bananas, out of almond milk. The shake was so terrible he gave up on it after a few swallows, pouring the rest out. He stared at the broken glass in the sink, now coated with grainy, milky fluid.

He could just call him.

(Who? Jesse. And apologize. For what? For the coke? For everything? For the whole shebang, from the beginning? But from how far back? From the time they got the house, from the time Jesse moved in with him, from the time that Jesse and Drew spent delirious weekends together and Drew had to all but bully Jesse into going to class? Earlier? Or just this weekend, this week, the month of June, the year. Oh, but Christmas had been weird, too. Every holiday was weird. Family. The simultaneous urge to honor and observe the familial bond, and to turn their backs on the whole world altogether, and be only amongst themselves, all they ever needed. Except obviously now that was no longer true.)

(Or Michael? Ask his whereabouts, why he'd left. Whine about Jesse. Beg Michael to save him. To fix this mess.)

Undecided, Drew went out and sat on the terrace, glaring at the wall. He felt like a chump. No wonder he was alone. Fatigue and annoyance dragged his eyelids closed, and he rested his head on his hand.

He woke to a hot, red-gold evening, his left forearm tight with sunburn, the house behind him as silent as before. His stomach made a drawn-out gurgle like a Jew's-harp symphony. Grabbing the handset for the house phone land line, Drew flicked through his folder of takeout menus, deciding on spinach salad, half a chicken, a slab of aged Manchego, and a baguette from Rotisserie Georgette. He put some aloe on his burned arm and put a bottle of *vinho verde* into the quick chiller, promising himself he'd just eat way too many carbs, have a few too many glasses of wine, and go to bed early, like a virtuous, normal American gentleman of nearly forty. Hey, it was just an ordinary Saturday.

Rather than going to the fussy coffee shop nearby, Jesse had gone to the bodega on Lexington and got a liter bottle of Pepsi. He preferred Pepsi to coffee the morning after doing drugs; there was something so refreshing and restorative about carbonation and corn syrup. Thus fortified, Jesse skated over to the subway station and got on a downtown train, headed to Brooklyn.

When he first got on the Metro, he thought he was going to go to Prospect Park, but instead rode two stops past it and got onto the 2 line, going through Crown Heights, into East Flatbush.

He hadn't been to visit the Landons' graves in a while, not since Christmas, and that had been almost unbearably strange. Drew had come with him then. At the time, Jesse had imagined himself grateful for his presence, but by the time they reached the plot where Jesse's father had been planted, along with his grandmother and grandfather, Jesse had felt physically jolted and had to find a trash can so he could throw up.

His mom's body had been sent back to Italy. It was Landons only in this place. He wondered if he'd end up here, too, eventually.

Jesse usually managed to visit twice, sometimes three times a year. He'd been to the cemetery plot dozens of times. But there was something about last time, something that yanked him back to the trauma of his memories, and the fact that Drew would not and could not understand what it had been like, punched him in the guts. He had laughed it off afterwards, joking that he experienced genuine Sartre-like nausea, the violent realization of the utter solitude of sentient existence, and that he could probably pass that French lit class if he were taking it now. But it hadn't been a joke, even if he'd laughed giddily as he told the truth. Drew had accepted his words at face value, taken him home, put him to bed, brought him saltines and 7-Up when what he'd wanted instead was cheap blended Scotch out of a plastic bottle.

The near-summer sun shone pitilessly bright on the plain, flat marker, carved with neutral, unsentimental, inexpensive block capitals: *JOSEPH HUGO LANGDON , 1953–1997. BELOVED SON.* No bullshit about him being a beloved father or husband. The decision had been left in Jesse's hands, and he'd only grudgingly conceded to his grandmother's request for the line that was there. Now he was glad that at least he could be reminded that Grandma Landon had been fond of Joey.

Jesse's folks weren't in very good shape after the accident. He'd had to identify his mother by her hands, so he wouldn't have to try to look at her face. Drew's mother had identified Joey first, since she was in town. With the scope of the damage, she couldn't identify Cosi, so Jesse had had to do it. A thousand miles away, his classmates at Beloît were buried under three feet of Wisconsin snow, and with protective selfishness, he was glad he wasn't stuck back there. Stacked brown scars , parallel on his mother's arms, were like the marks of repeated suicide attempts, but they were actually burns from the oven racks at the restaurant. He had them, too. Her wedding ring, gold with a ruby and a sapphire side by side, that she had pawned and retrieved over and over, twenty bucks each time, was actually on her finger that night for some reason. In Italy she had been cremated, and the ring was still over there. Jesse didn't want it.

It didn't *mean* anything. Objects. Little rocks and ashes and letters stamped in cement. Why would Jesse ever want any of that?

He hadn't bothered to return to Beloît. They shipped his stuff back to New York. There was no way he could try living there again, even for a few days. Life without Drew in it just hadn't worked. It wasn't just "other people" he needed; he needed that *one* person, that one man, that relative. That lover. Only Drew provided any meaning to anything.

He lay on the grass and closed his eyes, wishing he could talk to his mom about what was happening with Drew. She'd understand. She'd had to deal with his father's drinking and violent urges. What do you say to your lover when you can't stand what they do, and it's never going to change?

He was going to explode if he didn't talk to somebody.

He sat up, stood up, and wandered to the nearest tall tree, seeking the shade. He pulled his phone from the front pocket of his jeans. He almost reflexively hit the button to speed-dial Drew, but just in time stopped himself. Instead he scrolled to a number in his saved contacts, did a quick calculation in his head.

It would be dinnertime in Portugal. Probably okay.

"*Boa noite . . . Chamo mé* Mary Farrow." An authoritative woman's voice answered far more quickly than he'd been anticipating.

"Oh! Hi," said Jesse. "Hello. Um. I hope I'm not interrupting you."

"Who is calling, please?" she asked crisply, precisely. Every once in a while that formal, prep school diction had even showed up in Jesse's father's voice, no matter how much he tried to scorch it away.

"It's me," said Jesse, faintly upset that he didn't show up on her caller ID. "It's Jesse Landon. Your . . . " *Son-in-law. Your child's not-a-fuck-toy. Your brother's mistake.* "Your nephew? Your . . . brother's son."

"Oh," she said in surprise. "*Jesse* .Wow. Hi. It's good to hear from you. Unexpected. Forgive me." Voice gentler now.

"Is this a bad time?" he asked reflexively.

"No, it's fine. I'm just a little surprised. How are you? I can't remember the last time you called me. Is everything all right?" she asked.

"Yeah, everything's square. I'm fine." He had almost never called her, in fact. They hadn't spoken in years. She was all but a stranger to him, but for what he knew from Drew.

Jesse's father had rarely mentioned his older sister. It was as if they had grown up in different houses with two different sets of parents, one quietly pleased, well-groomed, accomplished, "comfortable," and one exasperated and horrified, confused and hostile, incoherently drunk. Rich, established, proper tax-paying citizens who got wasted on gin and threw each other down flights of stairs on Saturday nights, then went to Mass on Sunday mornings in crisp, expensive, immaculate outfits. To Jesse, this was like some kind of science fiction, a foreign language, incomprehensible. But he didn't dislike Aunt Mary, who seemed like a perfectly nice lady. She was just far above and far away.

He didn't know her at all.

"Is Andrew all right?" she asked.

"Yeah, he's great." He fell silent, waiting to see if she were going to ask more about Drew. It would only be natural. She was his mother, after all. But she didn't, and the stretched silence quickly became uncomfortable. *She doesn't know about us, and it's not my place to tell her.* As far as she knew, Drew and Jesse were cousins, friends, co habitants of the house on Sixty-First. As far as she knew, Drew was an eligible, childless, divorced bachelor, doing what unmarried men did. *It's not my place* . He sighed heavily, and rather than telling her anything, asked for something he never had before.

"Tell me something good about him? Your brother," he said. "My dad. I'm at the cemetery right now, and I'm feelin' kinda . . ." He exhaled long and slow, then added a pained, eloquently wordless moan.

Before replying, she paused for such a long moment that Jesse thought the connection had dropped, and he glanced worriedly at the screen of his phone.

When she did speak, the restraint in her voice spoke more clearly of deep-seated anger than any shout could have . "Well, he lived his principles," she said. Immediately Jesse felt a kinship—*Oh, yes, we're related, all right. We both knew this guy, and he was an asshole.* He softly laughed with relief. "I never agreed with them, but. . . He was his own man. Incredibly strong-willed. He walked away from a loving family, and frankly, a lot of money, to . . . live the life he wanted to live." Mary Landon laughed a little, too. "Pig-headed. Resolutely impractical. But, without a doubt, he was crazy about your mother."

If he closed his eyes and flared his nostrils, Jesse could beat back tears, but the pain in his throat, the cold feeling all over—that stayed. "Thanks. That's—yeah."

"Are you sure everything's all right? Do you need anything?"

"No, I mean yeah, things are fine. I'm okay." He stammered into silence. "I just, uh, wanted to make contact. See if your number was still good. But, you should call Drew, 'cause I think you guys should talk."

"What about?"

What did mothers talk to their adult sons about? Jesse had no idea. It wasn't something he had experienced. "Just, like, talk. Be family. I think he could use it right now." He had never told his own mother about him and Drew. Now it seemed important, and he couldn't do it. "It's nothing to worry about or anything. He's doing great. I just wanted to say hi. I've gotta go. Bye."

So easy, so quiet to hang up with just a touch of a button. He slid the phone back into the pocket of his jeans, balanced one foot on his skate deck, and rolled noisily down the cemetery path. Once he was outside its gates, he brought out his phone again.

"Hey, Charlie. What's up? I'm in your neighborhood, wanna grab a bite to eat? I need to run something by you."

As Drew received and signed off on the delivery at the front gate, Jesse came casually gliding back up Sixty-First Street, extra tan and wind-tousled like a catalogue cover model. There was nothing about him that implied a drug-fueled night before. "Hey there," Jesse said cheerfully to the delivery boy, a moped-riding, black-skinned teenager in a green-and-white striped soccer jersey. "I'm Jesse. I'm a runner, too. You been ridin' long?" The delivery kid just gave Jesse a weird look, nodded at Drew, revved up his scooter, and disappeared up the street. Jesse watched him go, bemused. "Hmm! Oh well. He was hot."

"He's from Côte d'Ivoire. I'm pretty sure he only speaks French."

Jesse rolled his eyes. "Whatever."

"Anyway, hey," Drew said.

"Hey."

Jesse went inside. Drew followed, and they up went to the

kitchen. Drew wished he'd put some music on or something else to dispel the weight of the silence of the house, but now it was too late. If he did it now, it'd be weird. He set the bags of food on the countertop and opened the cabinets, fetching down plates, glasses, a pair of trays. "Thought I'd watch a Monty tonight," Drew said calmly, opening the chilled wine. "Was thinking *I Confess*. Sound good?"

Jesse snickered faintly, still not looking at Drew. He regarded the broken glass still in the sink and sighed. "Feeling a little penitent, are you?" Jesse suggested.

Drew smiled thinly. "It was that, or *The Heiress* .I figured that whole class struggle business would hit a little close to home." He kept his voice and expression neutral. He poured one glass of wine.

Jesse blinked rapidly a few times, eyes downcast. Drew thought of a favorite line from *The Heiress*: *Since you couldn't love me, you should have let someone else try.* So much for avoiding "close to home." Still, it was just a movie. How many times had they watched it together? All of them, every Montgomery Clift movie, scores of times until the visuals and dialogue became mandala and mantra. Jesse could have always said no when Drew suggested they watch one together, but he never did. "I'm feelin' more Hitchcock, anyway. I don't have the energy for *The Heiress*." He changed the register of his voice to suggest the vitriolic snarl of Olivia De Havilland, and quoted, "'*Come in, Morris.*'"

It made them both laugh.

"Hungry? There's salad. Cheese." Drew dished salad onto plates, tore the loaf of bread, put half on each plate. Despite his attempt to be careful, the plating was sloppy and graceless.

Jesse grabbed a dish towel, dropped it over the glass in the sink, and swept it all up into a neat little bundle, which he dropped in the trash. The whole thing had taken him exactly two seconds. Without comment, without pouring himself any wine, he took his dinner plate from Drew and went and sat on the floor in front of the television.

Drew took his food and wine on a tray, setting it onto the side table next to the Kroll sofa. He opened the *I Confess* DVD case and slid the disk into the player, picked up the remote, and sat on the sofa.

"Did you hear from Michael?" Drew asked casually, pressing the play button.

"Nope," said Jesse, mouth full of salad. He chewed and

swallowed. "You?"

"No. Nothing," said Drew.

"Hmm," said Jesse distantly. "Did your mom call?"

"What? No." Drew frowned. "Why?"

Jesse rolled a bit of bread into a cylinder between his fingers. "Was talking to her earlier."

"*Why?* Why were you talking to my mother?"

"I just wanted to talk to someone who knew my dad. She's my aunt. I'm allowed to call her," Jesse pointed out.

"You wouldn't just do that," Drew said. "I mean, you haven't been, just, talking to her all this time, right?"

Jesse shook his head slowly, staring at Drew with the black-and-white images on the television flickering on his eyes. "No. Like I said. It had nothing whatsoever to do with you. Nothing. Okay?" He sighed.

"You'll forgive me if I find that a little hard to believe."

"I forgive you, all right," Jesse said. "You know, I gotta tell you something I decided."

"Oh, yeah?"

"I think . . . I'm gonna go. I'm gonna move out. I think that, maybe, we need a little space."

The drugs had kept Michael from sleeping deeply, and he turned over in bed, away from Jesse's warmth, at the sound of wasp-like buzzing coming from the floor where his jeans had been tossed in a heap.

He was too warm anyway, sweat congealing on his sternum and neck. He got out of bed and dug the phone from his pocket, intending to silence it. But even with blurred, uncorrected vision, he spied the caller ID message on the phone's glowing data window. **MOM. 9:27 a.m.** And a voicemail already racked up.

"Fuck," he muttered, swinging himself out of bed, sliding the phone into activity. "Yeah," he answered, grabbing his jeans and walking out into the silent hallway.

"Oh, Michael, thank God. It's serious. It's your father. You have to come home."

She was in tears.

"What? Slow down. Tell me what's happening." There was another bathroom on this level, next door to the guest room. Michael shut the door behind him and ran the sink's tap, just a trickle, not too loudly.

"Your father's in the hospital. He took a turn for the worse last night and he's still there. It's bad. They don't think he's going to make it."

"Why aren't *you* still there? Are you sure?"

"You have to come home, Michael. This is so much worse than last time. I think this is it. I think this really might be it." Her words paused momentarily, replaced by hysterical gasping. "I don't know what I'll do without him. I'm all alone here and—"

"Look, calm down. Don't get too worked up. You know that's bad for you. I'll—I'll be there as soon as I can." Michael stared at himself in the mirror, his face somehow flushed and gray at the same time. And it seemed his eyebrows had grown back together in the middle overnight. He wet his hands and scrubbed them over his face and neck. "Which hospital? Should I go straight there?"

"No, just come back here first, please. To the house, I mean. We can go back to the hospital together. They sent me home. I'm supposed to lie down and try to get a little sleep. I've been up all night. If the situation changes in the meantime, I *will* call you. My head is killing me. Oh, I hate that place. Those doctors don't know what they're doing. I'll call you if—Does your cellular phone work while you're outside the city?"

"Yes, Mom, it works. Look, I'm on my way. I'll be there as soon as I can. I'll get a car and drive. The stupid fu—the stupid trains don't run often enough." He had almost said a bad word to his mother. That was the last thing he needed. "I'll still be a couple of hours, though. Call me if there's anything I need to know."

"All right." Her breath shuddered, as though she had been sobbing her heart out. "I'm so scared. I need you here. He needs you. I hope he can—can hold on until we get there. You should see him again one last time."

"I'll be there as soon as I can," he replied. "I love you. Be strong, okay? This is when it really counts." He hung up, not even sparing himself the comfort of a sigh, and splashed more cold water around his face, neck, chest, armpits. He stank to high heaven, the kind of stink that only amphetamine drugs can produce, and he remarked bitterly to himself that at least he knew the Ecstasy hadn't been bunk.

He had to return to the guest room for his underpants and shirt, his socks and boots. In the violet-sheeted bed, Jesse slept on, nude, tousled, smiling, his hands still curved where they had rested on Michael's. No Drew; the older man was probably already up, probably running his daily miles. Michael tugged the bedspread back over Jesse and grabbed his things, taking them out of the room before putting them on.

He waited until he was outside, on the street, before he called information to locate the nearest car rental place to his apartment. A taxicab came by and he hailed it without any problems. It was barely nine-thirty in the morning, on a Saturday, and he felt like the only person in the world who was rushing and anxious. *Dad.* His heart pounded viciously, echoing in his head. It could be so many things: the cancer's damage to his bowels, the renal crisis, the hypertension. It was no wonder. Michael had known for years that his father's time was limited, but why now?

Either it was a random coincidence, or some kind of punishment.

It was awful but he had to go to his apartment first, get a change of clothes and shoes, and take a fast shower that only rinsed off a single layer of the slime, the terrible smell. More crap surged in his veins, ready to ooze through his pores. There was no time to make matcha properly, so he had to settle for a couple of tired bags of green tea in a travel mug, and even preparing that made him feel guilty. *He's dying, you fuckhead. You don't need your sissy tea; get going.* The sound of his mother's gasping repeated in his head. She had bad lungs. This wasn't good for her, either. She needed his help.

To calm the fuck down, if nothing else.

Michael sprinted to the rental company nearest his apartment. They only had one car available immediately, a four-door Altima in dark blue. It was far more car than Michael needed or wanted, but he signed for it surely enough, slung his overnight bag into the back seat, and was on the road within minutes. After the initial bone-deep terror of trying to remember how to get to the highways he needed, and dealing with traffic, body memory reasserted itself, and even after ten and a half months since he'd been behind the wheel, it was as though he had been born in the driver's seat.

He used to love driving. Getting away.

Once he reached I-80 and could continue thoughtlessly for a while, he plugged his mp3 player into the car's stereo and thumbed the controls until he cued up Boards of Canada's *Music Has the Right to Children*. Classic. Soothing but stimulating, traveling simultaneously backward and forward in the current of sound. Nine years ago, Michael had been eighteen and listening to this very album as he drove away from Altoona, the music a surreal statement on leaving childhood behind. Of course he couldn't completely leave; this was who he was, these gold and green country fields, the beige brick of half-abandoned strip malls, the scarlet of Pennsylvania rust.

Only belatedly, after he'd been sitting upright for a while, did he feel the ache of last night's exertions. His back, his hips, his guts, his sore asshole and dick—they throbbed like a bruise. He got hungry and thirsty, too, but only set his jaw and kept his eyes and his wheels on the road. He could manage all of that once he got back home, saw Dad. Saw Mom. They needed him.

Three hours, three and a half hours, more. He leaned on the gas, effortlessly making ninety. Even a speeding ticket didn't matter in the larger scheme of things, unless he found himself once again regularly dependent on driving a car. If he had to stay for a while. Help with arrangements. Mind spinning with variables, he returned the album to the first track and played it all again.

The neighborhood was the same. The house was the same, except for the garden full of dead or overgrown plants. There was no car in the driveway, but Michael parked on the street in front anyway, just in case. His hand shook on the parking brake. He grabbed his bag, jumped out of the car, and sprinted to the front door. He still had a key, and it still worked. "Hello?" he called, stepping inside. It was dim, with curtains drawn, but it was the same, too: the same furniture in the same place, but with extra dust. Too warm, the smell of urine underneath a horrible fruit-scented air freshener. "Mom? Are you here? It's Michael."

Only ticking answered him. That horrible cheap clock in the kitchen, the same one with the loud ticking that had tormented him when he had a fever with the flu when he was seventeen and terrified that he had somehow caught AIDS, his bedroom right on the other side of the wall, inescapable. Michael grimaced and took the clock down, pulling its cord out of the wall. Grabbing a screwdriver from the utility drawer—right where it had always been—he cracked the clock's plastic case and disconnected the wires from the mechanism inside.

"Mom?" he called again, putting the screwdriver away and putting the clock and the cord in the garbage can. "Are you asleep?"

His parents' room was empty. His own room was changed, thank God, but not enough. New paint job, new bedspread, but— "Mom? Are you here? Mom!" Michael rushed out of the room, back to the front room, sliding the curtains open, and when that wasn't enough, he opened the front door, letting in some air. He stepped back outside, feeling lightheaded, overwhelmed by dust, choking on it, his hands icy cold despite the sunlight.

He was too late. He was too late and his mother didn't have a cell phone . He leaned against the door frame. Legs suddenly weak, he slid down it to a sitting position, pulling off his glasses and burying his face in his hands.

Before panic could truly set in, he heard the sound of a large vehicle pulling into the driveway. He put his glasses back on and stared at the van, painted in taxi company phone numbers. He scrambled to his feet as the side door opened, disgorging the sound of his mother's fussing voice.

"—in a year, who knows? Now, look, we're home. Sit tight and I'll have him get the chair."

"Mom!" Michael shouted.

"Oh, Michael, good! You're here. You can help your father. Look, John, it's Michael. He's come back."

"Michael?" His father's voice, a quavering mumble. He sounded about a hundred years old.

His mother had gained some weight, which was good, but her clothes fit badly and she wore a pair of fuzzy house slippers instead of shoes. But it was definitely her, and Michael went to her and hugged her tight, burying his nose in her hair. "Mom. Mom, I'm so sorry—I thought—"

"Michael, please." She grasped his upper arms briefly, but also used her grip to disengage him, move him away. She stared up at him, her eyes behind their bifocals flickering as she looked him all over.

She smiled a tense little smile. "Please help your father?" She stuck her head back inside the van. "Get the wheelchair from the back, would you?" she said to the driver.

In the middle seats, slumped against the fake leather, Michael's father seemed to have nodded off in the last few seconds, his chin resting slackly against his chest. He fortunately didn't *look* a hundred years old, but he did seem much older than the last time Michael had seen him, just a year and change earlier.His thick, wolfish hair was all gray now, and his glasses thicker, his body thinner. "Dad?" Michael asked softly, and his father opened his eyes and focused blearily on him.

"Michael," he slurred. "Oh, hello. It's true."

"Feeling okay?" Michael asked with a smile.

"No pain," his dad said, shaking a white paper bag in his grasp, rattling multiple bottles of pills inside. "Tell your ma I don't need the stupid wheelchair."

"Don't listen to him," his mother shouted back.

"Hey, take it easy, all right? Just take the ride and be grateful for it." Michael went around to the other side, opened the door, and helped his dad down onto the pavement.

"Ironic, you telling *me* to be grateful for something."

"Isn't it?" Michael agreed.

"Put me in that chair, your ma will just roll me down to the highway and push me into traffic."

"I doubt that. What happened, Dad?"

"Let's get him *inside*," his mother said testily. "Out of this sun."

Fortunately it was a folding manual wheelchair, and not one of those automated scooters. That would have taken a while to figure out, and Michael didn't feel like risking the further agitation of his mother. His dad sat in the push chair with a laugh so giddy and drugged that it made Michael jealous even as his hangover sent a stabbing pain through his temples. He wheeled his father inside the house while his mother haggled with the taxi driver. "Can I help you with that bag?" Michael asked mildly.

"Sure, sure, just set it in the kitchen." As soon as he was inside, John Kaminsky stood up and shuffled over to the sofa, sinking down on it. "Ah, that's better. Bring your old man one out of the bottle of Cefalexin and a glass of water. Hell, bring me a Roxicodone while you're at it. I'm at home, I can tie one on if I feel like it."

"Not for another hour, John," said Michael's mother, coming in and shutting the door. "You should have it with food. I'll get dinner started."

"Ma, you don't need to do that," Michael said. "I can cook something."

"You don't even know what we eat, Michael." She blew past him into the kitchen, returning with water and a pill in her hand. "It's fine, I'll just put something together. Do you still not eat meat?"

"Still," said Michael faintly.

"Sit down for a minute, Martha," said Michael's father.

"Did you even take a nap?" Michael asked her.

"Both of you, stop it and leave me alone. I'm fine."

"Make whatever," Michael said. "I'll—I'll eat around it. I'm starving."

Michael's father rolled his eyes. "Take an Ativan, Martha. You could use it."

Michael wished for one himself. "So tell me what happened," he said quietly, looking into the pupils of his dad's eyes. Instead of establishing a connection, he only established that his dad was fairly wasted on whatever he'd been given at the hospital.

"Ah, it's not great," John replied. "Just some edema. In the lung. Had some breathing issues. It's taken care of."

"It's serious, Dad."

His father frowned. "I know it is. I don't need you to tell me it is. I'm the one pissing blood."

"Of course. Right. Yeah. Sorry."

Michael briefly thought of Jesse on this couch with Drew's head between his legs, weaving gently, and Jesse holding his hand out towards Michael, seeking touch. He blinked the idea away, focusing on the sight of the pain below the surface of his father's face.

"There's bedding in the linen closet as usual," his mother called from the kitchen, "if you don't like what's on your bed."

"What?" Michael asked. "No, what's on the bed is—I'm not

staying."

"Of course you are, honey. What if we need you to drive tonight? It's brown rice, honey, I hope that's okay. No salt, but I'll put on a little Mrs. Dash."

"I hate brown rice!" Michael's father shouted back, and laughed.

Clattering of pans in the kitchen. "Should be ready when it's time to take your pill."

Michael and his father met eyes, sharing a moment's silent understanding. "Did the doctors say you might need to go back tonight, though?" Michael asked quietly.

"Nah, no, nothing like that. Got fixed right up. They couldn't wait to see the back of me! I can't stand that damn place. I know what I'm doing. I'll be fine right here." Michael's father patted a couch cushion. "If your mother doesn't try to kill me with dietary fiber, that is. I told you," he added, raising his voice and directing it toward the kitchen, "it'll come out when it comes out! Brown rice just makes me gassy. I don't even like white rice. I'm not going to die if I have some mashed potatoes. With *butter* !"

"Dad, please."

"Leave the skins on! Jesus! It's fine!"

"Why can't you have potatoes?" Michael asked softly.

"Tomatoes, either. Some nonsense about the nightshade family. Seventeenth-century nonsense. You'd think she'd be trying to put some weight on a man with cancer."

"You're in remission," Michael pointed out.

"Don't *you* start telling me what my life is," his father snapped. "Get enough of that here. That damn woman."

"Michael, please come set the table," called his mother.

He gritted his teeth behind a smile and did it.

They ate brown rice and cole slaw (with carrots and raisins), the latter gone lukewarm on the plate. Otherwise there was grocery store-brand prepared chicken salad out of a plastic container. Michael didn't complain; he was hungry enough that the food was welcome. He sat at his side of the table, cleaned his plate, and said nothing, the net on the tennis court, occasionally shuddering as a comment jogged against it. "I'm not going back to that one. There's St. Joseph's, on the other side of town. That Advantage, or Advert, or whatever, they're incompetent. Half the nurses are fairies and the other half are fat ladies. And they all come in and grab right for the family jewels like they can't wait to get their hands on 'em."

"Better a catheter than sitting in a wet bed all night."

"I can do that perfectly well at home, and for free."

"I don't want you to. You think it's a picnic, cleaning up after you? It's hard enough to look after myself, with my back. Just grateful that Edward helps out now and then. You remember Edward, don't you, Michael? Lived across the street? He's only around the corner now, him and his wife—"

Michael had spent so many hours hoping that Edward was actually gay like him, and was just putting on a self-protective front, and would eventually come out and they could maybe go on a date or something. How many guys he'd gone to school with that he'd secretly hoped were like him, and not just taking advantage, and how he'd come to love being taken advantage of, as long as it meant the physical oblivion of an orgasm. No matter what they were, no matter what he was, he could make them come. "Yeah, I remember."

"Where's the clock?" his mother asked.

"I threw it out," Michael said, shaking high school out of his head. "It's a piece of shit."

His mother arched her eyebrows and scoffed. "Michael, you know you had no right to do that."

"Hey, now, don't say 'shit' to your mother," his dad put in.

Michael tightened his mouth, neatly folding his napkin onto his empty plate. His voice was calm and chilly. "You *do* know I'm a fag, don't you?"

Both of his parents went silent, and blinked at him. Emboldened, Michael showed his teeth in a reckless grin. "Yeah, *I'm* a fairy. I'm queer. I'm gay. In fact, I just had sex with *two* men last night. At the same time. We put our dicks in each other's butts. I'm pretty sure we're in love."

"What are you talking about?" His mother's voice was hardly more than a whisper.

"I'm in love. With a guy. With two men," Michael elaborated. "They're cousins, actually. We have sex all the time. They have sex with each other. I worked with them both on the play I just did that just wrapped. *Viridian*? I told you about that, Mom. By the way, Dad, I did lighting design on an off-Broadway play. I don't know if Mom mentioned it to you. But I have an actual career as a lighting designer, and I just did a play, and I met these two guys, these two cousins, and we started sleeping together, and I feel—I really like them. I love them, even, and I thought you should know. So, saying 'shit' to Mom is pretty low on the offensive list, I'm thinking."

His smile softened to a genuine one. "Are you done with your plates?" he asked, standing up, picking up his own. "I can take these to the kitchen." Neither his mother nor father said or did anything as he cleared their places and loaded the dishwasher.

The day still had plenty of light left in it, slanting in dusty beams toward the living room carpet. Michael's parents sat as if frozen in place. "Nothing to say?" Michael murmured, wiping down the table with a dishcloth. "I mean, yeah, Dad, you were right about me. Guess you knew even before I did. I just don't like sports." Michael paused to kiss his mother on the top of her head and pat his father's shoulder. "Since you don't want fags and fairies taking care of you, I'm gonna get going back home. How 'bout I go to Mass tomorrow, and pray for you? Would that be okay? Because I do care. I do. I just don't care enough to stay in this shitty little town any longer. You want to move to New York, I could maybe find a place for you—hell, move to Pittsburgh, move to Philly. Move to fucking Miami. But I am not coming back here."

"Michael," said his mother, "think about what you're saying."

"Oh, I've thought about it." He had almost camped out, and called her *honey*. "I've thought about it for years now. And, ah, you know what? I'll help out with money, and all that, but I'm not coming back here. Not to this town, not to this house. I'm done. Anyway, you've got my number." He took a deep breath and nodded to them. "So. See you later." He smiled again. "Come visit. I'll take you to a show. Oh, and give Edward my regards. He's not circumcised, by the way. Did you know?"

Michael grabbed his bag and went back outside to the Altima parked on the street. He made it to the state line before he was weeping so completely that he had to pull over and wipe his face so that he could see the road.

Jesse maintained eye contact with Drew, though his pulse thudded in his throat so hard he could hardly breathe. Across from him, on the red sofa, Drew stared with complete incomprehension.

"You're leaving me?" Drew asked.

"I'm moving out," Jesse clarified. "So, yes, but no."

"When? How.—It's really that bad? I'm—that bad?"

"I'm saying that I think it would be a good idea for us to get some space. I need it. For me. And I think it'd be maybe good for you, too. So you can learn to live with yourself."

"You're breaking up with me?" Drew's voice was flat, caught between anger and sadness.

Jesse clenched a fist and stared desperately at the ceiling. "You're not listening. I am not breaking up with you. I love you, and I need you. But I need to live somewhere else for a while. Get out of this fucking house. I don't want to live here anymore, okay? And I . . . I don't want to live with you anymore, not right now. I need to see if what we have is actually real, or if it's just a habit. If it's just me being weak. I've got to have my own thing. Right now I just borrow yours."

"I made you coffee this morning," Drew whispered.

"I know," Jesse replied gently. "That was . . . nice of you. But that's—that's part of it, you know?"

Into the silence that followed those words, their phones gave off their respective tones of an incoming text message. Jesse and Drew looked at each other, then at their phones.

From: Michael Kaminsky

I think I'm in love with you.

"Okay, wow," Jesse remarked.

"Is yours from Michael?" Drew asked. When Jesse said nothing, Drew showed Jesse his own phone, with the identical message.

"Well, that complicates things," Drew muttered.

Before Jesse could reply, Drew's phone pinged again in his hand.

Can I come over?

"Why'd he only send that to you?" Jesse asked.

"Jealous?" Drew said, and smirked.

Jesse shrugged. "Tell him to come by."

It seemed as if the doorbell sounded as soon as Drew sent the text, as if the sender had been standing just outside, waiting for permission. Drew roused himself to go down to the foyer and opened the door to Michael, who was visibly agitated, even a bit sweaty and out of breath. "What, did you run here?" Drew drawled.

Michael didn't respond to the sarcasm. H e didn't even seem to notice it. He came inside, eyes wide behind his glasses, grinning nervously. "Hi. Thanks for—I mean, whoa. What a day. I know it's probably not a great idea, but is there any way you could fix me a drink?"

"It has been a day," Drew agreed. "Sure, come on up. I'm afraid that we're down to the wine, but it'll do the trick, if you'd like a glass." Drew waved Michael toward the staircase. "Jesse's here," he added.

"Is he? Good. I really don't want to have to tell this story more than once."

In the kitchen, Michael accepted his glass of pale green wine and drank it straight down in a few gulps. Drew raised his eyebrows, but wordlessly refilled his glass. Jesse shuffled in from the other room, smiled at Michael and added a quiet "Hi," and grabbed a wine glass from the rack, holding it out for Drew to fill.

Rather than responding as casually, Michael reached for Jesse, pulled him close, and pressed a kiss against his temple, sighing as if the touch restored something inside of him. Drew took the glass from Jesse's hand, and slowly emptied the bottle into it. "I'm so glad to see you, I can't even say." Michael looked up. "Both of you. I just–I *needed* to see you."

"Come here, sit down," Drew said, heading back to the sitting room and the movie paused on the TV. "What's going on?"

Michael sat on the red sofa, Jesse sat next to him, and Drew chose the chair across from them. Michael sipped from his glass, took a deep breath, and said, "I just came out to my parents."

"Wow," said Jesse, impressed.

"And not just that. I told them that I—that I have feelings for you. Attachment. That . . ." He chuckled and lowered his gaze. "That we've been fucking up a storm."

"Jesus," Drew replied. "You don't do things half way, do you?"

"I just had enough. I just—okay, first thing, I just got back from there." Michael shrugged. "My mom called me, freaking out, saying my dad was dying right then, and demanding I come back to say my final goodbyes—"

"Seriously? Oh my God!" Jesse broke in.

"No, see, that's the thing, he's not dying. I mean, not any more than he was before. He was just in the hospital overnight. And so she took that excuse to call and flip her wig. And I just . . . God, I was so hung over. Just, like, overwhelmed, with everything that's happened. I just acted totally on instinct. So I went."

"This all happened today?" Drew asked incredulously. "You went to Pennsylvania—what, did you fly?"

Michael laughed. "I drove. I drove all the way there, and I drove all the way back. I'm parked around the corner, actually. I can't believe I found a parking space."

"That's like finding a unicorn," Drew said.

"I found *you*," Michael pointed out.

"So," Jesse said, "you're just a total basket case right now."

"I'd say that's correct." Michael sighed, shook his head, sipped wine. "Yeah, so. Fuck. I'm really sorry if I'm interrupting you, and I'll leave in a minute if you'd rather be alone—"

"Actually," Drew said, standing up, "that's the last thing I want. No. Please. Stay." He glanced at Jesse. "As long as you want."

"You're not the only basket case in the room," Jesse put in, sipping from his own glass. He used the remote control to power off the TV. "You and Drew have a lot in common right now. "

"Oh?" Michael asked.

"Yeah," said Drew. "Fun times. Jesse's just . . . announced that he's leaving me."

"I'm not leaving you. I'm leaving this *house* ."

"What?" Michael shook his head in confusion. "You're moving out? From here? Why?"

"Look, man, you live here for ten years as this guy's live-in coffee maker and sex slave, and see how much you like it!"

"That sounds . . . great, actually," Michael replied.

Drew allowed himself a laugh. "It does sound great."

Jesse smiled thinly at them both. "You two. You're so perfect for each other."

Michael reached over and took Jesse's hand. "He's kidding, Jesse. C'mon. What's really the problem?"

"You know what it is," Jesse said. "I've told you."

"Ah," said Drew. "More communications about me that I don't know about."

"I didn't talk to your mom about you, dude, okay?"

"I'm lost," said Michael.

"Jesse had the bright idea to call my mother, in Portugal, for some reason," Drew said, saluting with his wineglass.

Michael raised his eyebrows, focusing on the younger man, who slumped against the sofa cushions as if wishing to become one with them. "Really? Why?"

"Why's that any of your business?" Jesse asked, his voice quiet and resigned.

"I mean, it's not," Michael admitted. He rubbed his thumb against Jesse's palm. "It's just unusual. I want to know what's going on. You don't have to tell me, of course."

"It's nothing, though," Jesse said. "I just wanted to talk to one of the only people in the world right now who's alive and remembers my dad. Because sometimes I feel like I made up everything about him. Like, he couldn't have really been like that. Like it couldn't have been real. Like, nothing in my life is really real. So . . . " He sighed deeply. "I need to . . . experience life outside of this weird bubble I'm in. With this house and this neighborhood. It's never felt like me. I feel like there's been nothing I've had that's been authentic. Like I've never suffered."

"But you suffered a thousand times more than most people ever have to," Michael pointed out.

"Yeah," Drew agreed. "When you were just a kid."

"And you were there to swoop in and save me," Jesse replied, smiling sadly at him.

Drew looked away. "I didn't," he said. "You saved yourself. *You* saved *me*. And you know that. Or I thought you did. This—all this—this is all just gratitude. There's nothing I wouldn't do for you."

For a few moments no one spoke, no one moved, held immobile in invisible amber. It was so quiet that the hum of electricity in the walls formed a peculiar harmony with the shivering of lighting filaments.

The first to break the silence could only be Michael. "So," he said to Jesse, "when and where are you moving?"

Jesse took a very deep breath before replying. "Soon," he said. "I was toying with the idea of not staying tonight, even, and just getting that part over with as quick as I can. It seems better that way, y'know? My friend Charlie said I could crash on his couch tonight, and maybe even for a few weeks while I try to find a place. But . . . I haven't really worked out the practical specifics," he confessed.

"Well, I'm sure Drew won't turn you out onto the street tonight," Michael said.

"Actually, could I maybe sleep over at your place tonight?" Jesse suggested with a laugh. "I've made it weird."

Michael laughed, too. "Yeah, I can see that."

"Please," said Drew, "don't."

Jesse and Michael looked at him.

"I don't want to be alone tonight," Drew said.

"Well," reiterated Jesse, "I just don't really feel like sleeping *here* tonight."

"I know," Michael piped up. "Why don't you both come over?" He held up his hands. "I've got the car. Hell, let's get a hotel room. Let's just none of us sleep at home tonight. But, let's be together. Okay?" He looked back and forth between them. "I really want to be with you both right now. I mean, I want to be with you. Both. I don't really care where. But my bed's really not going to be big enough for all three of us to sleep, and I really don't feel like ending up on the floor." He shrugged. "We can go wherever we want. We can go out of town."

"I have to work tomorrow," Jesse muttered.

Michael smiled at him. "Okay, well."

"My bed is big enough," Drew pointed out.

"Of course it is," said Jesse, rolling his eyes.

Michael sighed. "Jesse," he said, an edge of pleading in his voice. "Just for tonight. All right? I'd really, really love to be in bed with you as soon as possible. Compromise, just for tonight, for me. Please? We'll get started working it out, in the morning. We'll get up early, go out for breakfast, talk things through. But I want to be with you tonight. Both of you." He reached over to Drew, took his hand, took Jesse's hand in his other, holding them both, linking fingers. "I know we can make this work," Michael said. "We're all really tired. Let's just go to bed." He paused and glanced back towards the kitchen. "Though, I gotta say, I'm kinda hungry, so . . . maybe we could order a pizza?"

Jesse broke into low, slow laughter. "I could go for a pizza," he admitted.

"Oh, Jesse," Drew sighed, and chuckled.

"Hey, my appetite just came back. Can't live on salad alone." Jesse leaned over and kissed Michael on the lips, then stood, approaching Drew, holding out his free hand, grasping Drew's arm and drawing him in close. They kissed, lips and cheeks, and settled into a gentle, nuzzling embrace. Michael stood up, too, and leaned against them, enfolding them both in his long arms.

"I think we can make it," he murmured. "Together. I think we can make it. Maybe?" Michael kissed Drew's lips, then Jesse's. "Maybe we could try."

He looked between them, his expression imploring. When Jesse sighed, and smiled, Michael brought their hands together, hand holding hand holding hand. When Drew smiled, too, Michael held up their joined hands and kissed them.

. . .

www.ingramcontent.com/pod-product-compliance
Lightning Source LLC
Chambersburg PA
CBHW070831250626
47159CB00003B/736